BLACK GOLD

A. JAY COLLINS

FriesenPress

One Printers Way
Altona, MB R0G 0B0
Canada

www.friesenpress.com

ISBN
978-1-03-830116-1 (Hardcover)
978-1-03-830115-4 (Paperback)
978-1-03-830117-8 (eBook)

1. FICTION, ACTION & ADVENTURE

Distributed to the trade by The Ingram Book Company

BLACK GOLD

The ORB Chronicles Continued

A. JAY COLLINS

Table of Contents

Cast of Characters vii

Iran – 1979 1

Leaving Iran – 1979 12

Thoughts from a Wolf Lookout 18

ORB – 2017 25

Friends of Iran – 2018 34

Cinema Rex: A Time to Die—2018 44

Not Tudeh 51

Black Again—March 2019 53

A New Challenge—March 2019 57

Istanbul—March 2019 61

Interstate EPC at Your Service—April 2019 73

Brussels 81

Domar Oil 86

Heading Out—2019 91

Sari—2019 97

New Day, New Town 104

Settling In 108

Hossein 118

Richard and His Mountain 126

The Commander 136

Blackmail or . . . ? .143

Plato 156

Matthew in Chalus .170

Plato and Ali 179

Moving On 192

Emma 206

Matthew on Site 218

The Guys at Site 226

Those Ruskies. 230

Leila 233

Chalus Revisited 240

Ali 255

Sabotage 260

Catching Up 266

Istanbul Revisited. 278

Final Impact—Mid-2020. 287

One Last Call and It's Off We Go. 303

What—No Refinery? 308

Figure 1—Iranian Oilfields and Pipelines

Figure 2—Northern Iran

Cast of Characters

ORB Operatives and Associates

Murray Stockman (Stockman) – president of ORB, Organization for Reorganizing Business and ex-CSIS

Matthew Black – senior field operative for ORB

Lucy Stockman – wife of Murray and an ex-CSIS operative

Emma Stockman – field operative for ORB, and Murray Stockman's daughter

Colin – ORB operative responsible for IT

Brian – ORB operative responsible for pipelines

Dave – ORB operative responsible for politics

Ken – ORB operative responsible for power plant, port, and shipping

Alan and Tony – ORB operatives responsible for legal

James Peters – ORB operative based on site as Resident Engineer at Sari refinery

Jenny Peters – James Peter's wife living in Sari

Anthony, Elliott, and Bradley – children of James and Jenny

Ali – ORB operative, friend of Plato, responsible for communications with Jafaar and Amir, and a successful businessman in the US

Plato – ORB operative, lives in Chalus but works for Melli Bank in Tehran

Margaret – Plato's wife, has a powerful father who works with the US diplomatic service and maintains trusted diplomatic relationships with Russia and China

Eddie S. Sloan (Sloan) – owns the London-based Sloan employment agency that provides labor as required for ORB

Mickey and Phil – Sloan-ORB operatives on mechanical at refinery construction

Arnie and Walt – Sloan-ORB operatives on electrical at refinery construction

Pete – ORB operative on instrumentation and controls at refinery construction

Dick Elliot – president of Interstate EPC in Montreal, ORB operative, and responsible for the Sari Petrochemical Project, including foreign contractors

Doyle Crower – construction superintendent of the Sarnia petrochemical plant and responsible for bringing Matthew Black to Stockman

Simon Beatty – senior representative for Domar Oil

Sari-based Personnel

Dick, Jane, Greg and Barb – Canadian expats based in Sari in the late 70's.

Tom Ardeghali – works at the refinery, Afghan educated, and a Russian transplant who befriends James and Ali

Mansourian – owner of Mana Construction, friend of the Regime and holder of a large portion of the mis-appropriated offshore funds for the Regime

John Charlesworth – Design Engineer's rep onsite, responsible for plant start-up as a technically competent Canadian who has started five refineries, and an unwitting participant in any Iranian, Russian, Chinese, or ORB plans

Jafaar Sazesh – father of Amir, advocate and leader of the New Workers for Iran Union

Saphir Sazesh – Jafaar's wife

Amir Sazesh – Jafaar's son and leader of the Friends of Iran movement

Abdul Reza Ansur – bombed the cinema in Chalus

Max Divet – Madcap Construction superintendent at Sari refinery and initially James's boss

Angel Divet – Max's devoted wife

Hossein and Liz Daneshkah– local but Western-educated, potential ORB operatives working at the Sari refinery

Gorgan Listening Post Characters

Richard – works at the communications center for the US in Gorgan, friend of James, as well as the driver for the commander

Commander – Richard's boss, works at the Gorgan facility, and Leila's lover

Leila – local girlfriend of the commander

Iran – 1979

The dawn Salat al-Fajr prayers echoed eerily over Tehran from loudspeakers mounted in mosque towers throughout the city. The wailing was interrupted by the sporadic sound of recorded machine-gun fire rattling from apartment rooftops. Few people were outside at this hour, but those that were, instinctively looked furtively around for any sign of trouble.

Dick and Greg left their young families sleeping in the company apartment near the city center of what would become a hot, bustling, jostling, noisy, and brutal mix of traffic and crowds just a few hours later with the streets shrouded in clouds of carbon monoxide fumes. It would be good to get away before being caught up in that kind of day. But 'away' was not necessarily a better place to be right now.

Greg quietly closed the iron gates of their apartment yard compound and he and Dick moved cautiously over to their small, pale-green Citroën Jyane tucked in close to the perimeter wall of the apartment, looking like a frog waiting to get back into the reeds, and climbed into the rudimentary canvas seats.

As the dangers of the times crushed down on the two families after just a couple of days in Tehran, they had little choice now but for at least one of them to go back to their apartments in Sari, on the north coast, to collect whatever they could, return to Tehran and be prepared to exit the country quickly should the situation worsen. It was highly unlikely they would be returning to Sari afterward if it was true that the revolution was really heating up, as it appeared, into a frenzy of expectation as the news spread of an impending forced exodus of the shah and his family.

This is what it had come to. Despite the warning signs over the last several months, some of the expats in Sari felt naively immune and isolated from the dangers closing in on them. But the realization of what was happening gelled for Dick and Greg as soon as they arrived at the outskirts of Tehran with their families and were greeted by demonstrations and militia on the streets, people running in all directions, store fronts covered with plywood, some buildings – banks they thought - burned out and what seemed to be pockets of mayhem they had to pass through or find a way around to get to the apartment. At that point, they began to truly grasp the futility of trying to remain impassive to the situation, as though this was just a passing phase. The town of Sari had been comparatively isolated from the dangers of revolution. It was, after all, a geographically central point in the north for supplying and harboring both the revolutionary forces and the militia along the Caspian coastline, with both sides being careful not to destroy their own provisions and resources; but Tehran was the centre of chaos.

None of them—neither Dick nor Greg, or their wives—had been aware of the full extent of the increasing tensions before they left Sari for Tehran. They simply weren't seriously attuned to any serious social issues that might affect them. They were, after all, just a couple of young Canadian families, unaccustomed to the cynicism and ruthlessness of politics and the manic drive of religious fervor that inspired the majority of the Iranian population to rise up at this time. The bravado of youth had clouded any thoughts they had of the possibility of impending doom and their company, Interstate EPC with an office in Tehran, had provided little information, or advice, on the situation. Instead, like all good expats did in times of crisis, they settled for the comfort that gin and tonic and the like brought, and went about their days practicing a simple, low-profile life, staying away from potential trouble spots. That meant ignoring the increasing show of intolerance leveled at them by the locals whenever they had to leave their apartments. While the expat wives would normally have been guaranteed immunity from uncomfortable situations when accompanied by their children, especially blond-haired boys, that protection was getting less effective these days. For them, it was as though being western foreigners who couldn't speak the native language, provided them a license to ignore whatever in-country problems there were. They thought themselves above such things.

In Sari during the latter half of 1978, the louder-than-usual voices coming from the rooftop-mounted loudspeakers around town as well as the mosques became increasingly intimidating and angry. But, other than the occasional sound of recorded gunfire, there didn't appear to be any physical danger for expat families as they went about their business of living – just a feeling of unease on the streets. Not that they could understand what was being broadcast, although the voices did sound tinged with more anger than usual. That anger increased in tempo as the weeks passed to a point when the mullahs expounding their thoughts over the microphones must surely have led to at least some cardiac arrests in their efforts to become louder and angrier than the day prior. But in Tehran the revolution was on their doorstep. They didn't have to understand the words—the whole city was tense. Anger and unrest in the streets were pervasive, and the incessant screaming of machine guns sounds blasting over the loudspeakers, tore the nights apart as the unnerving cacophony bombarded them.

They should have been more sensitive to the signs long before they got to Tehran. Even at the project site in Sari, security guards had been brought in to protect the expats, if needed, when lawful government protection appeared to no longer be available or visible. But still they felt immune to the unrest.

They should have paid more serious attention to their project security chief, an upper-class Iranian. When responding to Dick's question about what he thought was happening in his country, the chief simply lifted his Khomeini-shaped gray beard, put a finger against his unprotected neck and mimicked a slice across his throat, and told Dick he was sure Domar Oil, the most dominant western oil company in the Middle East, was at the root of the problem. They were ready to rid the country of the Pahlavi family who had the audacity to want to take control of Iran's own oil assets and were insisting on playing a greater part in the governance of mineral development. Domar were being pushed to one side, and they didn't like it. Odd, and strangely revealing, especially if true. It was also the beginning of Iran's anti-west movement under a devoutly Islamic regime that Domar had not considered when they got tired of the shah and decided to replace him.

The situation in Sari was becoming even more unnerving as stories were told of SAVAK, the shah's secret service of not-so-secret agents, taking local people in the middle of the night to unknown destinations, for unknown reasons, never to return. But, so far, no *ferengies* had been abducted, although it had become increasingly concerning that some of Dick and Jane's Iranian friends were disappearing for no apparent reason. A couple of Iranian technicians working with Dick at the project site had been spirited away from their homes one night and not heard from again – reasons unknown.

In the bazaar, locals began staring at *ferengies* more than usual, only now it was with an intensity as though they suddenly wondered one day what these people were doing amongst them during these times. "Don't they know there's a revolution coming?" was a common searching, but silent, question on the faces of the locals. "Don't they realise they shouldn't be here?"

Despite the growing antagonism shown towards them by the locals, Dick and Jane still seemed to be outwardly immune to the not-so-subtle warnings, and they continued to laugh things off with the bravado of youth and naiveté, while inwardly they started to struggle with the possibilities of what may come.

Then, one night, the entire crew from the other Canadian consultant, a contractor, at the Sari sawmill construction site providing guidance to the Iranian contractors, disappeared. In the morning, those who remained from Dick's company discovered that the contractor's personnel and their families had been evacuated in the middle of the night from the Sari airport in a privately chartered 737, without a word to anyone.

Wow! This was getting serious, and yet Dick's own company, Interstate, remained silent on any thoughts of evacuation. Instead, they argued that since the contractor, who had flown their people out, had invested nothing in the project to this point, might as well move out until things settled down. Dick and his associates thought this a reasonable conclusion and just carried on as though there was nothing for them to be concerned about. Plus, the very thought of evacuating on one's own, with a young family, was much too difficult to consider, although it had often passed through Dick's mind. It was well known that the trek to the west of Sari was logistically very difficult at the best of times, but the potential for a journey to the east was worse, with Russia waiting at the end of the road and only the prospect of help coming from a large leper colony straddling the only ground route out.

The embassies provided no information—if one could even contact them. The Germans were theoretically the embassy responsible for Sari-area expats of all nationalities because the majority of those working on the construction of the nearby Neka Power Plant were German. But they never made contact, never reached out.

The small contingent of ex-pat families that remained in Sari near the end of 1978 were starting to worry for their security and wondering how on earth they would be able to leave Iran without some substantial help, if it came to that. Despite some sketchy planning by Interstate, nothing had been committed, and one day all suddenly went silent and they realized they were on their own.

Immediately before Dick and Greg had left for Tehran with their families, they had been increasingly jostled, pushed, spat upon, and generally hassled by the local Sari population, who had once been such a pleasure to walk among. As the revolution progressed and its tentacles reached the more remote areas, the volume of the rooftop loudspeakers increased with religious rantings, the sound of machine-gun fire, and continuously broadcast prayers while the mullahs vented their anger and fired the populace up into frenzies. Gangs of youths began to roam the streets armed with machine guns, looking for any reason to let out their frustrations on anyone and anything that reminded them of why there was a revolution. While *ferengies* were uncomfortable with the situation, it was the SAVAK agents, and government offices and officials that were the primary targets of aggression for now. They represented the shah, and the shah had to go.

Villagers, from nearby small satellite settlements around Sari, demonstrated in the streets and carried placards warning of revolution and denouncing the shah, but those groups were primarily uneducated farm workers deliberately brought into town by the pro-revolutionaries. They had been paid to hold the placards and chant their "apparent" anger in a loud, monotonal groan as though with a single voice. While the vast majority couldn't read and had no idea what the words on the placards said or meant, the few rials they collected for showing up inspired them enough. Such was the power of money, despite it being equivalent to only one dollar.

It was time for Dick, Greg and their families to at least take a break and consider the situation.

They had intended to go to Tehran just for the Christmas period, stay in the company apartment for a week or so, collect all the alcohol they could manage to take back to the expats in Sari, and get through the rest of their contracts as best they could, despite all that was going on around them. They still really had no clue as to what was happening on a global scale, and it all seemed like a temporary hiccup in their lives.

The English-speaking news available from short-wave radios in Sari at the time was less than sporadic, with only Voice of America, the BBC World Service and Radio Moscow offering some commentary, but at a very high level. In some cases, the reporting was contradictory making the truth somewhat murky.

No news came out of the Interstate office in Tehran, despite the constant requests for a plan—any plan – from the employees. There seemed to be something always about to come, but it never did.

It was during the first two days of their Christmas break in Tehran that Dick, Greg and their families listened to the unsettling stories of social unrest, on the various local English-speaking television and radio stations – and the news was current, reporting events that were happening as they listened. It was all-consuming. Before that, they assumed that the winds of change would somehow bring about a resolution, on way or the other, over the next couple of weeks, and they could return to Sari. But it was troubling to them that their own company had still made no attempt to contact them and had apparently disappeared without notice.

As the two families thought more seriously about the situation in those first few days in Tehran they convinced themselves the social unrest far surpassed anything that could be resolved in just weeks, months, or perhaps even years. It would now be impossible for a foreigner to live unscathed even in the communities outside of Tehran, but they did agree that one, and likely two, of them had to go back to their apartments in Sari soon, to collect whatever they could fit of value into a single suitcase for each family. That was likely the extent of checked luggage they would be allowed to take with them if, or when, the time came to evacuate.

Then the news hit the airwaves that thousands of Iranian protesters were killed in the streets of Tehran by the remnants of the shah's militia and mercenaries imported to do the job that many Iranians wouldn't do to their own people. The news was the catalyst that Dick and Greg needed to take immediate action. They left for Sari in the early hours of the following morning.

*   *   *

The sun rose in a shimmering, dusty haze of trembling heat waves; a reminder of scorching conditions to look forward to on another hot day. Dick and Greg's Jyane raced north through the streets of Tehran to the outskirts of the city and started the long, gradual climb up the southern foothills of the Alborz Mountains. That narrow strip of mountains separated the dry and dusty 1,300 miles of southern Iran from the twenty-mile wide strip of lush, humid coastline that formed the southern edge of the Caspian Sea, where Dick, Greg, and their families had called home for the last two years.

It was fully daylight by the time they reached those southern foothills and focused on the next three-hour, mountain-hugging journey over the mountains to Sari, a town with a population of about 100,000, close to the Caspian Sea. They lived and worked there as expats for Interstate, constructing a large sawmill as a part of the shah's industrialization plan.

They knew they would have to run the gauntlet through at least two small towns on route. If stopped and recognized as foreigners, or *ferengies*, as the locals called anyone who wasn't Iranian, they could face unknown but likely very uncomfortable consequences with the locals. The natives had grown so angry and frustrated with their government that the violence of revolution over the last few months had increased in tempo, fueled by the words of the mullahs, and they were ready to take their angst out on anyone who didn't "fit", and *ferengies* didn't.

Leaving behind the dry conditions to the south of the mountains, the little Jyane slowly climbed to the summit of the Alborz and started dropping into the high humidity of the northern foothills as the road led down to the Caspian Sea. The lushness of their surroundings was familiar to Dick and Greg as they came down from the mountains and felt easier as they came into more familiar territory, and perhaps a less dangerous one.

The end of the Alborz foothills on the north side was marked by the small town of Amol, a center for roads traveling in four directions. There was no other way for them to travel but through the middle.

Fortunately, the small mountain villages on the route seemed to be untainted by even the concept of revolution. It had all happened so fast that the villagers never caught up with it. Whether through ignorance or apathy, their lives were the same as always. It was hard enough living in the arid mountains without adding the burden of revolution. It wouldn't change anything for them.

On the outskirts of Amol, the townspeople were beginning to come out into the streets, looking to start their day. Some were pulling carts, getting ready to set them up with fruit and vegetables. The local bakeries were alive with customers; not even a revolution could stop the baker, nor the people, from the delights of this simple, basic food and no one could resist that smell of baking bread and the taste of fresh naan...

But not all was peaceful.

Dick and Greg's comfort level dissipated as they witnessed the signs of unrest and violence as soon as they penetrated the perimeter of Amol. Some local SAVAK agents, the personal henchmen army of the shah, had been maimed and hung in the streets. Their vehicles had been overturned, and all manner of tires were stacked across roads to stop or at least slow traffic for inspection. By now, gangs of marauding youths paraded with guns slung across their young shoulders, their knuckles white on the triggers as they readied themselves for any resistance. Shops and banks were closed. Schools were shuttered. Markets were closed. Gas stations had long lines of cars and people with oil cans patiently waited their turn for petrol and kerosene for cooking —if it ever came. All this havoc had happened in the last few days while Dick, Greg, and their families were in Tehran. It was unbelievable. There had been little evidence of this amount of chaos when they had driven through this same area on their way to Tehran just that short time ago.

As inconspicuously as possible, the little car slowly made its way through the back streets of Amol, avoiding obstacles such as the barricades of car tires, with Dick and Greg's faces hidden behind colorful scarves. Dick focused on the people around them, but none were looking. Meanwhile, Greg concentrated on keeping the little car out of the jubes, the open sewer and water runoff ditches, along the sides of the road. Some renegade fruit and vegetable stalls were being set up along the way. The population started to avail themselves of the products that were still available before the confused local militia shut them down by pushing the street vendors to one side. It was unclear whether these were protective or punishing acts, and the local militia didn't appear to understand what their role was now that a revolution surrounded them. SAVAK had pulled them one way and the people pulled them another. Now there was little evidence of SAVAK, and the local police had disappeared.

Dick and Greg made their way to the outer eastern limits of the town and raced on to Babol, the last town before Sari. They avoided talking between themselves about the potential dangers and obvious signs of revolution all around them, but the threat grew in their minds. Panic began to replace complacency as they felt the urgency to do what they came to do and get back to their families as quickly as possible before things got more violent.

They couldn't help but be increasingly concerned as they worked their way toward the religious city of Sari, where mullahs had a huge impact on the rural communities, and the safety of *ferengies* would likely be threatened. The local population—especially the younger people who smelled revolution—had been driven to distrust the shah and government and instead place their trust in their religious leaders. They smelled the impending departure of the shah and were likely to be much more antagonistic toward foreigners, especially Americans and Brits. Once Iranians realized that Canada shared a border with the US, it would be their turn to face the antagonism.

During the short time Dick, Greg, and their families had been away from Sari, the local Iranian newspapers and television broadcasts along the Caspian coastline braved the potential backlash from the last of the shah's forces and announced the undermining and fall of the despised SAVAK. The news spread quickly and inspired the population further as the revolution gathered even more momentum. The dissent had ratcheted up several notches overnight.

Strangely, Sari appeared relatively intact when Dick and Greg reached it in mid-afternoon. They intended to spend no more than a couple of hours there before returning to Tehran. Things were only going to get worse the longer they stayed. As they discovered, while Sari was the most religious center in the north, it was also a principal distribution center for both the army and the rebels. It seemed protected by all parties, for now. But it was also becoming a lawless city, with no police or militia, and no one to call for help if needed. Gangs of youth with machine guns slung over their shoulders marauded through the streets in pickup trucks, hate in their eyes, and revolution on their minds.

They had wasted precious time cruising through the city, looking for friends, both local and ex-pat, and helping where they could. By the time they reached their own apartments, close together at the end of an alley, daylight was fading, and there was no power. They each sorted through their piles of belongings, trying to assess what their wives said had to be taken and what must be left behind. It wasn't hard to fill a suitcase each, but all the books, extra clothing, linens, ornaments, toys, everyday living articles, games, and the like had to be left behind. After the hour they'd allowed themselves had elapsed, they met at the car, threw the suitcases into the rear seat, siphoned petrol from a neighbor's car, and raced down the alley, onto the road leading out through the city toward Tehran. There was no other route.

Sari did not escape the fullness of the revolution; it just happened to be a calmer island in the storm at the time the expats were there. The surrounding towns had been devastated. Babol, to the west, had experienced riots, killings, and barbaric gestures of revolt. Gorgan, to the east, had been set afire. There was a severe shortage of gasoline and heating fuel as the southern oilfields were shuttered and supply pipelines to Tehran ran dry.

By the time Dick and Greg left their apartments, it was dark, and the city roads were barricaded with burning tires of all sizes, piled on top of the other. There was a narrow gap through each barrier guarded by a small group of youths with guns, intent on stopping, questioning, and hassling any suspicious-looking characters, especially foreigners.

Dick was driving as they raced toward the first barricade. He saw the gap and decided to take a run at it rather than stop and be faced with potential brutality. He rammed down on the accelerator, but the little Jyane only had a twenty-nine-horsepower motor. While its speed could get upward of sixty miles per hour on a good day, it could only reach that point after a fairly long warm-up through manual gear shifting and acceleration levels on relatively level terrain. Regardless, they had built up some reasonable traction by the time they reached the first obstacle and plowed their way through the gap as the young inexperienced guards dove out of the way, dropping their guns and failing to regain their balance or aim in time as they fired uselessly into the night. No one followed the Jyane as Dick and Greg sped toward the next barricade where they did the same thing, with the same result.

They whooped as they hurtled on to Babol. The Jyane shook and rolled as it maintained a steady sixty miles per hour, its chassis rattling and rear doors occasionally flying open as the car swerved to avoid potholes or animals in the road. Their adrenaline boiled. They saw the lights of Babol in the distance but knew that this time there was an alternative route around the center. Dick jerked the Jyane left onto the barely discernible bypass and sped toward the Alborz. They passed a small group of excited youngsters who had hoisted a Mercedes, with its lifeless occupants still inside, up onto the second floor of a bombed-out building on the side of the road, leaving it dangling there with SAVAK-uniformed bodies slumped in contorted positions. Dick and Greg recognized the building as a SAVAK house that had been intact when they had passed it earlier on their way to Sari. Now, it had clearly been gutted. The crowd seemed intent on destroying everything SAVAK. By the time the crowd had started throwing their oil-soaked flaming torches up into the Mercedes, to catch the bodies alight, the Jyane was heading to the outskirts of town and the building was fast disappearing in the distance behind.

Amol was the last populated town on the route, but they managed to get through with little problem, despite a small crowd that appeared to want to block their path but decided at the last minute it wasn't worth it and drifted over to the sidewalks.

It was a relief for Dick and Greg to reach the northern foothills of the Alborz and start the steady climb to the top. The speed of the Jyane waned as the little car climbed higher, but it was a stubborn, reliable engine and just kept moving forward until they slowly reached the peak and then coasted the rest of the way down to the Tehran city limit in the middle of the night.

*   *   *

Leaving Iran – 1979

Dick and Greg reached their Tehran apartment just before midnight. Their children were in bed and had not been allowed to wait up for them to get back. They hugged their wives, as well as a glass of straight Scotch, and gabbled to them about their trip, Sari, the other expats, rooting through their belongings, making their choices on what to take and what to leave, then dashing back to them through the turmoil on route.

Their adrenaline pumped as they told their story but gradually settled to a calm as they took comfort in being back with their families again – albeit them only being away for less than one day. They all sat around the fire, shared a few more drinks, and discussed their strategy. None of their plans included returning to Sari in the near future, although they wondered what would happen to their personal possessions and where the heck Interstate people had disappeared to without so much as a phone call. Finally, they decided that the loss of their 'stuff' would be worth the escape should the situation worsen. The consensus was that it would.

The following day, Dick and Jane ventured out of the apartment to 'take the temperature in the streets' as they told the others. Jane wore a kind of chador that covered most of her body. Dick tried not to look too westernized, dressed in jeans and a simple t-shirt. He had already started to grow a straggly beard and his now weather-beaten face from his time in-country helped his attempt of disguise. They walked the neighborhood streets, looking for some semblance of the Christmas season they had missed, perhaps something that would cheer everyone up. There wasn't much around although one street vendor still had small fir trees for sale to the Christians, but they were not reduced in price despite Christmas Day having been two days previous. Perhaps he didn't know, or more likely didn't care. Dick and Jane smiled as they thought of the unwitting faux pas, and made their way through the neighborhood, circling back to the apartment. They felt refreshed by having come through their outing unscathed and feeling better having gauged the sentiment around them outside as best they could tell. They hadn't witnessed any demonstrations and the militia seemed to be missing from the streets. The people looked depressed, angry and unsmiling but were not collecting in large groups. It was difficult to tell how serious the situation was for themselves, but certainly the recent killing of thousands of demonstrators would be taking a toll on the population. While things seemed quiet right now, Dick and Jane knew it wouldn't last. Something like that was bound to ignite more rebellion. It was just a matter of time.

Although it was not a good situation, they—again naively—felt no impending threat to themselves as long as they avoided trouble spots where levels of emotion appeared threatening and kept their children close by as a possible antidote against personal threats. Supporters of the shah versus supporters for the mullahs—that was how they looked at it. This was not a fight with foreigners. *Ferengies* didn't seem to be in the equation of discontent to any great extent at this point, but the whole experience encouraged them to try harder to get some more definitive information from an embassy—any embassy. They were no longer so naive as to believe they would be safe no matter what, despite having children. There were always extremists.

Somehow, with youth on their side, they relaxed in the comfort of the apartment and consoled themselves with the intimacy of their friendships, further tempered by the intoxication of a steady flow of exotic cocktails. Their bravado, bolstered by the alcohol, made everything and anything seem possible. They just had to wait and be ready at all times.

The call came in mid-morning, three days after Dick and Greg returned from Sari. Again, it was a Canadian embassy staff member in Tehran who instructed them to gather at the Tehran Hilton hotel in the north of the city over the following two days. Rooms had been reserved in their names under the banner of the embassy. The day after the call, the two families drove over to the Hilton, on one of the hills overlooking much of the city, parked their Jyanes in the parking lot and left their car and apartment keys under the driver's seats. They had no idea who would ever collect the cars, let alone find and use their apartment keys, but by now they weren' concerned about those details.

They waited in the hotel for several days before the ex-pat group was suddenly rounded up in the lobby, hustled onto a coach and chaperoned by an embassy representative across the city to the cargo gates at the Mehrabad International Airport, that were opened by another civilian, on their arrival. It was a chaotic frenzy of disorganization, but somehow it all moved forward. They collected on the tarmac at the north end of the main terminal. Other Canadian expats joined them from all over Iran and they all stood in solemn silence with one suitcase per family. What a sorry lot they were, as they waited, and waited some more, before they spotted a dark-green camouflaged Hercules C100 plant itself onto the runway and taxi over to their location. There was a small, inconspicuous Canadian flag sticker, placed just below the tip of the aircraft tail about thirty feet in the air. That's all there was to identify the ownership of the plane.

The last they saw of Tehran was from the tail ramp of the Hercules as they climbed into the hold of the aircraft and onto the strap seats strung in four parallel rows running the length of the plane. Their passports were taken to the main terminal building by an Iranian official for examination to ensure that all in-country taxes had been paid and there were no undesirables attempting to escape. The engines of the plane never closed down, and it felt like they may make a fast getaway. But the pilots were cautious. The waiting seemed to take an eternity, mixed with a huge amount of angst, before the passports were returned and the pilots were given the authorization to leave.

Ankara, Turkey, next stop.

At the moment of takeoff, Dick, Greg, and their wives realized the enormity of what was happening and their attention turned to face and consider the uncertainty of their future. They were subdued during the flight as they wondered what was ahead. They had no experience to draw on, and no-one to offer guidance.

It was a three-hour flight to Ankara. The Hercules was incredibly noisy, cramped and with only a couple of toilets at the rear of the plane, hidden behind curtains. There was no food, but bottled water passed around. No-one was available to talk to who might know anything about what they could expect when they landed. Everyone tried to sleep but it was difficult to relax in the simple slung seats and with the anxieties of the unknown weighing on their thoughts.

The Hercules landed in a discrete location to the east of the main terminal in Ankara and taxied to an open tarmac area away from other planes where the expats deplaned and clambered onto buses waiting for them. It was nighttime as they travelled through the city streets where ghostly, armed military figures clad in heavy, dark woolen overcoats seemed to be guarding the entire route, their breaths misting the evening air around them. The faces couldn't be seen, despite Jane and her children pressing their noses into the condensation on the cool windows of the bus as they tried to identify whether the soldiers were actually statues or humans. It was difficult. The figures never moved and the eyes were hidden by the peaks of their helmets.

The five-star Bayuk Ankara Hotel was to be their temporary home. There were militia posted throughout the embassy district where the hotel was located. They arrived at the hotel entrance and were greeted by someone who seemed to be a government official as each family exited the buses. Dick, Greg and their families were assigned a suite of three rooms each, on the sixth floor. No one on the hotel staff mentioned payment, checkout times, or who their contacts might be. Neither Dick nor Greg thought to ask.

The relief of being free of the uncertainty of Iran was palpable. It wasn't an immediate sensation but one that gradually came over them. They eventually relaxed and, after a few days, realized they could leave their children to sleep in the care of a newfound teenage babysitter from another ex-pat family while they unwound in the Sky Bar at the top of the hotel. It never occurred to them that they couldn't pay for the hotel rooms nor the expenses they were accruing. The adrenaline of escape from Iran clouded their logic—for now. How could things get any worse? Surely someone other than them was on the hook.

After a few days, with no news and no contact with anyone who might be able to claim any kind of representation of authority, it became clear they had been abandoned in Turkey by Interstate and everyone else it seemed. They needed to be proactive if they ever expected to return home.

While Greg and his wife headed to the New Zealand embassy in search of help from their home representatives, Dick and Jane tramped the streets visiting various other embassies and consulates including the Canadian and US offices. But given their British landed immigrant status in Canada, the British embassy was high on their list of potential benefactors and initially seemed to be the obvious way to solve their problem of abandonment. It wasn't. In fact, the British embassy essentially held the view that Dick, Jane, and family were not as destitute as the inhabitants of the colorfully graffitied school bus full of hippies – after all, it was the 70's still - parked in the embassy driveway while the staff tried to figure out how to help them do whatever it was they needed.

While they had no money on them, Dick and Jane told them they had the funds in a Montreal bank but had no access to it. The fact was that, in those days, it was very difficult to access overseas accounts when there was no internet or reliable phone lines. It wasn't a straightforward matter of contacting one's bank, anywhere in the world, and providing them with wire instructions. It just didn't happen like that in 1979. The embassy didn't seem to take account of those problems and just treated them as though they could somehow pay their way.

However, the Brits did offer to buy their way by second-class rail passage from Ankara to London. The caveat was that they were to climb out of the Bayuk Ankara sixth-floor suite windows to avoid paying the bill. The thought was laughable, with or without three seven-year-old and under children in tow, but the Brits never raised an eyebrow at their suggestion and scowled when the idea was rejected.

It eventually took the Canadian embassy to find a way out of their ex-pat dilemma and, with a simple promise to repay if demanded, the families were airlifted to Toronto, Ankara hotel bills paid.

From there, Dick made contact with Interstate who apologized but refused to make reparation for the lost personal effects – after all, this was a force majeure event and the contracts were very clear in so far as the company absolved itself of any responsibility for anything as a consequence of such. It was short-lived fight as Dick succumbed to their invitation of another project position elsewhere. And so, the lives of Dick and Jane tumbled forward in their usual chaotically naive way to the next adventure.

Whether by luck, by chance, or just by fate, Dick Elliot went on to become the president of Interstate. In 2016 the company secured the long-term contract from the Iranian Islamic Regime to engineer, build, and operate an oil refinery in northern Iran – close to Sari. Dick was once again destined to become embroiled with that country, but this time at a higher level and with a plethora of knowledge and understanding he had built upon from those early days, forty years ago. While he struggled with the prospect of working in Iran again, he accepted it and decided to watch over this one very carefully.

* * *

Thoughts from a Wolf Lookout

It was mid-2015, over thirty-five years after the Ayatollah had returned from France, when Hossein Daneshkah climbed the rough wooden ladder and stood on the uppermost platform of the wolf lookout, as he had done so many times in his youth. He crossed his arms on the rough wooden ledge, rested his head on his forearms, and squinted through the blue-tinged haze of the early morning over the beauty of the Mazandaran Valley as it stretched majestically across to meet the north-eastern tip of the Alborz mountains in the distance. Only a few days ago, he had heard that Iran's National Petroleum Company (NPC) received the last of its permits to construct a new world-class oil refinery right here, in the valley adjacent to the Tajan River.

There was already some construction activity, with earthmoving equipment preparing the site and tearing away at the vegetation, piling it in preparation for burning when the rainy season arrived. The topsoil was being stripped, piled separately and covered with huge plastic sheets to keep it dry. It would be used later for the reclamation program. The project would employ up to 8,000 construction workers to build the facility over a five-year period. It should be ready between 2020 and 2022 depending on many complex situations that had to come together, any of which could have a negative effect on schedule if they should go wrong.

By the time the refinery was completed, it would be the climax of a forty-year endeavour from concept to completion, with all the studies, permits, reports, land purchases, financing, even more reports and on and on and, of course, the politics. It also included time when nothing at all happened as the Iranian Regime "collected" its thoughts during the first fifteen years of its rule from 1979.

The local population who lived around the Caspian coastline considered the complex would be a scar on the landscape. It was one of a number of industrial endeavors that Shah Mohammed Reza Pahlavi had idealized during his reign to create a self-sufficient, modern, and prosperous Iran, as fast as possible. The projects had most often been financially supported by Western companies interested in exchanging that support for equipment they would sell to the Iranians at top dollar, operation of the facilities they sponsored, and a share of the profits. They had repeated that kind of support so many times they had become entrenched in the Iranian industrialization program such that it could not be sustained without their participation.

But by the end of the '70's the shah's days were numbered as he attempted to wrest control away from the foreign investors. In little more than a generation under the rule of the shah, Iran had changed from a traditional, conservative, and rural society to one that was fast becoming industrialized, modern, and urban. But the shah had attempted too much, too quickly, for a country so steeped in a mature culture of simplicity and faith. After thirty years of Pahlavi rule the ordinary Iranian concluded the shah had failed through corruption, incompetence, or a complete lack of understanding to deliver what the people really needed - solid welfare, healthcare, educational and social systems. Instead, the shah had paid homage to the Western world and pushed, intimidated, and tortured the Iranian people into accepting industrialization without benefits.

The time had come for change. Under the guidance, persuasion, and promises of improvements in the lives of ordinary Iranians, their chosen but exiled imam, Ayatollah Ruhollah Khomeini, was being urged to return to his homeland. But just before he did, his supporters forced the Pahlavi family to flee Iran for their lives. This time the politics of the West was powerless to protect them - or perhaps they didn't want to.

In January 1979, in what was officially described as a "vacation," the shah and his family fled Iran on a Boeing 727 with the shah, himself at the helm, heading to Egypt after thirty-eight years on what was referred to as the Peacock Throne. It was said that, while he was in power, he had squirreled away some $20 billion in holdings and cash diverted from the profits of Iranian oil sales, in particular, and invested it in other countries for the personal use of his family. It has never been recovered.

Khomeini arrived in Tehran from exile in Paris to replace the Pahlavi dynasty amid wild rejoicing on February 1, 1979. He eventually declared Iran an Islamic Republic, promising to purge the country of Western influence. Khomeini's Revolutionary Guard replaced SAVAK, the shah's own cruel, and often, secret service. One of the Revolutionary Guard's prime objectives was to prevent a CIA-backed coup, such as the one that had brought the first pro-Western Pahlavi family back to power in the 1950s. It operated principally in the same manner as the SAVAK – except, perhaps, better organized, but still just as ruthless and secretive.

During the first twenty years of their rule, the Regime—with support from the Revolutionary Guard—developed far-reaching anti-western policies intended to suppress western influence and replace all foreign senior positions and companies in Iran, wherever possible. However, it was impossible to totally avoid the help of westerners', and remnants of their technical support teams remained in-country.

Facing persecution and violent upheaval, many of the Iranian elite fled the country on Khomeini's return rather than be forced from power and into compliance with the mullahs. The middle class essentially deserted their homeland and found new homes in many countries around the world. Most never returned. Thousands of youngsters from all levels of life also left Iran, seeking an education in Europe and the US, that wasn't available to them in their home country under the Regime.

But, just as the shah had only been in power for thirty-eight years, it seemed as though the Islamic Regime was running out of political favor with Iranians after a similar period of rule. Between 2010 and 2017, there were constant street demonstrations and youth riots and, while they were brutally resisted by the Regime using the muscle of the Revolutionary Guard and out-sourced mercenaries, they continued to gather momentum and became unified. Again, the political and social scene in Iran was targeted, bolstered by internal strife, this time with a more educated population.

Hossein had been one of the young people who had joined the mass exodus of youth when Khomeini first came to power, having left for an education in America where he met and married Liz, an American and fellow student. But he returned to Iran in 2015, with Liz, and they settled in Sari. There, through conversations at small social gatherings they started to subconsciously impart their thoughts, about the potential for a better life, to the Iranians around them, based on what they had learned in the US and travels through Europe. But their strategy for change, if they ever knowingly had one, had a long fuse.

On the other hand, Amir Sazesh, a young Iranian from the city of Chalus west of Sari, had also returned home with an energy for reform that was palpable. He had been back home in Chalus since 2012, when his American education inspired him to start a movement for social change called Friends of Iran. Unlike Hossein, Amir had maintained a web of contacts throughout Iran of like-minded, newly Western-educated youth who had also returned home.

Since 1999, long before Amir's arrival, there had been demonstrations voicing anti-government frustrations, in the streets of cities throughout Iran. But now, fueled by the more educated and cohesive Friends of Iran, a new wave of anti-government demonstrations swept the country in 2017, expressing broad discontent and a desire for both radical political and social changes.

Amir's following increased exponentially over the years to the point that the Regime eventually recognized the movement as one to be carefully monitored. They planned to do something about it if Friends of Iran presented a real political threat.

While Hossein was aware of the demonstrations and the Friends of Iran, he tended to keep a low profile, as was his nature. But he continued to watch from the sidelines and attended their local meetings along the Caspian coastline. All like-minded people were welcome.

Meanwhile, NPC, with its Western partners, continued to control the 5.4 million barrels of exported crude, unrefined oil from Iran—at least in the short term—while the Islamic Regime developed its strategy for the future. Most of the crude oil flowed to the southern coast from oilfields located in Tabriz, Tehran, Esfahan, Abadan, and others, for export through the Strait of Hormuz to the US, Europe, and countries west, to be refined and consumed.

But times were changing, and Iran was being heavily courted by China and Russia while, at the same time, continuously sanctioned by the Western world as a consequence of its anti-west politics, terrorist support, and a nuclear program that was deemed by the west to be a serious threat to world stability.

In addition, both China and Russia were aggressively focused on replacing the US dollar with the petrodollar as the universal currency. As a consequence,

Iran was looking to break all commercial ties with the West, particularly Britain and America, and join its new allies as it searched for autonomy. That meant a dramatic reduction in oil exports to the West, without diminishing revenues.

Before his exile, the shah had conceived of a new, world-class, refinery to be built near Sari on the north side of the Alborz Mountains, close to the Caspian Sea. The shah envisaged processing Iranian crude oil before exporting it and reaping the rewards from oil derivatives rather than sending 'his' crude to offshore processing facilities for them to benefit. He wanted to build a new seaport to handle the refined oil products, adjacent to the recently completed 2,035-megawatt Neka power plant, on the Caspian shoreline, that would be expanded. His plan was to reduce freight costs and piracy risks by avoiding lengthy transport route through the Straits of Hormuz in the south to western ports for at least a portion of the oil.

Before the Khomeini Regime came to power, Iran's plan was to redirect some 30 percent of its national oil output from the southern oilfields to the new Sari refinery for processing and then pipe the final products to the Neka port for export to the West through Turkey.

Over the ensuing reign of the Islamic Regime, different ideas on how they wanted to manage Iran's resources were developed as they kindled relationships with Russia and China and pushed themselves further away from dependency on the West. When Khomeini died in 1989, the Regime he created still planned to build a 400,000-barrels-per-day oil refinery close to Sari and redirect about 30 percent of the country's oil output to the new facility. But the processed products would be re-directed to Russia and China, and away from Europe and beyond.

The Regime also proposed a phase two to increase the capacity of the refinery to process almost 60 percent of the country's oil production. At a production rate of some 800,000 barrels of processed oil per day (BPD), the Sari refinery would be second in size to the largest in the world—the 1.24-million-BPD Ramnager Refinery in Gujurat, northwest India. The second phase would dramatically reduce the flow of crude oil to Europe by sending it all to the east, not to the west. Iran's oil revenues would increase as a consequence of the refining process, and financially support their continuation of cutting ties with the west. Autonomy would follow and the influence of the west seriously jeopardised as thoughts of a petro-dollar international currency standard started to sound possible.

The Islamic Regime's strategy for the future was a bitter blow to both the US and the UK oil industries and governments, who had already funded phase one of the new refinery and its infrastructure. They had provided and paid for the engineering, and were currently supplying the construction management, know-how, and senior operations personnel, as well as secured contracts to manage the oil distribution. They were also guaranteed a share in the profits from the sales.

The Islamic Regime's plan hamstrung NPC's western affiliates. The NPC agreements were with the traditional western oil companies, including Domar Oil, which controlled 50 percent of the world's oil refineries through its operations. Such a radical departure from these commitments was untenable and financially ruinous to the West.

As Hossein looked out over the valley, he didn't like what he saw. Unbeknownst to him, neither did the Friends of Iran, let alone the western oil companies and their governments. It wasn't so much the new refinery that riled him as what it represented for the future of the Iranian people. The Islamic Regime was severing traditional Iranian associations, and the future of its people was about to be put into the hands of the Russians and Chinese—notorious, untrustworthy and historic enemies located too close for comfort. For the ordinary Iranian, another loss of Western influence was not something to look forward to. It would undoubtedly be followed by more sanctions, and life was already hard for the ordinary man in the street suffering from import and export limitations of household goods as a consequence of Iran's refusal to de-nuclearize, combined with their clandestine support for international terrorism. This was just one more nail in the coffin.

Something had to be done by the West, and perhaps by the newly aroused social antagonists, to manage the status quo, if not improve it, and prevent any long-term alliances with Russia and China.

This is not a story about the 1979 exodus of the shah of Iran, nor the arrival of Khomeini, nor the hostage taking, nor the forty years between then and now. It is a fictional story mixed with facts, based on the author's experiences in Iran during the 1978/79 revolution, combined with much research. It tells a tale of potential when, forty years after Khomeini's return to Iran, the Iranian people eventually rise up against the dictatorial Islamic rule with its medieval methods of population control. It is a story of how the West sets out to reverse the anti-west actions of the Khomeini-created Regime and restore some semblance of positive relationships with a "refreshed" Republic supported by the Iranian people.

Even though Khomeini died in June 1989 after ten years in power, during which his Regime essentially created a surprisingly stable but anti-Western government, the Regime lived on in this version of history and is referred to as the Islamic Regime, the Islamic Republic, or just the Regime, throughout this story. Regardless of its name, it had its roots in the brain of Khomeini.

* * *

ORB – 2017

Murray Stockman, or Stockman as even his friends called him, stared over the scene of Montreal spread before him from the window of his fifteenth-floor northeast-facing office in the Sun Life Building on René Lévesque Boulevard, although he didn't actually notice the view. He clasped his hands behind his back and his lowered head revealed him to be deep in thought as he muttered to himself. The deeper he thought, the less he noticed his surroundings.

Stockman was an inch under six feet tall, powerfully built, sharply intelligent, and in his early sixties. He sported cropped graying hair and a matching beard trimmed in a short point below the chin. He dressed in his typical casual style, this time a black-and-white houndstooth jacket that reminded him of his Scottish heritage, black chinos, and a plain black Burberry T-shirt complemented with well-polished but well-worn black loafers. He wore socks, unlike his younger counterparts, who somehow believed that a lack of socks proved something of their character. Maybe it did, but he didn't get it.

Rocking gently back and forth on the balls of his feet, Stockman asked and tried to answer his own questions but occasionally stumbled in a barely perceptible murmur. He talked to himself a lot when he was thinking his way through a problem. His hand would go to his beard, and he would slip his finger and thumb through the whiskers, feeling the tingle on his skin as they bristled in different directions. His coffee remained untouched on his desk, next to a pile of unanswered messages received during the brief absence when he had taken his thirty-six-foot Hunter sailboat out for short trips on Two Mountains Lake. Unfortunately, he had to mix business with pleasure, given the urgent nature of the circumstances his new clients had briefly described in a twenty-minute call before he left.

He had met some representatives of Domar Oil, one of the world's largest

US-based oil companies, at the sailing club for a few hours to discuss their problems of operating in Iran and the difficulties they were experiencing with the Islamic Regime. Afterward, he spent two days on the lake, clearing his brain and distractedly catching up with his sailing, thinking over what had been discussed, and what they needed from him and ORB. Their request was clear; the solution was not. They wanted to continue with their control over the Iranian oil-processing and -distribution system, and the Islamic Regime was working vigorously in the opposite direction.

This was the first time he had been in the office, since those few days away, to review the problems Domar Oil had put before him. It was not the first time the issue had raised its head. A short while ago, some representatives from the US and British governments had visited Stockman in Montreal and described the problem as it affected politics. They wondered if it was possible for Stockman's group to help the situation. But they had an additional problem. The Islamic Regime and their new alliances with the Russians and Chinese were threatening the balance of power between East and West by planning to cut oil exports to the West and increasing them to the East. Sanctions had failed to change the Regime's course, and the West was at a loss as to how to resolve the problem without having to take military action.

After the visit with the American and British government agents, Stockman began formulating an action plan. His meeting with Domar only helped him to flesh out the plan. He relished the thought of government and private industry working toward a common goal, and he was ready to put the project before his board.

* * *

Stockman had come a long way from where he had been when Domar Oil had first hired him. Those were the days when the oil cartel, comprising OPEC members, had come to rely heavily upon the imagination and initiative of Domar Oil, which controlled some 35 percent of the total world oil development and refining, to maintain their influence in the industry. Based in the US, with their European office based in London, Domar was the natural leader in this initiative, needing to protect its acquisitions and operations in more than the twelve basic areas of the world. The individual areas were each represented by a security chief. These chiefs were distanced from the internal politics, operations, clients, and all manner of business clutter that might get in the way of their work. They identified and resolved obstacles, from those associated with employees to governments that got in the way of control by Domar.

These chiefs had the authority to protect Domar's interests, whatever the costs. They had met many times over the years as their plans became more formalized in an attempt to find common ground in a single plan to establish a solid obstacle to the progression of power and control by other oil companies throughout the world.

It had not been easy, keeping control of this group of security chiefs. Their backgrounds were varied. Some had a violent nature, emanating from their warfare experiences, while others were experienced in the more sophisticated warfare of business. The mix of ideas was interesting indeed. At one point, it really seemed as though there would be neither common ground nor any common understanding of what was needed. But at the start, there really hadn't been a leader among them. They each individually answered to the CEO of Domar Oil and no one else.

But they needed a leader, and Stockman was the natural choice. He was well-liked and respected, knew all of the chiefs, knew the CEO on a personal basis, had years of experience, and was eager to consolidate the thinking. He listened to everyone, consulted with each security chief, and combined what he could into a manifesto for the chiefs to help guide them. Of course, he had consulted with the CEO before his position was advertised. From that point forward, the security chiefs would be coordinated through Stockman.

To date, the evolution of new developments and subsequent refineries was on the increase throughout the major oil-producing Middle Eastern and near-eastern countries at a rate of one per year. That added a capacity of between 200,000 to 500,000 barrels of new oil each year to the already swollen available stocks. Prices increased as OPEC manipulated them at will, despite the glut. But the glut was causing long-term availability to be restricted. There was worldwide panic as the West and Japan realized that not only were stocks depleting rapidly because of an over-abundance of oil on the market and the natural urge by humans to consume oil as fast as it was produced, but the major oil producers were also calling the shots on costs and power. Somehow, since the OPEC nations seemed not to be interested in open and reasonable debate, there had to be other means of control. That was not easy when foreign governments were in and out of power within four years or so and depended upon their popular vote to stand any chance of re-election.

Re-election was not going to be possible if they insisted that their populations had to become restrictive in their oil use. It was an almost unthinkable idea for a politician to conceive. Somehow there had to be other solutions to controlling the market price and volume of oil available. It was most unlikely that the general public would be able to be relied upon to help in that initiative, what with second, third, and even fourth cars being added to the family garage. It was far more reasonable to think that it was possible to control the oil-producing nations' output. This was the basis upon which Stockman and his group worked to find their solution.

Somehow, they had to find a way to slow down the progress of the eastern oil-producing nations in such mammoth proportions that the world would have to stop for long enough to enact new initiatives, establish new policies, and introduce a new order of things.

Stockman turned to a long-term associate of his, Eddie S. Sloan or Sloan, as everyone called him.

Sloan ran an agency out of London for skilled tradesmen willing and able to go overseas through his Sloan Agency. He had been a center for recruitment for all manner of industrial projects for the last fifteen years. As his reputation grew, so did the different requests made of him by disassociated parties.

It had been thirteen years since he had been first offered a substantial amount of money to attend to the partial destruction of a gold-mining operation set to open in southwestern Australia. It was so high in grade, so inexpensive to mine and process, and so high in forecasted output—using a massive lineup of the largest grinding mills in the world—that it would have unsettled the price of gold through over-supply as soon as the product hit the world market.

Sloan had sent a small team of electrical and mechanical people to infiltrate the contractor's forces and delay start-up of the plant by almost a year. It was long enough to bankrupt the plant owner, who couldn't survive the lengthy period without revenue, and for Sloan's client to buy the property out from bankruptcy for twenty cents on the dollar.

Sloan liked the work. The problems his people created were hard to trace, and the rewards were incredibly high. No one suspected such highly skilled tradesmen to be saboteurs.

Sloan started to take a harder look at the companies he had become involved with. He made sure that he circulated by attending whatever business functions he could, including getting closer to the Domar Oil security chiefs. He learned a lot about where the responsibilities lay within the company. He had learned a lot more about the politics of the energy business in particular, as well as precious-metals markets, the fierce competition for these markets, and their subsequent power. Sloan laid himself open to being invited to help each and every one solved their little power struggles. It was Sloan who had overheard three of the Domar Oil security managers talking about the state of the industry and the problems with the Middle Eastern countries and their power gains. It was Sloan who had awkwardly suggested, through a flippant maneuver of words, that maybe they ought to be slowed up and that maybe he could help to do it.

Within twenty-four hours, Sloan was being led through that back lane off Nathan Street in Hong Kong to the painted-out room that Stockman liked to use for some of his clandestine operations. There were several of the Domar security chiefs with Stockman at the head of the table. The security chiefs soon realized that here among them was the potential answer to their dilemma of slowing down the Middle Eastern oil suppliers—through sabotage at such a low level that it would be virtually impossible for anyone to suspect a national or international plan of any kind.

Over the next six months, Stockman met with Sloan every few months to take things a step further. Stockman had been set up as a clearing center for the security chiefs. If there was a problem, they would go to him, and he would assign resources as needed to resolve the issue. Sloan was effective in responding and his loyalty was never in question, but he was still a contractor and free to take work wherever he saw it.

After a couple of years, other parties who had heard of Stockman's methods of working began to seek his advice on how to handle their "special" problems. They came in all manner of types, sizes, locations, and groups, including governments. It didn't take long for Stockman to leave Domar and set himself up as an industry consultant, available to help companies and governments execute projects they could not easily manage themselves. He formed the Organization for Restructuring Business, more commonly known as ORB. Sloan became an associate and service provider.

Stockman was now the director of a loosely bound group of experts—ranging from finance to oil and gas, from legal to political, from builders to ex-CSIS, from industrialists to architects, from authors to pilots—a mixed group of professionals who called ORB their center and Stockman their conductor.

ORB received funding and credentials from trusted governments around the world, and it remained a mystery, cloaked in secrecy, to the mainstream. Each of the "consultants" were gainfully employed—or retired—within their own industry but answered ORB's call when requested to provide advice, action, or background for a project. Projects ranged from company takeovers to reorganizations, from political interference to coups, military interference, re-branding, and all other manner of intrigue that more visible groups, political or otherwise, could not reasonably perform without raising substantial, difficult-to-answer questions. All projects were generally dealt with in a non-military style, although there were the occasional "accidents" when field operatives had to take matters into their own hands for the good of the project.

Projects were presented for consideration by the ORB directors who had political and industrial leadership experience and were handpicked by Stockman. The directors vetted the projects, voted on them, and either accepted or rejected them as ORB targets.

Now, it was the petrochemical companies, as well as the US and UK governments, that sought ORB's help. The Islamic Regime's anti-West Iran was becoming a huge problem. With the end of the twenty-five-year pro-West Pahlavi rule, the oil-rich nation was turning away from the West and naively looking to the likes of Russia and China to fill the gap left by departing Western companies and secure its future on the world stage—as though they would be any better help than what they'd had previously.

Somehow, ORB was expected to help reverse the anti-West trend and get things back on track for the western oil companies and governments. It was certainly a tall order, but by all accounts, it would seem that Iran could be ripe for change again.

Stockman put a brief together for his directors. They would have an emergency meeting at the beginning of the following week in London, where the majority of them were based. It was still the center for business, despite many attempts by the Russians and Chinese to change the financial world's focus to other venues. It was too entrenched in the complex web of people, services, and information to move without losing an awful lot of power and resources along the way.

Stockman had left for England on the following Saturday and allowed himself a day of rest in London before meeting with the directors in the Canary Wharf office they had mutually agreed to keep for ORB business. It was a useful location on the banks of the Thames River and had served them well over the years.

The meeting was quite brief, and there seemed to be more personal catching up to do than business, but they covered some of the loose ends from other ventures that had been completed but still needed some massaging.

Stockman was on his way back to Montreal the following afternoon after he had spent a very enjoyable, if not decadent, supper with the whole group. It was an occasion that only happened two or three times a year, but it gave everyone a chance to catch up and provide a solid nod of approval to the new project that Stockman had brought before them. He was pleased with the approval, although he still had some concerns about the complexity of the project, and he had certainly not yet ironed out a strategy that could be put into motion as soon as he would have liked. That would take more thinking.

As Stockman sat in the business lounge at Heathrow before his flight, he listed some of the names of people he would need on the Sari refinery project in northern Iran. Matthew Black was certainly his choice for the field operations lead. He had all the qualifications needed as a saboteur, as well as being discrete and timely. He knew how to handle people and was quick enough on his feet to beat the best. Yes, he would work out very well.

Ideally, Stockman needed folks who could both read and write Farsi, but not all had to have that qualification. There were always interpreters, and he didn't want to compromise his choice of the best people for the project on the basis they had to speak the language. His daughter, Emma, would be a good choice because of her welding experience, understanding of ORB objectives, and support of Matthew on previous projects—sometimes without his realizing. This time, she would be used in field construction as a saboteur.

Stockman remembered Dick Elliot, another associate of his. Dick was now managing Interstate EPC, which, if he remembered correctly, was the prime contractor for the Sari refinery and likely to remain so for the second phase. Dick was old guard, a remnant of the '79 revolution, and had escaped with his wife and family at the time. He would have the insight and knowledge needed for this particular area, and likely still had good contacts to call upon. Stockman had to contact Dick to see if he could help him place people on his team in the field. Yes, that would be a great help.

Gradually, Stockman put a concept together in his head. He would need people to sabotage the new pipelines and the power plant expansion. He would need people to communicate with Domar Oil and the Americans, the UK, and other "most interested" parties. He would use his directors to communicate with governments.

There were so many other details he had to work out but he knew that if he selected the right team members, they would do a lot of the thinking for him once they kicked into the project. They had done it all before. The only thing that left him anxious was the situation with the Islamic Regime. He would have to think harder on that problem but was optimistic that the internal politics of Iran were ripe for change given the number of uprisings that had occurred over the last twenty years.

Stockman knew he had to do more than sabotage the refinery to accomplish the task. He thought about how the Islamic Regime spent the revenues earned from the sale of oil and gas, and how critical it was for them to maintain that level of income to support their other endeavors. He remembered Plato and his wife Margaret, whom he had used a number of years ago to help ORB manage relationships between the Peruvians, Chileans, and Ecuadorians after the no-fly zone was established on the Ecuadorian-Peruvian border. They had got that well under control without resorting to military action, and the border was still intact, although Chile and Peru still couldn't get along, and Ecuador didn't trust Peru. Plato had brought his financial wizardry and manipulation to bear on the decision makers and brought them to the table.

Stockman needed to locate the two of them and see what they were up to. He thought he remembered that Margaret had a father who was in the US Diplomatic Corps and had some substantial backdoor influence with foreign regimes. He was fairly sure it included Iran.

Stockman boarded his plane and as soon as the chance came, leveled his seat to the bed position and got comfortable for the flight back to Montreal. It would be long enough for a nap and short enough not to seize up.

* * *

Friends of Iran – 2018

Jafaar Sazesh gathered his family around the low dining room table for their evening meal. After the short prayer of thanks, he tore the naan into strips, as was his custom, and invited his five sons to take their places. He passed a strip of the bread to each of them. His wife, Saphir, stood by his side, waiting for a sign from her husband indicating that everything was as it should be. It came in the usual form of a twitch of the wrist above the tabletop—that was her sign to return to the kitchen, where she and her daughter would clean up and listen in on the men's conversation.

The women would eat later, after their men had finished their meal of rice, dried smoked fish, and diced mixed salad plus naan, plenty of naan. They had ignored Saphir's retreat as the five of them scooped their food between thumb and spoon from the large plate placed in the center of an otherwise sparse table, heaping it onto the dish in front of them and from there onto the naan, a spoonful at a time. They pinched the food between the folded naan and sandwiched it into their mouths. The first few mouthfuls were enough to satiate the initial pangs of hunger. Conversation began, occasionally interrupted by further mouthfuls of food washed down with sweet chai or water. There was laughing, jostling, pushing, and insulting each other in a way only brothers could. Jafaar just looked on and smiled. He was so proud of them.

With rice falling to the table from his talking-eating mouth, Jafaar looked at Amir, his eldest son. Jafaar was on the advance team for the operations of the new refinery in Sari. They were a group of originally untrained locals, considered to be of high intellect—including Jafaar, who had started at the plant four years before it was due to operate—and would become thoroughly accustomed to the details of the facility as it was being constructed, then set up the operations manuals and define the test systems for pre-operational testing when the time came. It was a mammoth chore with over 300 utility and process systems to be checked out as they were physically completed. That work would start in about twenty months with the utility systems first—power, air, and water.

"Work is going well with construction, and I'm really looking forward to helping operate this new plant." Jafaar looked around at his sons. In addition to his day job, he continued to be the leader of a movement of workers intending to legalize their union status with employers. He had started the formation of the loosely bound group while his son, Amir, was getting his graduate and post-graduate education in America. Even before Amir had left for America, he shared a common ideological belief with his father, albeit unencumbered by experience, that life for the ordinary Iranian had to improve. After the first five years of the Islamic Republic rule, it was clear that Khomeini had not, could not, or would not improve the lives of the Iranian people despite his promises in those fiery rhetorical speeches in March 1979.

Jafaar was proud of what he had accomplished since 2005, when he first formed the original social group with a number of his friends in Chalus. He had made it out of the fields, where so many generations of his family had toiled to scrape together some kind of a living and where so many still toiled. He knew, and his friends knew, there were better ways to live.

"I think we are almost ready to declare ourselves as a union under the laws of Iran," Jafaar smiled broadly. There was already a union to represent the oil industry workers, based on US standards, but it was the only union in Iran at the time. He smiled and squeezed a mouthful of naan and rice into his mouth.

"That is good, father," Amir responded. "Do you think the companies and the government will accept it, though? You know, actually legalize it and allow it to flourish?"

"I think so, my son." Jafaar looked serious as he pondered the question. Clearly, he was 100-percent sure it would pass the scrutiny and approval of the Regime. "Well, so far, so good, and my senses tell me that they have to know it would be good for them, and us, to have just this one group to deal with instead of so many individuals, each with their own desires and demands. It will be good, I am sure." Jafaar looked down at the table; he was optimistic but still troubled.

Nothing was guaranteed. The Regime could be so unpredictable, and it would only take the influence of a small group of radical mullahs to set him back years. He reached for another piece of naan. He was not totally unconcerned, and there was still a lot of work to do, a lot of convincing, a lot of talking needed, but he had been doing this now for many years and felt the time was coming when his close supporters would push for legitimization.

Despite the exploding populations of many Iranian cities, there was still no integrated federal or provincial welfare system and no representation for the common man in the workplace. The children would still have to leave Iran to find higher education. They might never return, and life would have provided little for those who remained or didn't have the wherewithal to understand how they could improve their lives. Jafaar had realized this many years ago and had formed a club of sorts that met weekly in a coffee house to secretly talk about things they had never been able to talk openly about without recrimination from the authorities. But now, after all the talk and all the planning, they concluded that they, the forefathers, should initiate the first step to create some kind of collective body to represent the working person.

It was a bold imperative given the circumstances of Iran, and none of them had the fortune of experiencing similar plans in other countries. Some had experience of unions from their work in the Iranian oilfields, where unionization had a strong hold, and they advised Jafaar on the pros and cons where they could. He never realized the extent of unions for everyone that already existed in many parts of democratic society outside Iran's borders.

There appeared to be some unspoken support from the mullahs, who claimed to advocate for improvements in the lives of the common man, although they remained suspicious of the motives and what the longer-term consequences could be. They maintained a close watch over Jafaar and his group for any threat to their politics, but it wasn't yet clear.

As Jafaar's group gained strength in numbers, it also gained the strength to talk about members' thoughts more openly. Their first "open" meeting had attracted many who came to hear the speeches more out of curiosity than intent to pursue further at that time. But it had been a success in so far as it was not a failure.

Support had been warm, considering the masses had learned to be nothing else over the years but apathetic to change. They had always been lulled by the Regime into believing that their lives would improve with time and resources—but they were becoming increasingly suspicious as the Islamic Regime did not appear to be improving anything at all. Fear of retribution from the SAVAK in the time of the Shah had done nothing to help the plight of the ordinary man, and now there was the Revolutionary Guard to replace them and control the population. It was becoming more and more apparent that nothing was really changing for the ordinary person. Even strength in numbers meant little if the numbers weren't completely dedicated to the cause, and the thought that the ordinary Iranian working man could change the whole basis of society was beyond imagination for most of them. But they listened and gradually absorbed the ideology. There were no repercussions. There were no disappearances in the middle of the night. Jafaar was still there. He was still outspoken but respectful.

Jafaar assumed the leadership of this group that had created a loosely held and fragile worker's union with just enough impassioned glue to prevent it from coming apart. But membership was growing faster than anyone had expected, as social media expanded so rapidly and touched the lives of many. People became more educated through access to the internet. The educated youth were returning from their studies overseas. More education meant more discontent with the same old, same old.

Employers looked on with amusement as their workers talked among themselves. They considered them their children. Rambunctious, questioning but ignorant, suggesting but not demanding for fear of retribution, workers remained compliant. Corporate management had often met to discuss the desire for unionization, but it always seemed almost an afterthought to the meeting and was relegated to the last item on the agenda. Discussions were brief and mostly ignored as the new group was acknowledged but considered an idle idea, born more out of boredom than reality. It seemed to be a good idea that the employees were taking an interest in collaborative ideas. They might as well carry on as the corporations looked the other way.

But no one had anticipated such a forward momentum of Jafaar's union movement as it gathered more membership and more interest. The private world remained aloof from the government world and neither collaborated on the potential for another stronghold in the country. But both were ignorant of the infiltration of communist antagonizers who willingly became involved with the people to fan the embers of underlying discontent. The powers-to-be in the Regime had not understood that their foreign compatriots—with whom they had shared meals in Paris or London or New York or Munich—were subversively encouraging the new movement of Jafaar and his friends as they foresaw a long-term potential to undermine the Regime. Jafaar's group was only one of many that were rising at the same time all over the country.

Once ORB got involved, they recruited a small group to keep their eyes and ears on extremists planted in Jafaar's supporters and acting whenever they had to remove the irritation. Not all of them were Russian. Some were from the West, paid to run rampant through the Jafaar's organization, sowing seeds of misinformation, claiming communist ties, and running counter to what Jafaar's people were doing in trying to increase interest and membership. Some were sponsored by Eastern governments and private industries looking out for themselves, but many were hired by Iranians to upset the momentum and turn people against unions. It wasn't easy to keep up with the dissenters, but regardless the union still continued to gather momentum.

Little did the Regime grasp of the significance of this new union movement until the returning Western-educated young Iranians started their own movement, Friends of Iran. Suddenly, there were at least two new major alien groups to contend with, and it seemed they could be considered to augment each other—the power of the new union and the upsurge of the rebellious, educated youth looking for a future that the Regime could not, or would not, provide. It had the potential to threaten the very cornerstone of the autocratic government policies the Islamic Regime used to control the Iranian masses.

The time came for Jafaar to present his much-prepared message to a national audience. Jafaar's followers, all over Iran, had waited for this moment when at last they could tune into their radio station at precisely the same time to listen to someone they trusted, who had not been perverted by wealth, power, the immorality of Iran's politics, or the extremism of religious zealotry. Jafaar's proposal was fully supported by the union workers in the Iranian oilfields who believed any potential additional union would strengthen their own position. The listeners were galvanized by the very thought that they might actually get to control and manipulate their future. Indications had been arriving from all over the country that other groups had been formed and were following him closely. Jafaar had received a number of coded messages from Western countries and corporations that indicated their support and wished him luck. ORB was among them.

"What do you think?" Jafaar stopped eating and looked up from his plate to his son's face.

Amir had returned from a somewhat low-grade university in the US, where he had graduated with a diploma in political sciences and returned to an Islamic Regime-run country. His intent had been to simply gain an education not available to him in Iran, where his father held the post of a refinery operator, one of the many that had benefited from some industrialization in the north. He had received more than an academic education. Unlike many students, he had developed an intense interest in his subjects once he realized the worth of such knowledge to his family, friends, and country. The education had turned into an experience in a land where freedom of speech was considered a right. He looked around him and had seen democracy, even with its faults, and concluded that his own culture could benefit from some of this with a little massaging and control.

After graduation, Amir had worked for a year with a social group in America, which showed him the good and bad side of life there. The social structure was defined by well-worn boundaries and money was so obviously ill-distributed. The poor knew they were poor, and their desire for democracy betrayed them. The constant barrage of commercialism led the people like sheep and the rich got richer in the name of free enterprise. Somewhere there had to be a compromise. He didn't realize this was a condition even in his own country, but it was to the extreme in America.

Amir had wandered back through the countries of Europe, Turkey, and on to Iran and his home in Chalus. During his travels, he experienced different social structures, new ideas, and novel, unique, and workable political systems. Little did he know that he was just one of the thousands of youngsters throughout eastern Europe and the Middle East who were finding out the same things.

Arriving home to his family, he quickly realized the import of his learning and the changes that could be made for the better, if only...

It had taken Amir and a small group of friends almost a year, through the formation of their group, Friends of Iran, to gradually surround themselves with like-minded youth to listen to some reason based, in part, on the ideologies of the communist Tudeh Party, routed to near non-existence by the shah and then Khomeini, not because of their communist ways but because they posed a threat to the Republic's domination. The Friends of Iran were still formulating a comprehensive manifesto, but they had already become an irritant to the Islamic Regime. Better for the Republic to stamp these things out early than allow them to fester and perhaps eventually gain momentum to become a force to be reckoned with. So, the Regime formulated a plan.

Amir's father listened, in a paternal but envious way, as a proud father might with a son who has achieved an educational standard denied him when he was younger. His son's words started to mean something as Jafaar realized that despite all his work to orchestrate a union to represent the worker, his own sons might one day be forced to follow him into the refinery, where they would still be met with a future leading to little else but managing to provide food and shelter for their families without the cultural simplicity of their history, unless something greater was accomplished to change things dramatically. Otherwise, it didn't seem the future would be a lot different from the old ways of surviving, except that they would now be able to buy stuff. But here was Amir, the originator of the Friends of Iran, a group dedicated to far more than just unionizing the worker. It was a group dedicated to national change on a scale that the ordinary Iranian man was incapable of conceiving.

Amir sat opposite his father and returned the stare, while each of them took those first few mouthfuls as though only they realized their shared secret.

"What do I think, Father?" Amir grinned and continued to stare at his father as though their minds were coming together.

Within a few minutes, each of them broke into a grin that widened to split the face from ear to ear. A moment later, their grins had turned to laughs as they continued the unspoken secret. Before either could secure the next mouthful, they broke into raucous laughter, and as Amir started to choke, his father rose and walked around the table to pat his son heavily on the back while both gradually regained control.

"It will be a great day, my sons, when we embrace each other and state our common cause. There has been no time like this that I can recall in my lifetime. You will all live to benefit, and I thank you, my son, Amir, for opening our eyes," Said Jafaar as he waved his arms at his sons in an all-inclusive gesture.

None of the others really understood the common denominator Jaffar and Amir were referring to. But they joined in regardless and laughed out loud and reached out to touch each other and revel in this new fervor. It was contagious.

Jafaar looked at Amir with tears in his eyes and stretched his hands across the table, reaching for him. Amir responded by holding his father's hands tightly. Jafaar stared at him for some time before talking.

"We are only the teachers, but you are now the power. As youngsters in a land of old leaders, our words could be meaningless. But even though you now have the education and the wisdom we have provided, you must not ignore the dangers all around us. Our government will not readily succumb to a new order simply because it would be good for the people. They are far too important for that," he said with a hint of sarcasm, "and they may not even realize the effects that you are having on the young people of our country."

Jafaar retracted his hands, pinched the naan into his mouth again, took a sip of chai, and waited for his son.

"Our movement is becoming well known, as you know, Father. It is true that it is composed of the youth of our country who have hopes for changes. While many elected to return to Iran with an education and remain cloistered with their families, they are no longer numbed by apathy. We are uniting with a common cause that we can now identify."

Amir looked as though he wanted to say something but, instead, sank back in his chair and slowly chewed another mouthful of rice and naan to help stop him from talking. He washed it down with a glass of water and sat still.

Jafaar was eating and watching. He looked around at his other four sons and realized the conspiracy. He still said nothing and realized, in that moment, that while he and his friends were fighting their small battles for unionization, the larger one went on without them. And his sons were a part of it all. Jafaar broke into another laugh, developing into a heavy guffaw. He

looked about him and raised the rice-filled naan above his head as though in salute to each of his sons.

"You must go on," he said after the boys broke into smiles of realization that their father understood, "and thank Allah there is something stronger than us old men who will fight and be satisfied with our small victories. But I am puzzled." Jafaar smacked his lips, wiped the naan around the large platter in the center of the table, and looked up again. "You say that you have identified the cause, yet I had always thought it to be such common knowledge that was better left unspoken."

Amir met his father's eyes again.

"You may not fully understand, Father," Amir said with no malice intended. "Perhaps there is much that mars your view. Perhaps this cause that we have identified is too large to imagine, and it will shake the very foundation that you have been building upon for these last forty years."

It was Jafaar's turn to hold up his hand to stop his son from continuing.

"Before you go on, let me tell you a little of how we have arrived at this point, and then we shall see if I understand your cause. Perhaps you may conclude from this that we really are not so different in our vision for the future." He stopped for a moment and wiped his mouth free of the few grains of rice caught up in his beard. "When I was a boy, our lives were simple. We owned land, supported ourselves, looked after each other, and reveled in our culture. When the first Reza Shah came to power from nothing in 1925, there was no objection from Iranians—neither rich nor poor. He was one of us, but he was also a leader. We had no real enemies at that time, and the adversaries we did have were not attracted to our desert lands or the small amount of agriculture in the north.

"But Reza Shah grew hungry for power. In doing so, he invited explorers as well as the wrath of our religious leaders, who had been only too pleased to maintain the simple lifestyles based on Islam. Still, we did nothing, expecting Reza Shah to see the errors of his ways and bend to the will of the mullahs. It was not to be. Before we, as a nation, realized it, we had become too divided to unite behind a common cause. When Reza Shah left his son to reign, with the power of the Pahlavi Dynasty becoming firmly established and supported by Western powers and their oil companies, his son, Reza Pahlavi, inherited the idea that he was the 'King of Kings.' It took only a short time for him to break the system apart while we, as a nation, stood by and watched without moving to stop it.

"Before we really understood what was happening, our country was being sold to outsiders, with the profits being pocketed by our self-professed political leaders.

"And then, the Pahlavis were replaced by the Islamic Republic. Did things change for the better? Of course not. We know that now. In fact, they got worse with the religious persecutions and extremist authority. We were sent back 100, 1,000 years or more in time.

"No, my sons, we are not blind. But believe me when I say that we understand the cause. It was only the bellows that were needed to fan the embers that we lacked, and as we get old, change becomes an inconvenience. We see no chance for us to achieve utopia for a country where the ordinary man would have rights with welfare and social services to provide security for his family, but perhaps we can at least unify our people in a simple cause as one small step forward while you, who have so much time, get on with the main event. I am happy it is all happening in my lifetime."

Jafaar looked around at his sons.

"If I died at this moment, I would be satisfied in the knowledge that my boys are the bellows and are kindling the fire, and that we have all played a part, no matter how small."

Amir nodded his head in understanding and looked around at his brothers. "And we thought we knew it all," he said as each of them started to laugh once more.

"Do not be jubilant too early." Jafaar became serious. "There is still much to do. We must continue to act independently to avoid discovery. There will be trouble yet, and we are a long way from uniting the people to the point where they will be willing to shed blood for the cause. It will take time, and it may still need a miracle. The embers have been fanned, but the fire has not yet caught."

They finished their meal in silence while Saphir stayed quietly in the kitchen with her daughter, thinking in which direction the women of Iran would lead their men next.

* * *

Cinema Rex: A Time to Die—2018

As dusk approached, Abdul Reza Ansur worked his broom from one side of Cinema Rex auditorium to the other while watching the rest of the cleaning staff head toward the storage room with their equipment. Having finished their work, the others stacked their tools and coveralls and dragged the garbage bags of litter to the yard outside for pick up in the morning. Without returning, they went back to their homes for the rest of the evening. Ansur, concluding that everyone had left except for the manager, who was occupied in the front office, as usual, wandered casually over to the storage cupboards. He looked cautiously about him as he placed his cleaning tools carelessly inside and closed the doors. He walked to the side entrance, made sure that the locking mechanism was intact to prevent entry from the outside, then sat in one of the cinema seats to wait for the sounds of the manager as he left on his nightly visit to the restaurant next door to partake in a lengthy meal before the next event. The Friends of Iran were holding a symposium in the auditorium in a couple of hours.

The slam of the exit door sounded the manager's departure. Ansur stealthily made his way toward the foyer, looking around corners and into offices before edging over to the front entrance, where he checked that the main doors had not inadvertently been left unlocked. Satisfied that the building was at last clear and secure, he made his way to the service area. Over the last few months, he had become accustomed to the layout of the building with a deliberate plan in mind to be executed now at this pre-determined time. This was the beginning of the culmination of his training that had begun four years ago with the Islamic Regime. Ansur was a dedicated, loyal extremist who would do anything, including committing suicide if asked, for the good of the Republic. He was a simple religious man with minimal mental peripheral vision. He thought of nothing but his orders. This was what he had been working toward, to please the Regime and earn a place in it.

Ansur had been an intense student with the Regime, cloistered in the mosque, avoiding social situations, never going out, never reading Western articles or books, and totally homed in on whatever task he was set. He was seriously embittered toward the regime of the shah, which had exiled his family for no reason other than for their support of the right to practice their religion. Their exile had been tragic. The family split and wandered aimlessly through Iraq as nomads. The impossibility of their return to their homeland had taken its toll on his parents, who had died during one of their attempts to return. His brother had been caught by SAVAK and had lived the remainder of his life behind the walls of the infamous Evin Prison in Tehran. By the time Khomeini came to power, his family had disappeared but the Regime had taken him in, cared for him, and indoctrinated him in the physical ways of defending the faith.

Ansur had wanted to leave his mark and had sought the guidance of his teachers, who assured him of his usefulness. The time had come some months previous, when a senior mullah with the Regime had called on him to discuss the situation with Friends of Iran—a youth group that appeared to be on a collision course with the Republic. He didn't know anything about these young men and didn't intend to find out. It would make no difference to him who they were. He was only concerned with what had to be done for the good of Islam and the Regime.

Ansur reached the service area and broke into the mechanical room. The metal door was secured with only a flimsy latch. He closed the door and turned the light on, although he felt that he could accomplish his task blindfolded. After blocking out the light from under the door—an unnecessary precaution but one borne out of his paranoid nature—he emptied his pockets of tools and unwrapped the rubber hose from around his waist.

The building was heated by hot water fed from the boiler fueled by three 20,000-gallon propane tanks crammed against the mechanical room's exterior wall. Pipes exited the building through the masonry wall to the outside, where they would be connected to a tanker refueling truck when needed. Inside the building, the tank feed piping was connected via a manifold leading to a vaporizer and into the boiler, where the fuel ignited and heated the water tanks.

Ansur swiftly located the manifold and traced the joined pipes back to the individual tanks. He isolated one of the tanks by turning the gate valves at each end to the closed position. Taking out a small hand drill, he bored a quarter-inch hole in the section of isolated pipe and allowed the propane to escape and dissipate before he continued.

Drilling a larger hole in the same place as the first, Ansur prepared to fit the specially made adapter in place. Using a small drift pin, he positioned the tee section over the hole and temporarily secured it with an epoxy resin. Using two circlips, he fastened the connection more permanently. Taking the rubber hose he had brought with him, Ansur fitted one end over the adapter and led the other end up to the air duct that led to the washroom. He pulled the two-hour timer from the bits and pieces he had spread out on the floor. The timer was a simple mechanical device that operated a flap that closed until it was activated to open by a timed release. He fitted this at the end of the hose and connected a short section of hose from the timer to the aluminum ducting. The ducting presented little problem for him to bore through and secure a small-diameter tee held in place by a small threaded metal flange.

He completed the total connection and reactivated the closed valves to permit propane to once again flow from all three tanks. After clearing all the tools away and making sure that the room left no trace of his presence behind, except for his handiwork at the tank and ducting, Ansur set the timer for two hours to coincide with 7:30 p.m., when the cinema would be quickly filling. He made his way from the service area and out through the side door into the alley, where he escaped under cover of dark.

He didn't congratulate himself. It was just a job, and now he needed to go back to Tehran. Back to the mosque and back to the safety and security of his religious family.

* * *

Amir and his brothers had finished their meal and left the table for Saphir to clear. While she labored over the cleanup and settled down to her own meal at the table with her daughter, the five brothers prepared themselves for the talk that was being given at the local cinema by the Friends of Iran. It was the only place in town that could hold that many people, unless they chose a mosque, and that was definitely out of the question. The topics on the agenda were far too sensitive for any of the truly religious community to attend, although it was very likely some would be present at the theater to learn more about what this potential enemy had to say.

It would be the largest gathering they had managed to get together. Amir was intending to give a talk, and this would be the evening he would officially assume leadership. He would nominate captains who would report to him from the forty-five local groups created throughout the country. Influence was another matter and had not yet come to the group, but that would follow if they ever grew into a political party to challenge the mullahs sometime in the future. But for now, it was enough just to be established as a nationally recognized group that promoted political change. If this gathering was a success, who knew where it would lead next.

The brothers' excitement mounted in tune with the rest of the crowd as they approached the theater. It seemed as though this event was attracting the majority of youth from the city and outlying areas. Though too early for the speakers to start, the enthusiastic young people busied themselves in passing the time by rushing from group to group with such exchanges of greetings that it was difficult to imagine that they actually saw each other almost every day. With much handshaking and arm-waving, they acknowledged each other as though long-lost brothers who had at last come together for a family reunion. This sort of camaraderie was their way of life, and while some might think it over the top, it was a necessary part of their culture. It reinforced relationships and bound them even tighter, as though they were the last of their kind and any loss would be unbearable.

So it was on this cooling evening.

The one double door to Cinema Rex opened and the seemingly unruly crowds spilled into the lobby. Part of the pleasure was the pushing and shoving to secure seats on a first-come-first-served basis, as often occurred in Middle Eastern and Asian countries, whether at a theater, airport, or bus stop. The only queue that appeared to have any semblance of orderliness was when fresh-baked naan was sold at the street bakeries twice a day.

Once inside the lobby, the ticket holders delighted in seeing who would be the first to get to their place within the auditorium. Amir, sporting a broad grin of victory, was the first of his brothers to reach a group of seats located roughly in the center of the theater. Amir left them and went up to the stage, where he consorted with others who were also speaking that evening. The other brothers sat with growing excitement, carelessly sharing provisions between them while continuing to acknowledge the greetings of surrounding friends as the building filled to near capacity.

At 7:40 p.m., Amir decided that a final trip to the washroom might be wise. He was not alone as a number of other members of the audience also made the last-minute dash before the speakers came out and took their seats on the dais. He made his way through the crowd by elbowing and shoving the less forceful to one side. The smell of the latrines went unnoticed by the occupants, who had come to accept it as a part of life, and the added smell of the infiltrating propane vapors remained undetected, causing no undue comments other than a casual puzzled look at one another as people concentrated on their task in hand. While Amir waited his turn, he caught a friend's eye who had decided to light his final smoke before the movie. For some unknown reason, Amir sniffed the already pungent air as though something had attracted his attention. His nostrils strained once more as his friend's cigarette caught. In that fleeting instant, it was as though something was trying to warn him, but too late. The realization flashed through his brain, and he dove under the sinks.

* * *

Sharp splinters of pain shot through his legs. Parts of the building spalled and several pieces fell on him, making him shrink back. He had no time to think about his friends or what had happened as the shock waves continued with a rumble. With the look of a terrified animal, he raised himself first onto one elbow and then to his feet. Screaming came from the rubble around him and from the auditorium. It was pandemonium.

On the verge of panic, he realized that he must get away. There were a number of lifeless bodies around him on the floor of the toilet. Making it to the double door at the entry, he threw himself at the bar lock but bounced back with an equally resounding force. Startled by the unexpected rejection, he got back up, but this time examined the door a little closer only to realize it was locked from the outside. The moans and screams behind him became secondary as he looked for an alternative escape. With hardly a second thought, he realized that a retreat through the auditorium was probably impossible and his only recourse was likely through the delivery door in the concession. He battered against the door, falling through to the outside of the building as a second blast compounded the devastation of the first. Those who had managed to grope their way to the auditorium exit had been prevented from further advance when the upper portions of the building collapsed over the lobby and doorways.

His hysteria reached a new high as screaming continued around him. It seemed to give him the additional strength he needed to break through and land head over heels in the alley off the main street. Just as he breathed a sigh of relief at having at last seemingly escaped the tragedy, a third blast ripped through the building. As he looked at the theater walls only feet away, cracks appeared and rumbling started.

Getting on all fours, Amir half ran, half crawled away as fast as he could, seeking refuge in a doorway across the street. As he turned back to Cinema Rex, it seemed to disintegrate before his eyes with the collapse of the load-bearing walls and the twisting of roof trusses. The buildings about him were now devoid of windows, and the streets alarmingly deserted of people. He watched with dust in his eyes as the picture cleared before him to reveal the mass of rubble. Straining forward, he waited as locals ran to the cinema to help, and he abstractedly started to dust himself off and fiddle with the tears in his clothes. He moved his limbs, checked for blood, felt over his body for damage, and tried to clear his head of the noise from the blast.

He could wait no longer as he examined the wreckage from a distance, beginning to identify the colors of clothes as it all became a silent picture on the landscape. There was no movement. His panic, which had started to subside, rose again. This time it was accompanied by a desperate feeling of loneliness as though he had become the only surviving person in a global disaster.

Rising once more, with a picture of friends and family swirling in his head, he ran, screaming for help. No one appeared. He reversed direction and raced toward the police station, only four blocks away, his cell phone lost in the melee. Collapsing on the floor inside the lobby, he began to blurt out what had happened, while desperately clutching the clothes of those who surrounded him. He screamed for help, but most had already mobilized after hearing the first blast.

He was pushed over to a sofa in the waiting room as someone tried to console him. He screamed and leaped up. Strong hands held him back, but they couldn't hold him down. He heard the clamor of running feet and shouting as the station emptied. Everyone rushed over to the cinema. The reality of what had happened set in as the small group from the station with Amir, now in the lead, rounded the corner and saw the rubble that remained of Cinema Rex. There was already a crowd of people pawing through the ruins, searching for life, but it had become silent as the screaming gave way to the moans of death.

*　*　*

The only four survivors sat in silent shock in the emergency room of the Chalus hospital, still too dazed by the sudden loss of so many of their friends and the incredible speed with which it had all happened. Amir had been one of the lucky ones. As he sat with his head in his hands, he gave little thought to the superficial wounds he had received during his escape. They had not yet been treated other than for a casual cleanse to remove the possibility of infection and a quick tetanus shot. He would have to wait until later for the antiseptic and dressings to be applied. Amir remained stunned, dried tear streaks staining his dirt-splattered face, at what little attention was given to such large traumatic events as these. But then, there had never been an event like this. The city had been stunned into shock as to what to do next. The pictures in Amir's mind's eye were too vivid. Each time he thought of his brothers and friends, his tear stains would be rewetted, and again each time he thought of his near escape, his family, the families of his friends, and even the loneliness of the days to come.

Not Tudeh

Abdul Reza Ansur had made his way from Cinema Rex to his car three blocks away. He had packed only those belongings that were needed, leaving the remainder at his lodgings to avoid any suspicions too early. He knew that it was only a matter of time before the authorities put the facts together, identified all the occupants of the theater, accounted for the staff, and realized there was one missing. Association with political and terrorist groups would be investigated, and so on, and so on.

Ansur's prime objective now was to head back to Tehran.

As his green, dusty Paykan sped out beyond the city limits, Ashur gauged that he had about three hours before there was likely to be any newscast of significance. Meanwhile, he could relax a little to reflect upon his deed. He hoped his masters would be grateful.

It was 8:35 p.m. when Ansur pulled the green Paykan over to one side of the road, applied the handbrake and reached back to his bag to make sure for the last time that his identification papers were in order. As he sat there with his belongings strewn about him, he didn't notice the lone, gray '68 Mercedes heading toward him. There was no other traffic. He didn't raise his head as the car came up opposite his. The window wound down to reveal the muzzle of a Kalashnikov PL-15. In the jerked reaction of intuition, Ansur lifted his head just enough for the single bullet to pierce his skull, between the eyes, blasting the back of his head against the passenger window. He fell back before slumping forward against the steering wheel.

The Mercedes crept forward, looking for a spot to get off the road and out of view of any traffic. Its occupants, having concealed their car, stealthily returned to the Paykan and slid into the back seat. Leaning over to the front, they removed all belongings that might identify the driver. In their place, the killer threw a wallet onto the floor of the car. It contained a Russian driver's license, passport, and several personal documents that identified the driver as Boris Stanislav, a resident of Kyiv in Ukraine. His identification would lead any investigation to his origins and associations with the outlawed Tudeh Party, which continued to promote communism in Iran through the younger generations. The other items that were placed in the car included a lighter with a pattern on it that could be traced back to being purchased in Chalus, some remnants of rope that were the same as that used to tie up the propane tanks at the cinema, and a layout of the cinema itself.

Having made sure that no additional clues had been overlooked, they got out of the Paykan. One soaked the vehicle in petroleum, the other struck a match and flicked it onto the body of Ansur. It exploded in flames before enveloping the car. The killers beat a hasty retreat to their own vehicle. As they pulled their Mercedes back onto the roadway leading to Tehran, the driver could see the smoke from the Paykan in his rear view mirror. Neither of them smiled or looked satisfied with themselves. Instead, one of them wiped a tear from the corner of his eye and returned his attention to the road in front of him. Their part of the job was complete, as was Ansur's.

There would be others.

* * *

Black Again—March 2019

Matthew Black turned in his business class seat to peer out of the scratched window as the 777 lunged into the clouds and he lost sight of Vancouver below. He felt somewhat compensated for his lack of a clear view once the plane gained enough altitude and speed for the stewardess to serve him a vodka tonic. He turned back to the window and stared at the blanket of cloud with just a tinge of expectation and a tightening of his stomach at the uncertainty of the near future and what it might bring.

In many ways, he enjoyed this moment the best—the prelude to the execution of a project. This time, he was headed toward Istanbul, where he would meet the new team and receive his instructions for his next assignment from Stockman, his commanding officer and the head of ORB. This was the best part. The mild anxiety of waiting for the inevitable call with nothing marked in his calendar was over, and the expectation of what was to follow held him in limbo. It was a time to reflect. His skills as a saboteur and industry manipulator were always in demand.

Matthew Black had been in the industrial construction business for twenty of his forty-four years. He had only been a saboteur for twelve of those. There was still a lot to learn. There were always new ways to develop— and new ways to destroy. He was a tall, slender, sandy-haired guy, quietly spoken, patient, and rarely driven to panic or aggression. He fit in with the construction crews, who knew little of his background and eyed him with a certain amount of curiosity and respect. Matthew was a bit of a loner and not particularly given to creating waves or off-site bouts of drinking. He flew below the radar of people who seemed to be looking for problems. His engineering background gave him some level of equality with the management of both his employers and their clients. Both would seek him out when remedial measures needed his kind of skills.

Matthew had learned a lot since graduating with a mechanical engineering degree but he had preferred to carve out a career in construction and avoid the world of engineering. He started as a site engineer for one of the larger construction companies in the world but watched and learned as he gradually settled on the trade of his choice. He decided to weld. It fascinated him. To Matthew, welding exotic metals was one of the most respected and interesting jobs in the industry. And it was an industry he loved. Money was really good, and the work was always there. He spent four years as an apprentice and the next five years working as a journeyman in the construction of petrochemical plants around Alberta and Ontario, building more of the complex parts of the plants using his welding skills. He had seen a lot, learned a lot, and absorbed the good things as well as the bad. He knew how to work fast and be assured of his next job, and how to work slow to drag the work out until the next job came up.

There were lots of tricks to pull if he wanted to earn more money. Hell, you could make as much in one week as you would normally earn in a month if you knew how to really screw around. He could work just six months of the year—and take the other six months off rather than pay the taxman if he wanted to. When he did, he went on training courses, conferences, and business seminars. He learned about the business world and white-collar professions.

Matthew always wanted to work. He had no family and just wanted to do more. His love of the industry meant he could travel anywhere in the world to do the job. The compensation packages were good. And he was well looked after. The guys were straight, the work was interesting, and he never backed away from a new task. He saw the pranks that were pulled as workers neared the end of the job, or when the company pulled a fast one that somehow took money out of their hands. Then, tools and rags were left in the pipelines, bolts were only partially tightened, the wrong thickness piping was installed, or the wrong pipe material was used. There was rarely ever an occurrence that actually caused bodily injury. These mishaps were designed to interfere with the plant start-up, but were always made to look like an accident that could have been. Nothing deliberate could be identified. Nothing could be pinned on anyone in particular. And nothing was illegal—at least nothing anyone could prove. They were good days, until the boredom started to set in.

After he had welded all materials in all positions, things started to get repetitious...

Matthew's work was nearly over on this latest project. The process operations team was on site and testing the systems for completeness. This was a time when construction took a back seat to the operations forces who would take over the plant. Matthew was always sad to leave a plant but excited by the next job prospect.

One lunchtime, in 2003, as he waited by the window of the site trailer staring out at row upon row of vessels in the ethylene unit, his thoughts were interrupted by a faint tap on his arm. He turned to find one of the admin girls standing behind him. She invited him to come to the main office later that day.

"I think Doyle Crower wants to see you. Maybe he wants to show his appreciation for your work on the job—and maybe talk a little about future prospects..."

Crower, the senior site manager, had become a well-known face around the plant site. Matthew had first met Crower one day when his inquisitiveness got the better of him. He couldn't help but ask the stranger what he was doing as he leaned over the wooden handrail around an open excavation and stared down at the piping crew below. Crower just looked at him, smiled, and said, "Not much." Then he just sauntered off, hands buried in his pockets. He was just smiling. Neither the question nor the lack of an answer was taken or given as a slight by either of them. It was just a sort of understanding between them that Matthew would eventually ask and Crower would eventually tell him, but for now there wasn't anything to say. After that, all they did was nod to each other as their paths crossed. A strange kind of respect. But after that introduction, Matthew often noticed Crower watching him on the site. He didn't think anything of it.

"You ready to go?" asked Crower, in his Texan drawl, as Matthew knocked on the open door and wandered into the office.

"I guess," Matthew shrugged with a touch of impatience that questioned the need to ask at all.

"Tell me," Crower slowly turned to face him. "Thought about the future at all?" Crower paused, waiting for an answer that didn't come. He looked down at the floor and carried on. "How'd you like to travel a little and do some real interestin' work, son?" This time Crower looked up and stared Matthew in the eye. He carried on without waiting for an answer. "Hell, you may even like it!"

As Matthew remembered, there had been a glint in Crower's eyes as he said that. The bait had been set and Matthew had gone for it, hook, line, and sinker.

Before the month was out, he was off to Toronto to meet with Stockman, a man who was unfamiliar to Matthew, but who seemed to be the one who was interested in his career moving forward.

*   *   *

A New Challenge—March 2019

Matthew and Stockman's meeting took place in a boardroom on the top floor of one of the principal mining companies in the world in Toronto's financial district. The boardroom meeting area was capable of being shuttered in by a retractable, oval-shaped screen that opened or closed at the press of a button. Once closed, the meeting space became sound- and wireless-proof. Only landlines were permitted.

Stockman was relaxing in a high-back green leather chair at the end of a 30-foot-long oval-shaped table with an overly large monitor on a stand behind him. The area was open to the floor around him until Matthew stepped forward to shake Stockman's hand, at which time the screens closed around them.

"At last." Stockman smiled and held his hand out. "I've been wanting to meet you for some time now, Matthew. I've heard a lot about you. Come and sit. Call me Stockman. Now, I know this may be a strange way to start a relationship, but I want you to help us out…" Stockman led him to a chair next to his and invited Matthew to help himself to coffee and sit.

Stockman turned out to be the head of an organization known as ORB, and he quickly indoctrinated Matthew into their activities and purpose.

* * *

That was fifteen years ago or so ago, and here Matthew was now, on a flight to Turkey to look at another project that needed his expertise.

In his dozing state, he noted there were only seven hours and fifteen minutes remaining before they arrived in Frankfurt from his home base in Vancouver. The seat started to get uncomfortable as he shifted and adjusted his position from sitting to horizontal. He didn't enjoy traveling as much as he used to, but at least the amenities offered in business class helped him get through. He took a last sip of his vodka, pulled his eye mask down from his forehead, pushed his earplugs in farther, pulled the thin blanket up over him, and slept fitfully. He would have to transfer to Turkish Airlines in Frankfurt for the flight to Istanbul.

* * *

Istanbul Airport is located in the northwest Arnavutköy district of Istanbul, on the European side of the city, about forty-five minutes by cab to the Hilton Istanbul Bosphorous, where Matthew was scheduled to stay and meet the team. The direct drive from the airport is unremarkable. Matthew preferred to take the longer Highway 7 south route to intersect Kennedy Caddesi, close to where the now commercially unused Ataturk airport is located. The cadessi, or avenue, skirts the shore of the Marmara Sea and provides one with an immediate vision of Turkish history dating back beyond the fifteenth century. There are a number of mosques along the route, not least of which is the Blue Mosque, or Sultan Ahmet Camil, named for the ruler who is interred there. It's probably the most famous mosque in the world, but residing almost next door is the Ayasofya Camil, or Hagia Sophia, a mosque that pre-dates the Blue Mosque by some 100 years, although its origins as a church reach much further back in time.

As the cab came out from the peacefulness of the grounds around the mosques and reached the Golden Horn of the Bosphorous, Istanbul came alive on the roads and water. This is the confluence of where the Marmara Sea meets with the Bosphorous Sea and the Golden Horn, a canal-like strip of water leading up to Istanbul's port. There were watercraft crossing in all directions at all speeds, from ferries to fishing boats to pleasure boats and ships. Liners, naval warships, recreational craft, and tugs all vied for a place to get through the Golden Horn. Tankers of all sizes crowded to pass through the Bosphorous, which allowed sea traffic from the Mediterranean, through the Aegean, through the strait of the Dardanelles, and the Sea of Marmara to transfer to the Black Sea, and return. It was the busiest stretch of water in the world, where ships crossed under the famous mile-long Martyrs Bridge, one of four crossings connecting Europe with Asia.

The cab made its way around the tip of the Golden Horn, leaving its intersection with the Bosphorous, and crossed the Galata Bridge, where Matthew could look through to one of the largest natural harbors in the world. This peninsular nub of land that sticks out into the Sea of Marmara, with the Bosphorous to the northeast and the rest of the Golden Horn running northwest, defines the city's peninsula, home to "Old Istanbul." It was once a center for shipping during the Byzantine and Ottoman Empires, when Istanbul was known as Constantinople, and continues to be one of the largest and busiest deep seaports in the world. Matthew had visited Istanbul several times, on both business and pleasure, and he loved this section of the city as it conjured up the history he had read so much about over the years. The area was a thriving mass of movement and excitement, and he promised himself to take a few hours to visit during his brief stay.

The Hilton Istanbul Bosphorous overlooked the continuous stream of tankers making their way to and from the Black Sea through the strait of Istanbul the hotel was named after.

At the entrance to the hotel, all traffic arriving was being stopped, and the occupants questioned. More often than not, it was guarded by armed militia, accompanied by two armored vehicles with their armed turrets pointed at the stop point. Each vehicle was subjected to wand mirrors pushed under the vehicles to search for bombs. This was a hotel that was often used as a temporary home for visiting foreign diplomats, and security was borne out of necessity, given the political situation in so many eastern and Middle Eastern countries.

Turkey was one of those countries that seemed to be continually under some kind of 'underground' martial law. It was common to see groups of militia traveling in armed vehicles through crowded streets or guarding government buildings, as though they knew something that the rest of the population didn't. Control was key in this country, which used to be the last stop for the camel caravans that traveled the Silk Road from China, India, and Persia all the way to Venice. To a great extent, many still traveled it from East to West, or in reverse with the same intent of searching for buyers and sellers of wares and services, although these days, the goods were often illicit. Turkey, after all, was, and always has been, a strategically located country for access to East and West, not to forget many Russian-influenced countries to the north and Middle Eastern countries to the south. It was a crossroads of international intrigue, collaboration, and deception with a culture that seemed to welcome everyone—but with suspicion.

Matthew made it through to the front desk, where he was assigned a room on the secured floor in the club section of the hotel that allowed him free access to wander, relax in the comfort of quiet reading areas, read a news-paper or magazine, have a drink or a snack, or use the services of the floor concierge. There were small meeting rooms dotted around the floor, and it was in one of these where he would be meeting Stockman and the team the next morning.

In the meantime, a trip down to the sauna for some rest and relaxation seemed to be warranted, after the long journey, to prepare him for a good night's sleep. Matthew headed down to the hotel sub-level that was equipped with a well-stocked exercise room, a sprawling beauty spa complete with in-ground pool, loungers, and a bar that opened out onto the grounds overlook-ing the Bosphorous.

The traditional Turkish bath is a two-hour experience that starts with a sauna to soften the skin, then a dip into a cold-water bath, followed by a second visit to the sauna before heading into the hammam, a marble-lined room complete with massage slab. Here, Matthew lay on his back and sub-jected himself to a pair of strong male hands that soap-massaged, rubbed, stretched, and exfoliated the top layer of the skin from his body, all washed away by the continuously running warm water that dropped into the trough below. After about thirty minutes, a quick flip of the masseur's cloth told Matthew he was finished and to go through to the resting room, where he could lounge for a while and enjoy some tea until he was ready to leave. By 9:30 p.m., Matthew was in bed and snoring.

* * *

Istanbul—March 2019

At 9:30 a.m., a tap on the door alerted Matthew. Stockman stood outside with a copy of *USA Today* in hand.

"Good morning, Matthew," he greeted Matthew cheerfully. "Shall we go and meet the crew?"

"Morning, Stockman. Anything world-shattering in the news today?"

"A few more wars, a couple of plagues, and United lost against Arsenal again. But that's about it," Stockman glibly responded.

Matthew followed Stockman to the end of the corridor and a door with a simple "Occupied/Vacant" slider that Stockman slid to "Occupied'" as he pushed the door open. They were the first ones to arrive. The others would be there shortly. For security reasons, the ORB crew members stayed at different hotels around Istanbul and would need a little time to gather.

Gradually the crew drifted into the room. Everyone shook hands. Some patted others on the shoulder as they recognized each other from other ventures. Stockman knew everyone and had worked with each at some point in the past. They poured themselves coffee or tea and took seats at the conference table, silently waiting for Stockman to start.

There were eight members in the room, including Stockman and Matthew. Two private security bodyguards stood outside in the hallway. The screen at one end of the room was alive with a picture of a large petrochemical plant under construction. There was no title.

Stockman shuffled papers until everyone was seated and attentive.

"Good morning, everyone. It's good to see you all again. I know not all of you know each other, but I think I will leave the introductions to each of you after we are through here, and you can exchange contact information, although, as usual, you can get all that stuff, and more, on the website for this project. The website address is in your project folder. Needless to say, you need an access password, and you all have one, so please remember it and don't pass it out to anyone. Only you and I know it."

He pressed his palms together, fingertips touching his lips, then slowly rose to his feet, picked up his chair with both hands, and moved toward the screen. He placed it carefully to face the other seven in the group and propped a foot on the seat and an elbow on his raised knee. He looked up at the group before him and clasped his hands together.

"Hope your hotels are okay." Stockman's hands dropped away to the back of the chair. "I know you have all made your own arrangements to leave here at some point. Some may need to stay around for a while, others need to head off to other foreign places, and some will head back home. Remember that all travel arrangements have to be made through Lucy so we know where you generally are at all times."

Lucy was Stockman's wife. She had been a long-time operative with CSIS until her retirement a few years ago at the youthful age of fifty-five. Now she helped her husband, and he used her as his sounding board. Everyone at the table was familiar with Lucy and knew how effective and efficient she was. They all knew some of her background and had learned to temper their dealings with her with a great deal of respect. She was no ordinary clerical person.

"All cash requests and expense submittals go through Lucy," Stockman continued. "You all have three passports in your name, international driver's licenses, and embassy clearances associated with the passports in case you need their help, as well as a couple of international credit cards, each with $50,000 limits. Matthew, your cards are unlimited, as usual. Anything else, ask Lucy, and if she can't help, she'll get hold of me. You also know you can contact me at any time using the usual email address and phone number."

"Now, let's see what we have." Stockman paused and looked up at the image on the screen.

"This," he pointed to the screen, "is the new Sari refinery under construction in Sari, Iran, in the province of Mazandaran up near the Caspian Sea. By the time it's completed, it will be the second-largest refinery in the world behind the Jamnagar refinery in India.

"As we understand it, and it isn't entirely clear just yet, the Iranian Regime's plan seems to be in two phases. The first is to redirect about 30 percent of the crude oil flowing from Tabriz, Tehran, and the southern oilfields up to the Sari plant, where they'll process it; the rest will continue to be transferred to the Gulf for distribution to the West, but at a much-reduced volume once the refinery is operational. That means that Iran will no longer be exporting only crude oil; it will also be in the business of refining and exporting all the processed derivatives from the crude that gets delivered to the Sari plant. All those products will be shipped on-demand to Russia and China with little, or likely nothing, heading west."

Another overhead flashed up on the screen. It was a large four-turbine unit power plant. Stockman pointed to it.

"The Neka power plant, or the Shahid Salami Power Plant, as it's called these days, located close to and east of Sari, currently provides energy to the province of Mazandaran. It's one of the largest steam-powered thermal plants in the Middle East, with a nominal capacity of 2035 megawatts. It's fired by natural gas, with light fuel oil as a secondary source, both supplied by the Iranian Power Corporation, or IPC.

"The capacity is currently being doubled, to around 4,100 MW, to add power for the Sari refinery. Also, oil storage tanks and a deep seaport are being constructed at the Neka facility shoreline for the oil tankers that are going to be needed." Stockman looked over at Matthew, who just nodded and smiled.

"The problem is that it was originally intended that a refinery located up on the Caspian coast would make it cheaper and easier to access the West's end-users, as well as provide some substantial industry to the north coast of Iran that is, as I think you all know, in a pretty poor state and lacks any kind of modern industry to help support the infrastructure and jobs that the young people need if they are going to stay around. At least, that was the shah's vision. Now, that's all gone in the crapper with the anti-West Islamic Regime running things." He paused again for a gulp of his coffee.

"Their plan is to complete the refinery, process that 30 percent, just like the original idea, except now they intend to export the processed products to Russia, China, and others to the east.

"The second phase is to increase the capacity of the refinery by diverting a total of about 60 percent of the nation's crude oil output, which would totally cut off the supply to the West and send it all to the East. Russia and China will use what they need and likely sell the rest to places like North Korea, Vietnam, and Cambodia. That would leave only 40 percent of Iran's crude oil." Stockman could see the shocked looks on the faces in front of him.

"Now, save your questions. Let me finish." Stockman looked around the room.

"Overall, their plan sounds plausible, the only problem being that we can't allow it to happen." Stockman raised his eyebrows and paused to gauge the reaction of the group before him.

"Sounds fairly straightforward, Stockman." It was Colin, the IT systems specialist. He had a smirk on his face. "I guess the idea is to knock out the refinery and the power." There were some guffaws around the room, as though they all saw that coming.

"You're right, Colin, but there's more to this than just that, I'm afraid." Stockman watched as all the eyebrows went up. "We also need to calm down the radical side of the Islamic Regime a few notches and get some common pro-Western sense to prevail. We have to make sure their oil flows west, not east, and it's going to take a massive effort to turn them around." Stockman looked around.

"Wow… wow." It was Colin again. He was trying to grasp the magnitude of the project. "That is one hell of a project, Stockman… is there any kind of a plan yet?"

The rest of the team pulled their chairs closer to the table. Some rested their elbows in front of them as their focus sharpened further. Some fiddled with their facial hair, tugged at an ear, or fidgeted as they wrestled with the magnitude of what Stockman was confronting them with. Most of them wondered what their role would be. This was a substantially bigger project than any of them had ever been involved in previously.

"Well," Stockman continued with a smile, "it's not all bad. You can imagine our clients are more than the petrochemical companies. We have at least six participating governments acting through their secret services, with us being the lead agency. I think we can tackle the sabotage of the refinery, power plant, and pipelines, but we will need help with the Islamic Regime 're-education'. It's not a given that we will be able to do that, but all our partners are actively engaged in infiltrating the anti-government movements in Iran that we need to cooperate with. Our job will be to sabotage the refinery and coordinate with the anti-government groups to get them to act at the right time and in the right place.

"As you may imagine," Stockman continued, "plans for this escapade were being put in place quite a while ago. Actually, it all started as soon as Khomeini returned from exile. Some of the work that has been accomplished to date requires some of you to support the effort as we move forward, from the back room, so to speak. Some of you will just need to monitor and advise, especially on the social and political fronts, and some of you will have to take an active part in the field." Stockman looked at Matthew.

"What's the timeline?" It was Colin again.

"It will happen in stages, Colin." Stockman paused. "The first stage is to prevent phase one from starting up, but we don't want to interrupt the flow of oil to the Gulf, so it has to be done ahead of when the crude oil direction changes from south to north. If we are successful with crippling phase one, there will be no need to focus on phase two because there won't be one." Stockman stopped when he saw Matthew raise a hand.

"Is that just a matter of plant sabotage?"

"I think so, Matthew. It will involve some quite sophisticated planning and execution. We already have the refinery design team on board, and they'll essentially build self-destructive coding into the control system. You're going to have to coordinate with them. You need to work on disabling the mechanical and electrical systems.

"There's also the pipeline, power plant, and port facilities to deal with. We need to push any disruption we can that will cripple everything associated with the plant and stop it all from operating. This is going to be a bit of a dance as we manage interferences in production from the new plant while at the same time preserving flows from the Gulf.

"For the sabotage activities, we have somebody already on the site, getting familiar with things and looking for where we can get the biggest bang for our buck, apart from blowing the whole place up. The fact is, once everything calms down, there are those who will want to put that refinery into operation, so it's vital we don't destroy everything—just hobble it and make sure we know what has been sabotaged. I don't know how long that will take, but we are working on ways that will help."

"Can you elaborate on the anti-government side of things and how it's going to help us, Stockman?" It was Colin again.

"Let me just say that there is a silent war against the Regime being waged by some educated young exiles returning to Iran who have, for want of a better term, alternative views of where Iran should be headed. They call themselves the Friends of Iran. Clearly, they don't want to revert to being a country treated as a puppet by the West, but at the same time they aren't interested in going back a thousand years to the old religious ways and the country bullied by the mullahs. Anyway, their work is vital, and they are making headway.

"You may or may not be asked to help them, but we must make sure we maximize their usefulness by controlling the timeline for their demonstrations. We have to be cautious with them. They're not a part of ORB; it is only that their initiatives and plans coincide with what we want. Hopefully, we can get their timing to coincide with the sabotage of the refinery and create an enormous problem for the Regime. They will be turning in circles, trying to figure out what to do with a dud refinery and masses of young people taking to the streets. That means we council with them as much as we can so we are not all going in different directions.

"There is also a substantial Iranian movement, continually gathering momentum to unionize the ordinary workers. That will undoubtedly be a thorn in the side of the Regime, and we hope to have them distract the Regime on the same timetable as the Friends of Iran when needed. All the while, Matthew and his team will be hobbling the refinery." Stockman caught Colin's eye and pointed to him.

"What about the Americans? They're surely getting involved and wanting to go in with guns blazing," Colin said. "They couldn't keep out, could they?"

"No, Colin, they can't keep out, and we don't want them to. But before I leave the subject of the new youth movement, let me tell you some sad news, which is propelling the Friends of Iran forward with even greater fervor.

"Just as the founding members of Friends of Iran were about to convene a general assembly of about 200 young people in a cinema in Chalus west of Sari, it was bombed using the propane distribution tanks that feed the heating system. There were only four survivors. We still don't know who was responsible for certain, but we do know that a body in a car was discovered an hour or so south, on the road to Tehran. It had been burned beyond recognition. Forensics has told us the person was shot through the head at point-blank range. The local police managed to find some identification in the burned-out remains, and it turns out the person was apparently a member of the Tudeh Party, the banned communist group that operated in Tehran for years before being hunted down by the shah, and then the current Regime. The person had Ukrainian papers on him, which showed he was from Kyiv. True or not, we don't know, but that's what we have to work with." Stockman stopped and looked around at his audience.

"What do you think the Russians' angle is?" It was Matthew.

"Difficult to tell," Murray looked pensive, "but I think they might have had a lot to lose if the Friends of Iran gained any momentum and altered the course of a pro-Russian Islamic Regime, don't you?" Stockman searched the room for comments.

"Well, do you have any personal thoughts on this, Stockman?" It was Matthew.

"I do, but don't spread it around until I can get a positive on it." Stockman looked at each member of the group as he said it. "I have a hunch this may have really been the work of the Republican Guard, and that the Russian story is trumped up. The word I have is that the Regime wants to keep the youth under control, and they just got tired of them getting in the way. If that proves to be true, you can bet the fathers of those boys who died in that cinema are just hankering for revenge, so God help whoever it was who really pulled this stunt if they're discovered." Everyone looked blank as they contained their own thoughts. It wasn't something that anyone knew anything about. There had never been a mention of the cinema blast in any newspaper outside Iran, and even inside Iran the news had been stifled.

"Okay. Let's move on." Stockman took a couple of mouthfuls of his coffee.

"Now, where are we? Oh yes, well, the Americans are definitely very much involved. Domar Oil, out of Texas, is right in the middle of all this. They've been trying to negotiate with the Islamic Regime, which seems like a lost cause but they're out of pocket by billions of dollars on what they have invested in capital projects in Iran so far, including the Sari plant to date, and were looking to spend more until the Regime reversed the original strategy. They're not going to give up, and we're continually in contact with them. As you can imagine, they're one of our clients in this mess.

"In addition, the Americans still have a listening post in Gorgan, fairly close to Sari, that picks up all the traffic going back and forth between Iran and the rest of the world. It isn't the only one the Americans had set up, but we know that at least three of them were raided by Iranian guerrillas of various factions, way back in the early years of the Regime. I can't tell you why this one is still operating, although I suspect the Regime not only knows about it but somehow uses it to its advantage. Our problem is we need to better understand whether the Iranians know about our current activities and if they are just playing us, or whether they care and are just listening in on us instead. Matthew, that's your territory and you can work with our man at site to see what he knows. He's been on the ground for several months now and seems to have picked things up really well."

"My guess is that the folks at the Gorgan post will have been hearing some very interesting dialogue going back and forth over this Friends of Iran issue." Stockman raised his eyebrows quizzically.

Matthew sat back, deep in thought.

"Any other questions so far?" Stockman smacked his hands together, looked up and around at the group from under his bushy eyebrows and held a smile on his face as though he was looking forward to this new project.

"I think it would be helpful if you outlined what you want each of us to do in the usual way, Stockman," Matthew suggested.

"Good idea. Now let me see." Stockman looked around the table.

There was an assortment of talents, and each person was expected to take some part in the venture. All would report to Stockman, who would disseminate the information and pass it on, where and when needed.

"Matthew, I think we are all aware of you being our man in the field, so to speak. You'll need to coordinate with a number of people and groups in and around Sari in particular, bearing in mind that there are things associated with the project in other places such as Gorgan, Babol, and Chalus, and maybe Tehran on occasion.

"The engineering boys at Interstate are located in Brussels, and your contact will be Dick Elliot, the director. The Germans are in Munich, working on the Neka plant expansion. You'll need to coordinate site work with a chap called James Peters, who works at the plant and lives in Sari with his family. He is not a direct ORB operative, and really works for Dick Elliot on site engineering, so he answers to him. He's the one who's trying to get a handle on what's going on with the Iranians behind the scenes on the Gorgan listening station, as well as local talk about the project and what the Regime folks are up to.

"The Islamic Regime has a government technical branch called IDRO, or the Industrial Development & Renovation Organization of Iran, that's looking over the engineering and construction of the project for the Regime. It's a private company that essentially took over the duties of Technolog, the government department that did these things when the shah was around. I suggest you avoid them as much as you can but at the same time understand their involvement in the project. Not to be trusted, you know." Stockman paused as he searched for his next target.

"Ah, Colin. You'll be using your skills in the world of IT to help with anything that may be needed at the listening station in Gorgan. More importantly, you need to get close to the refinery control system and work with the Interstate guys who are doing the programming, if needed. The chap we have there now is pretty good with these things but if he needs a second opinion, I'd like it to be you." Stockman took another sip of coffee as Colin nodded in understanding.

"Brian, you're our resident pipeline expert; I need you to do some research on the crude oil transfer pipelines as well as get up to speed on what's going on with the new pipeline from Tehran up to the coast. I need timelines in particular, as well as routing." Stockman looked around at the faces in front of him.

"Geoff, you need to dig into the Islamic Regime structure. I know you speak Farsi, and you look like an Iranian." There were chuckles and nods from the group. "So put it to work for us and develop an organization chart with names, positions, and commentary on personnel, addresses, profiles, personal information on each, and all the rest of it. Do any of them have any weaknesses or things to hide? We may need inside help at some point. I hope we don't.

"You may need to set up a base in Tehran, so keep in touch with Matthew so he knows if you are in-country. Rent an apartment, and maybe we can use that as a base station for all of us. Colin will help with setting up a state-of-art communication system from there." Stockman looked around.

"Ken, take a look at the power plant with Siemens, the designers, and see what you can find out from them about the port facilities as well. I'm pretty sure they're responsible for the tanker facilities, although they may subcontract the design out to others. Find out where the refined products are going to head from Neka. A few ports on the western and northern Caspian coastlines could handle the tankers. You may need to head over to whichever receiving port is most likely on the other side of the Caspian and let us know if any of them are expanding their facilities.

"Dave, we may introduce you to some of our in-country operatives, so you'll likely need to use your Farsi and see if they need any help. Keep in touch with Matthew in case he needs your help. I would like you to meet some of the Friends of Iran, see what their plans are and determine whether there are any conflicts. It's important they know where we're headed, although I don't want them knowing anything specific. Find out how the explosion in Chalus and the loss of that group are affecting them going forward. Has it stopped them, motivated them, and so on?" Stockman turned.

"I'd like to talk to you, Alan, and you, Tony, about some other issues that are more on the international legal side of things. We can talk about those afterward if you can hang around. I want to find out more about what our position might be on transferring ownership of the refinery and so on, and what we may be able to do about interfering with the sales contracts between Iran, Russia, and China. Is there anything we can do to hold things up?" Stockman put his hands together and looked at each person in turn.

"Right, are we all okay with the plan? Any questions?"

There were none. They would come later as everyone wrapped their heads around what was expected of them. "Well, I guess we should get on with it then. Can you each call me at least once a week? And don't forget to get each other's contacts before leaving. Oh, and make sure you file your weekly reports on the server. I think we need to give this about six to eight months to complete depending on what Matthew finds when he gets into Sari."

Everyone rattled their chairs and slowly made their way out of the room, talking to each other.

Tony caught Stockman's eye before he and Alan left the room. "We'll see you in the bar."

Stockman nodded to them and went over to Matthew. "I think you need to get your stuff together and head up to Sari as soon as you can, Matthew. We'll arrange a hotel for you, unless you want to do that when you get there; maybe you'd prefer an apartment, but I'll leave that up to you. It really depends on your plan moving forward, but you'll need some sort of a base to operate from. Make sure you keep in touch with our guys here. You may be able to use them, but maybe not.

"Of course, another good place to hang your hat could be Chalus. It's right on the beach and has some better facilities, although it's a bit of a drive to Sari. There used to be a lot of tourists going there from all over the world until Khomeini came home. I'm not sure what it's like now, but I would guess a lot of the tourist-type infrastructure is still in place. We've also got a man in Chalus, Plato, who's doing some background work for us on the banking system the Regime uses. He actually works in Tehran at the Melli Bank and heads up to his place on the coast for weekends. I think you'll like him and his wife, Margaret."

"Sounds great," Matthew said. "Would you let Plato know that I'm going to be heading up and will stop in and talk for a while? I think he's going to be a key for us. I also want to get a feel for what went on at the cinema and what the local population's thinking. Maybe also throw a few ideas around about what we may be able to mess with on the financial side of things. See if there's a soft underbelly we can go for."

They laughed.

"I think both Plato and Margaret speak Farsi," Stockman said, "and he looks a little like an Arab, so he'll fit right in and help root out some of the comments from the locals. Remember to keep in touch and get hold of James over at the plant. I'll send you a list of contact names and numbers, including hotels.

"Now, take care." Stockman looked over at Matthew. "Safe travels, and I'll likely see you in a month or so. Well, we'll certainly talk, if not see each other. I think we'll all get together here just before the shoe drops, say in about four months, and we can see if there are any holes in the plan that need fixing.

"Oh, by the way, Emma's on board and already up on the construction site, welding her little heart out. She knows you'll be there shortly, so you need to make contact."

Matthew smiled. "I'm glad to hear that. I'll get hold of her as soon as I get in contact with James."

Emma was Stockman's daughter, and she had worked on a couple of projects with Matthew. She had worked well behind the scenes on one of them, shadowing Matthew in case he needed help, although he hadn't known she was there. But she had been watching, just in case. On another job, she was more involved. For this project, she would be doing both and using her skills as an exotic-material welder. That was how she and Matthew had originally met, as they lay near each other under a steam drum, welding high-pressure tubes and working toward each other on their backs, their faces hidden by welding masks. They met at the center of the drum, where they introduced themselves.

Matthew liked to think of Emma as his best bed-buddy. They really liked each other and often hooked up in their downtime where they lived in Vancouver, one on each side of the city. Sometimes one of them stayed over at the other's place. Other than that, they lived quite separate lives with other soulmates and interests, but they always managed to catch up with each other without letting too much time pass in between.

Stockman and Matthew went their separate ways. Matthew was heading back to Vancouver on the evening flight. Stockman was heading back to London the next morning and on to the west country, where he and Lucy had a getaway cottage by the sea.

* * *

Interstate EPC at Your Service— April 2019

The National Petrochemical Company (NPC) is a subsidiary of the Iranian Petroleum Ministry, owned by the government of the Islamic Republic of Iran and responsible for the development and operation of the country's petrochemical sector. It's the second-largest producer and exporter of petrochemicals in the Middle East. The speed of growth since the Islamic Regime took control of the country was supported by many foreign companies around the world, whose existence remained confidential and closely managed to avoid conflicting relationships with the Republic and their own governments. Unfortunately for Iran, it was impossible for the Regime to do without foreign expertise in almost everything highly technical, including petrochemical, chemicals, pharmaceuticals, agriculture, and, of course, nuclear. Work on the Sari refinery was no different, and it was the Regime who had contracted Interstate to deliver the new refinery.

Dick Elliot sat in La Chaloupe d'Or, on the perimeter of La Grande-Place in Brussels, studying the menu. It all looked so good, and Dick was a sucker for French food, especially with a Belgian twist. He loved the brasserie style of eating, with warm, crusty, soft-centered bread, a robust red wine that stayed on the palette, and a healthy plate of locally pressed olive oils for dipping before the three courses of food. He looked his part, in a blue suit, white shirt, club tie, and brown brogue shoes, slightly scuffed and well-worn at the heels. He was the GM of Interstate EPC, better known as just Interstate, one of the largest engineering companies in the Americas and Europe. In addition, it had hub offices in London and satellite offices worldwide, including Brussels, where the engineering was being finished for phase one of the Sari refinery and about to start for phase two.

Dick had come a long way from those heady days when he and his wife, Jane, lived, worked, and were evacuated from Iran back in the late 1970s. But here he was, in the center of Brussels, preparing to meet with his engineering team. They had been working on the project since 2011, including all that was required for the studies needed to satisfy the financiers, the environmentalists, and the government. It was time for a project status meeting now that they were into the last year of construction and finalizing documentation and system controls.

Construction had started on phase one in 2015, four years ago, after all the studies had been completed and the permits received. While IDRO, the owner's surrogate for all things technical, theoretically oversaw the work on site, it was Interstate who provided the support technology, contracting out, construction management, and know-how on how to put it all together. They just had to be extremely discrete about it. In fact, having people on site was a substantial risk. There was no consulate or embassy to appeal to in the event of problems in a place like Sari. Even in Tehran, there was little or no representation of friendly countries other than France, which still had an embassy there. All the other Western ones had pulled out of the country a long time ago. If a Westerner ran into trouble and had to get out of the country, the only way out from the northern part of Iran—without access to a flight from Tehran—was by road through the border of former Russian states, either to the east or to the west of the Caspian. Unfortunately, if one ventured east by road, one would have to travel through a leper colony. By far, the preferred route out was to the west through Azerbaijan.

While the shah had already left Iran, the Sari project was starting to emerge from being a concept when Khomeini arrived in Iran. The project went dormant for fifteen years until the new Regime realized its value to the country while they strategized their future and revitalized the plan for the refinery. In 2011, it went into the study stage and was subjected to the scrutiny of environmentalists. Once the IPC received the permits, the wheels of financing started to turn, and construction started.

A number of offshore oil companies were financially supportive of the development, albeit cautiously, provided they could operate the facility and take a portion of the profits. Domar won the auction and poured millions of dollars into getting the engineering underway with Interstate, which had also taken a major role in the study phases.

As the project manager, Dick had taken the Sari project from concept, pre-engineering, and planning phase through to the engineering as Domar paid the bills, and on into the construction of phase one of the project. It continued without losing a beat when the Islamic Republic flexed their muscles, changed their minds about who they wanted to align with in the future, and added a phase two to the project, doubling the refinery capacity.

Phase one of the plant was now in the final year of construction, and Dick had by then progressed to become the general manager of Interstate worldwide but remained heavily involved in his pet project in Sari. He often remembered those days nearly forty years ago, when he and his family lived there while he worked on a sawmill. Those had been some of the most interesting days of their lives, and some of their most dangerous ones, as they got caught up in the revolution and had to escape first to Turkey and then eventually back to Canada.

He often wondered whether he would be able to go through all that again, but he doubted it. Youth had been on their side in those days, and their children were a constant distraction from the problems surrounding them. And here he was now, setting off on another Iranian escapade, this time into the mouth of the Islamic Regime where Western logic and ideals failed.

Dick also became involved with the phase two expansion, with engineering scheduled to begin as soon as phase one was operational, although some construction on the earthworks had already started in anticipation. It seemed that the expansion would be funded by Iran and its new friends—Russia and China—and Domar would be financially neutralized, despite having financed much of phase one and having a contract to operate phase two. Help from the West had been terminated by the Republic, including the Domar contracts. There were no options. Domar was more than just disappointed, but no amount of international legal or political pressure could change the situation. Domar needed to do something more.

The status meeting was a ruse for a second meeting on phase two with the Islamic Regime, to follow in Dick's offices. Of course, Interstate's help was on a confidential basis these days since Iran had outwardly isolated itself from

Western aid. It was imperative that the expansion merged seamlessly with the design and control systems for phase one. The same would apply to the expansion of the Neka Power Plant, where Siemens, a large German engineering and manufacturing company, was the lead but the expansion remained under the control of Dick Elliot as the lead engineer for the overall project. It would be impossible for the Iranians to terminate all the West's services without seriously compromising the technical merging of the two plants.

IDRO would be at the meeting to make sure the Iranian Republic wasn't being technically bamboozled by a bunch of foreigners. But they really irritated Dick by continually putting unimportant administrative obstacles in their way, as though they wanted Interstate to fail... or perhaps to cover up the fact they really knew little about the technicalities of the project. There was clearly a jealousy there that IDRO was unable to manage. The issue did not escape the attention of the representatives of the Regime.

But Dick had a plan to stay ahead of IDRO for phase two with the support of the Regime, who considered it a top priority to get the plant into full operations rather than be hampered by the negative minutiae IDRO continually presented, as they had done in phase one. It was as though IDRO wanted to prove their worth, although Abbas, their on-site chief, was often embarrassed by the constant nickel-and-diming by his site staff. The Regime more than encouraged Dick to bring whatever resources he needed to get the plant to completion. They had known him for some eight years now and, despite him being a *ferengi*, they trusted and liked him.

Within the month, Dick would have the basic administrative framework for phase two in place, and within two months, expatriate representatives of the engineer would be on site with the general contractor to start preparatory construction and planning for the merger with the current project. The first year, at least, would be devoted to structuring the framework for the main construction activities. It would move so fast that IDRO would get bogged down with having to deal with the myriad approvals placed in front of them. They would be unable to cope, and hopefully, Interstate would sail past them with the support of the Regime, which was impatient to get into full production.

While expatriate participation would be minimized to ensure as great an inclusion of Iranians as possible, the main contract was open for consideration to foreigners, provided they were in a joint-venture relationship with a native Iranian company that had a majority share hold. However, the first general contractor, Mana Construction, had already been insisted upon by the Iranian contingent and was working on the current phase. It had no foreign joint-venture partner and didn't need one. No foreign expertise was needed for what Mana had to do with the civil construction matters. Their owner, Mansourian, was a man to be wary of. One could not doubt his aspirations to politics and his tight affiliations to the Iranian establishment. No one quite understood them. He didn't hold any government office. He was not considered a high-ranking member of any particular mosque, yet he held substantial power outside of his contracting business. He was known as someone who played all sides, except the Regime to whom he was totally loyal.

Dick had enjoyed his role in coordinating all factions, but he was somewhat unnerved by what to expect. It was the first time he had met with this new Iranian group, and he wondered how politics might work itself into the project, regardless of his supervision. But, armed with a signed letter of intent, all parties seemed ready to work together to get the expansion underway, so here he was, enjoying his last meal.

The delicious aroma of the *coq au vin* placed before Dick wafted up his nostrils as he reached for his knife and fork.

Simon Beatty, a long-time associate and one of Dick's principal clients, touched his arm and quietly asked Dick if he could join him to dine together. Simon was the senior representative of Domar Oil, associated with the Iranian portfolio. It had been the largest petrochemical company operating in Iran before the shah was expelled. Now, while they still operated those plants, they were playing a waiting game until they understood what the Islamic Regime had in store for them. It had been almost forty years since Domar had last asked that question when Khomeini came to power. But nothing had happened during those forty years that affected Domar's business until now, as phase two of the Sari refinery was put on the table. Now it was being shut out from operating phase one, and very likely with no compensation for the money Domar had already spent on it.

Simon was in Brussels to discuss the situation with Dick initially and to feel him out on what he knew about the future control of the refinery, as well as Domar's other refineries in the south. Simon would also be attending the project update meeting in the morning with Dick in attendance. Then he would try to meet privately with the representatives of the Regime to, once again, push for clarification of Domar's position in Iran. After all, Domar Oil was still a client of Interstate, paid most of the bills, and could essentially still end up being the operator of phase one of the new plant until it was (probably) going to be taken over by the Iranians.

Only time would tell, but Simon hoped to get better information over the next couple of days. He was scheduled to meet with Stockman, who was also in Brussels to be close to the eyes and ears of the project meetings without participating in them directly. Simon's meeting with Stockman would be a chance to go over the plan that ORB had put together to eventually wrest control of the refinery back into the hands of Domar.

"Hey, Simon. Good to see you." Dick almost got to his feet, but Simon put a hand on his shoulder and gently pushed him back down.

"You too, Dick. How's the family?" Simon took the seat opposite Dick and looked at his meal with a hungry expression.

"Great, although I have to say, I don't see them as often as I would like." Dick seemed anxious to pick up his fork again and not lose out on that wonderful first mouthful of Belgium cuisine as it steamed in front of him.

"I guess it comes with the territory for us both, as the globe-trotting individuals we are." Simon smiled and Dick joined him.

"What'll you have?" Dick slipped the menu over to him.

"Ah," Simon let his eyes wander over to the meal in front of Dick again. "Same as you, I think. It looks and smells delicious." With a gentle wave, Simon stole some of the fumes from Dick's plate.

Simon caught the attention of the waiter and ordered the *coq au vin* with a glass of rich red, local, wine.

"How are things, Simon? Are you coming to the meeting tomorrow?"

"I'll be there in the morning for the project update, but I don't think they would want me at the afternoon session, do you?" Simon hung his head a little and looked up at Dick. "It's not like they need us anymore."

"No, I can't imagine so." Dick gave a sort of *c'est la vie* shrug as he held his hands up. "Mind if I carry on with my meal?"

"No, not at all. Go for it."

Dick was sure the kitchen would rush Simon's order through, knowing he was sharing a table with someone who had already started their meal.

"Have any words of wisdom, Simon?"

"Well, in fact, I do, Dick. Not quite so many words of wisdom as a request."

"Intriguing." Dick spooned up some of the sauce and pushed a little chicken into it.

Simon leaned across the table a little farther. His elbows planted in front of him, he lowered his voice. "Dick, I don't know if you have ever heard of a group known as ORB?" Simon waited for some kind of facial response from Dick.

"Yes, I worked with Stockman a few years back on a little escapade in Spain. Funny project, but I didn't know much about the full story. I just did my bit for queen and country, so to speak."

"Well," Simon sounded conspiratorial and whispered, "he needs your help again."

"Oh, what now?" Dick showed no signs of negativity, just contemplation. He knew that if Stockman were involved, there would be a major play ready to unfold, and he always needed the best help he could get.

"He would have contacted you himself today, but he knew I would be here, and since I am a part of the ORB's project moving forward, he asked me to ask you to meet up with him at his hotel after you've finished up on the project meeting tomorrow."

Simon accepted the plate put in front of him and let the scent of the food waft up his nostrils. He picked up his fork, spiked some chicken and carrot, drenched it in the sauce, and slid it into his mouth. His eyelids partly closed as he savored the taste. In that second, he was oblivious to his surroundings.

"What hotel and at what time?" Dick was also enraptured by his food and could only use a few words at a time to converse between the mouthfuls.

"Novatel, off Grand-Place, room 1415."

"Oh, I know it. That's right near the office. We're on Rue de la Loi, a few blocks away, overlooking the Parc de Bruxelles. Once the meeting is over, it'll take me about fifteen minutes to get to the hotel, but I can't say when I'll get to the Novotel. It just depends on how long the meeting will last. Could even be late evening."

"That's fine. Stockman's not flying out until the next morning, so go on over when you can."

They finished their meal after another glass of wine and then tucked into a generous helping of *la dame blanche* with warm chocolate, cream, and butter sauce liberally poured over it, and a small glass of peppermint liqueur to help it down.

They wandered out of the restaurant and up La Grande-Place for a stroll in the cool but pleasant evening air. They chatted about things other than work and eventually said their goodnights and went off to their hotels.

* * *

Brussels

Following a relatively uneventful day of meetings, first with his project team and then with the client's team to review the expansion project, Dick wandered over to the Novotel Hotel at around 5:30 p.m. after freshening up at his own hotel. He was thinking about his meeting with IDRO and a couple of shifty-looking representatives of the Republic. Clearly, none of them really wanted to work with Interstate, but they knew they had no choice in the matter. They met to consider a reporting organization chart and timeline for the project, but nothing was mentioned about costs and Dick didn't ask. As far as he was concerned, the client would be responsible for funding, reporting, and monitoring project costs. His concern would be engineering and construction. He was happy with that, although he wasn't prepared to go through another five years of battling with IDRO.

But that would be a matter for another day, just before Interstate released the final drawings for the expansion and he would have the most leverage to impose his conditions for managing phase two. By that time, all his people would be home from building phase one and wouldn't return unless they had guarantees of improved communications and a more constructive working environment. Well, he'd at least ask but whether it was really possible to get IDRO to actually improve was another matter. And this time, Dick would want a three-month advance payment and monthly payments up front.

He reached the Novotel and called room 1415 from the house phone. Stockman answered and told him to come up. He would leave his room door open.

"How long has it been?" Stockman held his hand out as Dick came into the small suite.

"God, it must be six years now, Stockman. How are you doing?"

"Getting into all kinds of trouble, as usual. And you?" Stockman led Dick over to the sitting area. There was a plate of fruit and pastries on the coffee table, together with a bottle of Beluga vodka, two glasses, and a bucket of ice.

"Well, still going at it with the Iranians, you know. I think we're the last ones standing these days." Dick looked at the iced vodka and stretched his hand out.

Stockman handed him the vodka but left the ice to Dick.

"There are still some groups hanging around helping out, Dick. Down south in the oilfields as well as on telecom and, of course, in the nuclear field. God knows they're going to have to get out of there soon."

"Wow, I'm surprised they're even allowed to work there, given how sensitive the industry is." Dick took a sip of his vodka. It went down well as he settled back in the armchair.

"I know, but it's a small group that operates out of Switzerland, so we don't have a lot of pull on them. Still, we'll get them out soon. In the meantime, the Russians and Chinese are filling our boots everywhere else." Stockman sipped at his neat vodka.

"I guess I wondered why the Iranians didn't bring them in on this project, except we hold a couple of the refinery processing patents and that's likely stopped them."

"I think you're right, Dick."

"What is it you need me to do, Stockman?"

Stockman took another sip from his glass and put it down on the coffee table. Dick took a sip of his and selected a pastry from the table. He was famished and was hoping this wouldn't take too long. His mouth was watering just thinking about the menu at La Chaloupe d'Or. He was heading back there as soon as he could. The beef bourguignon was on his mind.

Stockman sat a little forward in his chair.

"Dick, ORB is working on a solution to a bit of problem and part of that is related to the plant you're looking after."

Dick just raised his eyebrows, showing some surprise despite what Simon had talked to him about.

"As you know, the Iranian Regime is heading in a different direction from what we had hoped. Now, without getting into the politics of it all in any detail, let me just say that our task is to reverse their policy of terminating the oil flow to the US and Europe. We can't afford to let that happen and, more than that, we can't afford to let Russia and China get their hands on it instead." Stockman paused.

"And?" Dick sat forward and hunched over, elbows on his lap, as he waited for an explanation from Stockman.

"Well, we need your help, so I'll come right to it. We need you to design problems into the control systems so the plant doesn't operate as it should. In the meantime, we're preparing our team over the next six months to do some other damage that will stop the plant and pipelines from operating while we come up with a plan to make them change their minds about supplying the West."

"Wow. That's quite an ask, Stockman. I guess this is all coming from the new friendships Iran is working on with Russia and China."

"That's right, Dick. We can't have the Ruskies running away with our oil, can we?" Stockman gave Dick a grim smile.

"Okay, we can do that, Stockman." Dick knew that when Stockman was involved in these projects, they were well considered and backed by sub-stantial parties, including governments. He wasn't about to argue and knew where his duties lay. "It won't be easy with IDRO breathing down our backs, but the fact is they don't really know what they're looking at when it comes to processing and control. We haven't started the programming yet, but when we do it'll likely be out of this office, so we can draw on our European boys to help out. I'm going to have to find a lead that I can confide in if this is going to work, otherwise the rest of the team will wonder what's going on."

"I'll let you work on that, Dick, and if you need any help finding someone, let me know. I've got a handle on some good people I've used before. They can likely mobilize pretty fast."

"Let me think on it, Stockman, and see if I can find someone I know who would help."

"Okay but see if you can get it organized by the end of this month." Stockman looked at the calendar on his watch. "That's about twenty days from now. Think you can do it?"

"I think so. I already have someone in mind who has been highly recom-mended. He's been working with a very good associate of mine. Someone

I trust. He helped me the last time you and I worked together, so he better understands these kinds of situations without going through a learning curve and asking a lot of difficult-to-answer questions."

"Good job, Dick. Now, one other thing."

"Okay, shoot." Dick had temporarily forgotten his hunger and the restaurant.

"We need someone on the inside on-site with your team right now. I need him to keep his ears to the ground and find out if there are any problems we may face when we have to go in with our guys." Stockman pursed his lips, lowered his eyebrows, and gave Dick a questioning look.

"Okay. What're you thinking?" Dick sunk back in his chair, vodka and ice in hand.

"I can't say too much, but one of the things is that we're pretty sure the Iranians are on to the Gorgan station, which could pose a threat. There's a listening post in the mountain near that location, and it's been there for quite a number of years to pick up the voice traffic in and out of Iran. I don't need your man to become a spy; he just needs to keep his eyes and ears open and try to figure out if we have a problem. We're sure the Iranians know about the station, but they likely don't want to expose it just yet. It may be too useful to them for passing on information they actually want us to hear. We can't be sure, but we want to find out so we can play the game a little better."

"Sounds intriguing." Dick raised his eyebrows and had a twinkle in his eyes. "I should be able to get the right person. Leave it with me. I'll contact him as soon as I get back and see what his plans are, but I highly recommend him as a practical hand as well as being discrete."

"Also, Dick," Stockman smiled, "you're in the best position to get some people of ours onto the site. Right?"

"Yes, I probably am. They just need me to sign them off; the Iranians apparently do a background check, and away we go. I don't think they're suspicious of me at all. I've been around them too long, so they seem to be quite trusting of my judgment and requests. So far, so good, at least."

"Good. I'm going to need to get some trades on site as well as a couple of operations people when the time comes, so I'll be in touch. They'll all have scrubbed and authenticated backgrounds that will pass the test. You okay with that?"

"Sure, no problem." Dick shrugged his shoulders. "Just let me know who and when and get me their passports and paperwork but give me a week or so before you give them the go-ahead to travel."

"Okay, Dick. All sounds good. Make sure we keep in touch, and if I don't hear from you at least once a week, you can be sure I'll be contacting you myself, or Lucy will."

"Is that a threat?" Dick asked as they both smiled. Lucy could certainly be a tough one when she needed to be.

Stockman smiled as well, got up from the armchair, and swallowed the rest of his vodka.

"Wish I could join you for supper, Dick, but I've got some tidying up to do on another project. We'll be getting more active on this one in about six months, but please make sure you get your man on the ground as soon as possible." He held his hand out to Dick.

Dick swallowed the last drop of his vodka and shook Stockman's hand before slipping out the door. His taste buds were working again as he walked briskly toward La Grande-Place in search of food.

* * *

Domar Oil

Dick sat in the same booth as the previous evening, this time nibbling on Belgian endive with *gruyère* and prosciutto as an appetizer for the beef bourguignon that would be well lubricated in a rich red wine.

The tap on his shoulder was reminiscent of the evening before, but Dick didn't turn to see who it was; he instinctively knew.

"Hi, Simon," he said, not missing a beat. "Come and join me." Dick picked up the plate of appetizers and placed it on the table in front of Simon as he sat opposite.

"Great to see you again, Dick." Simon smiled and settled into his seat as he peered over at Dick's plate and the crusty bread to one side. "Hope you don't mind, but I just wanted to catch up and give you some background on where Domar stands now that you and Stockman have agreed to work together again." Simon winked at Dick in a knowing way. It was likely because Simon really didn't know all that was discussed between him and the Iranians on phase two, nor with Stockman afterward. So here he was, to put Domar's case forward in the event Stockman had not been clear.

"News travels fast, Simon." Dick smiled. He was quite happy to have the company while he ate; plus, they had more in common now than they did the previous evening, but he really wished they didn't have to go over all this again. He already clearly understood what was expected of him on behalf of ORB and knew that Domar was in the plan somewhere.

Simon ordered the same as Dick again and sat back with the glass of wine that seemed to materialize out of nowhere.

"You know, Dick, you're a good man. Domar likes you. We think you'll do a great job for ORB and therefore us. But it will be, shall we say, a little different from your normal duties. Bit of a departure from the norm, and we really need you to keep us in the loop."

"I assume ORB will do that, Simon. What are you expecting from me that could be more than they'll offer?" Dick was a little taken aback, but he wasn't concerned. He knew he was in a safe position, especially now with the expansion of the refinery.

Simon tipped and twirled the wine glass and raised it to his lips in a sort of conspiratorial manner. He raised his eyes at the same time. He sipped at the wine as he met Dick's eyes and waited for a reaction.

Simon and Dick had known each other for quite a number of years now. Both had acted as managers of the Sari project for their companies as Interstate became involved. They now knew each other on a more personal level, even though they were, in effect, employee and employer.

"You look very pensive, Simon. I get the distinct impression that you'd like to say a lot more. Come on. It can't be that bad—can it?" With that, Dick picked up his drink and took a good slug before placing it back on the table and letting out a nervous chuckle.

"Dick, with the expansion taking shape the way it is, and considering what ORB is planning, Domar Oil has to consider its future here. Despite the Iranians' funding and controlling the expanded project, we believe that Domar Oil will eventually be back in control. Anything you may have to do to fulfill ORB's needs must consider that the plant has to eventually be operable."

"Okay, but..." Dick was starting to respond.

Simon raised his hand to let him know that he wanted to continue further before letting his friend interrupt.

Their meals arrived, and while Dick would have preferred to savor the flavors without interruption, especially about work, he had no choice but to discuss the project.

"As you know," Simon continued with little regard for the feast set before him, "Domar Oil essentially pioneered the Iranian oil industry. As the years rolled by, we poured money into the country and acted virtually autonomously in the development and marketing of the products internationally—with the consent of the Regime. It seemed like things would go on like that forever. But it didn't, not after the Islamic Regime found its feet and caught up with how international business worked. It may have taken them twenty to thirty years, but everything was a learning curve for them outside of religion. The fallout from Khomeini's arrival and his anti-West Regime eventually left us flat-footed. We should have known better, but I guess we lulled ourselves into a false sense of security and focused on other countries." Simon stopped just long enough to scoop up some of his beef bourguignon, dip some bread into the sauce to help spread the flavor, and gulp a mouthful of red wine.

"You may not understand the real politics of the country these days but believe me when I tell you that Iran was not quite the stable political country that most of the world believed, before or after the shah. There have always been players just wanting to tear the country apart for its oil and gas, including the Russians and Chinese, not to mention the usual culprits—the US and the UK."

Simon paused as though he needed Dick to have a silent moment for his own thoughts. Simon took advantage of the silence to spoon another pile of beef into his mouth, push some saturated bread in after it, and wash it down with another mouthful of wine.

Dick never really got involved in international politics, other than reading about them or watching CNN. Now he realized that he was likely to become involved in something he didn't really understand or want to be involved in. He held up his hand for his friend to give him a chance to say something, then stopped eating, put his fork down, and squirmed a little in his seat.

"I have this sense that what you may want to involve me in is something that I might not wish to become involved with. I don't have any doubts about the project, nor what my responsibilities are to it now that I've talked with Stockman. But I have to tell you that for a fleeting moment here, I thought you were about to suggest there was more to all this than meets my simple little eyes."

Dick relaxed back in his chair and sipped his third glass of red wine. He felt that he had more than adequately expressed himself.

"Look, Dick," Simon raised his hands in defense, "I just wanted to make sure you keep us, Domar, in the loop. Remember, we may need to own and operate this refinery at some point in the future, so we want to know what goes on there. ORB's mandate is to sabotage the refinery. My mandate is to get our capital asset back and make some money. That means whatever happens to the refinery has to be reversible. So whatever ORB does—and that essentially means your site operatives—there has to be a record of what has been done to cripple the plant, so that we can put it back together. It may take some time, but we cannot start from scratch." Simon watched Dick's face and went back to eating.

Dick didn't want to divulge too much about his discussions with Stockman on the same subject. He didn't know the extent of Domar's involvement in ORB's plans and preferred to call Stockman later to get his views on what Simon was asking for.

At this point, more wine arrived. After the prerequisite tasting and subsequent serving were completed and the waiter was gone, Simon carried on while twirling the wine glass by its stem and abstractedly attempting to spread some spillage across the table.

Simon sipped at his wine and let Dick have a chance to ask any questions that he might have. The waiter brought a dessert tray. While they spread napkins on their laps, Simon digressed into small talk concerning the latest weather conditions in Toronto and Montreal compared to those in London. In fact, he got so involved in his comments about the apparent worldwide shifts in weather patterns, as only English people can, that Dick thought the serious discussions were over. Before he had a chance to open his mouth, Simon started once more.

"The bottom line, Dick, is that this project, and its proximity to the Russian borders, makes it one of the most important locations in the world for Domar to be. Our distribution could be tripled with Russia and China as new clients under our control and an increased oil production in Iran to supply them.

"The Americans have been listening in to the talk through their Gorgan facility, and the future does not look good for the West right now. But if we can get it to work our way, that would be better for everyone."

Simon stopped, looked at Dick, and then started to eat in a slower, more deliberate manner. There was a silence for a few moments before Dick put his utensils down, put his elbows on the table, and gracefully placed his hands together.

"I get the drift, Simon. From what Stockman tells me, there's really little choice in the matter from ORB's viewpoint but to—at the very least—delay the operation of the plant for some indeterminate time. That isn't quite what you're suggesting, but I do understand what you're asking." He smiled and continued to stare at Simon as his friend hesitated before placing the next forkful of *gâteau au chocolat* in his mouth. Simon wiped his mouth with his napkin and smiled. When he finished, his smile became a chuckle.

"I'll check things out with Stockman." Dick was prepared to leave it at that.

They smiled at each other for a few more moments before Simon changed the subject completely and started to discuss the local politics of the two countries.

Dick reciprocated in the best way he knew how; by taking part in the chit-chat. But beneath the facade he knew that this time the rest of this project, as well as the expansion project, was not going to be as straightforward as he would have liked. Still, in a strange way, he looked forward to this new role that Stockman, and then Simon, had described to him. They finished their meal with a glass of Grand Marnier, followed by Simon's cigar, and left the restaurant together to wander around La Grande-Place before going their separate ways. They would meet again, but tomorrow they would both be flying out.

* * *

Heading Out—2019

Dick Elliot's' thoughts were interrupted by the knock on his office door. He turned to see a strange face poking around the edge.

"Are you Mr. Elliot?" Without waiting for an answer, the face and attached body slowly slid into the room and thrust a handout toward him.

"James Peters. Pleased to meet you," said the figure who shook Dick's hand vigorously.

Dick was brought back to reality from his thoughts of Iran and what lay ahead and what he had already gone through there forty years ago with his family.

"Oh yes, James Peters, the man from Bud," said Dick as he broke into a smile. "Sorry, I was miles away for a moment. Come in and sit," Dick waved him over to a chair at the round table by the window. "Mary, can you get a couple of coffees, please?" Dick spoke into the intercom to his assistant.

"We have a copy of your résumé, and I'm impressed." Dick rested his feet on an open desk drawer while he reviewed the file to refresh his memory. Bud Bourhis, his long-time friend, had recommended James for the job in Sari— although Bud was oblivious to the world of ORB and what Stockman was looking for in an on-site engineering operative. Bud and James had worked together on the refinery construction in Sarnia, where James was not only a site engineer but also a control systems engineer, and a very good one. Bud had a direct line to Dick Elliot and had seen strength in James that didn't come around too often these days with younger people. There was a sense of urgency about him that impressed the people he worked with, and his name came to be a respected one on the project. Bud had no doubt James could recreate his usefulness for Dick in Iran, although Bud didn't understand the full extent of usefulness that Dick was expecting.

Dick had sent the résumé with some notes on to Simon at Domar Oil in London and, in turn, Simon had developed a dossier on James that fleshed out his work history, contacts, education, marriage situation, finances, and anything else that came to light. It wasn't a kick-ass dossier but was one that was impressive enough for Simon to respond positively to Dick. Neither of them was looking for anyone that would stand out in the crowd, so to speak. They wanted someone who could do the job and had initiative while at the same time keeping a low profile. Neither of them had thought about it before, but the fact that James was married with three blond-haired sons under the age of seven could well be an advantage. He would definitely stay below the radar of suspicion and give some authenticity to his poking around when he had to. In Iran, young male children, especially blond ones, always caught the attention of the black-haired Iranians who also particularly revered the mothers of sons. While strange to the Westerner, blond-haired boys helped open doors in Iran that others would have difficulty entering.

The twenty-eight-year-old James seemed to be perfect for what Stockman wanted.

Dick closed the folder.

"So, James, you would like to go on an overseas assignment? Think you're ready?" Dick smiled as he looked over at James.

"I think so," James fidgeted a little but looked Dick in the eye. "We came over to Canada a few years ago and would prefer to go overseas with a Canadian company so we can keep our immigration status here. Hopefully, we can get citizenship when we get back." James smiled and fidgeted a little. "But I would like to know a little more about how we're going to fare as foreigners in an Islamic Republic. Times have changed, and I have to wonder whether we are safe as a Western family."

"We think about it every day, James," Dick replied and smiled. "Fortunately, we work in a fairly remote part of Iran, away from the political mess in Tehran. Regardless, we still have to be very careful, although we have extremely secure arrangements with the Republican Guard—we think. The fact is, they know we need to be there if they're going to be successful in getting things up and running. It gives them a lot of motivation to keep us happy. No one hangs on to our passports anymore, and we get safe passage wherever we go." Dick paused.

"You can appreciate my concern, Mr. Elliot, but at the same time, we know some folks who are already over there for IT installations and programming, and they say the same as you ... I think we are okay with it."

"Call me Dick and, okay, I think you already know a little about the project and you'll fit in just fine." Dick pushed his glasses up over his forehead as he thought about how James might fit into his role on site.

The coffee arrived, and James put a couple of lumps of sugar in his cup and stirred.

"There are some things you're going to have to do for us while you are over there, James—that is, if you take this assignment on. It's a little out of the norm."

"Oh." James took his first sip of coffee and looked up at Dick.

"Well, to start with, we don't want the plant to operate as planned." Dick lifted his coffee to his mouth and took a sip.

James gulped and was clearly shocked.

"What? Run that by me again." James pushed himself to the edge of his chair.

"Look, James. We can't let that plant get into the hands of the Islamic Regime. It's too dangerous and upsets the balance of power, so to speak." Stockman looked concerned and spread his hands out on the table, palms up in a display of frankness.

"Oh, and what is someone like me supposed to do about that?" James was in shock and squirmed in his chair.

"You're going to have to act as the controls engineer to make sure that the plant doesn't actually get into operations." Dick looked over the top of his glasses. He wasn't sure this was going to fly with James.

"By doing what?" James asked, a little unsettled. He slouched back in his seat with his hands raised and shoulders shrugged.

"By building problems into the systems—like the control programming and operations. We'll have a number of operatives on site doing their thing on the physical plant itself. You'll get to know them in due time, but for the first six months, I need you to settle in and strategize on what needs to be done."

"Is all this kosher, Dick? I mean, is it legal?"

"It's not legal in Iran, but it is to those of us who have to negotiate our way through the problems the Islamic Regime has created. They've threatened to stop the oil flow to the West, cut all ties, and align themselves with Russia and China to create a petrodollar. That's a problem. But listen, I'm not the one running things. There are others far more powerful than we are in the driver's seat here. One of my jobs is to find the right people for the project. And, by that, I mean people who will do what they have to do." It was Dick's turn to slouch back in his chair as he studied James. It was a lot to take in for the young fellow, but then no one said it would be easy to recruit the "right" people.

"Okay, I guess," James responded, not knowing what else to say right then.

"Now listen," Stockman perked up a bit at James's response. It was not a negative. "We also need you to interact with the local population as much as you can to gather information that could be useful to us going forward." Dick paused.

"Boy, this is getting more absurd by the minute. What kind of information?" James asked with a puzzled expression.

"Well, the comings and goings both on site and off site of people who appear somewhat out of place. Foreigners who speak, say, Russian or Chinese. Military people going back and forth to and from places like Gorgan, Babol, and Chalus—all small cities, close to Sari, where expats live. Listen to people in the Armenian stores, take Friday drives along the coast, and look for anything that seems out of the ordinary." Dick raised his eyebrows in expectation of a response.

"Boy, that's a tall order for somewhere that everyone is going to seem out of the ordinary to us." James smiled.

"Yes, but there are going to be people, places, and circumstances that will seem particularly odd after you've been there a while. Faces that don't seem to fit in or that appear to have you under surveillance. Look, I know this isn't a specific role I'm asking of you, but over the next several months, there's going to be activity in the Sari area that we need to know about. For instance, there's a US listening post buried in the mountains just south of Gorgan. Everyone seems to know about it, but it's still confidential. No one talks about it. Odd? Yes, but it's still operating, and the Iranians aren't messing with it—why? We don't know and would like to know."

James seemed to be growing into the role as he absorbed the potential for excitement and intrigue. It offered him an oddly attractive challenge and likely came with a substantial financial reward.

"All sounds pretty intriguing, Mr. Elliot. I assume I still have to carry on as normal on site; keep my eyes and ears peeled and make my time off constructive?"

"You've got it, lad!" Dick almost sighed with relief, having had to describe a very difficult-to-describe situation to an unknown when he really didn't know much about it either. In any case, his intent was to provide Stockman—and Simon—with all the help he could muster and maybe a little of it would help their cause, whatever that ultimately was.

"You may want to be discrete about all this with your wife, James. But I have to leave that to you to decide. I don't know how much you tell her about your work." Dick looked at James.

"We pretty much tell each other everything—I think." James looked as though he was questioning his own statement. "Anyway, I'm going to tell her. Jenny knows that if I'm okay with things, it'll likely be okay for her and the kids."

Once they had gone over things a few more times, James seemed to warm to the project and actually sounded excited about the prospect of getting involved in some nefarious activities for a change of pace. It piqued his interest, although he wasn't sure that Jenny would agree.

The session with James settled down to more mundane things, like accommodations and schooling for the kids. James and his family were to live in a second-floor apartment at the end of an alley in central Sari. That way, he would be more able to mix with the locals and visit the same places they did. He would also be able to stay away from project gossip and difficult questions that might pop up from his coworkers, who would mostly be housed in the camp complex at site. Some of the ex-pat managers would stay in an apartment block across town with their families. It would not be easy, but the intel on both James and his wife, Jenny, was positive; they appeared to be amenable to not living in an ex-pat cluster and seemed free-spirit types who could easily mix with the locals.

As for schooling, some ex-pat teachers would eventually be employed to open a small school in Sari for the expats' children, however many that might be and whatever ages they would be. Whoever was recruited would have a real job on their hands, coping with what was likely to be a range of ages among the school kids. But such is life in an ex-pat outpost.

Dick handed James a 150-page document titled "Culture Shock and How it Could Affect You."

James scanned it and concluded it was a generic template for an ex-pat living almost anywhere in the world. It certainly wasn't directed at Sari, but James would find out more about that soon enough.

Their meeting ended with a strong handshake, a farewell, a pat on the back from Dick, and a promise that he would be visiting Sari soon and get caught up with the family. He had forgotten his own difficult days of having to adjust to similar circumstances. He had eventually concluded it was a necessary but traumatic step to take to a more successful future—provided he made it through his contract. How soon he'd forgotten.

James checked in with HR, made his way back to Dick's assistant to arrange for travel, signed all the documentation for visas and expenses, and sought help on establishing non-resident status in Canada that would allow him relief from domestic taxes. He was cleared to leave for Iran as soon as the client's approval was received. A date was set for two weeks' time for him and his family to head out. In the meantime, they needed to pack up their belongings and get them shipped as soon as possible so their things might arrive at the same time they did. There was so much to do. James figured there would be eleven pieces of luggage, three young boys, and a wife to corral to this new country with all its new experiences and where they didn't understand or read one word of the language. Of course, being so young has its advantages in those kinds of circumstances; one just doesn't have the experience to panic.

*   *   *

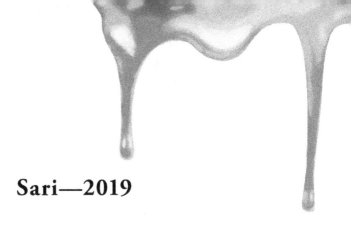

Sari—2019

As the Varesh Airlines 737-500 came out of the clouds and passed over the summit of the Alborz Mountains, Jenny looked over the lush fields hugging the Caspian coastline, a sharp contrast to the rugged red and brown of the south. She could just make out the main population centers and roads as she nudged James to lean over and look out at the scene as the Caspian Sea came into focus. It was a welcome change from the dryness of Tehran and reminded them a little of their own part of England, where they had by the sea and greenery. They relaxed back in their seats and pushed the boys over to the windows for them to see. Amid the oohs and aahs, as the children excitedly planned their first trip to the beach, the plane turned to the east and started its descent to Sari, a city with a population of more than 300,000.

"Well, it looks relatively modern," James said, looking anxiously at Jenny and then over at the boys. "It can't be any hotter than Tehran when we arrived there." He paused and waited for Jenny. "Remember how that blast of heat hit us as they opened the plane door, and we thought it must be the heat from the engines? Not that it was that bad as we acclimatized. It was just a bit of a shock after leaving Montreal, with all that snow."

He slumped back into his seat and passed one hand across his brow as he remembered back to their first five days in Tehran. They were numb from the exhaustion resulting from their preparations to leave and then the seven-hour flight from London with fifteen pieces of luggage and three kids. But they rose to the occasion as they thought of the possibility of a good night's rest only a few hours away. Jenny just smiled, a sort of cynical smile as though her anxieties had by no means been left behind, and she pushed herself forward with bags and kids hanging off her. Thoughts of what the future held for them zipped through her mind every now and again. She wondered for the hundredth time if they had made the right decision in coming here. She'd had her last chance in England, on the layover en route, to back out but, despite her trepidation, they had decided that they must go on together and, while reluctant, Jenny had felt that the commitment had been made and there was no turning back.

The 737 descended more steeply than expected as it swung once over the city of Sari before landing at the Dasht-e Naz, a small international airport with all the modern conveniences.

James and Jenny looked at each other and smiled with satisfaction before they started arranging the children, using them as a distraction from the unfamiliar surroundings with Farsi signs and instructions and the disembarking passengers impatiently pushing toward the plane's exit. At least they were supposed to be met by an associate and, while they had not met him before, they knew Max was also an employee of Interstate; in fact, as a site superintendent, he was apparently James's boss for the time being. They knew little about Max except that he was French and had been on the project for nearly two years.

As James reflected on the clues that people had given him about Max, he realized that very little had, in fact, been said about him. The picture he had been shown was of a middle-aged hippy-type man, personified by the mass of gray curly hair hanging almost to his shoulders and matching bushy beard. Unfortunately, the photo had been taken more than three years before, when Max was in Algeria. They hoped they might still recognize him as they disembarked.

Having retrieved their luggage from the small, crowded arrivals area, they somehow managed to hold on to the three boys and four luggage carts and push their way through customs, waving their entry permits at a completely disinterested official. A shout echoed from the back of the crowd, and a tall, hairy man leaped toward them with arms extended and hands waving.

Max had the rough and tumble character of a person who had got his education from the countries he had lived and worked in. Born in Brittany, he had since served his time in a number of third-world countries, where he was often the only Caucasian, and had dutifully and single-handedly managed small World Bank sponsored projects for Dick Elliot as an employee of Interstate. He had become used to a sort of nomadic existence over the last almost forty years and used a twenty-six-foot recreational vehicle as a home base to which he and his small family returned after each contract. In this instance, the vehicle was parked in a long-term storage facility in Montreal.

He had lived this way for so long it became a relative mystery as to why he had decided upon wedlock. One could only conclude that it was the continuation of the Divet name rather than companionship that he sought. Using all of the cunning he had developed over the years of being the only white man in a black man's world, Max had established himself as the local politician in power, rather than a construction manager. His résumé had gotten longer over the years and represented his biography rather than a work profile. It even cited the late President de Gaulle as a reference, just for good measure, although the president was discreetly listed halfway down the full page of references since he had died some time ago and was thus unavailable.

Max approached his life with the tenacity of a leech, refusing to let go at any time and draining the energy from all who got near him. He was the type of person who could exist without defining his prime function yet survived as self-made and recognized as indispensable. Upon meeting him for the first time at the airport, James and Jenny's preconceptions about first impressions were strewn into disarray. In fact, there was no lingering on any one first impression at all since there seemed to be so many of them and it was difficult to distinguish which was most apparent. But if forced into describing that first thought about this odd man, James might say he appeared to be out of sync with his surroundings.

Strangely, and despite the heat and humidity, Max wore a three-piece gray suit, waistcoat buttoned, with matching tie and white shirt. His black galoshes brought the look down some, as did the white construction hard hat tilted to one side atop his mass of tight long gray curls. The thin-lined mustache that clung precariously to his upper lip, as though one twitch of his nose would cause it to slip sideways, completed the picture. The overall effect gave an impression of Salvador Dalí in disguise among a crowd of people but undecided about whom he was masquerading as. Whoever he was, he was not in sync with the local Iranian population, who had no idea how to interact with him. His French accent provided the listener with the usual earful of mispronounced English, including dropped h's while the word toilet sounded like a sensual paradise in which to indulge one's erotic fantasies. This effect was exemplified by the twirling raised hand to make it seem as though each normally uncomfortable or mispronounced word was being thrown out to the general public to see if they could do any better.

Their first encounter with the man was as though a cloud of dust had risen suddenly and swirled them off to settle in an apartment in the middle of a strange and uncertain world. Max had handled the baggage with as much concern as a fly being swatted from the butt of a cow. He maneuvered them into his dusty green Jeep Wagoneer with room to spare for everyone to clamber aboard. They sped off into the distance, heading toward the city of Sari while Max blabbed on about the job as though James had only been gone for a few days' vacation. In the confusion of that first meeting, there was no denying that they had been invited to supper but nothing had been said about how to get to Max's house or where they were now headed. It also became immediately evident that Max expected James to turn up for work at the crack of dawn the following morning, which he did not intend to do. His first priority was to his family and getting them at least partially settled.

The drive into town had been relatively uneventful except for the shock of what appeared around them as they sped from the airport to the apartment through the outskirts of Sari. The route led them through a squalid area of the city, where the streets went undefined except for the open sewers or jubes. Everyone appeared to be dust covered, as they got the full treatment from passing traffic. The accommodations were slightly less than decaying single-storey residences and little more than mud huts. The women struggled to wherever they were going with huge loads balanced precariously on their heads, while the menfolk all seemed to be either playing in the jubes or squatting against the mud walls of the decrepit buildings, smoking hookahs and generally lounging about. Children and dogs were scattered all over with apparently no ownership.

It was not until later that both James and Jenny realized that had they approached the city by road from Tehran and not from the airport, which was on the other side of the city to the east, their first impressions of Sari would have been quite different.

Compared to this, Tehran seemed like heaven despite their cursory thought of Sari being modern as seen from the plane still a couple of thousand feet in the air. While not exchanging one word between them, James and Jenny knew from the look on the other's face that there was no need for comment. If they had been armed with return airline tickets, there was little doubt that the plane that had just brought them to Sari would also take them out. But it was not to be, and they endured that first trip in stony silence, determined not to dwell on the subject, and resigned to continue with their commitment since there was no obvious option available to them.

With little ceremony, the five of them were dumped in the second-floor apartment of a two-storey building at the end of an alley. It seemed to be close to the center of Sari, yet one had the impression of almost living in the country if one looked out of the back windows over the countryside to the south.

Max had left within a few minutes of dumping them at the apartment. He had described little yet said a lot. They were left to feel that everything was under control, while at the same time not knowing what was really going on. With a sigh, they wandered around the three-bedroom apartment and found some relief in the fact that someone had left butter, milk, bread, and beer in the refrigerator—a little touch of creature comforts that they could grasp.

It took them only a very short while to sort out their luggage and distribute the bedrooms among them. Apart from that, there was little else to do indoors except to think about provisions and wonder how they were supposed to use the unfamiliar style of eastern toilet, where cockroaches lurked and peered up at them from the blackness of the drain and the smell of the open latrine permeated the apartment. Clearly, one had to squat, but after that it was a mystery to them with no toilet paper and a tap with a hose attached to the wall. But they were fast learners. Meanwhile, the children busied themselves at the window, watching the locals go about their business in the alley.

Though adventurous by nature, James and Jenny had silent pangs of anxiety as they thought about venturing out into this foreign land where English wasn't even a second language in the north. It started to dawn on them how little they had previously appreciated and how cut off they would feel by not understanding one word, one number, or one road sign. Certainly, the degree of difficulties was not explained in the company literature prepared for expats.

Nevertheless, they went about what little business they could find to do as they embarked upon trivial conversation in an attempt to lessen the reality. At least their belongings had miraculously arrived, and in later months they would wonder how that could possibly have happened in such an apparently haphazardly managed country.

James and Jenny were actually relieved when Max arrived early in the evening to lighten their anxieties of moving in. But there was little greeting from Max, and certainly no interest in whether they were coping with the new situation. Max had, after all his years in foreign countries, no reason to suspect that other people had settling-in problems, and the thought could not be further from his mind. James's mind was not like that, having associated mostly with people like himself, who would actually go out of their way to ensure that these first few days were made as easy as possible for newcomers as they got their feet wet.

Temporarily relieved from the stress, James and family scrambled into the Wagoneer and it sped along the alley. For some reason, this trip back into the unknown didn't seem so bad, and both James and Jenny started to relax a little. They listened to Max with his heavily accented English and actually seemed to understand some of what he said, although they weren't certain.

Within a few minutes, they pulled up outside a single-storey house, surrounded by a five-foot-high iron rail fence. It could have been almost anywhere. The garden bloomed with an array of local blossoms, and the mere act of having to take their shoes off at the front door was a comfort that they welcomed, having just come from a country that insisted on such a habit.

They were met by Angel, Max's wife, and his two under-five blonde-haired daughters. Max's character took on a new dimension surrounded by his little family of femininity. He exuded an "inherited from birth" macho image exemplified by the very appearance of his dependents. It remained questionable as to whether the apparent weakness of Angel was really true to character or in keeping with the image that Max expected.

They got the impression that there was not much of a long-lasting relationship between Max and Angel but more a job that needed to be done. Angel, an unassuming brunette from a long line of pinched, loving, and hardworking Québécois, had readily accepted the offer that Max had made to save her from a stable but predictable future. They had traveled to and worked in a number of countries during their five years of marriage, where Max had dutifully but masterfully ensured that the surrounding populations in Algeria and Togo partook in the birth and subsequent raising of the two girls.

The evening went pleasantly enough, although James really wasn't too sure if there was anything he had in common with Max, since every time they broached the subject of work, one of Max's eyes would close over, his head would tilt to one side, and a rather oblique set of only partially clear statements would issue forth that James couldn't grasp the meaning of in the slightest. It seemed as though Max was just rambling with no particular subject in mind. But, if nothing else, they had settled a few basic facts concerning everyday living. Despite some obvious deliberations by Max, they were assigned a Citroën Jyane as their personal vehicle and a Land Rover Defender with a driver who would be at James's disposal for working hours.

Angel had spent the whole evening cooking, serving the meal, and then preparing her children for bed. There was almost no interaction between her and her guests, although now and again, she would lean over Jenny and say something like, "*Ne t'inquiète pas. Je vais te montrer, ma cherie.*" Don't worry. I'll show you, my dear. But she never did.

After enjoying a simple meal—as well as one can in your bosses' house on your first meeting while at the same time trying to control three young, tired sons as they tumbled around the floor with their two new friends—the evening ended relatively early with everyone departing in good spirits and promising to get together again soon. They never did, but it was the thought that counted.

Max insisted that James be picked up by his driver at 6:30 a.m., but James resisted and told Max he needed a few days to acclimatize. Max shrugged, bottom lip protruding, and clearly considered this to be the first sign of weakness in his new resident engineer.

"Well, if you must... you must, I suppose." He twisted an end of his thin mustache and turned away. "*Adieu* and goodnight."

* * *

New Day, New Town

As sunlight streamed through the barely opaque curtains and spread throughout the room, James and Jenny peeked out from beneath the bedclothes. Almost afraid of finding themselves where they thought they were, they dragged the bedclothes farther over their heads and huddled into the mattress in relative security. Reasoning that it was impossible to remain there for the rest of their lives, they both gradually emerged into the sunlight, inch by inch, before finally accepting the situation and reluctantly folding the blankets down to expose themselves to the world and let it take its toll. If nothing else good had happened over the last few days, at least the bed was large and comfortable. Despite the apprehensions they had felt the previous day, they had slept soundly and now awoke refreshed.

This first day after their arrival brought its own natural refreshment to the two bodies that had limped to consciousness, acknowledging each other with sheepish grins of expectation.

"Do you think it's a mistake?" James asked as he leaned up on one elbow and stared at Jenny from the corner of his eye.

She didn't answer.

"You know, coming here in the first place. It's a bit of a shambles, isn't it?"

Jenny lay still, staring up at the ceiling.

"To think, we could still be in Montreal right now, getting ready to drive down to Fairview for the weekly shopping." Jenny turned to him, and they both broke into a fit of laughing at how ridiculous it seemed that they could even think of those normal everyday activities when spread out there before them was so much unknown.

"I hope you're satisfied," Jenny eventually managed to gasp, "dragging us halfway 'round the world to this God-forsaken place. I can't believe I gave up so easily. When I think back to that last chance I had, I feel stupid for not staying there in London and letting you come here by yourself." Jenny looked serious as she said these last words and James avoided her stare.

"Oh, come on, it really can't be as bad as it looks, although I have to admit that if we turn out to be half as crazy as Max, I'll eat my words." They both laughed, and James relaxed a little and looked back at her.

"Listen," he said, "we have to at least give this whole thing a chance. After all, we don't have the fare for return air tickets and even if we did, we don't know where we'd go or what we'd do when we got to where we would go." He shrugged. "Things will turn out just fine." He paused and shrugged again. "Despite everything we've seen so far, I can't possibly think that it can get any worse. We simply have to look on all this as one hell of an experience and enjoy it when we can. There'll be other people coming out soon, so think of us as pioneers." James stopped and smiled at Jenny, who returned his look with an impish grin.

"I have to admit, though," James continued, "this character, Max, is a little overbearing. I'm beginning to understand why the guys in Tehran didn't say too much about him. It could be a bit of a battle. Still, what the hell, I'm game to give him a go. Anyway, it's all sort of intriguing, what with this business of lending an ear to the locals that Dick was talking to me about. There's a lot more to all this than crazy Max. We might actually find out some interesting things to tell our grandchildren." James paused as Jenny put her hand up to her mouth. He had shared the highlights of that first meeting with Dick Elliot in Montreal but had played his role down as best he could. Jenny just took it in stride, overcome by the anticipation of an adventure.

"God don't tell me they're still sleeping," Jenny remembered. "I can't believe it. It's nearly 10 o'clock. Let's go find them. If they've got any sense, they'll have packed their bags and got on the first plane out of here. On the other hand, perhaps they've decided to spare the country their interest and are still asleep." They both ambled out of bed and wrapped themselves before opening the door and peering around the jamb.

The three boys had their backs to them and were staring quietly out of the window. Bradley, the youngest, at two years old, had pulled a chair over and now stretched up on tiptoes to look out at some obviously enthralling happening down in the alley outside. Elliot, their middle son, aged five, was standing on the floor with just his eyes level with the bottom of the window. James and Jenny crept over and casually glanced over their shoulders before Jenny wobbled backward at the sight before her. Bradley sucked harder at his soother and the other boys were obviously having trouble keeping their eyes in their sockets. James stood there aghast at the scene before him, unable to take his eyes away.

Below them, in the garden of the house opposite their apartment, for all their innocent eyes to see, was a live sheep hanging from a small tree by its back legs. The family was standing around while what appeared to be the youngest son held a large knife poised above his head. An elderly man seemed to be chanting. James guessed what was about to follow and suggested that the boys might rather go into the kitchen for breakfast. None of them wanted to move and miss the action, and even Jenny was peeking out from her fingers in anticipation as she held her hands against her eyes as though trying not to look but looking all the same. While she might have been trying to avoid the scene below, there was no avoiding the blow-by-blow account that Anthony, their eldest son, the seven-year-old, was determined to provide of what was happening.

"He's cutting its throat," shouted Anthony in a strangled cry. "It's bleeding all over the ground. Ugh, it's wiggling all over the place. Dad, how can it keep doing that when its head is hanging off? Elliot, it's not funny. Ugh. He's catching all the blood in a bowl. I'll bet they're going to drink it now. His dad's got the knife now. I wonder what he's going to do." Anthony paused, waiting for the next event while the family below watched the carcass run dry of the rest of its blood and Jenny beat a hasty retreat to the bathroom. Bradley sucked harder on his soother with a sort of unconcerned look on his face.

"He's started to skin it now," Anthony continued as the elderly man cleanly stripped the wool and skin from the dead sheep. James quickly pulled the curtains together before the story continued, much to the chagrin of the boys.

"I think that's enough for now," he said, "especially since we haven't even had breakfast yet."

"God, I hope they don't do that every morning, James. Can you imagine what it would be like after a month with blood and guts all over the place? Well, so much for our introduction to the finer points of life here in Sari." Jenny laughed a short, hysterical kind of laugh.

"I don't remember HR them telling us about this in Montreal." James laughed at the thought of what his reaction might have been had they told him of such rituals.

"On the other hand, it's just as well they didn't. Can you imagine how they would do it?" Jenny paused and held up her hands as though showing off a photo to friends. "Oh, and look at this," she mimicked, pursing her lips, fluttering her eyes, and talking in a false falsetto voice, "you'll enjoy their little jokes. Here's one of the locals slicing the head off their pet sheep. See all that blood spurting over everyone. What a beautiful color it is up against that magnificent, peacock-blue sky!" She laughed again, but this time with a more guttural sound as though someone was slowly choking her. James put his arm around her and led her out to the kitchen.

Within minutes, the event had turned from trauma to interest as the boys demanded answers to all their questions concerning the slaughter. There is little else one can do in the face of childish innocence but to treat such a subject as a casual event. Amid all the discussions, it seemed a miracle that breakfast of one kind or another appeared on the table.

*   *   *

Settling In

The first few days are always the worst in a strange new place—unless it's on holiday, of course. Well, that's what everyone seems to say and more often than not, they're right. It took James and Jenny a week before they felt confident enough to venture out into the main shopping area to get a reasonable supply of food without merely dashing to the corner store where they would stock up on items labeled with a picture they could recognize, since the script on everything was in Arabic.

It was usually with a sound of surprise when one or the other actually recognized what they had discovered tucked away at the back of one of the upper shelves. The storekeeper had never been as lucky as he had been in those early days, when these strange folk would enter his store, complete with three blond-haired boys, and would start immediately searching through his goods. They would sift and sort and now and then a packet or can would appear on the counter. He had learned to start making way for the piles as soon as the young Iranian boys from the nearby alleys warned of the *ferengies'* arrival five minutes before they got there.

Still, times had been good then. They were buying all the stock the storekeeper had been landed with by those slick city salesmen who had promised him that these new things were going to go fast as people started to develop new tastes. Of course, they were wrong, and most of the stock remained unsold for more than a year.

The storekeeper couldn't remember what most of the goods were and had instead made space for the more routine groceries by moving all these normally unsalable goods out of the way, relegated to the uppermost shelves.

While the storekeeper was adding up the bill on his old well-worn abacus, the kids would continue piling up bits and pieces on the counter and the old man would keep smiling at his newly discovered wealth. But this wasn't going to last as James and Jenny continued to venture farther into the town. Of course, the bazaar was still pretty foreign to them and while they passed it often as they wandered around, it took them a month to pluck up the courage to dive in.

In the meantime, as they drove around in the Jyane, James had been keeping a careful eye on where everything was in the town center. He often led Jenny and boys in circles as they did some "sightseeing" for James to understand the lay of the land, often walking with Bradley in an umbrella stroller so that James could discover more things in detail. He carefully absorbed the directions to various places outside the town. To James, Sari was more of a town than a city. It was relatively small for a city by North American standards, with a population of about 300,000, but it happened to be roughly in the middle of the rather inhabitable Caspian coastline. All roads led to the center and Sari was likely considered a city because it had the only international-designated airport along the coastline due to its runway length of about 9,000 feet. The airport actually had no international destinations, only connector flights.

They ventured farther and farther from their apartment location any time James was not working. It was a welcome change for Jenny, who had the three young boys on her hands all day. She only ventured out alone as far as the corner store at the end of the alley during that first month, although she was getting more and more adventurous as time went on and soon was off and working her way through the maze of lanes leading to the main road and beyond. She never drove.

Observing this rare breed of English-speaking people in the city brought amusement for the locals, who made games out of following the blond-haired tribe around at every opportunity. At first it was amusing to turn and confront a gang of giggling youngsters, who would scatter at the prospect of bringing down the wrath of some unholy terror. But the novelty gradually wore off and James and Jenny preferred the relative anonymity of being ordinary shoppers who wanted to go about their business without the distracting hordes of locals watching their every move. Eventually, the locals ignored Jenny and her family, realizing that they were not really that different from themselves, except for the boys' blondness and skin color.

Those early days were filled with experiences to be remembered, when even the ritual of buying food felt like it was pioneering. The mere act of going out to buy meat became an experience never to be forgotten. Those were days of having to point to particular parts of the carcass, hanging outside the older meat stores in the markets with flies landing everywhere, and having to ask for a kilo of *gushte* or minced whatever. More often than not it was unrecognizable as mutton and likely wasn't, but all meat was better minced than not. The mincing sort of hid the product, which might have hung for days in the store window as the flies made their home on the juicy body. The butcher would hack away with his machete-style knife at the part of the carcass Jenny pointed to, letting the hunk of meat drop into a plastic bag. He would transfer it to the mincer and lean on the meat with both hands to push it through. The meat was collected in a piece of unlined newspaper, wrapped around the product as though the butcher was serving fish and chips old style.

James had gradually become accustomed to the traffic flow, directions, and government office locations, and recognized numbers as well as some of the words, or at least some letters of the Arabic alphabet. It wasn't easy, but slowly he absorbed some of the information he thought he might need for the future, such as the direction to Gorgan, to the airport, and to the coastline about twenty miles to the north.

It took about three months for James and Jenny to discover meat stores that they considered to be safe, where what they were eating didn't look as if it had been hanging outside in the heat for a while. Jenny was brought to reality one day as she inadvertently wandered around the back of one of their "safe" butcher shops, only to come face to face with the meatless head of a horse, hanging out of an open garbage bin. Naturally, it put her off meat for a while, but the ensuing diet of milk products, naan, vegetables, nuts, fruit, and milk products didn't inspire her either, so it was back to the meat.

They had fleetingly considered that maybe this *was* civilization of a sort when they discovered that milk could be ordered from a delivery service. The vendor in this instance was a short, rather fat man who rode a moped weighed down with large vats of milk hanging off every available hanger. He would stop at the end of the alley and cry out with some completely indecipherable call that was presumably intended to signify his arrival. One of the boys would be shunted off with a large saucepan to have it filled by the fat milkman. This had gone on for two weeks before Jenny was told that the milkman only sold unpasteurized goat milk, the most notorious carrier of tuberculosis. Jenny was not prepared to have to boil milk every time she needed it. Once again, a fast rethink was needed and it was back to the market for supplies.

They discovered plucked and cleaned chickens after just a month, and it was the welcome end of trying to build up the courage to buy a live chicken and prepare it themselves for cooking. They bought six and hurried back to the apartment to count their blessings and start cooking. True, the birds needed a little cleaning, but then they had been living here now for over a month and could handle it. They tossed a coin to see who would be the lucky one to grapple with the innards. Jenny won the toss and James was given the job. Armed with plastic bags covering every exposed part of his hands, he spread apart the legs of his first chicken, only to be confronted by a beak staring menacingly out at him from the security of the parson's nose. James went into shock, Jenny into hysterics, and the bird was thrown across the kitchen and smacked into the wall. They considered tossing the little troop of chickens into the garbage and returning to the *gushte gaft* but thought better of it, cleaned all of them all and froze five.

James had continued, sometimes alone, looking around the city, as well as the area around the site. When he ventured out to the towns to the west and east, he would take the family but always took careful note of all the pertinent exit routes and government buildings. There were good maps available and he marked them up, making notes as needed. It was likely overkill, but he wasn't sure what he might need and it all played into his sense of adventure. It couldn't hurt.

If there was one thing that would be remembered as being a gift from heaven unloaded on them during that first month, it was probably the fact that booze became readily available to them, albeit at a high cost. In many ways, it was a shock to stumble upon the supplies that they did after hearing all the talk about Muslims and alcohol. But one only has to follow a white man for a short time in a foreign country before the inevitable alcoholic drink appears like a mirage in the desert.

The Armenian store was in itself like the discovery of civilization to people who had lost themselves in the mountains. Stocked with an incredible variety of European delicacies, like Corn Flakes, salami, wines, and caviar, it became for them a veritable delight to wander from shop corner to shop corner, seeking out new delights. If the truth were known, it wasn't just the relatively limited selection of foodstuffs that drew their attention so much as a chance to discover other foreigners that were actually located in the vicinity of Sari. It was comforting to realize that there were, in fact, quite a number of other expatriates in the area, working on one project or another. However, it was quite obvious that the vast majority were not English speaking. On the other hand, it was at least better to receive a friendly nod and give one in turn than not to have one at all. Not that there weren't lots of cursory nods from the locals, but to get one that seemed genuine was one small success in this foreign land.

While the store wasn't stocked to the brim with a tremendous variety, it certainly didn't lack in quantity. The assortment of drinks, however, would have done justice to any North American liquor store. Beer was more than in plentiful supply, and while the brands generally varied from week to week, there was at least the old faithful Skol International to keep the palate active. Within a few more weeks, several other Armenian stores were discovered hidden around the city, and James derived a certain satisfaction from going from one to the other, searching out the newly arrived selections of food and drink. Unfortunately, to only shop in these stores was relatively prohibitive as the selection was simply not great enough to establish a healthy diet and the prices were extortionate, as one might expect for imported goods. Nevertheless, they were a very big plus, supplementing one's otherwise truly native diet with a spot of the old recognizable—it was a needed safety valve.

The arrival of their soft furnishings from Montreal had made life more bearable. In itself, the apartment was spacious and airy. Planned on the same basis as any good-sized three-bedroom apartment in Canada, it was equipped with marble floors and covered liberally with carpet. A balcony ran the length of the rear side with French windows opening onto it from the master bedroom and the main living area. Furnishings provided by the company were sparse but adequate and reminded them of rent-a-room decor.

One could make up for what one lacked, like shelving, with cement bricks and wood planking. It was fortunate that they had brought a small portable stereo and some of their favorite CDs and bought a cheap shortwave radio in the bazaar. The combination of CDs and music on USB drives, together with the BBC World Service, sufficed on many an evening after they had forgotten what it was like to settle down to a good evening of television.

Fortunately, internet was available and more often than not they amused themselves watching streamed entertainment, although it needed patience to cope with the intermittent signal strength and continual booting up. However, James was very happy he could easily communicate not only with friends and family back home, but also with Dick Elliot, whom he called every week to report on his findings. Many of the findings were of no particular interest to Dick, but he was impressed by the consistency and quality of the reporting from James, who talked about everything from the site situation, his understanding of his location relative to everywhere else, and, of course, his family.

Since the winter months were approaching fast, it was interesting to discover the delights of heating with kerosene or *naft* as it was known locally. Three large burners were positioned strategically around the apartment. Each was a permanently installed device equipped with a day tank and tin chimney that exited to some point on the roof. One would simply turn the valve to allow *naft* to flow into the smaller reservoir in the underside of the apparatus and wait for the right time before throwing a wad of burning paper in through the top. This should have had the effect of setting light to the now-soaked wick. Unfortunately, on the majority of occasions, the timing proved to be inefficient, and the wick would drown in its own fuel, or the supply line would plug with the ashes of the burning paper.

On rare opportunities, one would have the unmentionable pleasure of grappling with the whole contraption, taking it apart piece by piece, spreading fine soot all over oneself as well as anything located within ten feet. One of the daily chores was to fill the day tanks with *naft* from the fifty-gallon drum located in the storage closet outside the apartment entry door. It was a weekly event to have the larger tank filled by some poor urchin who struggled up the stairs with a full drum of kerosene.

One could hardly imagine there would be a domestic water supply problem in northern Iran, where the lush vegetation and closeness to the Alborz Mountains suggested water would be in abundance. In fact, at times, it was in too great an abundance when the rainy season would cause the mud to flow and the street to turn into small rivers. As the rains emptied onto the city, James and Jenny could turn on dry taps while watching the rain splash against the windows. It was the greatest of frustrations to end a hot and sultry day by bathing oneself from a saucepan of water retrieved from the dripping of the taps.

There were days, it was true, when water was plentiful and the family would indulge themselves in bathing as long as the hot water tank in the kitchen could keep up with the demand. But more often than not, it became a constant struggle to store, heat, and use water at one's leisure. It had taken a good deal of research for James to eventually discover the real problem. It seemed that the adequacy of the water supply was in no doubt in other parts of the city and the problem for them was that they were located in a second-floor apartment at the end of an alley—at the end of a supply line. Such was life.

Obviously, Sari had expanded over the years, from a city of 100,000 to 500,000 in forty years. But it had made little provision to boost the water pressure to fulfill the needs of those dwellings at the outer limits of the city. A first-floor apartment would have solved most of the problem, but the second-floor location posed great problems for the trickle of water that lacked the energy to make the great climb.

The problems magnified themselves during the summer months when rainfall was scarce and any available groundwater would be used up long before it had even reached half the length of their alley. The greatest test of the theory could be witnessed each Friday when, as the Muslim day of rest, bathers were constantly washing themselves after the old Thursday night binge.

Little wonder James and company would look like piles of dust with eyes, at the end of each Friday. Fortunately there was always the beach, where a dip in the Caspian replaced the traditional method of bathing.

The idea of living so close to the Caspian Sea had conjured up all kinds of encouraging thoughts in James and Jenny's minds when they had been in Canada awaiting their departure. They had imagined it as the riviera of Iran, a holiday resort for the wealthy middle classes who flocked there from all over the world. They thought of it as a place where Russian families would spend the summer, frivolously indulging in the delights of the internationally renowned Iranian caviar and fresh fish combined with Russian vodka. They could see the fishing fleets in their minds, mingling with the opulence of wealthy playboy mariners who drifted around the world on their superyachts, looking for pleasure and adventure.

James and Jenny had bundled everyone into the car on that first trip and had headed for the beach, twenty miles away, with an excitement unprecedented since the last flow of water through the shower nozzle. They were a little more than disappointed with that first impression. Gray clouds loomed over the matching color of the water, the gray sand was strewn with garbage, and not a reasonable dune in sight.

There were no swimmers on that first visit, and none of the family had the urge to go in alone. They left before allowing the depression of disappointment to set in and drove at a leisurely pace back along the same route, hoping to spy something that could replace the disappointment they felt. They found nothing. This was not a seaside place that offered anything close to what they might find back home.

They had always lived near the sea and the first impression made by the dismal display of the so-called Iranian Riviera could not put them off from a second visit. The following Friday turned out to be one of those rare, glorious days at the edge of winter that warms the heart and fills the mind with thoughts of picnics, beaches, and swimming.

Refreshed by the day, they set off with even greater gusto than the previous week and headed toward the Caspian as though ready to do battle and prove that it could be all they wanted it to be. This time, they avoided parking at the first entrance to the beach at the end of the road, having realized that the majority of people seemed to be drawn to the easiest spot to park, get out, and stroll around within a few feet of their vehicle. Instead, they turned down a side road, parallel to the beach, and found a secluded parking spot some miles farther away. They saw dunes and what seemed like yellowish sand.

Armed with this new high, the five of them swarmed over the tall grass and rushed out onto the beach as though they had just discovered the lost city of Atlantis. The sands stretched for miles in each direction. Small groups of people strolled, headed for no place in particular but obviously enjoying the day. It was glorious. The boys tore off their clothes and headed for the sea, enticed by the relative calm, gentle swoosh of the tide as it washed over the sand. It was then that they stopped at the sight of a large black balloon floating in the water with more coming into view around it.

As the shape headed toward them, it was Anthony who recognized a human face hanging just above the surface of one of the balloons, expressing nothing in particular as it just bobbed there. There can have been fewer stranger sights than to see a chador-clad woman emerging from the water, acting as though there was simply no other way one could go swimming. The boys stood, their mouths agape, and watched her stride casually up the beach, headed toward a small group of people half hidden by the dunes. She disappeared from sight as the three boys looked at their parents in disbelief.

The Caspian Sea had lived up to some of its previous allusions, at least, and they now had something more to look forward to. As they frolicked in the dunes and on the edge of the water playing with the soccer ball, it was Elliott who decided to give it a mighty kick with the wind behind it. The ball disappeared toward the back of the beach, onto the sand dunes, away from them. Elliott chased it until he was almost a speck on the horizon. Meanwhile, James introduced the other two to sand throwing contests and for the next half-hour, Elliott was little missed. In the tradition of all true mothers, it was Jenny who realized the loss of one of her children when concern tugged at her mind. The games were postponed as they all headed toward where the ball had last been seen, drifting in the wind.

As they neared the dunes where Elliott had last been spotted chasing after the ball at a snail's pace, they saw rather than heard the two unevenly matched pairs of legs pointing up toward the heavens. James put his finger to his lips to signify to the others that they should approach in silence. Anthony fell to the sand and crawled commando-style toward the four legs, closely followed by Justin, who had arranged himself so that nothing but the flats of his hands and his feet touched the sand.

"So, you think it's gonna rain, little guy," A rather husky voice said in a genuine southern US accent.

"Yep. See that cloud over there. My dad says it's full of water," observed Elliott, as though he and his newly found friend had known each other for years. Elliott crossed his legs and placed his hands behind his head as he began to settle down for what could become a long day.

"You know, Richard, I like this beach. I'm going to come here every day. Do you come here lots?"

"Well, Elliott, whenever I can, I just drive over here and lay down in the dunes and relax. It sort of reminds me of back home. If you close your eyes real tight, you can imagine yourself anywhere you want to be. Try it."

"Oh yeah," replied Elliott, as though he reveled in the delights of his suddenly favorite place, wherever that was. At this point, James called Elliot's name, and the two of them turned quite casually toward him as he grinned back.

"I guess you've met Elliott," James said, extending his hand in introduction to Richard.

They all sat on the sand and talked a little about who they were and what they were doing in this part of the world. Richard told them he was working over in Gorgan for a US company and James told him he was working over at the new refinery. Richard was interested and wanted to know more. James wanted to know more about what Richard did, but Richard avoided saying anything other than suggesting he was assigned to a confidential mission and actually didn't know much. James didn't press him but guessed he was working at the communications center, and his interest multiplied. He would look for an opportunity to follow up on it later.

As the afternoon wore on, Jenny invited their newfound friend back with them for supper and for the first time since they had arrived in Sari, James and Jenny didn't feel quite so alone.

* * *

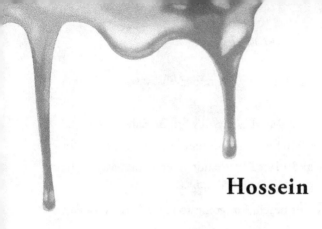

Hossein

Hossein Daneshkah rested his elbows on the rough wooden ledge of the watch tower and peered out over the valley, as he had done every week since he returned to Sari in 2015, to where the new refinery was being constructed. The thatched timber lookout was his favorite spot in the world to relax and think. His grandfather had helped build it nearly sixty-five years ago to watch over the sheep and protect them from wolf attacks. Hossein's father had used it when it was his turn to tend the flock, and Hossein went with him to learn. The memories of those early days were crystal clear as he remembered the simple life and ambitions of his youth.

Hossein was the youngest of eight children in his family and had thrived on being expected to maintain a minimum of responsibility, while his older brothers and sisters undertook the major chores of the family. His father, a shepherd first and metal worker second, had taught him all the rudiments of surviving comfortably among the villagers in the northern foothills of the Alborz Mountains to the east of Rasht, the largest city on the Caspian Sea, and some twenty kilometers south of Mehabad.

Life was uncomplicated and basic; the village existed almost as one family, attaining a level of self-sufficiency that would seem almost idealistic to the modern person in the Western world. Hossein's people had worked hard in the fields, fished in the Caspian, built their homes from the strong native clays and timber from the forests of the north, and tended their animals away from the complexities of urban communities elsewhere in the world. As long as they had rice, sheep, a roof of some kind over their heads, and warm clothes to wear, they were happy.

It was true their fields were not their own, but the demands of the wealthy local landlords were few and easy enough to satisfy—providing the weather was with them. Food was basic but plentiful, rice being the staple. The rains, at least, were to be relied upon each year. There had been a sort of peaceful understanding between religion and nature as the village thrived in those early days. The environment was respected, and it, in turn, provided for them.

Country and global politics were of little concern to them. Anything beyond the limitations of their village lives became the responsibility of the landlords who screened their tenants' exposure to the outside world. Although it had seemed strange at the time that those few who had been curious enough to leave the village had rarely returned. Still, it went a little deeper than idle curiosity and was certainly nothing that could be contrived as jealousy. The landlords selected what nationally important events should be communicated to the villagers through the elders. The elders, in turn, would choose if the news should be distorted with their own interpretations. Little wonder that Hossein and his peers knew little or nothing of Russians, British, Germans, Americans, social revolution, or industrialization as they started to become adults.

All visitors who spoke languages other than their own were treated as *ferengies*. Large doses of caution and heaps of make-believe hospitality were ladled out in short order during those uncomfortable confrontations when locals deliberately avoided contact with outsiders on the "advice" of their landlords. Hospitality inadvertently became the eventual ruination of the simple society in which Hossein had lived and loved. As those early years had drifted on, parties of foreigners traveling through their lands had become almost commonplace. Nearly twice a year, strange motor-driven vehicles, which got stranger as the years advanced, brought groups of white- or yellow-skinned *ferengies* in impracticable attire from Tehran through the Alborz Mountains. They headed for the sea as though they had been without water for months, laughing and obviously in high spirits as they theatrically plunged through the lushness of this narrow strip of land.

Hossein was almost fourteen, barbecuing corn for sale on an open fire on the beach, when a couple of *ferengies* from one of the visiting groups came to buy some of his food. Up until then, Hossein had been careful to avoid *ferengies*. Before he established the barbecue, he had just watched their antics, not understanding what they said or what they were doing there. His continual curiosity about the group that was staying nearby for more than just a couple of days convinced one of them—a tall thin man with very white skin, a sporadic growth of blond hair on his face, and a smattering of Farsi—to sit near Hossein as he cooked, gradually drawing him into animated conversation. At first, it was strange to Hossein to watch the antics of this strange man, who for some reason insisted on his attention. Hossein had been quite content to just stare and smile every once in a while when he felt that the circumstances warranted it.

Now, this man seemed intent on engaging Hossein in communication. After almost six days of picking up the occasional word here and there and the help of some sign language, Hossein began to grasp the significance of what was expected of him and his interest began to increase.

This particular group of strangers had come from a country so far away that they had traveled across oceans and deserts simply to quench their curiosity about Hossein's country. Their mission was to investigate the origins of the Assassins, who had once been the most powerful group of revolutionaries in the world. The Assassins had lived and operated from castles established in the Alborz some 500 years previous until they were eventually routed during the Mongol invasions. Hossein had some familiarity with the history but had little interest in such things.

He found himself now not so much interested in the foreigners' discoveries as his need to understand why they ventured into the unknown for what appeared, to him, to be little reason. He kept asking why but listened with increasing curiosity, asking for explanations when he couldn't understand. They showed him photos of all kinds of people from faraway places, strange buildings, odd writing, and maps of foreign countries. He saw a map of the world for the first time, and they pointed to where they had come from and where they were going. He started to understand how limited his knowledge was of everything outside his village. Some others wouldn't care and would rather stay close to home, but Hossein soon realized there were limitless bounds to the world that he had never imagined. He came to understand why others had left his village to seek out new experiences and why they never returned.

Hossein became excited at the prospect of discovery and began to plan for his own departure into the unknown.

By the age of sixteen, Hossein was ready to leave his village and Iran. He had friends who had relatives living in some place called San Francisco, in America, and they had agreed to take and support him while he went on to advanced studies. By the time he was ready to leave for America, having achieved the highest standards of education he could get at home by the age of eighteen, his English was more than passable and his application to study for a political science degree at the University of California, Berkeley, had been accepted. It was close to where his relatives lived in Oakland. A bonus was that the Persian Center was just blocks away on Durant Avenue, where he could meet friends and discover more about his own country. He was delirious with excitement and all he could talk about were the freedoms of Western life and his desire to see what the rest of the world could bring him.

Like many Iranian students living and studying abroad, he became more educated in his country's religious-political system, which then raised more questions. He could only compare what he learned with what he witnessed in front of him in America. He didn't like what he saw in either country. The shah had been too powerful, and the mullahs were much the same but hidden behind religion. America was based on commercialism and seemed to have little regard or respect for its leaders, while religion never played any sort of pivotal role in Americans' upbringing. It was all so mixed up, confusing, and repugnant to Hossein.

By the time Hossein was thirty, he had married an American lady, Liz, who had also studied political science at Berkeley, although their paths had not crossed at the time. They were several years apart in studies, but both settled in the same area of Oakland after university and met at an Iranian Studies evening at UCLA one evening. Their marriage seemed uneventful for several years until Hossein declared his need to return to Iran, his hometown, and his family. Liz was totally supportive and also wanted to put into practice some of the political science initiatives she had learned, and he was eager to put into practice the good things he had learned in America to help improve life for the poor Iranian. Was that possible? He wanted to find out.

*   *   *

It was not as difficult as they had thought to get visas for both of them. Iran needed and encouraged its citizens to return, especially if they had received an education. As for Liz, well, she was welcome to tag along but only because she was married to an Iranian. Of course, once she was there, it would be impossible for her to leave the country without the permission of her husband—some things never changed.

They settled in Sari, to the east of Rasht, far enough away from family to feel independent but close enough to visit. They rented a one-storey house a mile from the center on the east side of town, out toward the airport. It was difficult to get jobs. No one had any use for translators in an outback location like Sari, and political scientists that specialized in non-Persian studies were frowned upon by the local religious leaders. Regardless, Hossein and Liz survived by taking on menial chores that paid little but put enough food on the table and provided fuel for their heaters. Their lives slowed down dramatically as they acclimatized themselves and made friends around them. Liz had started to learn Farsi before she came to Iran and with Hossein's help she picked up the language fluently enough to feel comfortable when she went out by herself or mixed with neighbors and vendors in the bazaar.

Hossein buried himself in the local culture, went to the mosque on Fridays, attended the mullah's sessions afterward, and offered his help wherever he could. He and Liz became a popular addition to the community after only six months, with friends dropping by at all times looking for some educational pointers and discussions, especially about what it was like in the West. Was it as bad as the mullahs said? Was the shah really that bad? Where were they going as a nation? Was Khomeini on the right track? Did he understand the people?

Hossein soon became a local philosopher and someone to be reckoned with in any discussion where he was challenged about what he considered wrong about Iran as Khomeini saw it. But he also saw a lot of good and thought that somewhere between the excesses of the capitalist West and the religiously zealous Iran lay the truth of what they needed as a society, especially when it came to retaining their culture and history. Unlike the West, which seemed to have a need to constantly distance itself from the past and cherry-pick only some historical moments.

With rent to pay and a baby on the way, life was getting more expensive. They became desperate for transportation beyond the moped they had been using to carry both of them and their baggage. They needed furnishings, more clothes, electrical and electronic tools, and accessories, and realized this was their inner capitalism coming to the surface. It was impossible for them to devote themselves to anything unless they had at least some creature comforts.

And so it was that both Hossein and Liz applied for and got jobs at the new refinery being constructed just outside Sari, in the Sari Valley. Hossein became a document control manager and his bilingualism came in most useful since all the documents were in English but the contractors were mostly Iranians who had a decent yet not technically sufficient understanding of English. Liz did very well as an assistant to one of the more senior foreign design consultants and, again, her dual linguistic abilities helped a lot. While they both worked the six days a week required, they still found time to socialize with their Iranian friends away from the site. Everyone was interested in the project and wanted to better understand the benefits it would bring to them as a community.

Liz worked up to the last minute of her pregnancy, took two weeks off to have their son, Farhad, and went back to work. It was easy enough and inexpensive to find nannies in a society that doted on children.

But Hossein never forgot why he returned to his homeland. He was continually wary of his surroundings, what foreigners were doing, what the natives were doing, and what they were most interested in. It certainly wasn't money. The general Iranian population was extremely suspicious of the affluence of the West and its excesses, as they saw them on television. Many Iranians really wanted to return to a simple but more comfortable life away from the hardships they had suffered during the shah's regime and now from Khomeini's Regime as it slowly clamped down on any semblance of freedom. Religious zealotry was back with a vengeance. This was not why they had revolted, and many started to wonder if they had backed the wrong horse. The fact was, in Hossein's eyes, neither horse fit the bill and both had serious problems attempting to dominate an ancient population ingrained with a culture developed over thousands of years and built into their DNA.

No, there had to be a better way. Hossein was convinced. But how to start making a change?

Work at the plant was enjoyable insofar as both Hossein and Liz were popular members of the team; they were very much appreciated and mixed well with both natives and *ferengies*. They attended all the social functions of both and continually built on their knowledge of each, using their political science skills and constantly comparing notes. Liz was totally attuned to Hossein's desire to somehow influence his Iranian friends into understanding there was a better way.

After almost a year of being in the country, they came to the realization there was no fast way to move things forward. They had to start small and focus on the people they lived and worked with. Then they would go out and preach a new way to others.

One evening, while they shared a meal with some very influential Iranian friends not associated with the mosque, someone mentioned the crusade Hossein and Liz seemed to be fighting. It was an eye-opener for them both. They hadn't realized their discussions over the past year were being taken that seriously just yet. One of their friends called Hossein the father of the silent revolution in the north. It seemed to stick and people from all over came to visit, talk about the future, and ask what they should do. Clearly, the Islamic Republic's grasp on Iran had strengthened day by day until the religious rhetoric of the past had become the religious zealotry of the present.

Eventually, James discovered both Hossein and Liz in the market one day as they spoke in English to each other. They had introduced themselves and their association matured into a friendship as each reminisced about their Western experiences. At first, James was not the slightest bit suspicious of Hossein but as time went on, he noticed Hossein getting together with some of the security staff on site. It seemed odd but he kept his thoughts to himself.

James's position on site allowed him to pry into the lives of Hossein and Liz, and before long they were sharing food together in Hossein's courtyard. It appeared to be a delightful relationship, devoid of any politics or racism. They never talked about work and seemed to have common interests that sustained them. James and Jenny also took an interest in Hossein and Liz's ideologies and often listened to Hossein as he expounded on the virtues of his newfound social interest. James listened with acute interest; he needed to alert Matthew. Perhaps Hossein and Liz could help ORB's mission somehow.

What James could not have known was that the Revolutionary Guard had already identified Hossein and his wife as potential threats a few years previous. Through an intermediary, the Revolutionary Guard had come to learn of their philosophies and they were clearly not in sync with those of the Regime. There were many individuals like Hossein, educated overseas and returning to create dissent. They were not part of an organized group, like Friends of Iran, but just some rogue Iranians looking for attention with their big ideas about how things should be. These individuals could be dealt with easily and, more often than not, were somehow silenced. But Hossein and Liz now worked on the construction site of the new refinery and could be used for a greater purpose.

So it was that Hossein and his wife were coerced into reducing their philosophical rhetoric while at the same time keeping watchful eyes on their surroundings at the plant. Anything and everything was of interest to the Revolutionary Guard and they met every week to talk about what they had heard or seen while on the site. Most of the time there was nothing to report, but at one point Hossein had mentioned Matthew's presence and his friendship with James. While that might otherwise appear innocent since they were both employed by Dick Elliot, Hossein openly wondered about Matthew's qualifications and apparent lack of technical expertise compared to John Charlesworth. John had been brought into the project by Interstate to lead the initial operations team, and he was clearly a technical wizard when it came to petrochemical plants. That was enough for the Revolutionary Guard to start monitoring Matthew's movements on site and even follow him occasionally when he left the site.

* * *

Richard and His Mountain

It was several weeks before James and Jenny came to know Richard on a personal basis but realized they knew nothing of what he was doing in Iran. Not that they really thought they were owed anything in particular. It was just that... well, now that Richard knew them as a family, maybe he would like to become more of a part of it. They decided to talk to him that evening.

It had become more of a routine over the last little while. Richard would appear at their doorway for four evenings straight and then not be seen or heard from for the following three days. This was to be the first of the four straight days, and in keeping with the usual ritual, Richard arrived just after 7:00 p.m. He would be quietly reserved for the first hour or so, and they would sit around, enjoying the shared smokes and drinks. Gradually, as talk turned from the week's events surrounding the latest catastrophes that had happened while living in Sari—the "Iranian outback," as they referred to it—the conversation settled almost abruptly upon Richard's week.

As though suddenly sensing a conspiracy, Richard tried to evade the tone of the lingering silence and jumped to refill the glasses.

"Hell, don't give me those looks, you guys," he said almost with a whine. "There ain't nuthin' that's been happenin' to me. I just go to work an' back agin. There ain't nuthin' interestin' in that."

He kept his back to them, pretending to pour drinks, only it went on too long and Richard knew it. He turned and smiled one of those slow, deliberate Alabama smiles.

"C'mon, you guys. There ain't nuthin' to tell." This wasn't going to work and Richard knew it.

He'd been in Iran now for almost six months and missed his family badly enough that he really wanted to adopt James, Jenny, and the kids as an extension of his own—even though they really had nothing much in common. To Richard, that was a great advantage. They really knew very little about him but he felt safe in their company, a haven from the reality of everyday life. And yet he needed to confide in others the same way he used to come home from work and spend the supper hour discussing the day's goings-on with his wife, Bonnie. Those were good ways of at least partially unloading the boredom of work, the frustration of administration and rules, the guys he didn't get along with. Kept a man sane when there's no one else to talk to. Not that he could ever discuss that much with his family. It was more the routine of the day. The activities that had to be hidden, even on his home base in Alabama, were never discussed with outsiders. But now, with another year at least to go before he saw them again, the lack of communication was getting almost too much to bear for Richard. He was in a land where, away from work, you couldn't even understand conversations around you, read a newspaper, or share a laugh with a buddy in the bar. It was like walking around as though partially deaf and dumb. Able to hear but not understand. Able to see but not read. Able to speak but not understood. Even the look in the eyes, the turn of the face, the movement of the body—they all meant different things from what he was used to at home.

Richard passed the freshened drinks out, lit a Winston, took a deep drag, and let the smoke out slowly and deliberately, looking at the ceiling, then down to meet Jenny's eyes first, and over to James's.

"Richard," Jenny interrupted the silence as though she understood all the thoughts that were flooding through Richard's mind at the same time. "You don't have to say anything at all. We know that if you could, you would. It's just that we'd like to know something more about you than what your address is, what your wife and children are called, as well as what kind of drink you want. That's not because we're nosy." Richard smiled as Jenny took a breath before starting again.

"Richard, we just want to know you. Maybe for you to get to know us a little better. Maybe that's not such a great idea, but we need to know someone else. It's important to our sanity. Living here is sometimes like living on a different planet. Everything and everyone that we know is so far away. There seems no hope of getting back to them. It's as though we need to build a bridge. Get to know others who also need to build and gradually, maybe, we'll build another home away from home. Isn't that how it's done?" Jenny stopped and looked from Richard to James. She got the look of comfort she needed from her husband and turned back to Richard.

He looked at her and dropped his eyes to the floor. "Ain't nuthin' much to tell," he said, this time hanging his bottom lip a little as though he'd just been told off and was fighting to keep a secret.

He looked up at James, then over at Jenny. Flopping down onto a floor cushion, he took a short snap at his drink and an almost pathetic puff at the Winston. Cradling his drink as though it needed comfort itself, he looked up at the two waiting faces.

"Well, there ain't a hell of a lot I kin tell ya, cuz that's the nature of the game. I guess you think it's pretty strange that I only see ya on four consecutive days, then not for three."

"No," interrupted James. "We just figured that your job warranted that. There's nothing too strange about that. But we have wondered where you live and where you work. You're not from around here—that we do know. We have a pretty good network of informers in the drivers. They would know if there was another *ferengi* living nearby."

Richard looked a little surprised but sort of shrugged as he considered the logic. "Well, I shouldn't really be tellin' ya anythin'. But at least I can say that I work for the US intelligence nearby. You know, listenin' posts an' all that. Up there, near Gorgan."

He stopped and looked at the two of them studiously as though they really did know, especially now that he'd spilled at least part of the beans. Sure, they must know. As he looked at their faces even more, it dawned on him that maybe they didn't know anything. As he looked even more intently, he realized that they knew nothing at all. He laughed, then started to guffaw.

James and Jenny looked at each other, shrugged, and just stared at Richard, who started to compose himself as it really dawned on him that maybe, just maybe, not everyone was mixed up in the same business.

"You guys. You really don't know, do you?" he asked, now knowing what the answer would be. "I've been here in this God-forsaken place now for some six months just listenin'. Doin' nuthin' but listenin'. Course, I don't understand it all. I just make sure that we're tuned in to where all the talk is going and coming from, an' I tape an' listen, an' tape some more. We live underground, an' we work underground. It's as simple as that." He raised his palms in a gesture of nonchalance, as though it really was that simple.

James looked a little taken back. Jenny looked as though she couldn't understand what all the fuss had been about in keeping this secret for so long.

"Well, it can't be that simple," stated James as he feigned an itchy ear in subconscious distraction. "If you live and work underground, how come you manage to come here every day off that you have, almost bang-on the same time, every time. Your work can't be that secret."

"Well, I sort a play a little game," Richard started with a little grin breaking out. It spread into a wide smile as he remembered the simplicity of it. Something that had taken him nearly six months to perfect.

"I'm sort o' lucky in a way. We got this commander at the base. He's from a little place near where I come from. Sort o' likes the ladies. Well, when I first arrived at the post, the only person who was allowed free passage on an' off the base was the commander. He had to be somewhat discreet and couldn't be seen off duty in uniform. Well, he used to go into Gorgan all the time to see this lil' lady. Some German whose husband was out at Neka at the power plant most of the time. Well, one day, we got orders that a driver would be needed for anyone going off-base. So, he arranged it so's one of the orderlies drove him down into town and then went back to the base. At a pre-arranged time, one of the orderlies had to come an' fetch him.

"Well, this went on for some time before the commander, he sure got tired o' that. What with makin' sure that all the arrangements were made an' nuthin' got fouled up, it sort o' was a little sticky." Richard raised his hand and jiggled it to accentuate the trickiness involved.

"Course, all the while, I'm just sort of watchin' an listenin'—cuz that's what I'm good at." He chuckled. "Sort of a prerequisite for the job. Well, I could see the poor guy was havin' a tough time of it, all tryin' to git in town to see his gal. I sort o' got talkin' to him by accident when he was passin' me one day and stopped out of the blue to ask me if I knew Tom Perkins an' his wife. They lived two blocks from us at home, an' I sort of knew them pretty well, really. Well, I made out as though the wife and I knew them a little better than we really did, cuz I could see it might have been to my advantage somewhere down the road.

"Anyway, we started to talk a little more, although it's sort o' difficult tryin' to have a flowin' conversation with a superior officer. Hardly what you think of as a potentially long-lasting relationship. Still, he sort o' seemed friendly enough. So, we always stopped to talk whenever our paths crossed and eventually we really did sort of become friends, an' we started to eat at the same table.

"An' then we got a card game going in the mess. What with a few drinks an' so on, I started to learn more about the trials an' tribulations of this guy, what with not gettin' his fair share of satisfaction, and all that. Course, he never thought about the likes of me not getting' any at all. Still, what do you expect from a commander? Probably don't think of any of us as real people."

Richard stopped, his previous grin falling back to a sour look as a thought of his family probably crossed his mind.

"Anyway, what the hell. We really sort o' got to be quite friendly, an' I offered to do his chauffeurin' for him so long as I could go off wherever I wanted while he did his thing with the young lady. At first, he weren't too warm to the whole thing at all. Sort o' felt to him like a conspiracy. So, I only mentioned it now and agin, never thinkin' that seriously about it. Then, one day, he confides in me that the young lady is goin' home to Germany. Her husband's contract was up an' they were off.

"Well, that sort o' shattered him an' he stayed like that for some time. Then one day I sort o' put the bug in his ear that we should just go out for the night just to get his mind off it all. Well, he went for it an' we came here to Sari. Course, there's really not a lot to do in Sari but when a man's really desperate, there are all kinds of things that he could do if he really wanted, and in all kinds of strange places.

"We drove for a while, just sussin' the place out before we sort o' got the drift of the place an' found that some of the more Westernized ones with skimpier chadors and the like were goin' to a little pizza place 'round the back from the bazaar, behind the Armenians' place, called Nero's. Could o' knocked us down with a feather. It was almost civilized. Run by a couple of real neat Iranians educated at UCLA, of all places. I guess the only real thing they learned was how to make pizza, cuz it's good.' Richard grinned and licked his lips.

"You're going to have to take us there, me old mate," said James, pointing a finger at his friend, who started to rub his belly and roll his eyes at the thought of more pizza slipping down.

"Well, so you can guess what happens," Richard started again once the pizza ecstasy had subsided. "We sit down an' order an extra-large Nero special with two Skols. While we're waiting, in walks this five-foot-five-inch chador. I mean with just two eyes. She sits herself down next to the commander an' proceeds to look at the menu. The waiter comes over and says somethin' in Iranian to her, and without liftin' her head she asks for a small Nero special but hold the anchovies—an' then she ordered a Skol. Well, we were just flabbergasted, especially when she'd done all this ordering in English with a Midwest accent. An' to cap it all off, she called after the waiter to make sure the beer was cold and the pizza hot!

"As she placed the menu back in the center of the table, she sort of looked up at the commander in one of those long lingerin' type ways that sort of looks like it was all done with a slow-motion camera and she winked. Well, once agin, we were boggled. I mean, without speech... at all. So, while we're both gettin' over this, she looks around to see if there are any Iranian men in the place and there weren't, so she proceeds to stand up and take off the chador. Have you ever wondered what they wear under them things? I never really thought about it. Course, no one really encourages you to—not like a Scotsman an' his kilt. In a funny kinda way, I guess I sort o' thought there was nothin' under there. Just nothin' at all, not even a body. It always seemed to me like a pair of big brown eyes wrapped in black cloth. You sort of get used to it after a while. Well, there was definitely something under this chador. Wow."

Richard stopped this time to lick his lips at a different thought but an equally exciting one... well, maybe not as good as the pizza!

"The commander, he couldn't help himself. He helped her out of the chador and was about to help her get everything else off right then but the pizza and beer arrived—thank God. We started to talk to the lady, an' it turned out that she was back in Sari to visit her parents for a while. She actually lived in the States and had been there for fifteen years. Her English was perfect. So, we carried on talkin', an' it sort of became pretty clear that I was in great danger of becoming outranked and outflanked by my commander friend, who had obviously decided that he needed a replacement for his lost love—right now.

"Anyway, we kept talkin, an' I kept thinkin', an' I could see that this could lead to my gettin' some of my sanity back. She was sure a pretty little thing—an' definitely out for a good time—but I needed a longer-lastin' somethin' to keep my head loose. So, I started to tie these two people a little closer all the time, and soon they had made a date of sorts. Course, the commander needed a little help to get out and about an' here I was like a white knight—hurt at not bein' the chosen one by the chador, but true enough to still offer help to a friend. He sort of agreed as though it was fair consolation. Almost as though he would have become the chauffeur if it were me who got the date. Course, that's purely hypothetical. A thought like that could never enter that man's mind.

"So that was it. After the first date, it never stopped. I bring him in to the town for a seven or six o'clock drop off at her apartment that he rented just for the occasion and pick him up at around midnight. Of course, I spent most of the time up at the beach before I met you guys. I sure like it there. I like the contrast compared to living and working under that mountain all day and all night."

Richard talking so openly now about the mountain intrigued James, but it seemed Richard was letting go a little—perhaps too much. James lapped it all up.

"You know, "Richard started, "that mountain was carved out sometime during the seventies as part of a network of listenin' posts set up all along the borders of Russia, Turkey, and Iraq. This isn't the only one, but from what I know it used to be the central post. A sort of clearinghouse for all the rest, especially since we're close to the Chalus route to Tehran and with it being on the north end of the Alborz, and the air is clear all the way to Russia in one direction and Tehran in another. Anyway, I guess it's all pretty important stuff, cuz we get some pretty distinguished visitors. The prince used to be a regular visitor before the shah left. Of course, I wasn't here then but you hear the stories. Now I don't know whether the new Regime even knows we exist. They sure don't seem to show any interest."

"But what do you do, Richard?" asked James as he rose to refill the drinks. "Are you involved in all the intrigue—like who slept with whom last night, and who's going to push the big red button next?"

"Naw, nothin' like that really. Well... I don't think so. You see, I really don't understand all that talk. Sometimes I hear Russian, sometimes Iranian, or Arab-type talk, or Turkish or whatever. You can sometimes piece things together, particularly if you latch onto someone talking and then recognize the response. It doesn't happen too often, though. Sometimes there are long gaps between conversations, or maybe no responses at all on that frequency. Sometimes it sounds sort of important, you know, like there's a flap on, an' other times like it's someone just reportin' the time. Still, my job is to tune in to whatever frequencies there are where talkin' is goin' on, an' record it all; everything that makes a noise, really."

Much to James' surprise, Richard was winding up to say more.

"Another drink, Rich?" James wanted to keep Richard's tongue lubricated as he brought over a freshly mixed cocktail, took the empty glass from Richard's hand, and placed the newly mixed one into it.

"At the same time," Richard took the drink, nodded his thanks, and continued, "the recording automatically notes the frequency, time, date, and point of origin. There's a whole bunch of us tuning in to all kinds of things. They all go to central, where the tapes are sort of fed through a computer that matches frequencies, deletes the quiet periods, translates, and ends up with a sort o' long string of dialogue. The frequency messages are fed to another group of people who try to match conversations that might be occurring between different frequencies. The result is a bunch of conversations and a bunch of unmatched sort o' one-liners. I think it all gets passed back to the Pentagon to figure out. They have all kinds of contraptions there, includin' voice matchers, phrase recognizers, amplitude matchin', an' all this other stuff to help piece together the whole thing. Well, I guess it sort o' sounds pretty complicated, but most of the conversations are apparently pretty regular and for anyone's ears—whether they're really meant to be or not! So that's about it, guys. Now you know."

Richard sat back and gulped at his drink as though he suddenly felt guilty, but he was just tipsy.

"Well, I have to admit that it all sounds a little fantastic. But then, why not? I guess someone has to listen in," James suggested. Things started to click in his brain as he thought of the potential of a contact like Richard and the information that he must have access to. He shrugged it off with a slight shudder, as though it had gotten too late to think logically anymore tonight. He was tired. When he got tired, things started to get a little out of proportion. Maybe this was one of those times.

"I guess you're looking forward to going home, Rich," said Jenny trying to break the strange silence that had developed. "Does Bonny know what you do and for whom and all that?"

"Sort of. I tell her about life in general in the military. But then, on the surface of it all, it don't appear all that excitin' to the guys at home. So, I don't say much. An' besides, it ain't allowed." Richard had clearly passed the mark of sobriety. He looked at James and Jenny, put his finger to his lips, "I ain't saying anythin' more other than our mail all gets vetted going out an' comin' in. I shouldn't really be talking to you guys about all this but you're family—right?" Richard gave a big lazy smile with eyes half-closed. "Course, most of the countryside knows that we're in there but they don't know much about what we do.

"Course, when you think about it, we don't know that much either. All our recordings go to a bunch of other guys, an' they do their bit an' pass it on, an' so on an' so on. We don't get much of a chance to get to really understand anything in particular. Of course, on the other hand, we ain't that dumb. Even a totally foreign language sort o' rubs off. You get to recognize sequences of words, some of the same ones that come up over an' over again. Then you start to recognize names of places, then people. And the ways in which some things are said—such as questions an' the like. In fact, the more I think about it, the more I realize that I do pick up a fair bit of stuff. Not that I take that much notice. Just as well, it might frighten the hell out of me. Or I might start blabbing it around the base, an' that would surely cause me some trouble. I guess we've all sort of become numb to it all. Turned ourselves off, really, I guess."

"Gee, that must be interesting," said James, deep in thought once more. "I'd love to see the place."

Richard shrugged; his mouth turned down as though wondering to himself. "Well, you can always take a look at the place, if only from the outside. There ain't no barbed wire about, but you sure will be turned back fast if you come too close. There ain't much to see 'cept one antenna that sticks out the top of the mountain. Hardly visible from the road unless you look really hard. Still, if you wanna see it, you should take a drive on Friday."

"We may just do that. I can see all kinds of things in my mind. It sort of reeks of Napoleon Solo and Maxwell Smart and all those guys doing their thing for king and country. What a laugh. What do you think, Jenny?"

"Why not? There's not much else to do. Maybe we could head on up a bit farther afterward and check out the camels up there in Kurd country. I hear the Kurds use them quite a bit. I also heard that the Kurds are quite a bit different from the locals around here. Sort of a cross between the Arabs and the Iranians. A little more earthy than this if you can believe it."

"Okay, that's settled," James said with a quick rub of his hands, followed by a gulp of drink. He rose, started to hum a tune, and wandered off into the bedroom to get the backgammon set.

*   *   *

The Commander

It was just before midnight, as usual, when Richard left James and Jenny to pick up the commander. He jumped into the Land Rover, disappeared to the end of the road, and made a right turn as James watched from the window. Once Richard had gone, James bounded down the stairs, ran to where the Jyane was parked, and sped off after his friend. The roads were deserted. It wasn't hard to catch sight of the Land Rover as it turned the second corner by the school and headed west toward the gas station and on to Talebi Nataj. James kept the lights off, which wasn't unusual for Iranian drivers during clear nights with so little traffic about.

He followed the Land Rover to the corner of a narrow alley running along the back of the houses facing the main street. Richard had pulled back out onto the main road and parked outside the gates to the courtyard. James watched as Richard jumped out of the car and rang the doorbell on a pillar at the gate. Within a half-minute, another person stood next to him. The other was slightly taller and obviously well built. They both got into the Land Rover and silently drifted away down the road heading east.

James followed at some distance as the couple continued to head east toward Gorgan. There was little point in following them any farther. James turned the little car 180 degrees and headed back to town. As he passed the end of the alley behind the house where Richard had picked up the commander, he noticed to his right some movement roughly near the location of the back entrance to the house. It was only a split second, but something nagged at James. He stopped the car and backed up a few yards before switching the engine off and silently leaving the car, being careful to keep low enough that if anything emerged from the alley, he would be suitably out of sight, hidden by the pillars of the double gate to the courtyard of the apartment.

As he edged along the wall to the corner of the alley, he could hear low voices as two people seemed to be arguing. He made it to the corner and looked around cautiously, peeping with only one eye. Fortunately, the moon was shining at ninety degrees to him, providing his silhouette with partial protection. Despite the chador, James recognized the girl from the pizza place that Richard had described because the two figures seemed to be tussling and the chador had come undone. Then James recognized the other figure. At least he recognized what it was. The outline showed a military person of some type. James concentrated on trying to establish what was happening and then the other person turned sideways and James saw the cut of the clothes that indicated a uniform of some sort, likely militia.

"Well, he looks like a tough cookie. I'd say he's one of the Revolutionary Guard," he said to himself, remembering that all non-officer Revolutionary Guard personnel wore a sort of pillar-box cap and pants tucked in at the ankle. They also wore a rather loose-fitting combat jacket that had the general appearance of a sack of potatoes. On the other hand, the officers wore relatively well-fitting outfits, much like American officers, with flat peaked caps and straight-legged pants.

Suddenly, the girl was being led down to the end of the alley by the arm. She wasn't struggling so much as being urged to maintain pace. James followed and arrived just in time to see them both get into an unmarked black Mercedes. The door had hardly closed when it sped off down the road with that easily recognizable older Mercedes diesel rattle.

James raced back to his Jyane, cut through the alley with his car lights off for the second time that night and reached the other end just in time to see the taillights of the Mercedes disappear left around a corner a few blocks away. He raced to keep it in sight and continued to follow it as it headed east toward the Revolutionary Guard barracks in town. Just before it reached the Armenian store, it turned through the entrance to the base.

James stopped across from the barracks but around a corner of a side street, and sat pondering the situation. It was 12:45 a.m., and the streets were deserted. Something seemed quite wrong. But he just couldn't fathom the scene he had witnessed. Yet in the back of his mind, he could see the picture of a conspiracy forming. A picture he really didn't like at all. He pushed the gear stick into first and headed forward toward his apartment. Maybe he was too tired and the whole thing was just his imagination.

As he walked through the door, Jenny greeted him with a tired look as she headed for the bedroom.

"Nice walk, love?" she asked, having got used to James coming and going at all hours of the day or night. Sometimes for his job and other times just to get some air—to think. They went to bed.

James lay wide awake in bed, thinking over what he had witnessed. Then it came to him. Of course. The woman was bait for the commander. It was a setup, and the commander was the pawn in the game. James knew that had to be the answer, and he decided right then to do some more research before reporting the incident to Dick Elliot.

* * *

On Friday mornings, the kids woke early, knowing this was the only day of the week that the family got together. They usually left the apartment early, had breakfast on the way, and then headed to one of the other towns to look around. They might end up at the beach or having a picnic in some shady spot. James and Jenny had talked to Richard three more times that week. He had arrived around seven each evening and left around midnight. They had not discussed the topic of his work again, and Richard never offered any more information.

James had followed Richard to the apartment pickup point on the first of the four nights of the next week, and then followed both Richard and the commander out past the town's border until he was sure that they were really headed for Gorgan. Again, there was little point in following them all the way to Gorgan. At least not at this point in time.

The next night, James had waited for the woman to emerge from the house and noted the lights on the third floor of the three-apartment building. The lights went out just before the woman emerged. On that occasion, he simply watched as she disappeared around the corner at the end of the alley. Within a minute or so, the other figure emerged from the house, adjusted his clothes, and made off after her. James was almost caught as he started to edge down the alley after the woman. It was fortunate that the second figure came out dealing with some dress rearrangements that distracted him from anything else that might have been happening in the alley. James pressed close to the sidewall, mostly hidden by a utility pole. The figure slipped into the driver's seat of the Mercedes, with the girl next to him. It pulled away from the jube, crossed the end of the alley, and headed in the direction of the barracks.

James didn't need to follow. He headed back to the girl's apartment and examined the wall, looking for a way over into the courtyard. He quickly moved to the utility pole. Using the guy wire, he pulled himself up and over the eight feet height. As he dropped to the yard below, he stopped, held his breath, and glanced from side to side.

Feeling safe from inquisitive eyes and given the fact it was now something like 12.:45 a.m., James casually wandered to the wall of the building, trying to figure out how he could get up to the third-floor balcony. He got himself up onto the *naft* drum and reached up to the second-floor balcony, where he grabbed hold of the rail and lifted himself slowly up and over onto a tiled patio floor. A table was set out with two chairs. James climbed up onto the table and did the same thing as before. Once he reached the third-floor balcony, he pushed the unlocked sliding doors apart.

He stopped and stood listening for a few seconds, as though the sliding action was bound to bring figures rushing from inside to see what all the noise was about. There was almost no noise and with an almost imperceptible grin, James realized his own paranoia and continued to slide the window across. He squeezed through to the room beyond, closing and locking the window behind him. He didn't really know why he was here, only that something nagged at the back of his brain.

Fortunately, the night was well lit by a half moon as James crept over to one of the doors, which he guessed would lead into the front room. He had come in through the sliding doors to a bedroom devoid of anything that might lead one to believe it was used. From what he could see, the room appeared neat and tidy, and he told himself that a quick recce of the rest of the house was in order before settling into any kind of detailed search. In the kitchen, James discovered that the only window looked out into a sort of arboretum, which was approximately three feet square. It was open to the sky and only had the toilet window facing onto it, in addition to that of the kitchen.

He shut the two doors leading into the room, one from the dining area and one from the living room area. He turned the light on and looked about him. Opening the cupboards, James started to take a close look at everything while still not really knowing what it was he expected to find—if anything at all. So far, it all seemed like the arrangement that Richard had described—except with a twist. Whoever the girl was, she was somehow involved with the Iranian military.

There seemed to be the expected total lack of supplies that might otherwise indicate a settled domestic situation. But the fridge was filled with beer, vodka, lime, some other fruit, and little else. The cupboards were essentially bare, except for tea, sugar, coffee, and powdered milk. There were some candles, matches, and cigarettes by the carton. The drawer had some basic utensils, sufficient to stir drinks. Nothing of any great interest presented itself—but then, why should it?

James grabbed a candle and lit it, being careful to pocket the used match, and shuffled the candles that remained in the box, in order to hide the fact that one had been taken. He turned the lights off and opened the door to the living room. There was nothing out of the ordinary there either—only the stereo, with a mixture of Western music propped against the unit stand on the floor.

He made his way to the second of the two bedrooms and peered through the door as though he might inadvertently catch someone still in bed. The air smelled of sex but the bed had been remade and only a few additional items rested on the single chest of drawers—mostly perfumes and makeup. Only one bottle of cologne rested among the women's things. There was a change of men's clothes in one of the drawers but no sign of clothes for a woman. Everything seemed to point to a typical, homely type of sexual relationship. But the other figure. That really was the puzzling part.

As James made his way back to the French windows leading to the courtyard, he took a last glance about the room. The only door that he had not tried was the one to the storage area, which led off the front entrance and would be used to store the heating oil.

"Nah," James said aloud. "Oh, what the hell. I probably couldn't sleep properly if I don't just take a peek. You never know."

He made his way to the room and surprisingly found it to be locked. It didn't take long to find the key resting on the ledge above the door. James unlocked the door and poked his hand around the corner to flick on the light. The single ceiling-mounted lamp flicked on its 100 watts and lit the small room. Sure enough, the *naft* tank was there, upright right next to the open door. James almost closed the door before he noticed the backrest of the chair just visible behind the tank.

"Strange place to have a chair, in a storage room," James told himself as he bent his frame around the tank and stared at the voice recorder and other electronic devices resting on a small table in front of the seat. There appeared to be blank tapes and writing tools around the place. He picked up several things and played his fingers over the recorder. There were headphones, which he put over his ears as though expecting to hear something. He turned a few knobs and pressed a few buttons, noting the original position of each before doing so. He heard nothing but noticed the wiring leading to and through a wall into the room beyond. James's imagination started to get the better of him again. This time he allowed himself the luxury of continuing.

He followed the wire to the wall and measured by paces within the room, trying to map the house interior in his mind so he could locate the wire on the other side. As he entered the room on the other side of the storage closet, he peered at the wall, not quite knowing what to expect. It was the second bedroom. The king-size bed was centered against the wall with the usual bedside tables and lamps arranged in the normal fashion. James examined the wall, feeling with his hands down to the join with the floor. There appeared to be nothing unusual. Only the wall outlet for the lamps. He moved the bed out from the wall, placed one of the bedside lamps on the floor and turned it on. There appeared to be nothing unusual.

"There's got to be some kind of connection," James whispered to himself.

He reached down to the light plug in the wall and followed the cord to the lamp base. A single separate piece of wire, matching the color of the electrical cord, was twisted around it. Almost invisible, it disappeared into the base with the other wire. James examined the whole lamp, being careful not to damage anything. There was a small addition to the otherwise typical screwed-in light bulb. A small adapter with screen-like perforations. James reached for the lamp on the opposite bedside table and brought it as close as the cord would let him. He switched it on and turned the other off. After waiting for almost a minute to let the bulb cool a little, he unscrewed the assembly, burning his fingers a little in the process. The bulb unscrewed from the adapter, which in turn slipped out of the socket. James gently tugged at the adapter to test that it connected to the single wire from the wall. It did.

He returned to the *naft* storage room and sat at the tape deck. It was a typical home-type system with very little complications. James slipped a tape, which appeared to be new and lying out of the wrapper, into the tape deck and pushed the play button. He ran it for a full minute to satisfy himself that it was clean. He fast-forwarded the total side and turned the tape, making sure that it too played for a full minute. It had nothing recorded. Setting the counter to zero and pressing the pause button in the record mode, half rising from his seat, James released the hold button and ran into the bedroom, sat carefully on the bed, and spoke a few words into what he was already sure was the microphone. He spoke for only a few seconds before returning to the storage area to check if his voice had been recorded. It had, and he made sure it was erased.

Satisfied with his evening's work, James carefully arranged the storage area, turned off the light, locked the door, and placed the key on the frame above. He carefully walked through all the rooms before reaching the kitchen, at the same time correcting anything he had misplaced. He blew the candle out, placed it in his pocket, and closed the kitchen doors before reaching the French windows. He was careful to leave them unlocked as he crossed to the courtyard wall. Hardly noticing how he did it, James was up and over the wall in one motion with his back flat against it. He waited, stopping even his own breathing for a few seconds before being satisfied that he had not been seen.

His drive back to the apartment was without incident, while a jumble of different thoughts went through his mind. He slipped into the bed next to Jenny and curled into her, needing the comfort of her closeness.

He fell asleep immediately.

*   *   *

Blackmail or . . . ?

The new day helped to sort out the previous night's turmoil in James's mind.

Before reporting the string of strange incidents to Dick Elli0t, he felt compelled to establish whether the compromising of the commander was anything more than a simple blackmail attempt for cash. James arranged a loose plan in his mind with little detail attached to it other than to essentially ensure that he confirm—or not—his suspicions. Anything that involved the Iranian military or Revolutionary Guard did not leave one to suspect some petty occurrence. He decided not to divulge his thoughts to anyone at this time.

James prepared for work that day and set off on the ten-mile drive to the site. He started to think out a simple plan. He was quite sure that the commander and the girl, as well as the third party, had no inkling that he was following them; he was 100 percent sure of it. The girl would be preoccupied with ensuring that the identity of her "friend" doing the recording would not be discovered. She would have no thought about the potential of being discovered right now. The commander was the wild card. He had far too much to lose if he was discovered, but James couldn't imagine that he would have any idea of being watched. However, the thought did go through James's mind of what would likely happen if he were caught. The commander would likely have him shot.

James decided that during the next set of visits from his friend Richard, he would again follow him on the first night, simply to check that there were no new rearrangements. On the second night, all permitting, he would feign having to return to work just before Richard arrived and go to the apartment to check the time of the commander's arrival, while at the same time hoping to get there to witness the arrival of the girl and the third party. He wanted to see them in the fading light of day. On the third night, James decided that he should be in the apartment before anyone arrived. The second bedroom would be the obvious place to hide, although the room itself held little that would provide shelter from even a casual search. An attic might have been the answer but there was none in the typical Iranian home. But there *was* a roof. Too close to the house perimeter might cause him to be seen. Then James suddenly thought of the stack that took the *naft* fumes through the roof. Being relatively mild at this time, it would be very unlikely that the furnace would be used. He decided to locate the one that would be used to warm the bedroom in winter, as well as the other two that could be used to warm the rooms where talking might occur, and listen through the pipe, where the voices should be somewhat amplified.

It was a plan that sounded reasonable to him, and simple. James wasn't too sure what it was that he wanted or thought he wanted to hear. But without doubt, he felt that whatever he overheard may help to resolve his questions and help Dick.

The path he took after his escapades remained a little bit of a mystery and in most ways James preferred it that way. He was a person who had learned that as long as one had an overall (if scanty) plan, details were superfluous until one knew for sure the next step.

James settled back for the last mile to the site, enjoying the simplicity of the scenery, and watching as an enormous bundle of sticks came toward him at a laborious rate. As he drew alongside the bundle, he slowed down to take a closer look at it. It had feet. As he slowly drove by, an eye appeared from under the load. "*Salem alakom,*" an old woman said, not missing a step. It was another eight miles before she would reach the bazaar where she could sell the firewood for the few rials she needed to buy a few things for the evening meal that day. Tomorrow, she would do it all again.

* * *

It was another three days before Richard started the four-night saga of visits to James and Jenny's house.

True to his word, James followed Richard that first evening. Sure enough, the clandestine meeting went on the same as previously. Richard picked up the commander and headed back in the direction of Gorgan. Shortly afterward, the girl headed off down the alley, closely followed by the third party, who had now, apparently, come out from the storage room. *Guess all's normal*, James thought, twisting his face as a cynical gesture of contempt for what normal had become.

He decided to jump the wall and test if the sliding doors had been left open. They had been. It seemed odd to James that the doors had not been checked. On the other hand, he supposed that once the error in leaving them unlocked had been made, it was unlikely that it would be checked, since that entrance was not the normal passage of entry or exit. It only led to the balcony at the back of the apartment.

James returned home and lay wondering where the events would lead. There was little doubt that Richard was not aware of what was going on between the commander and this woman, but James couldn't make up his mind if he was that naive or just didn't want to think about it. The real question was whether he could, or should, confide in Richard. James decided not to raise the issue unless circumstances warranted it.

* * *

On the second night, James made his pre-planned excuse to Jenny that he had to return to the worksite on the pretext that the first of the concrete had to be poured. It really wasn't too far from the truth. That actual event had already taken place that day, much to James's chagrin. He had arrived on site at the usual time and set off for the location where the first foundation had been prepared for concrete.

For James it was of no great consequence, so he hadn't realized this first pour's impact on the working Iranians. Standing in the excavation, surrounded by bodies diligently attempting to clean every speck of deleterious material from the hole while at the same time being caught in every precarious position imaginable by the steel reinforcing that crisscrossed the excavation in both directions at the top and the bottom, he was suddenly aware that the rest of the bodies were fast disappearing to higher ground—out of the hole.

Without warning, one of the laborers reached over the side of the hole, dropped a sheep in while he held on to its back legs, its feet still kicking, and proceeded to swiftly slit its throat. The blood shot across the hole and hit James squarely in the chest. Totally shocked by the experience, it was only by reaction rather than good planning that he somehow managed to minimize the effect by leaping with one bound into the cheering crowd gathered around him. Strangely they weren't cheering for him; in fact, they tended to ignore him as though getting splattered in blood from a sheep's throat was too common to dwell on anymore. Rather, they clapped and shouted their praises as a blessing of the ground within which they worked. The concrete was poured and the blood mingled into the northwest footing of the new compressor footing. It would be there forever.

James reflected on the day as he drove over to where the commander would be arriving. He parked his car a few blocks away and walked over toward the alley, looking all the while for a suitable spot from which to gain the best view. He had plenty of time, and the evening would stay light until about 7:30 p.m. He felt it imperative to get a good vantage point and became all the more frustrated when he couldn't easily find one. He looked at both ends of the alley and cursed himself at not bringing a pair of binoculars.

As he returned to the other end of the lane for the second time, he noticed an apartment building that seemed to be only partially constructed. There were no windows and only a partial roof. The surrounding wall had been completely finished, including the decorative in-laid artwork on the walls and even the house number. To the casual passerby, it would have appeared as though there were occupants. There weren't. James looked about him and tested the gate. It was locked. He jumped the wall and was over in a flash, hardly stopping to wonder whether he had been seen. The house was some 80-percent complete but not yet habitable. The stairs had been roughed in but marble facing stones set.

James climbed the stairs and went to what he thought would be the best viewpoint. It was certainly reasonable and far better than he could hope for at ground level. He would be able to make out the faces of anyone who approached. He looked at his watch. It was 6:15 p.m. As he looked up, he saw two figures enter the alley and walk quickly toward the house opposite. Despite the chador, he could not mistake the body it helped to outline—it was the commander's girlfriend. The other party was a male, dressed in some kind of uniform that James recognized as typical of many in the Revolutionary Guard. He had very dark, almost-sunken eyes and great hairy hands. James noticed those particularly as the man grabbed the arm of the girl and almost swung her through the gate while at the same time having a last glance up and down the alley. He did not look over or up at the partly finished house and James brazenly stood to get a better view so that he would not miss their entry into the house. They closed the door behind them as they went through the hall. James could look almost totally into the second bedroom on the third floor and see at least the bottom part of the door on the opposite wall.

There was little else to see, other than to study the layout of the roof opposite to establish the location of the exhausts and air intake hoods before the next evening. The layout was simple, and it was easy to identify the one that would be of most interest to him. James climbed down the stairs and left through the front gate, leaving it unbolted from the inside. He drove home deep in thought as he wondered again what the situation's implications might turn out to be. But he was getting his thoughts in order before contacting Dick Elliot. Certainly, Dick had wanted him to investigate the listening post and it seemed that the commander and the girl had all the potential to be useful to whatever Dick was trying to do.

* * *

On the third night, James feigned a similar excuse, except this time it was a phantom meeting with the general contractor being held at the home of the manager. Jenny had no reason to doubt his word and simply asked when to expect to return. James knew he could be holed up for a substantial part of the night, depending upon the conversation that occurred and whatever light it shed on the commander's little meetings. He parked the Jyane in the same place at roughly the same time as previously. Walking quite casually down the alley, he looked around to ensure he was not being watched. There appeared to be no danger as he hopped over the wall. Eight-foot-high walls were becoming easy to conquer for him, what with all the practice over the past two weeks or so. Getting onto the roof was a different matter. It didn't seem that there was an obvious way up from the outside. Then he realized that all houses had access to the roof from the inside, usually from the small outside space beyond the kitchen window. Sure enough, there it was. Sufficient footholds to make it with relative ease up and onto the roof. It looked as though it might remain a cloudy but warm evening. James hadn't bothered to take precautions against the possibility of rain.

He walked around the roof, getting used to lines of vision from the surrounding houses and alleys. Trying to make sure that he positioned himself at the stack from the *naft* heater in the bedroom so as not to be seen from any angle, he crouched and placed his ear against the pipe, tapping it lightly to get a feel for the potential amplification. It actually sounded as though it might work. It was 6:30 p.m. when he heard footsteps in the alley but didn't dare to look over the small parapet wall to check them out. Someone entered the building. He placed his ear back to the pipe, anxious to check out his theory. He heard voices quite faintly at first. If they were from the bedroom, he was lost. He couldn't make out the words, or even the language. Suddenly the voices got louder. He could take his ear away from the pipe and hear them quite clearly. The people spoke in Farsi. He couldn't understand, other than for the very occasional word, and there was little point in concentrating too much since he didn't stand a chance of being able to piece the conversation together. Then he caught a few words in English from the girl. James was anxious to take a look at the pair of them since he had missed his chance earlier.

He had another fifteen minutes before the commander arrived. This time he felt compelled to get the whole thing over with on the same evening. He moved back to the access from the kitchen. The kitchen was dark. It would have had a light on if anyone was there; even though it was still light enough to see by it was dusk and the kitchen only received natural light from the roof access area. James peered over the edge, straining to see as far as he could into the room. He heard voices in the distance. If the voices stopped, he would go back up the footholds to the roof's safety. He descended in one clean movement, never hearing a stop or waver in the conversation beyond.

Climbing in through the window, he realized that this was probably the most vulnerable time and suddenly he became conscious of the beating of his heart and the dryness in his throat. He stopped inside the window to concentrate on the voices. They had stopped and heard the padding of feet. He darted to the door that led into the dining room after hastily deciding that it would be the most unlikely opening for a person coming from the bedroom to enter the kitchen. He was right, and he dodged into the dining room just in time to miss the figure entering the kitchen.

James spied the sofa in the front room and decided that it should provide adequate cover to allow him to spy on the persons from a close advantage. He waited for the figure to re-emerge from the kitchen and return to the bedroom before he made an almost clumsy pitch to the sofa. He held his breath as he settled down on the floor and waited for the possible repercussions of his maneuver. There seemed to be none.

The voices resumed at a low level. James guessed that they were simply checking off their list of things to take care of before the commander arrived. He peered cautiously around the edge of the sofa when he was certain from the volume of the voices that they were in the bedroom, concentrating on other things to do. The commander would be arriving momentarily.

James really wanted to take a look at the third person before he shut himself in the other room. He almost pulled his head back into the hiding position behind the sofa as the third figure started toward the bedroom door with his head turned apparently toward the girl, who must have positioned herself over by the bed. He suddenly got a look at the man as he turned his face toward James. His sunken eyes seemed even more so now than the other night. His mustache was neatly trimmed. He had removed his jacket and sweater, probably in preparation for having to be cooped up in the storage room for the evening. His discarded clothes were draped over his arm, neatly folded, as though the whole evening would be a repeat of so many before it, and he had become well practiced. He was tall, well built, and seemed to be typical Iranian military. There seemed to be no immediately visible distinguishing marks. As he left the room, the girl called to him. He turned as his name, Salamati, was hardly uttered and his military cap was tossed at him. He caught it clumsily and seemed slightly embarrassed at what was obviously a scolding from the girl. He left the room, locking the door behind him. James heard the sound of the storage room door open, then close. There was no more sound.

James stayed behind the sofa, hoping to catch a sight of the girl preparing for the commander's arrival. He decided to get a better view and turned to look around the sofa from the opposite end. He peered around the edge in time to see the flash of a naked body go behind the bedroom door. The girl stepped back into view at the door and wrapped a silk robe around herself. The air was filled with a musk perfume as she strode through into the front room apparently checking that all was in order. She turned the record player on and slipped it into a Fausto Papetti number. The saxophone seemed to transfer the previously sterile room into a comfortable little meeting place.

It was made even more so by the beautiful girl who moved before him. The smell of her perfume was almost intoxicating. She moved toward the kitchen, took two glasses from the small, wooden cabinet next to the entry and placed them on a silver tray on the table. She was oblivious to James, who remained quite still. He took in the sight of her and was almost jealous of the commander. She adjusted the curtains as though anyone could see into the rooms. She turned and headed into the kitchen and returned with an ice bucket, vodka, and a bottle of lime juice. The woman poured two drinks and took a sip of one. She lit a cigarette, took a long drag, breathed out her anxieties, and listened for the arrival of her lover while checking her watch for the time. It was 6:50 p.m. She took the tray into the front room and placed it on the small side table next to the sofa. She walked quickly to the bedroom and James heard the tapping, the international method of testing a microphone. All seemed in order as she stepped back into the living room and looked carefully about her, having one last check.

She turned toward James, undid the belt from her robe and let it fall apart to reveal her body underneath for a few moments before rearranging herself and redoing the knot in a loose bow. Just as she finished, a noise from the rear entrance attracted her and James's attention as the commander walked briskly into the room, held out his arms and grabbed the girl affectionately around the waist. He lifted her off her feet.

"What a day. Thank God that's over at last." He accepted the drink handed to him and downed half of it with little effort. He walked over to the sofa and sat heavily on the soft cushions, loosening his tie.

"That bad, eh? Well, relax for a while, at least. You should be used to all this."

The girl spoke perfect English with hardly an accent. It was almost uncanny how she had seemed to converse so easily one minute with her co-conspirator in Farsi and now settled so comfortably into English with the American commander, appearing for all intents and purposes as though she were simply a loving wife welcoming her husband home at the end of a long hard day.

The commander took a slug of the vodka lime, downing the second half as quickly as the first. He held the glass out for a refill. As the girl crossed over him to take it from his hand, the commander reached under the silk gown and ran his hand up over her thigh. The girl feigned shyness and pulled away.

"Easy boy. Let's get you relaxed a little first before you get going. You know you get a little savage if you don't give yourself a little time first. Let me get you another drink while you take a shower."

"You're quite a girl, you know. I have no idea how I'd manage if I didn't have you to come to. That place is getting at me just a little more with each passing day. I don't know what it is, but I guess with all the guys being so confined and our work always being without ending, it's like you get the feeling that things are going on all around but no one ever tells you what it is. Yet if they did, maybe the work would be a little easier to take. Maybe we'd be able to help even more. All I ever get are these damned abstract questions." The commander had gone into the bedroom to remove his clothes. He walked back into the front room naked and crossed to where the girl was making his drink. He grabbed her from behind and playfully, and carefully, pushed his hands down between her legs, while at the same time pushing his body into her.

She laughed and pushed him backward with her butt.

"Go take your shower, you horny son of a..." She couldn't finish the sentence as the commander pulled her to him and headed for the bathroom.

While she still clung to the glass, much of the content spilled out.

"No-o, my hair—it takes me ages. Son of a gun. Let me go." She swung a foot playfully at him but he continued to pull her.

"Listen, Jim, I'm serious. Let me go before I really give you something."

"Promise, promises. That's all you ever give me. Oh, all right, go get me another drink and I'll be out in a minute." He let her go and she stuck her tongue out as she darted back to the drink stand.

The commander laughed as he headed for the shower.

The girl shut the bathroom door quickly behind her—the smile disappearing just as fast from her face. She went to the bar tray, made another couple of drinks, then headed for the bedroom. The shower stopped as she turned the sheet down on the bed and went back to the music center to check the music. James watched as the commander walked naked from the bathroom, still rubbing his hair dry, his penis partially hardened in anticipation. Reaching the girl, he tossed the towel to the side and removed the robe from the girl. By now, his penis was fully erect. She led him to the bedroom before they got too carried away, too far from the microphone.

James craned his head farther around the sofa to catch some more of the excitement and hopefully talking but he could only vaguely make out some of the gyrations now taking place on the bed. James decided to get closer to at least catch what might be said, although he doubted that talk would be forthcoming too soon at the rate the bodies were moving.

He darted over to the side wall by the bedroom, not doubting his safety for a second as he heard the continued groaning and grunting coming from the bedroom. Creeping into a dark corner of the small dead-end passageway, James decided that he might just as well settle down for a while. There was little point in going to the rooftop. It was more comfortable right there.

At least an hour went by with little more than some giggles, muffled comments, and rustling noises coming from the commander and the girl. Then a different noise from the bed made James start and press back against the wall. The girl appeared in the doorway on her way to the bathroom. The commander followed her as far as the bedroom entrance, then headed to the drink tray instead. He poured a full glass, took a slug, and looked at his now limp penis. "Stand down, private!" he ordered as he laughed and headed back to the bedroom. He disappeared inside without even a glance down the passage to where James remained hidden. The girl followed, rubbing herself down with a towel. The noise of the bed gave away that both bodies were back in motion, except this time there was more giggling and talk. James crept closer to the doorway.

"Another hard day, darling?" She continued to stroke the commander.

"I can never figure out how come they have so much to say. You know I must hear a million strange things a day. Thank God I don't have to make sense of all of it. That English guy I told you about last week was on again." The commander took a long drag of the cigarette and looked over at the girl. "Remember the one?"

She looked puzzled for just a moment. "Oh, you mean the English guy who was talking about his camels wandering around in the jungle?" She laughed as she recalled the picture she had conjured up after the first time they had discussed the incident. Apparently, at approximately the same time each week, some Englishman transmitting from Turkey held a one-way conversation with no one in particular about his string of camels, which he had herded through various locations around the world and were presently embroiled in some antics in the African jungle.

"What I don't understand, even after listening to him all this time, is what he's up to. Oh, I guess the camels are more than camels and all these strange locations mean something in particular, but it sure would be interesting if just for once I could find out the ending to one of these little episodes."

"Well, maybe one day you will, darling. Just listen long enough and who knows what secrets you'll learn. What about that transmission from Basra? That sounds interesting, particularly since it seems like it includes so many different groups. Maybe they're all for real. Maybe all the pieces really do make some sense."

"You could be right, although I would doubt that whoever is doing the transmitting is really that stupid that they don't realize that half the world is listening to what they're saying. But if they really are that stupid—or at least pretending to be—then it all sounds very political to me. Of course, we shouldn't be discussing this at all." The commander grabbed the girl around the waist and started to tickle her.

"Promise not to tell," he whispered harshly in her ear.

"You don't have to tell me anything if you don't want to. I just like to hear you talk about what you do. You get so into it, and it all sounds so strangely fantastic. It's hard to believe that so many people are so covert if that's the right word. Maybe the majority of them have some strange desire to carry on secret conversations to pretend that they're something that they aren't." She paused and looked at her lover. "Perhaps?" Her face wrinkled in question.

"Maybe," he replied. "But I tell you, some of those folks out there are for real. Take the guy from France. He broadcasts into someplace that's right around here somewhere. That much I do know. He's really onto something, that one. Contacts some guy he calls Assassin, and from what we can tell, the responder we've identified as someone who refers to the other guy as Paris." The commander paused, reached over to the side table, and took hold of the vodka lime. He had one sip, then a slug, and looked over at the girl. "Strange, eh?"

"Maybe they're just amateurs," she taunted as though trying to get him to continue. There seemed to be a trace of nervous excitement in her voice.

"Remember I told you before that this guy Paris was talking about the southern oilfields. Well, he didn't make too many bones about that—at least in what the subject matter was. Well, I thought it was just going to all end in the same way as usual—you know—no ending. Well, last night, Paris comes on and calls his friend up at the usual time and says something like, 'The oilfields will burn in September.' Assassin held back for a few moments, then he repeated the statement and asked for identification of the fire. Paris sort of coolly said, 'The first field in the string, we will start there and fan the flames through Ramadan.'

"After that, there was silence. No more transmission, and I suspect that that will be all we'll hear as well. Can't wait until September." The commander rubbed his hands together and chortled, not noticing the girl's silence. He was clearly into forbidden territory but, for some reason, he didn't think of her as a risk. Her face set in deep thought. He turned to his drink and asked over his shoulder, "What do you think? A little strange, eh? Especially after all those other times when they got into talking about what I'm pretty sure must have been the shah and his allies around the world. It all gets a little difficult when we get into the oil stuff and the connections with those companies like BP, but maybe there's some sense in all this that I just can't figure. I just feed it all back to the experts and let them play with it. God knows what they'll make of it all." He stopped and looked over to his girl, who looked perplexed. "Problem, honey?"

The girl caught his look as though broken out of a trance. "No, no, I'm okay. I just came over a little strange, that's all. Must be the booze." She gave a short laugh. "I don't feel too good, honey. Do you think we could call it a night? I should get home and have an early night. Maybe I'm coming down with something."

"Sure, sunshine. You get yourself going, and I'll just hang around here and wait for my driver."

"How long will you have to hang around?" she asked.

He looked at his watch. "Oh, a couple of hours yet, but that's okay, I'll catch some shuteye for a bit and set the alarm. I could do with some catch up too."

James started to get agitated as the conversations turned to the two of them separating early. He stealthily crept back to the darkened corner and pulled the curtain around him while he waited for the girl to leave. She wasted little time and emerged from her bedroom already partly clothed. They kissed and hugged quickly.

"I'll see you tomorrow night at the same time, my darling" she said and quickly left, hardly giving him time to respond.

The commander came back into the apartment, took his almost empty glass over to the drinks tray, refilled it with vodka lime, and put on a Grover Washington CD before returning to the bedroom. James could hear him fiddle with the clock before the light went out. It was less than five minutes before he heard the commander's gentle snoring.

James made his way out of the apartment and through the garden gates. He headed home. Thirty minutes later, a second figure emerged and slipped silently through the gate and along the dark alley.

*   *   *

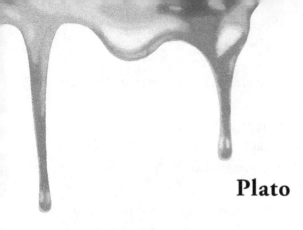

Plato

It took less than an hour for James to get ready for his trip to Chalus with Tom Aradeghali, his friend from the construction site. Tom worked for one of the contractors. He was a "displaced" Russian, educated in Belarus, and had worked his way over to Iran, where there was work in Sari. Even though it was something of an odd match, the relationship between them seemed to work.

Jenny had taken the plunge and flown down to Tehran with the three boys to spend some time with a friend who had recently arrived from the UK for a job in the city.

James had sped home from site the day Jenny had left, after a gruelingly hot and humid day in the sun and dust. He'd showered as soon as he had arrived at the apartment. *Thank God there's water today*, he thought. After he had changed into fresh clothes, he threw a few things into a small bag, not really caring what they were, and waited.

When his friend drove up, James almost threw himself down the stairs in his excitement to get away for a break for a few days and before Max had a chance to call him back to the project site on some trumped-up reason, as he often did on James's days off. Fortunately, Max would be moving out of Iran in a couple of weeks. His project experience didn't go beyond earthworks and concrete, and he was just too difficult to deal with.

James and Tom had planned to go for a "retreat" to Chalus, to enjoy the sun and relax on the Caspian with Tom's friend. They stopped at the Armenian store in Babol to pick up provisions to last them for a couple of days, including two bottles of vodka, a couple of bottles of Iranian rum, and an assortment of beer. True, the beer wasn't cold, but it sure beat the hell out of chai.

As they swilled back the first of their beers, they were tempted to go browsing around the city, looking for a little bit of fun in true Friday-night downtown fashion. But as they considered it more, they decided to move on to Chalus before they got themselves into any trouble.

It took them almost three hours to get to Chalus from Sari, and almost another half an hour to find the entrance to the house they were headed for. Tom had never been there before. All he knew was a general description given to him by his friend Ali and the approximate distance out from the main center. In fact, it was almost a miracle that they found it at all; the front of the place was well hidden by tall cypress trees, which didn't seem to want to divulge there was even a house lurking behind them. The only clue that they could make out to suggest that any domicile actually existed in that location was the occasional glimpse of a tennis court they knew was a part of the complex.

Tom drove back and forth a number of times before negotiating the narrow gravel driveway, and they spied two cars parked farther down at the end of the tennis court in front of what was clearly a beach house that only people of means could afford.

They parked next to a white Maserati and shouldered their supplies as they headed to the front door. It was getting dark by now. James really wanted to have a quick look at the surroundings before he went inside but his curiosity was curbed by a huge, bronzed Goliath of a man who flung the front door open and vaulted out to pick Tom up in one fell swoop, lifting him high off the ground and spinning him around like a rag doll before dropping him unceremoniously to the ground without so much as a "sorry." James drew back to avoid a similar experience and Tom slumped to the ground. He simply grunted and held out a shaky hand as the Goliath came toward him with a face-splitting smile.

"Hello, I'm Plato. Good to see you both. Come inside," he said all in one breath and held out his hand.

James held back a little in case this was a trick deliberately being set to catch him unawares just before the big heave-ho. Nothing more physical happened, apart from Tom's antics as he did slow press-ups from the ground in his attempts to get to his feet.

They stepped into the house to be greeted by a couple who came at them in the same excited manner as Plato but who fortunately didn't bother with the Herculean antics. Instead, they beamed welcoming smiles as Plato introduced his wife, Margaret, and his good friend, Mersadaghli, who they referred to after that initial introduction as just "Ali"—Tom's friend who had invited him over to Chalus.

Plato was truly what one imagined him to be with a name like his. He seemed to be a cross between an African and a West Indian, with a little of the white man thrown into the mix. His accent was a well-cultivated Oxford, as was his bearing, and it wasn't difficult to tell that he must have been educated in such an establishment. He possessed the aura of someone who could dominate a group discussion without really saying anything too important. Gesticulating with slow, rhythmic movements that seemed to blend in as a pictorial description of his narrative, one could hardly imagine him talking without the accompaniment of the other. And yet, by contrast, Margaret, his American wife, seemed almost lacking in character as she moved with a sort of gangly motion from one room to another, apparently getting a meal together. She said little as the four men sat down at the rough wooden table that looked out over the back garden. Beyond the trees, a dilapidated wooden fence separated the house from the white-grayish sand of the Caspian Sea. This particular stretch of beach was too far from the main population center to have any accountable amount of people wandering in the area. It was a peaceful respite from the hustle and bustle of the site and city of Sari. James and Tom visibly relaxed within the hour as they were amused by Plato's banter and Ali's prodding and lubricated with vodka.

It transpired that Plato had combined his natural talents for talking with the inheritance of a banking ability passed on from his father. He worked at the foreign exchange desk of the Melli Bank in Tehran and had used his relative freedom to travel Europe on business, cultivating his friendships in the financial and business community and making new contacts, while at the same time getting away to Chalus whenever a weekend presented itself. He had met Margaret on one of his many excursions to London, where he had been invited to a party at the American embassy.

Margaret had not particularly stood out from the crowd, unless one would consider that to be associated with a person who seemed to laugh uncontrollably at a drop of a hat and seemed insistent on spilling drinks and food on other people. The curious thing was that she needed no prompting and seemed more concerned with being herself. That was enough to suggest that she was somewhat unusual and stood apart from the rest of the crowd of would-be debutantes whose principal ambition seemed to be netting a suitable beau. True, she had shown a flicker of interest out of the corner of her eye as Plato walked toward the bar where she had propped herself up. He rested his hand on her hip to gently suggest he needed a little more room to maneuver past her. She, of course, reciprocated by turning and spilling her lime cordial over the front of his white jacket. That had been the start of their romance.

For some reason, Plato had considered her casual and natural approach to life as somehow complementing his own character. In many ways, this was true. There were few demands that he had to meet from their marriage, as Margaret virtually continued her same existence of chaperoning her father around the world on his political escapades. He had been something to do with the American embassy staff operating out of London but traveled to Europe and the Middle East, reviewing projects that were being financed by the American government. Margaret enjoyed the traveling, as well as meeting new people in the countries to which she traveled. She also needed those weekends in Iran when Plato and she could disappear to Chalus for a reclusive weekend together.

Rather than take a plane, they would drive at a leisurely pace over the Alborz Mountains from Tehran, taking time to stop en route for a refreshing bowl of mast, fresh naan, sliced melon, and an assortment of fruit while they watched the local people creating their own amusement along the dusty road. They would stop at roadside vendors and select trinkets of straw mats, handwoven baskets, and other works of art that the locals would swear had taken them hours of work to produce. If only they had removed the "Made in Taiwan" labels before they put them up for sale, it might have helped their cause. But it would have detracted from the novelty of it all. Plato and Margaret would reach Chalus by dusk, totally relaxed, and unload the car, grab beers, and wander down to the water of the Caspian Sea before the sky turned to night. Refreshed, they would wander back to the house, laughing and joking, waiting for Ali to arrive.

They had bought the beach house as a retreat; it was their only permanent home in what they considered to be a neutral part of the world for them and without telephones or mail. Ali had once been the owner of the beach house before going to live in the States. On his return, he had traveled on a nostalgic journey back to Chalus.

Venturing to take another look at the house from the beach, Ali had almost tripped over Margaret as he wandered past the fence without looking down at the sleeping mound on a towel on the sand in front of him. She squealed, he jumped, and the two of them had rushed off in different directions, each feeling that the attacker would follow. It didn't take either of them long to realize the mistake and they introduced themselves. From that day on, Ali had been a regular visitor to the beach house, opting to use it at every opportunity, whether Plato and Margaret were there or not. They had entrusted him with a key and he came and went as he wished, stocking the cupboard with food and the bar with drink. They had become more than good friends, especially after realizing that each had a common interest in this country.

James and the others smoked some Afghan hashish that Tom had brought from Kabul on his last visit, enjoying it with the casualness of lifelong users and relaxing in each other's company as the conversation grew easier. Rice and a variety of fish with sauces appeared on the table as Margaret sat down with the men and joined in the conversation as though she had never been away. It was difficult not to notice her as she sat in the barest of bikinis and picked at the chicken with her fingernails, as though she was alone with no one to see her. In contrast to her husband, Margaret was what one could only describe as relaxed, with relatively unkempt hair that fell in dark locks over her eyes. She was thin, with no particularly outstanding bodily aspects. It was difficult to imagine the two of them being considered partners. But they survived better than most and obviously thoroughly enjoyed their short times together.

When the table had been cleared, the five of them went out into the night air and sat around on the beach, listening to the waves break and talking of their adventures over the past few weeks. James felt he was with familiar friends. As the ambient air cooled a little, Plato, Margaret, Tom, and James climbed into the Jeep and sped off down the beach, while Ali went back inside to prepare the fire for their return. The four of them ended up in the city and casually drove around, taking in the smells and excitement of the scene as the population came alive again after their prerequisite siesta. Chalus was probably the only recreation center outside Tehran that such a cosmopolitan collection of people enjoyed at almost every time of the year.

As the principal resort area of the Iranian side of the Caspian, it was still a favorite center for tourists, who had discovered this relatively unspoiled part of the world where they could relax without the intrusions of obvious commercialism or the intrusion of the Islamic Republic—but that was likely contrived. The Chalus Hyatt had a reputation unbeaten by its counterparts in other parts of the world. The waiters still wore the uniform normally associated with the original pre-revolution days of the 1950s and wandered efficiently among the guests dressed in crisp white jackets, ballooning pajama pants, sandals, and open-neck, collarless white shirts—each item impeccably clean and of obvious pride to its wearer.

But this was not the night for the foursome to revel in the delights of continental company. This was a time for retreat and the joys of simplicity and close company. They chewed on fresh naan and sipped Coke as they drove the five miles back to the beach house. Ali met them at the door with a concoction of iced mast and cucumber. Guaranteed to cool them down, freshen them up, and lighten the head after the variety of food and drink that had been digested during the evening. They sat around on the steps of the Tayaki pit, watching the fire and sharing some quiet conversation, as James and Tom slowly drifted into the hypnotic state of slumber, heavy with the labor of the past week and the rush to leave Sari. Ali had collected spare blankets from the bedroom. Margaret headed for her own bed. It took James and Tom little encouragement to spread themselves out on the steps of the pit, sink down, and slip into a sleep comforted by the warmth of the fire and the security of the blankets.

But James dozed fitfully as Plato and Ali continued a quiet but discernible conversation while sitting at the table by the window overlooking the garden and farther out to sea, drinking shot glasses of vodka. James was lost as they talked in Farsi but Plato was clearly not all that comfortable with the language and after a while they turned to English, having satisfied themselves that their guests were asleep. Ali had lived in Kentucky for a number of years and spoke English with barely a trace of his native accent.

What sparked James's attention in the ensuing conversation was the occasional reference to someone that Ali kept referring to as "the Russian." At first, he thought they were discussing the same old problems that many of the local workers talked about concerning the old Russian families that had continued to live among them in Chalus. They had insisted on maintaining their old Ukrainian lifestyles with little regard for the fact that this was Iran. They were convinced their empire would again exert itself with a show of the dominance they had known after the turn of the century, when Russia had controlled the whole area including Gorgan. Pushed out by the British and eventually by Reza Shah, they considered this temporary setback would soon be rectified and all the problems of the locals would be solved. Of course, the natives didn't quite see it that way, but then who could be bothered to deflate the visions of these old settlers. No, the reference hadn't been related to that old topic. There was definitely something bothering Ali, and James forced himself to prick up his ears a little further and shake off the sleep he knew he needed.

"As if one wasn't enough, Kabul is sending another. They know something is brewing and, while I'm sure they know little about what we are planning, I believe it will not be too long before they realize what is going on. But two pairs of Russian eyes at the plant is at least one too many and ORB needs to be extra diligent, my friend." Ali paused.

James quietly turned toward them, feigning deep sleep, while he cautiously opened one eye to a slit and focused on the pair at the table. If they had noticed his movement, they didn't show it.

"I know Tom, my friend," Ali said. "He's no trouble to manage. I can't say the same for the new ones until we meet, but they both have to be managed. It's easy to become paranoid when we're the eyes and ears for so many. We have to be curious and cautious, but not too cunning. The Russians are, after all, at a disadvantage. While the Regime might appear to want to share their bed with them, their party would rather not deal with them at all." Ali paused and reflected. "Oh, true, there is discontent, and they will play on that. But the people are wise. If there is to be another revolution, it won't be inspired *by* the Russians *for* the Russians. It will be inspired from abroad and the people here will support them, according to our informants at least. We must be careful not to be caught in the crossfire with any of this business, and the Russians must not gain any advantage. Be cautious but don't sound the alarm before it's time.

"Plato," Ali placed his hand on his friend's arm, "this time, I'm sure they'll replace Tom. He's been a son to me since I returned from the States. I've never thought of him as being a Russian with subversive thoughts. I think he's just a simple pawn in their game. He reports what he finds, but he isn't looking for anything that would affect what we're part of. He doesn't know anything about these things."

Plato was deep in thought and just stared out at the darkness of the Caspian.

"There's so much corruption and evil. It's becoming an almost daily event for one of my men to report the disappearance of one of his family or a friend, just like in the days of SAVAK. It must stop. The people must support a change. I just hope they can do it soon." Ali looked at Plato as he waited for a reply, as though his friend would divulge some secret answer and solve their problems with one sweeping statement.

"I know ORB are watching; I know that my friend." Plato paused and looked over at Ali. "I know you don't know them, but I can tell you that they're working hard to secure a better future for all of us here in Iran. And there's more discomfort with each passing day as the money floods out of the country, but we know where it's all going and it's not into the hands of those that would improve the lives of the Iranian people.

"All I can report at present is that my contacts abroad are recording huge sums of money being deposited in safe accounts under what I've found to be fictitious company names in a number of countries around the world. Whether this money is being taken out illegally or whether it's for foreign investment, I cannot be certain. What I do know is that the money is being skimmed from our oil profits and diverted away from internal investment.

There's much bad feeling among our bankers, who think only the worst. These days are no different from when the shah did the same. Once we establish the money trails, we'll be able to effect change, but until then we have to follow the rules.

"As for the Russians, I would only give them a little thought, since I believe that while they're ever ready to foment discontent, they'll be the last to realize what is actually happening with the Iranian people. My main concern is to ensure the security of my contacts looking for the Regime's money.

"Ali, you have to establish fact not hearsay, and while we may see more of the Russians arriving that may signify nothing more than an increasing interest in their investment. That's natural and something that we must expect. You mustn't worry so much. Belarus is the breeding ground for Russians preparing themselves to move into Iran. It used to be Afghanistan, before the Americans routed them. Work visas are easy to get, and it's just a four-hour flight from Minsk to Tehran."

Plato patted Ali's hand and poured another shot glass of vodka for them both. They lifted their glasses to each other with a salute and downed the contents in one drink. As if his confidence was restored and his courage returned, Ali smacked his lips and smiled.

"You are wise, my friend, to think of these events so casually yet carefully. The time we talk about may not come at all, and maybe I've grown too suspicious in my old age. But not without some reasons." Ali chuckled and looked down at his glass on the table, twisting and turning it to make patterns in the condensation.

He looked up at Plato.

"You know," Ali started as he turned his head away to gaze out of the window, "I don't know why I came back when there's so little that I can do. The future will unfold no matter what you or I do now. My family needs me much more. This country sometimes moves too fast, and the people cannot keep up. Perhaps they are right. Perhaps the ship must stop and the captain be changed before Iran crashes on the rocks again. When I look about me and see our people disappear one by one into the hands of torturers who would lock away all our people, I wonder at the use of it all. For what? What has changed over these last 100 years?" Ali looked back from the window to his friend. He got up and plunged his hands deep into his pockets as though thoroughly dejected by it all.

"I can't agree with you more, if you must really know," Plato stated to a rather surprised Ali. "You know that we're not here to save the country nor to cause a revolution if that's what is needed. Our task is simply to observe and report on events to ORB. You know what will happen if there is civil war. First, the Iranian currency will become worthless on the international market and investors of today will not only lose their wealth but there will be no future opportunities for many years to come.

"Our job is to protect the future as best we can. No matter what may happen now, there will always be a need to provide for the people when the politicians have run their course. We cannot let the investment that's been made fall into the hands of those who'll take it and use it for their own devices." Plato paused to study his friend, who was deep in thought.

Ali shrugged.

"As usual, I never regret our little talks. You seem to have the knack of bringing me back to reality. I get so embroiled in the concerns of everyday life that I sometimes lose the thread of the overall plan. Perhaps it will come to a head soon and I can go home to Kentucky." He chuckled again, but this time with a little more humor than the last time.

"You know I've tripled the size of my company over the last four years," he said suddenly, changing the subject. "I think I may send Tom back to look after the construction of our new development in Florida. He'll like that, and I'm sure that he'll do well," Ali paused once more and placed a finger against his lips. "Yes, that's exactly what I shall do. He'll like that, and his parents'll be happy to see him back in America again. But I shall miss him badly. He knows that there's something going on but he doesn't ask and I can't tell him, so it's better that he goes." Ali seemed happier at the thought that at least one part of his dilemma had been solved, albeit the easier part. But, then, it was the only part he had some control over.

Plato and Ali continued their talk for longer than James could recall. It was with great effort that he had managed to stay awake to the point that he could concentrate on any part of their conversation. As he began to drift into oblivion, he managed only to catch some casual talk of Ali's relationship to his present situation. James tried to put the logic together as they talked and he wondered about this ORB entity they referred to. *Oh well,* he decided, *I'll piece it all together in the morning when I can think a little clearer.* At the moment, the effects of the warmth were getting the better of his consciousness and he drifted off into a deep sleep.

*   *   *

James bounced from the step to the floor of the Tayaki pit, having experienced that fleeting feeling of falling in his sleep, and shook himself awake, taking seconds to realize where he was and what had happened the previous evening. He lay where he fell, nine inches down from his marble platform and twelve inches from a smoldering fire. The smell of hashish hung in the air and the steady sound of gentle waves breaking on the beach reminded him that the Caspian awaited.

With a slow and slightly resentful start, James struggled out from under the tangled pile of blankets and crawled beyond the pit before daring to straighten up. His back ached and his head seemed thick as he stretched and headed for the refrigerator, intent on at least concentrating on getting to the mast before he hit the surf. It seemed that within a minute, the potion worked and his head started to clear as he made his way toward the back door and out into the garden.

The sky was blue and the air was freshened by a steady early morning breeze coming off the Caspian that helped him down to the water's edge. With little thought, he removed all his clothes and paddled his way into the water, not caring for his surroundings. At this moment, he could be in any country in the world and, for a few minutes, he wished that he was the only one in it. As he flopped around in the small soothing waves, his memory drifted back to the previous evening and the conversation he had overheard. From his perspective and understanding over the last six months, it seemed strange to him that so many people were seemingly involved in this general social discontent. After all, having gotten rid of the shah some forty years before, one would think the people had got what they wanted. And yet there was full-scale discontent.

People moaned and bitched all around at the site. His Iranian friends would complain when they came over to the apartment. He could see the discontent on the faces, at the bazaar, and in the restaurants. There were people watching others who were watching others and so on and so on. From what he had made out from the snippets of conversation that had come to him just before his final departure into the big blue yonder last evening, it seemed that Ali had been asked by a group of wealthy businesspeople in Tehran to return from Kentucky, where his own company was prospering. They had requested that he form a new company that would contract out to Mana Construction, one of the prime contractors at the Sari oil refinery, to keep an eye on the situation in the province of Sari, as well as on Mansourian, the owner of Mana. They had become very concerned about their investments and that Mana had got itself so embroiled with the Regime. That did not bode well. But Ali didn't seem to want any part of it and had backed away. He just wanted to get back to Kentucky as soon as he had finished helping Plato.

James really couldn't quite understand the Kabul issue, but he guessed correctly that Russians were making use of their hold on Kabul. If nothing else, they would use it as a collection point for their people to undermine the integrity of countries in the region. They were like a malignant growth, intent on consuming, destroying, and ultimately controlling the integrity of others. He guessed that they were being sent from Russia, educated in Belarus, and dispersed to other countries in general like Iran, Iraq, Syria, and maybe others. He didn't know where, but his mind was not expansive enough to understand. But he did know that, once in Belarus, they could be easily transferred anywhere in the Middle East, unlike the Americans who were just Americans in a foreign land.

The Russians really understood how easy it was to transfer their operatives into Iran, despite the fact that all their supporting education documentation bore Russian identification, and each carried up-to-date memberships of the Communist Party. None of this was a diplomatic transfer breaker. And yet, the West never managed to catch up.

Still, James might be able to prove that later when he was back at site and managed to associate with Tom's replacement. The thought hit him like a bullet as he remembered that his friend was to be replaced. He had always known him affectionately as Tom and, despite the fact that they were really on the opposite sides of the fence at the job site, they were still the best of friends outside the fence.

When Tom had first arrived on site only four months ago, he had obviously been brought in to relate to the Westerners' ways of working in Iran as well as to better understand whether James or any of his expat. associates were up to anything subversive. James didn't know this, and they worked well together in the field. But more than that, they had become friends, and Tom had visited James and Jenny on a number of occasions to talk about Iran, or America, but never Russia. It was difficult for James to distinguish between whether Tom was truly becoming a friend or whether it was all a clever facade on the part of a contractor to befriend the engineer—all for the good of his own company. Still, James had taken it all in stride after the first deliberation and decided that it really was not worth the trouble of putting the relationship to the test.

It was hard at first, but there transpired a bond between them that they realized had limitations, depending upon circumstances. During off-work hours there was no job talk, while on site they limited their conversation to their socializing. It seemed to have become a mature and open friendship that both could live with. It would be sad for them to part, but then all James's friendships were like memories that came and went with projects. It was an enigma he had to live with.

As James wallowed in the water deep in thought, half watching the gulls overhead and half thinking of the good times he and Tom had had, a great dollop of sand landed squarely in his midriff, followed by another that caught him under the chin. Tom, totally dressed, lunged toward him. In return, James scrambled to his feet, forgetting his nakedness, clutched at the sand on the bottom of the seabed, and hurled it with all his might at his friend with little impact. Tom raced back to the safety of dry land. James scrambled after him while replacing the missiles of sand with shouts of friendly abuse.

It was only when they reached an upturned rowing boat, some 500 feet from the villa, that James realized his naked circumstances and dove for cover and looked about him while Tom fell to the sand in hysterical laughter. As he looked over the top of the boat, James smiled when he realized that they were alone. He turned and mopped his brow in a feigned exaggerated relief, only to realize that a small group of people had actually approached him from behind, all apparently straining to see if their eyes could really be believed. Holding his credentials discretely, James slid along the length of the boat and around its bow to the other side, where he released his hold and frantically beckoned his friend.

Tom looked about him, "Who me?" he shouted back as though wondering if it was really him that was being called, pointing to his chest in a questioning way. Realizing he was unlikely to get any help from that quarter, James decided on a plan of escape and slowly lifted the side of the rowboat as he groveled under it for cover. He could just make out the small group as they sauntered by and stared at him in his one eye that peeked from under the side of the boat.

There were many questions in their looks, but apparently none they were prepared to ask openly. As they continued on their way, it was obviously difficult for any of them to maintain a forward look. Gradually, the group drifted off farther down the beach and disappeared to the point where James felt relatively safe in coming out from hiding and chasing Tom back to his own bundle of clothes. As James maneuvered into his clothes, keeping constant watch for more passersby, the two of them giggled at the scene as they recalled it over and over. They collapsed close to the fence and lay prostrate there for a while without talking, alternating between dozing and playing in the sand. After some time, Margaret came down to the beach and placed a large plate of fruit, cheese, and naan between them while she continued on her way to the water. She walked casually into the Caspian, laid down, and stayed on her back while floating. At some point, she left, but the guys hadn't noticed.

James and Tom stayed in the same place until sunset and watched the sky glowing through different colors over the Caspian. It had been one of the quietest days of James's life, to just lie there and wallow in the serenity of the clear sky and warming breeze—the type of day that should never end.

As the cool breeze of the evening chilled them, James and Tom got up, as though by a mutual unspoken arrangement, and headed back to the villa to find that the others had gone. They lit the fire, covered themselves in blankets, and shared a bottle of crude Russian vodka in continuing silence as though that was their destiny for this last day of rest—for now.

* * *

Matthew in Chalus

It was just over a nine-hour flight to Frankfurt, then an overnight stop, and a flight out the next day to Tehran. The Airbus 340 took off on time from Vancouver only partially full, although in business class one didn't have to concern oneself with the tangle at the toilets, the children running up and down the aisles, or the dinner service interrupting one's need to stroll about. It was also where one could stretch out to one's full extent and lap up the luxury of a horizontal seat-turned-bed, albeit distinctly constrictive after lying in it for more than an hour. There were, of course, things to occupy the mind on the route, like alcohol and *cordon bleu* food and a fine assortment of movies, magazines, and newspapers from around the world. But the best was the quietness and time when there was no possibility of interruption, if that was what one wanted. A time when one could get lost in one's own thoughts without having to pander to the thoughts or words of others. Where it didn't matter whether one mixed a vodka with a gin chaser and then had a wine with lunch, or just ate the prawns from the plate and left the rest of the meal. No one would make audible or facial judgments, and one could just stay there in limbo for at least three of the nine hours of flight time.

After the layover in Frankfurt, Matthew caught the 2:45 p.m. flight to Tehran. It was almost 10 p.m. when he arrived at the Imam Khomeini International Airport, about twenty-five miles to the south of the city. A number of years ago, it had replaced the Mehrabad airport to the north as the international airline hub. That airport now only managed the in-country traffic and was where Matthew would catch his flight to Sari the next day. In the meantime, he headed to the Tooba Hotel on Naseri Street, about eight miles from Mehrabad, a wonderful boutique hotel with a fabulous vista of the Alborz Mountains, particularly from the terrace restaurant.

He was too late for a meal and didn't feel like one after his flight, but he did wander up to the terrace for a late nightcap. Matthew knew that under Iran's Islamic Penal Code, consumption of alcoholic beverages was punishable by eighty lashes, and if an individual was convicted and sentenced three times, the punishment on the fourth was likely death, although none had ever been recorded. One had to really search hard and long before one could get an alcoholic beverage in Tehran but if one stayed more than a couple of days, it was possible.

When Iran became an Islamic Republic in 1979, it became illegal to produce or consume any type of alcoholic beverage, but it didn't stop the booze-fueled parties that were far from rare. At the last count, authorities noted there were more than 200,000 alcoholics in the country. Strangely, for an alcohol-free country with such rigid regulations and severe punishment, there were some 150 Alcoholics Anonymous centers around the country. Homemade alcohol was high on the list of hobbies in Iran, especially in the north along the southern edge of the Caspian Sea, and wine, beer, Cognac, and a kind of vodka-like moonshine called *aragh* were all concocted in abundance. But there was also the black market with a lot of the alcohol being smuggled through the border with Iraq.

Matthew forgot the alcohol and instead relaxed with a tumbler of yogurt and peppermint they called *doogh*, with a small side plate of *gaz*, Persian nougat with pistachios. Nothing too sweet before he turned in for the night. He was going to have to rely on melatonin to help him sleep—although he did manage to smuggle through a bottle of single malt in his baggage. Maybe just a sip before he put the lights out.

*   *   *

The hotel was equipped with one- and two-bedroom self-catering apartments, and Matthew negotiated a monthly rate for a one-bedroom suite until he could establish what he needed in the future. His rate was reduced for the time there was no one in the apartment but while he there was it would be dutifully kitted out with all the linens as well as a supply of food and drink in the fridge. In the meantime, this hotel was very well situated with many great restaurants and parks nearby. It would be an easy place to get to for any of the ORB people who needed to be in Tehran for any length of time.

His plane to Sari was leaving at about 5:00 p.m. It took only an hour to fly the seventy-five air miles to Sari but four hours to drive, maybe more. He thought about the options for a couple of hours as he had breakfast on the rooftop terrace. The day was warming up and the waves of heat were slowly rising from the blacktop and disappearing as the temperatures heated the atmosphere. He caught a whiff of bitumen now and again as the roadways softened under the heat. He also noted the traffic. It wasn't quite as bad as he had thought it might be but then he had substantial experience driving in Montreal, so what could be worse? Certainly, there didn't appear to be a lot of organization to the traffic patterns he watched below—not many traffic lights or traffic cops, and cars did seem to be cutting each other off a lot. But, what the hell, he decided to rent a vehicle and get a better feeling for the area as he drove north toward the Caspian.

The front desk helped him locate a Jeep Grand Cherokee and had it parked at the front doors by noon.

Now that he was going to drive, he decided to head over to Chalus first. He wasn't sure if Plato would be there. Matthew thought he worked in Tehran and headed to the coast only at weekends. He called, and a very English voice answered.

"Melli Bank, Plato here. What can I do for you?"

"Plato, this is Matthew Black." He paused, waiting for some recognition. They had never talked, and it was only Stockman who had made the communications with Plato so far.

"Matthew." Plato sounded excited at hearing from him. "How lovely to hear from you. When did you arrive?"

"I got in last night and am about to head out to Chalus. Just wanted to check with you first before I head out. Where are you?"

"Oh, I'm here at the bank in Tehran. Another couple of hours and I should be in Chalus myself. Are you coming over to the house?"

"Absolutely. That was the plan. Sorry I didn't give more notice, but I changed my mind about going to Sari first and decided to get some background information from you first."

"I think that's a terrific idea, Matthew. Why don't you head up there as soon as you like? Margaret, my wife, will be there and I'll call her to let her know you'll be arriving around 6 p.m. Does that sound good?"

"I think so, Plato. Just give me an address, and I'll put it in the GPS."

"Jolly good, Matthew. I'll message it to you now... there we go."

"Got it, thanks. I'll see you a little later. I'm looking forward to seeing you."

"Me too, Matthew. Drive carefully and call me if you have any problems. I'll only be a couple of hours behind you."

"Okay." Matthew clicked his phone off but looked at the message for the address.

The phone rang.

"Oh, Matthew." It was Plato. "I should have suggested you stay the night, or two, if you would like. No point in rushing off to Sari without us having a good chinwag first. What do you say?"

"Sounds good. See you later."

Matthew dressed down for the journey, grabbed his bags, and checked out. He punched Plato's address into the GPS and joined the traffic, all the while keeping an eye on the map showing him the way out of the city. The language was Farsi, so it was a little difficult for him to take verbal instructions. He muted the voicing and took off toward the mountains, following the highlighted directions on the GPS. He really couldn't go too far wrong getting out of the city, knowing the mountains were dead north, and only had to concentrate on making sure he didn't take the northeastern route to Sari. He needed to follow the northwestern route to Chalus. There was a coastal road between the two that would allow him to go back and forth easily when needed. At this point, he didn't know what was needed, but it would all fall into place soon enough.

He climbed steadily through the ever-winding roads of the Alborz Mountains to the highest point at around 11,000 feet, where he stopped and got out to stretch his legs and breathe in the freshness of the air at that altitude. As he looked over the scene before him, he felt, rather than saw, a sense of history, culture, and simplicity. Scattered below were some crude buildings with a few people wandering and goats and sheep grubbing for a living in the scarcity of green and abundance of arid, cream- and brown-colored soil and rock, throwing up small puffs of dust as the animals moved about. There were no trees, no growth that he could see, just a barren wilderness with a scrappy-looking creek way down in the valley meandering its way north to the coast. There was nothing else. No gas stations, no stores, no bars, not even a drink stand to be seen. There were no covers to take shelter from the sun, no buses, no landmarks, no junctions, no road signs. Just occasional trucks that belched diesel fumes and had deformed axles and drivers who looked tortured by the drive as they hugged their steering wheel and ratcheted down one more gear to reach the peak, and then would have to do it all again tomorrow. Regardless, there was a serenity about the place. The kind of peace that didn't exist in Matthew's world. It was a raw, tough, waterless part of the country where not even birds showed themselves.

The desert turned to rocky formations on more gently undulating topography as Matthew dropped down toward the coast. He could see the Caspian from miles and miles away—it must have been forty—a dark shadow reflecting the gray sky and rain streaks joining the two. The dry heat of Tehran and the run-up to the top of the Alborz and over the other side had been relentless, and the humidity of the north side as Matthew approached the forests of that fertilized and watered strip of land paralleling the southern coastline of the Caspian was also relentless. It would never cease until he returned to the south side of the Alborz, which seemed an eternity away by comparison and in all respects.

Matthew followed the GPS directions religiously and found the house with relatively few problems, although he had to reverse back and forth a few times before he spotted the driveway and a tennis court between the tall cypress trees. He parked on the gravel to the side of the house, grabbed his bags, and knocked on the already open door. He peeked around and almost butted heads with who he assumed to be Margaret.

"Hello, you must be Matthew. I'm Plato's wife, Margaret." Her smile was infectious and casual, and she grabbed Matthew by the arm and almost dragged him through the hallway to the kitchen.

"Hi Margaret," he said with a smile on his face, "and yes, I'm Matthew. What a pleasure to meet you." He took the offered hand and stared at this scruffy-haired, kaftan-clad woman who stood smiling at him with a couple of cold beers waiting to be opened on the counter next to her.

Matthew liked her immediately.

"Good drive up?" It was only natural for everyone to refer to north as "up." And "down there" would be south. "Over there" could be east or west; it didn't matter.

"Yes, I really enjoyed it. I stopped at the top to take in the sights. Spectacular and distinctly different between north and south."

"Ah yes. The great surprise." Margaret cracked the beer opened and offered one to Matthew. "It quite takes your breath away, coming over the mountains and seeing all that green and water below you after coming up from the Tehran side, doesn't it?"

"Yes, I guess it does. But I was also thinking about the country, the language, the people, and the problems. You tend to forget the anguish that has gone on here for hundreds of years, maybe thousands, and you look over the land from the top of the mountain and you get, or at least I get, this sense of history and foreboding as though it hasn't quite settled down yet and still has a long way to go."

"Well, I've never heard it put quite like that, but perhaps you're right. There is still a long way to go and yet they've come so far. But then, perhaps this is their second or third trip through history." Margaret smiled and cocked her head to one side.

"Come and sit outside on the deck with me. It's a little cooler with the breeze coming off the sea."

They walked together through the sliding doors that were extended right across from wall to wall and out onto a patio with loungers spread around, a wooden table and chairs that would serve as a place to sit and eat, and a grand view over the Caspian Sea. The fence at the end of the yard was in bad shape and only knee-high, enough to stop any dogs from wandering onto the property but not high enough to block the view of the beach and water beyond.

They sat on loungers facing the water. There was no one else around them, and it seemed to be deserted as far as one could see in both directions. The house was a few miles from the edge of Chalus and, while there were properties on either side of them and a few farther along, it seemed they were all homes away from homes—likely wealthier people from Tehran who came up to Chalus for a weekend at a time. In any event, Plato and Margaret had a beautiful private home here on the beach.

"What brings you here, Margaret? I mean to Iran, and Chalus?"

"Plato, I think. As you know, he works in Tehran and heads up here as much as he can, and I'm free to come and go as I please to do my 'stuff' around the world. We both enjoy our lives, and we certainly enjoy each other. Bit of a funny mix, I guess, but it works. Strangely, Chalus is one of the few places we've discovered in the world that seems free of all the BS in everyone's lives." Margaret shriveled her nose up and frowned at the thought of what she was saying. She shrugged and took a gulp of cold beer. "And you?"

"Business," Matthew said. "I have some business with Plato, and I'll be going on to Sari after that. Business again."

"Oh, I know all about that stuff, Matthew. You don't have to be shy with me." Margaret flicked at Matthew's shoulder and smiled a little wider. Her eyes were twinkling. "ORB and stuff. The project and things. Dealing with the government. You know, all those things. Nudge, nudge, wink, wink." Margaret winked a long wink at him and twisted her lips up at the same time.

Very British, Matthew thought. "Oh, you do, do you?" He was quite relaxed as he sipped his beer. Despite his wariness, he took it for granted that Plato and Margaret were a pair. Stockman had mentioned it.

"Don't be surprised if the two of them don't work on all this together," he had told Matthew. He was right, although Matthew was not sure of the depth of their joint understanding or their understanding of what each other was up to. He would wait for Plato to turn up and then they could talk.

* * *

Following his brief conversation with Matthew earlier in the day, Plato had met with a group of bankers at their Melli headquarters in Tehran to discuss the continued movements of cash offshore and what they should do about it, if anything. Bank Melli Iran was the largest bank in the Middle East with history that went back to 1879; very few, if any, movements of money between Iran and elsewhere went beyond its notice, whether it came through Melli or not.

Before Plato met with the group, he called Stockman.

"Hello, old boy," Stockman answered the phone to a number he recognized as Plato's. "How are things in the heat?"

"Hotter than hell, Stockman. But look, I just wanted to check in. Matthew has arrived and is heading up to our place on the coast. Margaret will be there to meet him and I'll get up there later, but I wanted to brief you on these financial transactions that are going out from Iran."

"What have you got, Plato?"

It had not taken much for Stockman to convince Plato to provide his services to ORB. The payouts from ORB were spectacular and the causes always worthwhile but often dangerous, as this would have all the potential to be. Plato was already in Iran and making a good living with the bank. It was perfect, especially since it was with the Melli Bank, through which most government money passed, and Plato was on the foreign desk. His knowledge of world affairs was impeccable. He knew so many people and whoever he didn't know Margaret did through her father's dealings.

All Plato needed to know of ORB's business was what was needed of him. Fortunately, what was needed was exactly what he was doing, reporting on the cash flowing in and out of purse. Apart from that, Plato's knowledge of the Chalus area could prove very useful, especially as a support for Matthew should he need it.

"Well," Plato continued as he relayed some of the shenanigans going on at the bank, "it seems as though our Iranian friends are continuing their entrenchment with the Russians and the Chinese. The wired funds we are receiving for the Republic are in the millions and coming in at a rate of about three a week. There are no special instructions other than one very significant one. The incoming payments are divided into two, with one deposited to the account for the Republic and the other to an account in the Caymans. The account in the Caymans is registered to a company called Mana Developments."

"Wow, that's quite a chunk of information to handle," Stockman responded and paused as he thought about the circumstances and the consequences. "Now, I'm guessing that the Mana account requires a signature of a fellow called Mansourian and if you look behind the corporate cover, you'll find a number of Islamic Republic senior members. Thoughts?" Stockman waited.

"You could be right, Stockman. I can't prove anything yet without tipping my hand, but I have a person down there checking things out. Let's call it some due diligence, or perhaps it's going to just have to be bribery, but hopefully I will be able to call you in a week or so and let you know." Plato paused and waited for Stockman this time.

"Sounds good, Plato. I have to think about all this but do you have any idea of the total amount we are talking about?"

"Without opening the laptop, I'd say the Mana account balance is sitting at about $15 billion US and could be a lot more if there are associated accounts."

"Okay. I'm going to need some time to gather my thoughts and see where it sits in the scheme of things. Anything else?"

"Not yet. I'm just going to go into a meeting and then head up to Chalus. Maybe Matthew and I will contact you from there. There are some other things that we should talk about."

"Look forward to it, Plato. Talk soon and drive carefully. I know what those mountain roads are like."

They hung up and Plato wandered into his meeting. They talked about the transfers and what they needed to do for their due diligence. The bank was trying to stick to the international rules related to money laundering and terrorist accounts around the globe. Everyone was concerned with supporting terrorists these days, and it was a general rule that sums of money transferred or withdrawn in excess of $200,000 US had to be reported to the government authorities.

Mellis Bank didn't want to do this with every transaction and it weighed on the institution as it tried to make sure the right ones were selected for declarations. The bank was doing that with only those transactions it could prove were not for terrorist reasons. It wasn't interested in disclosing laundering efforts. Due diligence was essential.

* * *

Plato and Ali

Plato arrived in Chalus just after 8 p.m. in his red '67 Austin Healey 3000 convertible, with a small black leather weekend bag tossed into the passenger seat, his oversize sunglasses, an open-neck white shirt, a silk scarf hanging loosely around his shoulders, and a red mesh cabbie flat cap. Perfect for a drive through the mountains.

The car was immaculate but daring, in so far as one had to search for a good mechanic in Tehran to take care of the fifty-year-old beauty and there weren't many. In fact, there was only one. Plato had had it shipped from the US, which was where more than 90 percent of the AH 3000 production line ended up, and he had bought it from the estate of an enthusiast who died having never driven the car. According to his widow, he had just liked to look at it, smooth it, polish it, and occasionally sit in it, but that was the extent of his affair. It gleamed with original spoked wheels, seats, and engine.

Plato loved the car. It reminded him of his English youth when he had driven all manner of small sports cars from MGs to E-types. But the Austin Healey had a special place in his heart, likely associated with his first attempt at trying to be intimately involved with a delicious lady but failing miserably as he was constantly outmaneuvered by the shift stick, no matter what gear he was in. Now he had a habit of always running his hand over the length of the car body as he left it after a drive, and it was no different when he arrived at the house in Chalus and parked in front of the entryway.

"Matthew, how great to see you. It's almost as though I know you from just Stockman's description. Although I have to say, he hasn't said much, so I had to construct this picture of you from what I did know. Not bad, if I say so myself." He shook Matthew's hand vigorously then turned to hug Margaret and plant a kiss on her cheek. Margaret, in turn, punctuated the air with a smack of her lips that missed Plato's cheek by several inches. Undaunted, she led her husband to the patio and placed a cold beer in his hand as they all sat.

"Great to meet you, Plato. How long have you been here?"

"Well, if you mean 'here' generally, it's been several years. If you mean 'here' as in ORB here, it's been about four months since Stockman convinced me to come on board and, naturally, Margaret comes with me. We're sort of a team, you know." Plato smiled at Matthew and looked over at Margaret for confirmation.

"Yes, I'm well aware. I think the two of you have worked on at least one other project with Stockman. Is that right?"

"Well, there have been a few, actually, Matthew," Plato responded. "Where was the last one, Margaret? Do you remember?"

Matthew didn't believe Plato had forgotten for one second, but it was fun to watch him and Margaret interact.

"It was down in Nassau, honey. Don't you remember that to-do with the banks down there and all that fuss with Price Waterhouse? They just couldn't get the hands of that bunch of crooked managers out of the till." Margaret guffawed, and Plato let out a roar of laughter.

"Yes, yes," Plato was recalling the incident. "Seems as though the bank in question was undergoing a due diligence exercise by PWC. Well, the bank managers were being investigated, really. PWC figured out that the whole bunch of senior managers, including the bank president, had set themselves up with alternative personal accounts and were squirreling funds away from unsuspecting clients all 'round the world. It was the Saudis who cottoned on to it and noticed they were short by quite a few million at their year-end audit. PWC and the Saudis brought ORB in to find out what was going on. Anyway, it all got resolved in the long run." Plato gave Margaret a smile and an air kiss. She responded in kind.

"Sounds interesting." Matthew was genuinely interested but didn't want to deviate too much from the project at hand. He sensed it could well go that way with Plato and Margaret at the helm. "I think you'll find this project a little more complex with a lot of moving parts, so let's see if we can kick things off." Matthew took a couple of sips of his beer and put the bottle down. "What do you think your roles are, and where do you think we are, and what do we do next within that scope?" He laughed. "Asking a lot, aren't I?" They both shook their heads. "I can tell you what I know, how I fit in, and so on, but Stockman is really the coordinator, so I think it's fair to say it all goes through him to sort out in the end."

"All agreed, Matthew. Let me give you a bit of a picture from our standpoint. Margaret, jump in whenever you need." They all looked at each other and smiled.

Matthew clapped his hands together in the style of their illustrious leader, Stockman, as a signal to start.

"Okay," Plato started, "as you know, I work in the Melli Bank in Tehran on the international finance desk with a few others who are not ORB people. I've been there for about four years and built a solid reputation. My part of the plan is to keep an eye on the financials associated with the Islamic Regime or, to put it a better way, on their spending habits. I'm not looking at the check book, just the major foreign transactions, and there are quite a few."

"What is quite a few? And how significant are they?" Matthew wanted to know.

"I mentioned to Stockman earlier today that I think the Republic's personal share is around $25 billion US so far, held in an account for a company called Mana."

"Are they the same company that's working on the new plant? Some fellows by the name of... Man... Mansourian?"

"You've got it, Matthew. Mansourian is the owner of Mana and is a very close associate of the Islamic Republic's most senior cronies. It seems that Mansourian set up a company in the Caymans, but in a different bank from the Islamic Republic, also in the Caymans, and deposits are split fifty-fifty between the two accounts."

"Where's the money coming from?" Matthew was getting very interested. This was a new side of things that he hadn't heard about before, but he guessed that Stockman had had some inkling, enough to bring Plato and Margaret in.

"The money's currently primarily coming in from Russia and China, although there are also substantial amounts coming from other countries, including the US, the UK, and some in Europe for what we assume must be oil revenue. That money doesn't get split up. It all goes into the Republic account, but still in the Caymans. Now," Plato went on before Matthew could interrupt, "the Republic also keeps a substantially well-funded account here in Tehran for their expenses, and occasionally we are instructed to deposit money from other sources into it. Remember, this is the purse of government and the expenses to run it are enormous. This is where all the revenues go for public spending. I don't get involved with that since I'm on the foreign desk." Plato sat back and took a sip of his beer.

Margaret brought over a platter of finger food and more beers. She lit some candles for the table, shut off the lights, and lit a fire in the grate as the men watched, and then she went and sat down again next to Plato.

"So, do we know why the payments come from Russia and China?"

"No idea, but I am pretty sure it's not for oil because it doesn't come through the NPC. So, they must be payments for something else." Plato licked his fingers after picking up some food. Margaret passed him a napkin and gave one to Matthew.

"Our sources tell us that the money is some kind of a sweetener for future business. Aren't these pastries good?" It was Margaret, and Matthew looked over at her, quite stunned.

"What makes you say that, Margaret?" asked Matthew.

"You mean about the pastries?" She looked over at Matthew, who said nothing. "Sorry, you mean the other. Well, Daddy says the bastards are getting too close to the Regime, but unless you're prepared to pay more money, you're out of luck. Of course, it would help if you weren't American or British or anything close. All a bit of a nasty business, he says." Margaret reached for another pastry and spilled some of her beer on the table. "Whoops." She trotted off to get a towel.

"What does your father do, Margaret?" Matthew called after her.

"Oh, a bit of this and a bit of that. He works for the American government as some sort of negotiator. He seems to have a lot of influence with quite a few countries—a kind of backroom, or should I say backdoor, guy." She was busy moving things around on the table as she wiped up the beer, then walked over to the fridge and grabbed another one. She cracked it open with the shovel end of a tablespoon. "He travels an awful lot and sometimes visits us here in Iran. I think he catches up with a few of the old guard who are hanging on in their executive bunkers; hard to believe that, isn't it, with all that's going on? But détente must go on, as they say, in the world of embassy politics. Anyway, he gets to meet with his counterparts in the Russian and Chinese embassies. He says the Chinese aren't that friendly but once you get some vodka into a Russian, well, off they go. You know how it is." Margaret looked up with a knowing look at Matthew and waited for his nod of understanding. Margaret was a mine of high politics. Stockman probably knew that.

"What's the word with them, Margaret? About the money, I mean," Matthew asked.

"Oh, as I said, Daddy thinks it's all parti-barsi money, you know, you scratch my back and all that. There are some huge prizes at stake in Iran, as you know, and all of us know where Russian and Chinese dreams are. Get rid of the US dollar, create a petrodollar, become the financial center of the world, and push the power of the West down the toilet. Iran thinks of it as becoming an Islamic world but they really don't know the Russians or the Chinese that well, and neither of those has much time for the other either. It's going to be a very interesting future." Margaret stared at the last pastry sitting on the plate, waiting to be eaten. "That money is supposed to be for the Iranian Republic and the Iranian people. But, same old, same old... the money disappears into the pockets of the least wanting. In this case, the Islamic Regime, their cronies, and I suspect some senior members of the Revolutionary Guard."

"Okay." Matthew was getting tired from his travels. "Let's move on. What's your sense of things around here? Well, from here through to Sari and the whole coastal region. I heard there was a lot of movement with the youth as well as with the unionization attempts. Not much news gets out, so tell me what you know."

"Well, we don't really keep in touch with anything going on at the refinery, nor what's happening in Sari. I generally keep to the financial side of things. We're a little out of the Sari situation. We go over there occasionally but we generally head over west to Rasht. It's a bigger city and a little more Westernized after all the industry that was going on over there a while back. Anyway, I'd like you to meet Ali, our very good friend, who used to own this place. He'll be a mine of information and is an ORB person. He has a lot of information about the social aspects of this part of the world." Plato waved an arm around the room. "He should be here shortly. He still stops by and stays, but he's really based in the US now. He went there about twenty years ago, started his own business in construction in Kentucky and is very successful. He has some good insights as to what's happening in Iran. In fact, I think I hear his car now." Plato got up. "I can tell his car a mile off. It's a Maserati with those extra loud exhaust pots. It sounds fabulous." Plato opened the front door, and Matthew could hear him greeting someone.

They both came through the house, Plato's arm draped over the shoulder of his friend. They were laughing at some private joke. Ali headed straight to Margaret and took her hand to his lips and kissed it gently.

"My Margaret. How are you, and how is this brute treating you?" he looked over at Plato, who was smiling.

"Oh, the same as usual, over-pampering and generally torturing me with kindness and gifts. It's all getting too much to take." She smiled and introduced Matthew.

"A pleasure to meet you, Matthew. I hope these two are helping you to get acquainted with things here."

"Well, we haven't had a chance to move from this spot yet but hopefully we will. Perhaps tomorrow before I head over to Sari. And you, Ali, may I call you that?"

"Of course, Matthew. I have no other name that you could pronounce, so Ali is good."

"Let's all sit and catch up on things." Plato guided them to the sofas inside the living area.

The place glowed as the candles and fire lit the darkness, casting shadows into the corners and on each other's faces.

"I don't know if you are aware, Matthew, but Ali is also with us on the ORB project. He provides advisory services and keeps his eyes on the Mana business dealings. He knows the owner, Mansourian, very well, and they socialize whenever the two of them are in the same area at the same time. That is not to say Mansourian is aware of anything our friend here is doing for ORB. Mansourian is, after all, a very suspicious character and one we are well acquainted with. Mansourian is just another source of information for us." Plato rested and gave his friend the room.

"No, I hadn't realized Ali was a part of the group, but I'm sure there are many others that Stockman has asked to help out. Please, Ali, perhaps you can tell me what you're seeing out there."

"I don't think I need to talk about Mansourian and the Caymans bank account. I assume Plato has filled you in on those things." He stopped and looked over at Plato, who nodded. "What I can tell you is that the Russians are increasing their presence at the site of the refinery. I don't think it will be more than two people working within the ranks, but it's difficult to tell right now. There could be some living in Sari but not working at the refinery who are there as eyes and ears only, and there could be more, perhaps Iranians on the Russian payroll, who are also working at the plant that we are unaware of. Who knows, but one has to be extra cautious." Ali paused.

"Where does Mana fit in?" Matthew asked.

"As you probably know, Mana is a large contractor that has civil work on the project, so it has no mechanical or electrical knowledge, and will be on site until the end, I'm sure."

"And, as far as I know, Mana will be on the next phase as well." Matthew interrupted.

"Yes, Mansourian mentioned that in our last conversation. Now, the Russians that we know about are on the Mana payroll in management positions. That means they're attending meetings, mixing with the client and the other contractors. I believe it's all about listening and watching and reporting. But I'm sure their orders are also to act if there's anything that seems out of sorts, shall I say. And, by that, I mean it would not surprise me if they were required to get rid of some people on the project who they thought might be a problem. Mansourian is on top of these things and I believe he reports directly to Moscow as well as to the Islamic Regime. I don't know if he tells them the same stories. He's very cautious with a history of playing all sides. I wouldn't be surprised if he hasn't already tried to infiltrate Domar's ranks." Ali paused again to take a skip of his chai.

"Okay, well, I'll keep my eyes open for him. Can you get me the names of his Russian employees when the time comes?" Matthew asked.

"The one who's there now will be replaced and one more added. I'll get you their names as soon as I know them. Now, let's talk about what's happening with the people." Ali sipped the chai that Margaret had made for him.

"Yes, I'd heard there had been some trouble as well as a bit of an uprising of sorts but, again, there is a blackout in the Iranian news on these things, so anything I know has been passed down to us from observers.

"There was an explosion a while ago in the cinema here in Chalus. There were more than 200 young people who died. They were attending the first open conference on the Friends of Iran, a new populist movement started by some educated young Iranians recently returned from their studies in America. No one, other than perhaps the Revolutionary Guard, knows for sure who was responsible but it's rumored that the Tudeh Party could have been behind it. We just don't know. And there's an alternative theory among the people." Ali sat back and watched the others for their reactions.

"Oh." Plato, Margaret, and Matthew perked up their ears.

"Yes, and a very strong candidate for the truth, I'm afraid." Ali paused more for effect. He clasped his hands together on his lap and leaned forward in a conspiratorial manner. "It is being said that it was the Islamic Regime or more likely the Revolutionary Guard who orchestrated this."

"What!" Margaret was almost out of her seat in surprise. The others sat with their mouths open, waiting for the follow-up.

"Yes, my friends, that is the word on the streets. It was the Regime itself, pushed to act to rid themselves of this young, revolutionary group, even though their leaders had openly promoted the concept of more freedom and religious tolerance. Chalus had the largest group of followers, and the northern part of Iran has always been ripe for dissension. Perhaps the rumors are right, but we just don't know for sure. If they are, then who knows what the future will bring but you can be sure that the Regime's screws on the country will be tightened even further." Ali stopped, drank the rest of his chai, and sat back in his armchair.

The fire sparked as Plato put another log on. It was getting late, but the conversation had not tired them. They sat in silence, staring into the new flames and feeling the warmth float over their bodies. Margaret went over and slid the doors closed. The breeze coming in over the Caspian was doing its work to move the humidity south to the mountains.

Matthew interrupted the silence.

"You know, I think I'm going to turn in. It's been a long day, and I have a lot to think through. Plato, I'm going to give Stockman a call from upstairs. Is there anything you want me to tell him?"

"I talked to him this morning, Matthew. I may call him in the morning, but I don't have anything new just yet. I want to find out more about the banking in the Caymans, so I'll call him once I've found out something. Just say hi from us all here."

"Okay, goodnight all. Are you staying over, Ali?"

"Yes, I'll see you in the morning. Goodnight, Matthew. Great to meet you."

It was clear that the others would talk a little more as they moved down to the steps of the Tayaki pit and brought out the hookah.

Margaret had already described where Matthew's room was in the house. It had windows overlooking the Caspian and they were wide open. A soft, humid breeze wafted through.

"Hello, Stockman. Matthew here." Matthew had put the call in to Stockman as he closed the door to the bedroom.

"Hello, Matthew. How are things? Arrive safely?" Stockman seemed jovial. It was about 8:30 p.m. in London. Stockman would be catching up on his paperwork.

"So far, so good. I'm staying over at Plato and Margaret's place in Chalus. Ali is here. Do you know him?"

"Yes. He's a player with us, although it's primarily as a watchdog over that fellow, Mansourian. You know, the gentlemen we don't trust. How's Ali doing?"

"Ali seems to have a pretty keen sense of him. He may be a very useful addition to take the temperature of the social-political situation for us. He and Mansourian sometimes lunch together and he has the same feelings as us. He has known him for quite a few years, and I gather he has always looked at him as more of a gateway than a friend," Matthew optimistically observed.

"I'm sure the reverse is true as well, Matthew. No love lost there, but the relationship is something that neither wants to give up on."

"I gather that. Anyway, it seems that Mansourian is the conduit for the Russians coming into the project from Kabul. He only knows of two that will be placed with Mana, but he is open to believing there could be more in Sari as well as on the project site. Ali believes they are there to just watch things, but he's also warning that they can be pretty unscrupulous and may be prepared to take people out when they think there is a reason."

"All the more reason to be extra diligent, Matthew. You had better get James educated to that when you see him. Have to have a word with him about his wife as well. We should put some security for them all when they're out and about, especially in the bazaar. They'll stand out like a sore thumb, and if the Russians think James is up to anything, well... you know what I'm getting at."

"I do. Are you going to organize security or do you want me to do it from here, Stockman?"

"Until you get your feet on the ground, it'll be a little difficult for you to arrange too much just yet. Leave it with me, and I'll let you know what I've done. I'll probably have a word with Ali and see what he may be able to find out."

"I think you're right, Stockman." Matthew paused. "Do you know anything about the social unrest going on up here? A cinema was bombed out a while ago in Chalus, and it sounds like there are fingers pointing at the Islamic Republic. That's not public knowledge, though. The word that's been officially put out is that it was a member of the Tudeh Party, so it sounds as though someone or some group is trying to implicate the communists. Any thoughts?"

"Yes, I heard." Stockman coughed. "But I haven't got any word yet that it was actually the Republic. But it wouldn't surprise me if it was behind it. There's maybe a tie of some kind to the refinery, but I don't think so. But I should let you know that the father of one of the main figures with the Friends of Iran, the group that got blown up in the cinema, is not only on the refinery operations team but also the leader of the new union movement. If he's successful with the union, it'll send ripples through the Regime as everyone will want to join it. So, he's going to have to be very, very cautious about who his friends are. See if you can meet with him next time you're in Chalus. Or, better still, see if you can have Ali talk to him. Intel tells me they know each other."

"Sounds good, Stockman. I'm off in the morning to Sari. If all goes according to plan, I'll be seeing James tomorrow evening."

"Great. Now look after yourself and keep a low profile if that is possible for you."

"Talk later." They ended their call at the same time.

Matthew leaned out of the window and took in a few strong breaths of air. He left them open but pulled the shutters over, undressed, did his ablutions, had a drink of vodka, and lay down. If he thought he was going to do nothing but stay awake and think all night, he was wrong.

* * *

Matthew was greeted by laughter as he reached the bottom of the stairs the next morning, travel bag in hand. There was fresh naan and fruit on the table with a pot of coffee and stainless steel and glass samovar with cups and honey sitting to one side. Margaret greeted Matthew with a wide smile and Plato and Ali nodded to him. He pulled out a chair and poured himself a coffee with a little honey.

The sliding doors were open wide, and the breeze from the Caspian freshened the place up.

"Any plans, Matthew?" Plato asked.

"I think I'm going to head over to Sari this morning and meet up with James this evening."

Ali interrupted. "That sounds like a plan. It'll take you just over two hours if you go through Amol and a bit longer if you drive the coast road through Babolsar. The coast road isn't much, though. There's no view and the road's in terrible condition. Do you know where you're going once you get to Sari?"

"I'm staying at the Ghorbani Hotel over on the east side until I can figure out what's what and where the best place to stay will be. It's in my GPS. I've got James's address locked in as well, and I'll call him from the road."

"Oh?" It was Ali. "You may find the Salas Darreh Hotel much better, Matthew. It's modern with a good restaurant and a view over the valley. It's only about ten miles to the east of Sari but on the road to the refinery. I think you'd really like it a lot more than living in a hotel in the middle of town. I'll make a reservation for you." Ali was standing a little off to the side. He put his hand out and Matthew shook it.

"Thanks, Ali. That would be great. Would you send me your contact numbers and the address of the hotel, please?"

"Of course. I'll do it right away. Plato has your number?"

"He has. Margaret, would you also send me yours?"

"Will do. Now drive safely and don't get into too much trouble over in Sari."

"I'll be careful, I promise." Matthew winked at Margaret. "Many thanks for the hospitality. Plato, I'll be in contact shortly. Would you let me know if there's anything that comes up that you think could be useful for me, even if you think it trivial? It might help complete the picture." Matthew shook Plato's hand as he led him to the door.

"Of course, Matthew. Anything you need, just call. If you need to get out of town, just come on over. You can stay as long as you like." Plato waved to him as Matthew threw his bag into the Jeep and got behind the wheel.

"Take care, you guys." Matthew gave a short wave, headed out of the drive, and suddenly hit the brakes before he got out onto the road. He reversed and Plato came out to meet him.

"Everything good, Matthew?" he asked, looking concerned.

"Just one thing for Ali, if I could just go back inside."

"Of course, come on."

"Ali," Matthew called as he went into the front hallway. Ali appeared and came to him.

"Ali, I forgot to ask if you could make contact with Jafaar Sazesh in Chalus."

Ali looked perplexed.

"He's a very good friend of mine, as it happens, old schoolmates, and he's the father of Amir, the regional leader of Friends of Iran who almost died in that cinema explosion. What do you want me to do?"

"I need to know how well he is doing with union membership and whether he has noticed any threatening subversive activity that could block them? Also, with nearly 200 young people killed in that cinema blast and his son barely escaping, I'd think the Friends of Iran are still recovering, even after nearly two years. But I need to know how well they have recovered and if Jafaar thinks there is any additional danger for them. He likely won't know but I would think his son is up to speed, having gone through that terrible night. Are you good with that?"

"Of course, Matthew. I'll look into it right away and contact you."

"Great." Matthew backed out of the door, jumped back into the Jeep, and drove out onto the road to Sari.

There was a lot to think about and he needed this time to mull it all over.

*   *   *

Moving On

The drive to Sari was uneventful. Matthew took the route through Amol, a fairly quiet city with little traffic, and nothing in particular attracted him enough to stop for a short break. The approach to Sari was grand compared to the other populated areas Matthew had come through. There was a dual carriageway with palm trees and neatly manicured grass through the center, and some small shops dotted the route. He passed a Kentucky Fried Chicken outlet that showed Colonel Sanders with long flowing red hair and matching beard. It made him smile, and he glanced down at the map for guidance as he came into the more built-up area of the city. He knew he was going to have to make a turn south in the middle of town onto Highway 81, which would take him about ten miles out of town to the Salas Darreh Hotel on Kiasar Road.

The hotel was perched on a terrace above the Sari Valley, just a few miles north of where the refinery was being constructed. It was a beautiful location outside the city. The air was heavy with humidity and the temperature up in the nineties, but the hotel was air-conditioned and well-appointed. Matthew's room was a small apartment with a living area, bedroom, and small kitchen with French doors that led out onto a well-kept lawn. He was pleasantly surprised; all he had read about Sari was that it was a somewhat rudimentary settlement in the north. That wasn't true, and the city was several notches above that. But he had only seen the better, western part at this point. There was a darker, poorer side of life in the eastern side that one didn't see when approaching it from Tehran.

Matthew called the front desk for chai and waited while he freshened up. The chai arrived with some sweet pastries and fruit. He called James, who was still at work at site.

"Hey, Matthew. Glad you made it. Are you coming over to the apartment?"

"Yes, I thought we might sit and chat for a while, James. Meet the family, and then perhaps we can spend an hour or so somewhere where we can have some privacy and talk about things."

"You bet. Now, you have our address. Would you rather I pick you up or…"

"No, that's okay. I'll find my way over. About seven?"

"Great. Are you stopping for supper?"

"I think I'm going to eat right now. I'm famished and haven't eaten all day."

"No problem. See you this evening."

Their phones switched off.

Matthew made it down to the hotel restaurant and tried out the *koobideh*, a kebab with ground meat seasoned with minced onion, salt, and pepper on a bed of *chelo*, rice with saffron and cooked in butter, with soda water on the side. No beer here. The *koobideh* was similar to the Turkish favorite of his called *kofta*. There they would grill the seasoned meat in flattened balls and serve the small patties with a naan-type bread. Simplicity itself but a delicious sandwich one could eat on the run.

It was still early and Matthew decided to head over to the refinery to get a sense of the activity, location, and degree of completion. He would take in the security as best he could. Then a trip through the city would be next on the agenda to get his bearings and identify any landmarks that might be important.

Matthew drove down to the refinery. It was well under construction with the vast majority of the towers standing and the cracking units installed. The turbines, generators, and compressors were being set, from what he could tell from a distance. The large bore piping had been installed and the cooling tower structure construction was well underway. The boilers were being hauled into place, and the pipe racks and electrical cable trays erected and being loaded. *Yes*, he thought, *the plant could well be on schedule for completion within six months or so.*

The place was crawling with construction people. The only security that stood out was on the gate at the entrance to the property, and it was substantial. The guards were armed, the barriers were doubled, and all vehicles entering or leaving were searched, including having mirrors under the carriages. Trucks had been pulled off to one side before entering and were being searched before being allowed onto the property. Trucks coming out were being diverted to a holding area and searched for stolen goods.

Two guard towers stood about 100 feet in the air with guard dogs and armored vehicles at the ready at the bases. The site was surrounded by double-wide six-foot-high chain-link fences, topped with barbed wire, and a flooded trench between the two. There were spotlights mounted high above the plant, facing in and out of the plant along the length of the perimeter fencing, with warning horns mounted on the poles. All passenger vehicles and employee buses were parked in an area separated from the plant by more double-row fencing sitting twenty feet apart, with an employee alley and ten-person timeclock runs for the employees entering and leaving the plant.

Matthew assumed everyone needed a magnetized badge that activated a responder connected to central security each time a person entered or left an area within the plant. Everyone was accounted for at all times.

The area was bound by the Tajin River on the east, the road on the west, and open valley on the north and south sides. Matthew parked on a terrace above the plant for a while as he stared down at the activity. It brought back so many memories of both good and bad times. In many ways, he missed them. After about fifteen minutes, he started the Jeep and circled back toward the city.

He passed James's apartment on Saba. His was the upper storey of a two-storey building with a courtyard in the front for parking. He didn't stop and carried on east before taking a loop around the residential area, looking for any signs that might indicate a government office of any kind, but all the signs were in Farsi. Matthew felt lost without being able to understand anything around him. He could need an interpreter but decided to persevere until it became a real problem.

He saw a signpost in English, showing the direction to the Neka Shahid Salimi Power Plant, probably for the foreign workers there, and decided to take a drive there to take a look. The plant was located close to the Caspian Sea shoreline, some five miles north of the town of Neka and twelve miles to the east of Sari. The plant was constructed as four steam units that relied on light-duty diesel for some 50 percent of its operation and natural gas for the other 50 percent, with all feedstocks provided from Iranian sources. This was the largest combined cycle plant in the Middle East and, despite the Iraqi bombing attack back in 1986, it continued to power the majority of the north of Iran with its 2,100 MW of electricity. The planned expansion would double the number of units to add sufficient power needed for the refinery and additional industry to service it.

Like the refinery, security looked extreme with the entire area fenced in, lighted, and guarded. The plant had been fully operational since 1981, when the last of the four units was commissioned. They were getting old and needed constant servicing. It looked as though the earthworks had already been started for the expansion to the east.

Matthew thought how useful it would be to have a technical person working inside the plant, preferably in the control room, for when the new refinery needed power. He would have to see how he could arrange that with Stockman. It was getting late, and Matthew headed back to Sari.

He parked his Jeep outside the apartment on Saba and rang the doorbell on the gate pillar. A female voice answered, released the lock, and the gate swung open.

"Hi, I'm Jenny. You must be Matthew." James's wife opened the apartment door, greeted Matthew, and led him into the living area where James was opening a couple of beers, and the three boys sat in front of a television watching cartoons in Farsi.

"Great to meet you both. How are things going here in the backwater?" They laughed.

"Oh, it's much worse than that." James handed a beer to Matthew and led them over to the sofa. "Well, it's not all that bad, really. I guess the biggest thing is the language. Can't understand a word of it and neither of us have any linguistic skills. It's tough enough keeping up with English." They all laughed again.

"How are the neighbors and the townspeople?" Matthew asked.

"Sometimes okay and sometimes a little off, I'd say. What about you, Jenny? Are you sensing any issues at the bazaar?"

"Difficult to tell, really. The men are the same as they always were, trying to pinch my butt and then looking the other way, and the women are so covered up you don't know what they're thinking, but everyone is pretty civil. There seems to be something going on in the background with groups mumbling, but I don't think there's any ill feeling toward us Westerners so much. I overhear some of them really getting into it, and there's some pushing and shoving these days that never used to happen. We were wondering if it has anything to do with what happened over in Chalus with the bombing. I think things started to deteriorate after that." Jenny looked over at James.

"Yes, I think you're right. That's about the timing. I know we had quite a number of people off work after that for a few days and when they came back they were all pretty sullen. But they don't tend to share their feeling with foreigners," James added.

"Other than that, I don't think we've noticed much else. Our would-be English-speaking Iranian friends stopped coming around for a few days, but they started up again and have been friendly enough, so..."

"How's work, James?"

"Pretty good. Things are really rolling along now. I have a completely mad boss—we call him Mad Max—but we manage to work around him and get things done. Fortunately, I have some good Indian friends who work with me, and they're excellent. They just ignore him. I don't put any stock in him being a problem to us for the future. In fact, my guess is that he and his wife, Angel, will be out of here over the next few months. Too many run-ins with IDRO, and he just doesn't have the brainpower to be indispensable at this point. He's a bit of a leftover from the old days and managed to stay while the rest of the *ferengies* left years ago."

"That would be Max, I assume." Matthew guessed.

"That's the man. Max, Mad Max. Oh well, in the end, he's just an irritant but he has no understanding of what we're building here. We have some pretty good guys here looking after things. They're all contracted through Dick Elliot or Interstate like I am," James explained. "They're professionals, and I hear there are quite a few more to come over as we ramp up to commissioning."

"What about the workforce, James? Are they all Iranian, or do we have some Westerners mixed in there?"

"There are quite a few Americans and Brits, some Germans and French, and even some females managed to get through. Most of the heavy trades are loaded with *ferengies*, and the female contingent is particularly specialized in things like welding, high voltage, and controls."

"Do you get to see the welders, James?"

"Oh yes, if they're out from their positions, I do. They need breaks fairly often. That's a crappy job, being in all those positions."

"Do you know if a lady by the name of Emma Stockman is part of that team?"

"She is, Matthew. Do you know her?"

"We worked on a couple of projects together. She's one hell of a welder. I should catch up with her."

She would be staying at the camp and Matthew wanted to contact her as soon as he could. It was time for them to get together. It had been far too long since their last romp. Maybe get her out of there for a night or a weekend over in Chalus. He liked that idea and put it on his list of items to do.

"There's no way the Iranians have the expertise to get involved with the kind of sophisticated equipment, piping, electrical, and instrumentation that we have here. In fact, we probably have about 400 *ferengies* on site. They all stay at the camp a little farther to the south from the plant. Did you see it yet?"

"No, I went down as far as the refinery, but no farther. I hadn't thought there was anything to see down there."

"The camp is enormous. I mean it's all concrete, huge recreation and canteen, and a lot to do for everyone. I'm pretty sure the Iranians want to keep the expats all locked up there rather than letting them wander into town where it's too difficult to keep track of them all. If you saw the plant, then you would have seen the security, and it's no different at the camp. If anyone does want to go into town, they get a driver, and the driver is a security guard. They can go in by themselves, but it has to be under their own power."

They each took a slug of beer.

"How are the boys doing here?"

"Pretty good, considering," Jenny responded. "They eat the food, sleep okay, and there's a bit of a school now, so that keeps our four- and six-year-olds busy for part of the day. Every now and again, I make a trip to Tehran. I have a friend there, and I stay at her place. It's a good break. There are also a few ex-pat wives here in town. They're married to some of the managers who live off-site." Jenny paused.

"It sounds as though you've all settled as best you can." Matthew waved his arm around the apartment they had decorated with native art. There were flowers, statues, ornaments, and all the accessories that go to make a house a home. They had done a good job.

"Thoughts on the project start-up timeline, James?"

"Oh, at this rate, we'll likely start to commission the utilities in four to six months, and it should take another four months or so to commission the rest of the plant."

"Are you keeping in touch with Dick?"

"We speak about once a month. He hasn't been up here yet, but there's nothing that he doesn't already know. I think he's coming up for a progress meeting with IDRO and operations in a couple of weeks."

"Any ideas about the new pipeline from Tehran?" Matthew asked. He hadn't seen any signs of it on his journey through the Alborz.

"We don't have much to do with the pipeline, but I go out there now and again to get a sense of progress. There are some ex-pat rig welders over there that I communicate with. It sounds as though they're on schedule. That's tough country to come through up in the mountains, but they have the right equipment and about twenty pipe-laying machines. All that pipe has to be x-rayed, so it's going slow but failure rate is low with those welders—they have to be some of the best in the world. I hadn't realized, but they build their rigs wherever they go with the latest equipment. They must earn a fortune."

"Where do they stay?"

"They move their camps with them every fifteen miles or so. There's a permanent crew that comes in to dismantle and move the camp to the next spot. There are two twenty-person camps and they leapfrog them, so there's always a place to stay while they dismantle or re-assemble one. Once they have one of the camps habitable, they move on to the next spot, get it ready for the next move, and dismantle the other camp. It's a hell of a system. I think everyone's on a three-month on and one-month off schedule, which is enough time to leave the country for some R and R."

"How many pipes are they installing?"

"Two thirty-six-inch wrapped steel pipes, with a couple of twelve-inch-diameter ones to carry other products up here."

"Sounds good, James. Can we take a drive and look at some of the interesting parts of the city?"

"You bet. Let me get my boots."

Jenny started to round up the boys for their baths before bed.

"I won't join you, Matthew." She smiled at him.

Matthew smiled back. "I understand." He gave the boys a pat on their heads and gave Jenny a reassuring touch on her arm. *Better her than me*, he thought.

They used the Jeep, and James guided Matthew around the city, pointing out places such as the mosques, the bazaar, and the local Revolutionary Guard facility. There was a small police station close by and, two blocks east of that, an apartment building on Taleb Nataj where they stopped for a few minutes.

"This is a part of the story I'll explain to you in a few minutes. I just need to give you a little background first." He looked over at Matthew. Matthew shrugged and they drove on.

"When I first came here, I wasn't sure what I was supposed to be looking for, if anything. Dick just wanted me to keep my eyes and ears open, on site and off." James started. "Well, for sure, on site there is a lot more security than I would ever have imagined, and I can tell you it runs from top to bottom." He paused.

"What do you mean, top to bottom?" asked Matthew.

"It's everywhere. I don't know who's employed to be official security at site, who's just a plain snitch, and who's just doing it for fun. But I can tell you that everything gets reported back to central; that's security central, located in a separate building from the main office. Then there are the IDRO crew, who seem to be both technically inclined as well as amateur sleuths who snoop around the expats all the time. Despite that, I'm pretty sure they really lack the high-end technical skills needed to understand the more complex aspects of this project. In other words, they may be spying on everyone, everywhere, but they don't necessarily catch on to what's really important for us—or for them, that is."

"Give me an example of what you mean." Matthew was fairly sure what James meant, but he wanted clarification as well as to better understand how deeply James was involved.

"Take the control system, for instance. Or the electrical circuits. Or the process itself. None of that is ever in question. No one's ever looking over the shoulders of the guys who actually do that stuff because they wouldn't know what they were looking at. They just spy on people, their movements, whether they're taking things, talking about things they shouldn't be talking about, not working when they should be, all that kind of stuff. But the real stuff gets missed, or should I say overlooked. You could get away with just about anything technical, and they wouldn't cotton on."

Matthew raised his eyebrows.

"What's your role on site?"

"I'm a bit of a jack-of-all-trades, but my reason for being here is really as a project engineer on the olefins side of the projects. That's the heart of the plant."

"Yes, I know. I've worked on a few. That's where all the refined products like ethylene and propylene and those things are distilled out," Matthew noted.

"Yes, sort of. But it also includes the distillation and cracking processes, as well as the steam generation, turbine and compressor station and cooling systems, so it's a part of the project where the main action is, and it's the most expensive part of the project. That's where the biggest bucks are spent and where the equipment can take up to years to manufacture and deliver. That's where we need to focus our attention and, strangely, that's where the least amount of security is. Other than lights, two or three guards wandering around with flashlights, and dogs, there's nothing else.

"I'm pretty sure there are no cameras because the angles change so much with everything being installed. You can't get any line of sight that would last for more than a few days before it would be blocked by a piece of equipment, a tower, a crane, pipe in the air, a millwright's shack, or whatever."

"That's good to know, James. What about off-site? Any activity that you're aware of that needs attending to?"

"As a matter of fact, there is. You remember the place we stopped next to back there on Taleb Nataj?"

"Yes, the two-storey apartment building with a courtyard just like yours."

"That's it. Well, I don't want to bore you with the whole story, but it seems that a commander in the US forces stationed at the Gorgan listening post... have you heard of it?"

"Yes, Stockman filled me in. It's one of the places I need to get to know a little better."

"Well, this commander has a girlfriend, and that's where they meet to do their thing, if you know what I mean." James paused as he looked over at Matthew and tapped the side of his nose in that "you know what I mean" type of way. Matthew nodded his understanding. "If that was all there was, it probably wouldn't be worth reporting, but I hung around a couple of times and watched the commander leave and saw the woman with another guy. It looked fishy enough that I took a look inside when they weren't there and it seems to me, at least, that this lady is being run by the Revolutionary Guard or the militia, and maybe both. While the commander is there with his lady, there's this guy who hides in a closet and records everything that's said. Once the commander leaves, the lady hightails it with the guy two blocks away to the military base and in they go. It's funny, but he always seems to have to drag her as though she doesn't really want to go. I don't know what the deal is with that, but it's probably worth exploring a little more," James suggested.

"Boy, that sounds interesting. Has anyone seen her leave the base after her visits there? Any thoughts?" Matthew was very interested in this latest piece of news. It was something he didn't know anything about.

James dropped his voice further as he whispered, "I've never waited around long enough to see the lady leave the base. But I have a friend who works at the Gorgan station, drives this commander, and tells me generally what's going on. It seems as though they listen to all the chatter going in and coming out from Iran, and Russia and China are the biggest talkers. Don't ask me what they talk about just yet, because I haven't got that far, and I'm not sure I can. My friend can't tell us everything about his job, and even my knowing about him working there and driving this commander is really more than he wanted me to know. But..."

"That's great, James. When do you see this friend of yours?"

"Four days in a row each week, with the first day of the next row being tomorrow."

"And your friend—does he drive this commander every time?"

"That's the only reason he's able to get into town. The commander wants his meetings with the lady and my friend does the drop off and the pickup, the same time every time. He comes over to visit with us and waits until it's time to pick him up at midnight."

"Let me think on this, James, and we can talk again soon." They drove on a little farther. "In the meantime, make sure you don't get caught. I think I'll do the watch tomorrow night and see if I can wait it out for the lady to leave the base. Maybe even follow her home."

"Sounds good." James was pleased his information seemed useful.

"Now that I think about it, James, see what you can find out about the woman, her name, where she works. We may need her on our side at some point. And see if you can find out the commander's full name?"

"Will do," James was quick to respond.

"Let's talk about the refinery again. I need to know what we have to do to get some people on the inside, in the trades."

"Oh, that's no problem, Matthew. Just work them through Interstate, and Dick Elliot will get them here. They are going to have to stay up at the camp, though. That means it won't be easy to liaise with them unless you're also on site."

"I will be, James. I'm going to come and go just like you, but I'll be attached to the operations team. My papers from Interstate should be ready shortly. I may even stay over at the hotel while I'm here. I really don't want to have to set up an apartment. If I'm going to be watched it doesn't really matter where I am, so I may as well be comfortable."

"I don't blame you. If you want to come visit any time, just say. Perhaps you'd like to come for dinner soon and meet my friend."

"Let me think about that. I don't want him getting suspicious, so it may be that I keep out of his way and just watch him from a distance."

"Okay, I'll leave it up to you. Anything else?"

"I was wondering about the Neka Power Plant. Do you have anything to do with that?"

"Nothing really, although every couple of weeks we have a coordination meeting, and someone comes over from the plant to make sure we're all in sync. Our main power lines come over from Neka, so there's some high-voltage integration that goes on with our substation guys. I can get you a name if you want."

"No, that's okay. I'll need to talk to someone over there at some point, but I want to make sure he's the right person. Dick or Stockman will know."

"Oh, before I forget," James leaned over, "there are some folks at the plant you should probably be in contact with. Hossein and his American wife, Liz. A very dynamic duo in the amateur politics of Iran, I would say. Likely future leaders or something like that. Very clever, articulate, and persuasive. They took on some temporary jobs at the plant, but they seem to be quite influential with the locals. You should meet them. Maybe they need to join forces with the other rebel groups and get something done." James smiled, but he was serious.

"Can you introduce us?"

"Absolutely. They're great company and very attuned to what's going on."

Matthew dropped James off at his apartment and headed back to the hotel to make a call to Stockman.

Stockman answered on the second ring.

"Hello, Matthew. Everything going, okay?"

"Stockman, you probably know about James's escapades with the listening post commander and so on, but I'm thinking of trying to enlist the commander so we can find out more about the verbal traffic at Gorgan."

"We already know, Matthew. I don't think the commander is going to be a help to us on the frontline. His first allegiance will be to his people, and I'd prefer him not to be blabbing to them about ORB. The Washington boys are already on our side with this, and they send me transcripts of everything they feel we should be aware of. That's probably a lot more than the commander knows. We started getting the reports about three months ago when the call came in on this project. We had to know what Iran was up to with the Russians in particular. Now our problem is whether the Iranians know we know, and if they're transmitting false information just to screw us up. We'd be better off to have someone on the inside of the Revolutionary Guard, but not even the Israelis have been able to do that, so we're looking at alternatives."

"It sounds as though you have it in hand, so let me think on how we may be able to find out. What about getting the girl involved?"

"You mean the commander's woman?"

"Yes. Let me do some watching and see if there's a way in there. If she agrees to help, we could have her talking to her military friends. A bit of a long shot, but she's the closest to them we know at this point."

"Well, you can try. We have no intel on her, but there could be a way in there. Go ahead and see what you can do."

"Will do. Other than that, there's not a lot to report. The pipeline from Tehran is well underway. Can you talk to Sloan about getting some field troops into the refinery here on the mechanical and electrical trades? That's where we will start with the initial delays."

"No problem, Matthew. I'll talk to him right after this call. He'll have to work through Dick Elliot, who can arrange all the paperwork. Shall we start with three of each?"

"I think we need a couple of millwrights, two high-voltage boys for the substation, and an instrumentation guy for calibration. Now, I had a look over the outside of the refinery and the power plant. Both are incredibly well guarded. They've got everything organized. Dogs, small arms, razor wire, armored vehicles, searchlights, lots of guards, and that's just what I can see on the perimeter. I'll know more once I get to site. Very suspicious lot, I would say."

"Well," Stockman interrupted, "I don't think they're getting anything from our side to make them that way. We're as tight as a duck's ass. Even the listening post isn't giving anything away, so it might just be the Russians they're antsy about. It sounds like the place could be crawling with them."

"I thought they were buddies with the Ruskies, Stockman."

"Yes, but not the most trustworthy buddies, as you know. Of course, it might just be them being a little sensitive to the international reactions to their plans, and they're just being extra cautious."

"I think that's more likely, but with the Russians you never know what they're up to. Anyway, they could just be bothered by the amount of *ferengies* they have on the property."

"Okay, Matthew, keep your eyes peeled and your nose sharp and keep in touch."

"Oh, by the way, I think Dick Elliot may be here in a couple of weeks. It sounds like he may be coming here for a project update meeting. Frankly, I wouldn't advise it. Perhaps you can let him know. There are just too many balls in the air right now, and I don't want him in the middle of anything."

"I'll take care of it, Matthew. Not to worry." Stockman went quiet. He was probably writing a note right then to Dick.

"One last thing, Stockman. I'm going to need a contact over at the Neka power plant that's on our side, so to speak. Can you arrange that?"

"Let me see what I can do. We have the Siemens people on board, and they'll likely have a rep we can rely on. They manufactured the generators for the plant and I'm sure they already have the order for the next batch for the expansion. I think they also have the contract for the gen sets over at the refinery, so we will definitely be needing their help." There was a pause. "Have you caught up with Emma yet?"

"I plan on it over the next couple of days. It sounds as though she's well entrenched with the boiler tube welders, and that's where she needs to be. I'll let you know how she's doing by the weekend."

"Thanks, Matthew. Talk later." The phones went dead.

Matthew took a walk around the grounds of the hotel. He could see the lights of the refinery, sitting down near the river in the distance. There seemed to be a lot of activity and clearly they were double shifting. Trucks were still going in and out. He would bring field glasses the next time he came out and maybe take a drive farther up the road, closer to the plant, and over to the camp just to get a better feel for things.

*   *   *

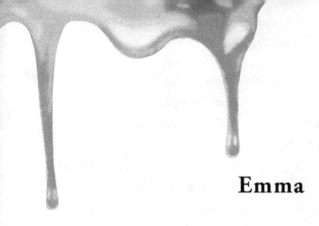

Emma

It was another hot, humid day with low-hanging clouds that smothered the view over the Sari Valley. Matthew sat in the hotel restaurant and planned his day.

He wanted to meet with Emma and called James at the refinery to contact her and let her know to call him.

She would be over in the boiler area, climbing in and around the tubes that needed welding. There were four sets of boilers in the new refinery to provide the high-pressure steam driving the turbines to run the compressors for the production of the petrochemical derivatives, including such things as polypropylene. The equipment included some of the highest-capital-cost items in the entire refinery, as well as the longest-delivery ones.

Each set of boilers comprised of one elevated steam drum and one lower "mud" drum joined by myriad steam tubes, each subjected to a top and bottom high-pressure weld and all x-rayed. Each drum shell was up to three inches thick. The tubes were the most difficult of all pipe welds because of the positioning of the body of the welder to get in and around the tubes that had to be first fitted into the matching holes in the boiler shells and then welded. Every pipe weld was subject to x-ray examination.

The tube shapes were prefabricated and the fit of each tube into the matching holes had to be precise. Once welded, these tubes would essentially be hidden from visual examination unless the boiler was shut down for maintenance when tubes might have to be changed out. A retrofit could last three months for each boiler island. Altogether, the high-pressure tubes had something like 3,000 one-inch-diameter welds.

Emma was in a perfect location for sabotage, and her history proved her to be one of the most successful welders in the business.

Matthew decided to take a drive up to Gorgan to look at the area around the mountain where the listening post was located. He took the highway from his hotel into the center of Sari, turned right onto Darab Boulevard, and headed east as far as Imam Reza Boulevard, which joined Highway 22, a twin-lane highway that went through Neka and on to Gorgan. It was an eighty-mile drive, and the traffic was light. Matthew headed into the center of the city, looking for a signpost to Ziarat, a village up in the mountains to the south of Gorgan. His GPS helped a lot. None of the roads ran in straight lines and sometimes the one-way streets were difficult to navigate, but he made it out to the edge of the city and looked up at the Alborz. He used his binoculars and searched the skyline for radio masts and communication towers. He spotted several, although some were for the city and others were for the listening post. He guessed which ones were for the post by their robustness and multi-faced communications-receiving plates mounted at the top.

There was only one road following the creek up to and through the village. The population of less than 2,000 lived in apartment buildings and houses built on terraces on the sides of a narrow road. The road needed maintenance; gullies had formed and small boulders showed through the rain-damaged surface. The runoff had flowed into the side ditches and jubes before over-flowing into the fields. Matthew drove through the center of the village, looking for a possible route up to where the radio antennae were. He found it going off to the east and followed the road around the multiple hairpins until he reached a fenced compound.

"This has to be it," he said to himself and spotted its coordinates on the GPS. Some vehicles passed him going down from the mountain and the occupants wore baseball caps and certainly did not look Iranian. No one took any notice of him as he parked near the gate but the area was well covered by security cameras.

The communications masts were up higher and farther to the southeast in what appeared to be a clearing on the flat top of a mountain. The only way to get up there seemed to be via a gravel trail likely only used for maintenance vehicles.

There was no point in Matthew going any farther. He saw what he had come to see. There were no peaks higher than the one where the towers were, and he assumed that there'd be the dryness of the desert beyond. Clearly, the sightlines for the towers would be excellent with a 360-degree view toward Tehran in the south and north over the Caspian Sea to Russia.

Matthew turned the Jeep around and headed back down through the village and on down to Gorgan, then back on to Highway 22 to Sari. He would save the sightseeing for another day. For now, he had a lot of other things on his mind.

"Hey Matthew," a cheerful voice sounded on the other end of the line as Matthew picked up on the first ring of his cell phone. "Guess who?"

"Emma, sweetie. How the hell are you?"

"I'm doing really well. It's a bit of a strange place, but I think I've been in stranger ones. What are you doing later?"

"Seeing you, I hope," Matthew responded without thinking about what he might have to do later. Whatever it was, it didn't seem as important as getting together with Emma. "Are you able to come over to the hotel after you've finished up there? We can share a kebab with a yogurt." He laughed.

"Oh, I'll bet you have all the girls coming after you with a line like that."

They laughed, and it felt good for both of them to talk to someone they knew in this foreign land.

"Listen, I have to get back to the job, Matthew. Can you pick me up at the main gate at around six this evening?"

"Looking forward to it. See you then. Take care."

Matthew cheered up considerably now that he had contacted Emma. Then he remembered his plan to track the commander's woman later that night. He decided that it could be better if both he and Emma followed her, and maybe Emma could sleep over. *Yes, things could turn out really well,* he thought as he cruised back to Sari and stopped near the bazaar to take a look around. He would buy something for Emma. It would give him an excuse to wander and kick back for an hour or so.

The Nargesieh Market was one of several in the city and the first one that Matthew spotted on his way through. It was teeming with life and saturated with stalls that displayed everything from socks, shoes, clothes, umbrellas, bags, figs, dates, nuts, coffee, and meat of every kind and every shape and size. Butchers stood ready with their machetes to carve off a chunk from whatever animal quarter one wanted as it hung there waiting. There were toys, candies, jewelry, collector's cards, electronics, CDs, DVDs, and games. The chadors flowed out from one end of the market to the other as they billowed out over the men. The older men wore suits, both grubby and smart. The younger men wore jeans and T-shirts. A smattering of mullahs created a gap through the crowds as they typically watched everyone with their sullen, miserable gray faces and long gray beards. Occasionally, Matthew would be suddenly faced with two or three black chadors pushing past with their spooky-looking silver beaks making them look like *Spy vs. Spy* from the comic book.

Matthew picked up a bag of assorted nuts and dried fruit, some nougat, and a handmade embroidered change purse. There was nothing else he could see among all the trinkets, cheap knockoffs, and sandals that appealed to him as any kind of a gift for Emma. He worked his way through the crowd, carried along by the crush of bodies, his nostrils taking in the pungent fumes of rotting fruit and vegetables, and meat hanging in the hot sun as he got an occasional nudge from behind. Nothing obvious, but it happened more often than it should. No one ever looked him in the eye afterward, and they were always careful to move in a different direction after it was done.

The women were no better than the men, but the younger ones gave him no trouble and, more often than not, wanted to engage him in English. Matthew patiently played their word games, laughed when they did, and patted them on their shoulders as he drifted away. He wanted to get out of the claustrophobia and smell of the place and was quite happy when he found an exit leading to one of the streets that bordered the market.

He made his way back to the hotel and spent an hour making some notes on his phone for his next conversation with Stockman. It was time to head down to the plant and pick up Emma.

She was already at the gate when he arrived, after going back to the camp to freshen up and change after a day in the cramped quarters under the boiler. She looked spectacular in a floral summer dress and a white scarf covering her head, or trying to, as some of short black hairs poked out to frame her face. *Fuck, she's beautiful,* he thought as his penis rose to the occasion—as it always did when he came anywhere close to her. *What's that all about?* He had asked himself time and time again, but it was true. He couldn't resist her proximity.

It was incredibly unnerving but sensual, intoxicating, irrational, and most likely pheromones. Who knew, but he was totally enamored by her proximity, her smile, her touch, and her aura. It was something that could not be explained in his world of thinking, but he fucking loved it.

She stood outside the security shack, trying to have some sort of a conversation with a friendly guard. It was tough going, and she was clearly relieved when Matthew arrived. She waved goodbye to the guards and hopped in the Jeep, smiling at Matthew as she threw her arms around his neck.

"Hi, babe. Not hiding this time around?" Matthew joked in reference to a previous project they were on together when her job was just to shadow him. It was all he could do to contain his impulsive erection again.

"Nope. I'm frontline this time, with Daddy's blessing." Her eyes smiled as well as her mouth. She was so glad to see him, and it showed in every way as they headed off to the hotel.

"How are you getting along out there with all that testosterone around you?" He really wanted to stop off somewhere and just make love, but...

"Oh, you know. I'm used to it, and after a while they just treat me like one of the guys. There are only two of us on the tube welding. The other's also a female. She's really good and almost keeps up with me. She beats the pants off the guys I've worked with before for speed and quality. We get along great and go out together on a night out now and again, not that there's much to see or do in the city for two gals, but we manage. It sort of closes down out there at around 9 p.m. and, of course, there's no alcohol and that means no clubs, no dancing, and no men, so we generally go back to the camp and play some pool."

"Living the good life, eh?"

"As good as it gets, you know. What about you? What's happening?"

"I only arrived in Sari yesterday. But I did stay over in Chalus on my way through. We have some ORB people over there looking into the government finances and a few other things. Great people. We should take a weekend out and head over there to spend a couple of nights with them. It's a beautiful spot, and the city has all the remnants of what the tourists left behind. They tell me there's even alcohol over there. Well, there certainly is where I stayed. "Matthew paused and smiled.

"Okay, I like the sound of that. Just give me the word, and I'll make sure to get away. What else have you been up to?"

"Well, I did go to the bazaar this afternoon for a look around. Boy, that's a bit of a scary place, what with black chadors everywhere, all pushing and shoving, and the men looking quite menacing."

"You know, I still can't figure out what to call all these chador things, so I call them all chadors. One day someone will take offense and put me right. Do you have any idea, Matthew?" She looked so beautiful yet fragile in these revolutionary surroundings. He wanted to lean over and kiss her, make love to her, but circumstances were not quite there...just yet.

"Well, the last time I was in London, I saw so many different types of Muslim women coverings that I asked a friend of mine to help me out. Let me see if I can remember it correctly. Do you really want to know?"

Her eyes said "yes" but her face wasn't sure.

"The hijab is really a headscarf that covers the head and neck but leaves the face clear. The rest is just normal everyday dress. It's the same as what you're wearing now. We see these a lot in Europe and North America with women who wear regular Western clothes. The niqab is just a veil that leaves the area around the eyes clear and is worn with a headscarf, again often with Western clothes. The burka is the most concealing and is a one-piece garment that covers the face and body, leaving just a mesh screen to see through. I've seen women wearing the burka as well as long, conical-shaped shiny nose covers, but don't ask me what that's all about because I never did find out. Then there is the chador, worn by most Iranian women when outside the house. It's a full-body cloak with the face exposed. Hope that helps."

Emma clapped just as they were pulling into the hotel car park.

"That really helps a lot. Now I know." She pecked him on the cheek.

"It's really even easier than that for us here in Sari, though. The women either wear a chador with or without a veil that only shows their eyes, or they wear a burka in which they're fully covered. There are some other derivatives, like the *shayla* and *khimir*, but we don't see them a lot." Matthew went silent, but Emma could see he was thinking. "You know," Matthew started, "the shah's father actually banned the chador back in the '30s and then had to physically enforce it. And here we are again, with women having to go through the same old, same old and covering themselves up. But it all comes from a long line of cultural DNA, you know."

"What?" What do you mean?" Emma looked over at him, looking for an answer as they got out of the Jeep and walked over to the hotel entrance.

"Well, way back, women were considered as pretty erotic creatures, you know," Matthew winked over at Emma, "but were continually giving trouble to men. They were regarded as imperfect, of ill repute, and had to lower their gaze and be modest by covering their bosoms with veils. And so, the chador, and its variants, came into being. But those poor guys were a little odd. They looked on their women as jewels to be sought after and admired, so they ended up protecting and guarding them like property and chattel. And here we are today, heading in the same direction."

They headed into the hotel lobby and over to the restaurant. They sat in a seat away from anyone else.

"So, you've settled in with the boys?"

"I have, Matthew. All's good. Have you talked to my father lately?"

"Just about every other day. There's a lot going on, and I need to keep him up to speed on what's happening here, although sometimes he's two steps ahead of me. Maybe that's because of you?"

"Well, we do talk, and maybe there is a little overlap now and then, but I can't imagine the two of us have that much in common on the project just yet. I just keep him up to speed on the progress of my work, and I think James does the same. There's really not much to say from my end at this point. We're still about four months away from testing the steam circuit, I would think, but I've been doing my bit for the cause." Emma winked at Matthew, smiled, and took a sip of her soft drink.

"Let me have it, Emma. What are you up to?"

"I know a fair amount about these boilers and have worked with them now for about twelve years. I think you know that from our time together. Well, you may not know that each boiler is capable of operating at 100 percent capacity with only 90 percent of its tubes open. That means there's an acceptable failure rate of 10 percent of the tubes. Now, that allows for some contingency for normal operations but once the tubes operate below 90 percent, because of corrosion or whatever, it's time for a retrofit. That usually happens every four years or so. In this case, where there are four sets of boilers they will take one off-line at a time and, as long as the tubes in the other three are good, they can still get enough steam to maintain plant capacity, but it's tight. If they don't maintain capacity, then plant throughput falls and that means less processed crude."

"Okay, what does all this mean, Emma?"

"It means that we need to make sure I plug enough tubes to get below the 90-percent failure rate but still maintain a high x-ray success rate on the initial welds. That's quite a lot, but I can handle it. There are about 3,000 tubes altogether, so 300 of them have to go first; that's the 10-percent contingency gone. It means I need to put something like 600 of them out of action, or 20 percent of the total, which would mean they couldn't operate at anywhere close to even the minimum volume of steam needed. To do that, I need access to weld 1,800 tubes. I just have to move fast enough to keep ahead of my buddy, Holly. She's the one I mentioned is really good, and fast. She'll end up welding the 1,200 others. As far as I know, she's not part of the ORB picture but, frankly, nothing would surprise me anymore."

"What do you plug them with if every weld has to be x-rayed? Won't they see it?"

"Not if you put the weld rod at least four inches into the tube and let it blob in there. It doesn't have to seal the hole—just provide a good barrier to prevent the water from passing up to the steam drum from the water drum below."

"Boy, that would really take them down for one hell of a time, Emma. By the time they figure that out and then have to remove all the tubes and replace them... wow. Now there's a challenge."

"That's right. Hopefully, I'll be long gone by the time they figure it all out; otherwise, they'll have my head. I figure it would take them at least six months to identify the problem, order up new tubes, cut out the old ones, and replace them." Emma winced at the thought.

"How would they know it was you, though?"

"My initials will be on the weld. That's normal for all high-pressure welds so that the quality control folks can identify who is at fault, and too many failures would normally mean you would be gone from there. In this case,

I'll already be out of there and, while they'll know it was me, there won't be much they'd be able to do."

"They'll certainly go after Dick Elliot for having got you in there in the first place."

"Yes, but he only has the recommendations on me. Nothing else. There's no history for them to track. Dick just has to sit back and claim ignorance. And he is if you think about it. He has no idea what we're really doing here."

"Right. Yes, that's right, and we don't want to tell him either. The less he knows, the better off he will be in the long run. By the time all the problems have been identified, he should be well and truly out of here. Plus, he has the support of Domar."

They had ordered a couple of thinly sliced lamb chops with the obligatory saffron rice. The chops were sliced and barbecued at high heat for just a couple of minutes. Delicious, although the side of vegetables was somewhat suspect in so far as neither of them could identify the greeny-brown globular mess that sat to one side of the rice. Emma tried it, liked it, and passed her comments on to Matthew. She was quite used to the meals at the camp. Most were of a similar concoction that weren't readily recognizable with tasting. None were pleasant looking but most were palatable. She never asked what it was and assumed that if it looked like vegetable it would be edible, and if it looked like meat or fish….well just hope for the best. There were no other choices other than just plain boiled rice, or nothing at all.

They finished up what they wanted and headed down to Matthew's room. He still had most of his bottle of vodka but was relieved when Emma told him she had plenty more and knew where to get hold of the hard stuff any time they needed it.

It didn't take them long to have a few ounces of vodka, kiss, undress, and get into bed with a rush of expectation and desire. It seemed such a natural thing for them to do and it was taken for granted that that was where they would end up that evening. They felt comfortable with each other after all the time they had spent together off the job. Now, there was a common bond on this mission, as there had been with others and, while they didn't talk about work once in bed, they were making their own history.

Their level of lovemaking intensified as they twisted and turned from dominant to supplicant position. Neither was giving in, and both were starting to sweat despite the air conditioning. The fighting continued until they found a suitably satisfactory position that seemed to satiate each other's desires, and they stayed like that until they were spent and each rolled to one side.

"Christ, I needed that," said Emma.

"Me too."

They both laughed and leaned up on one elbow to look at each other.

"Another one?" Emma asked with her eyebrows raised in question.

"I have to go, Emma. There's a little something I have to do and it's getting close to the time." Matthew looked over at the clock, threw off the bedclothes, got out of bed, and pulled his clothes on.

"Can I come?" Emma asked with interest.

"Sure, why not. I'm only going to do a little snooping, and I know you're good at those things." He winked at her.

"I am." Emma jumped out of bed and dressed. "You'll have to drop me at the camp afterward."

"Or you can stay here for the night. The camp won't care, will they?"

"No, there's no check-in and I can just go to my room and change for work in the morning. That's decided. Let's go."

Emma was keen and Matthew smiled at her eagerness. They headed out to the Jeep and into Sari. It was 11:45 p.m. when they arrived at the end of the lane on Talebi Nataj, where the commander would be with his lady. Matthew filled Emma in on what was happening and what he wanted to do. He didn't anticipate any confrontation that night and just wanted to better understand the movements of the woman and the guy who hid in the closet while the commander was in the apartment. The end game was hopefully to get the lady on their side and see if she could identify what the Iranians were up to with the commander. Matthew also wanted to find out if the Iranians were sending false information out via the satellite that was intended to be intercepted by the listening station in Gorgan and passed along to the British and Americans. It could be a long night. Matthew wanted to wait to see where the lady went after she had been over at the military compound. He assumed she lived in the city and wanted to follow her.

At almost midnight, a Land Rover pulled up outside the main gate to the apartment and someone got out and pressed the buzzer at the gate pillar. Five minutes later, someone came out of the apartment and got into the Land Rover. Matthew assumed it was the commander and that meant that the lady and her closet friend would soon be coming out to the lane. Matthew and Emma waited for ten minutes before two figures emerged from the back of the house into the lane and got into a black Mercedes. They drove east out of the lane and onto Talebi Nataj. Matthew followed a good distance back. There was no other traffic at that time of night.

The Mercedes crossed over a few blocks, took a left, and stopped at a security gate at the entrance to a courtyard. The gate lifted and the car drove through. Matthew assumed this was the Revolutionary Guard compound. He could see the Mercedes park and then two figures get out and go into a one-storey building. A light went on in one of the offices and Matthew could just make out some shadows.

Thirty minutes later, the woman emerged, exited alone through the security gate, and walked quickly along the road. She turned two rights and disappeared down an alley. Matthew followed cautiously and spotted her chador as it flowed through a gate midway down the alley. He went around the block, looking for the house she had entered. Matthew and Emma spotted a light coming on at about the same time and they parked outside to collect themselves and make a mental note of the address. This was a three-storey building and the light had come from the top floor. Like many of the apartment buildings, this one was narrow with one apartment per floor and no elevator.

They sat for only a few minutes and talked about how to intercept the woman at some point to talk to her about the potential to establish some sort of collaboration. They decided to wait until the following Friday, the Iranian holiday of the week, and stake out the apartment, front and back, and wait for her to come out to head to the stores. Emma would do the intercept and the talking. They knew the lady spoke good English from the report James had provided. Emma would claim she was new in town and really needed some directions to the market, then carry on and strike up a conversation, hinging on the woman's English skills and background. Hopefully, they would spend a little while together just talking, as women do. At some point, Matthew would accidentally bump into them and introduce himself, maybe as a friend of Emma, but he would have to play things by ear. It was at least a sketch of a plan but it could change in an instant, depending on the circumstances of the intercept.

They drove back to the hotel, had a nightcap, tucked themselves into bed, cuddled a while, and drifted off to sleep. The alarm was set for six. That was in four hours' time.

*   *   *

Matthew on Site

Three days after his arrival in Sari, Matthew received a call from Dick Elliot. Matthew's papers were in order and delivered to the security services at the project site. When he was ready, he could go at any time to get oriented and signed in. His official job description was Operations Manager, which meant he was able to visit any part of the plant he needed. He also had a small team already in place on site that was currently managing the pre-operational systems and looking over the shoulders of the trades as they worked in particularly complex areas where the team's advice would be most needed.

Fortunately, the small, already embedded operations team was led by John Charlesworth, one of the world's best process engineers and operators for olefins units. He had commissioned five in his career. Matthew would hide in John's shadow and defer to his knowledge on all technical matters associated with operations, allowing Matthew to intrude wherever needed to get his own job done.

Matthew needed to get to know all ORB operatives already on site, understand their functions, and understand who else might be needed to join the team. The call had already gone out for more trade support, but he was also likely to need administration support. That could wait until he assessed the situation better and got to know his partners in crime. So far, he was quite happy with both James and Emma's involvement. He also was sure that there were a number of other things they could do as a team to block plant operations for an indeterminate period.

He also had to get out to the new pipeline. Stockman had given Matthew the names of a couple of ORB pipe welders based there and he wanted to make contact. There were several avenues of potential sabotage to disable the pipeline. Things would not be as simple as blocking the pipes as Emma was doing with the boiler tubes. These overland pipelines were thirty-six inches in diameter.

Those were not going to be blocked by weld splatter. It seemed to Matthew that any attempt at sabotaging the pipelines had to be with the electrical at the pump stations and/or within the control system. He preferred both tactics but would have to rely on the abilities of whoever would be working with him from ORB.

Matthew's first day on site was spent with Charlesworth as they went over the system design. Charlesworth was not an ORB operative. He just did a great job. He was truly an expert, able to catch the smallest of issues before they became bigger ones, even though he wasn't a control systems person. It was unlikely that he'd catch the initiatives of ORB saboteurs since their work was much more involved with the physics of the system rather than the chemistry. In other words, the crude oil could still be refined and the by-products still produced but none of that would happen in the timeframe expected.

Charlesworth was a great guy to deal with, although his brain was often wandering in another world. He didn't seem to have the ability to come down to earth with everyone else but still managed to be a great person who people gravitated toward to solve technical problems. He essentially lived at site, and while he was senior enough to warrant an off-site address, he preferred to be close to his "baby," as he expressed it.

Matthew and Charlesworth found their common balance almost immediately. Matthew would look after the management side of life, while Charlesworth would manage the technical side. Charlesworth was very happy with the arrangement. He wasn't one to have meetings of a non-technical nature or interact with the administration personnel. Leave him alone to get the plant up and running; that was all he needed from life.

James communicated often with Charlesworth since his job involved the control and communication system for the process and, oddly, that was something that Charlesworth was not particularly fond of getting involved with or interfering with. Things advanced far too quickly in the world of computing and control systems for Charlesworth and it seemed to him that every plant he dealt with was controlled by the latest and greatest system, where only those born to such things were able to exist and succeed.

"Hey, James." Matthew opened the door to the site trailer where James "lived" on site. "What's happening today?"

James was well aware of the hidden ears that could be listening.

"Hey, Matthew. Wanna walk in the sunshine?" James responded with a smile.

"Sounds good, my friend."

They stepped out of the trailer and walked across to where the towers in the olefins unit were being dressed. It was a term they used when a piece of equipment was having all its appurtenances and paraphernalia attached—ladders, valves, instrumentations, electrical, level gauges, and all the rest. There was a general din in the area, so they could talk relatively freely without concern of being overheard.

"Do you interact with Charlesworth much?" Matthew wondered

"Yes, a fair amount. Good man." James was quick off the mark.

"What's your interaction?" Matthew wanted to know.

"Control system mainly. He sets up the operating parameters and my job is to make sure we have them all programmed into the system."

"Does he check for accuracy or correctness?'

"No, he shouldn't need to. Theoretically. And I don't think he can. That's not his thing."

"What are your thoughts about making sure this plant doesn't operate?"

"Oh, I have a lot of options, Matthew. The real problem I have is keeping them away from the prying eyes of IDRO and the Revolutionary Guard people on site, and I am pretty sure the Russians have people here as well but I haven't identified them yet."

"I thought they were a bit of a non-entity. They don't know anything about control systems or process and the like."

"You're right, but IDRO pokes its nose into everything whether its people know anything or not. I have to keep them satisfied with answers that appear to be right."

"And do you? Keep them satisfied, I mean?" Matthew squinted as the sun hit his eyes.

"Of course. It's not hard, but it still takes time." James was squinting now, and he put his sunglasses on.

"What now?" Matthew asked.

"I'm going to fuck with that control system like no one else has done before." James chuckled and crossed his arms across his chest.

"Tell me more." Matthew suddenly had the feeling he could be dealing with a bit of a madman. Maybe slightly off-kilter. Was this a misfit or just someone that felt really strongly about his commitment? He couldn't be sure.

"James, can you come to supper this evening somewhere in Sari so we can have more of chat?"

"Love to."

"See you at six at the gate."

"I should follow you to Sari, Matthew. Then I can just head home afterward."

"Good plan. See you a little later. Emma is going to be with us."

"Sounds good." James headed back to his trailer.

Matthew made another call. "Emma, are you there?"

"Hey," was all she said.

"Meet me at the gate at six. James is going to join us for supper."

"Okay. See you then." That was all she needed to say to understand there was an issue.

Matthew shut his cell phone off and headed back to his trailer, where he studied the plant layout drawings. He needed to touch base with the guys that Sloan had sent in through Dick Elliot. There were two millwrights, a couple of electricians, and an instrumentation technician. They were integrated with the rest of the expats and were already working on the site. Sloan had instructed them in what their roles were, but Matthew needed to understand what they were actually doing. He needed to make sure their timing was on track with the rest of the plan. Nothing was to go wrong before the steam systems were being commissioned.

Matthew walked back out on site and headed over to the turbine area where the generators and compressors were located. That's where the two millwrights would be working. He climbed up the stairway to the mezzanine operating floor and looked around for the workers. There were a number of them finalizing the precise location of the equipment with their steel wire lines and levels set up around the floor. There were chalk marks and tape indicating the various markers they would use as bases for their measurements. One of the millwrights was looking through a level at one end of the compressor train of four units, while another millwright stared through another level at the other end of the lineup. Two millwrights were using micrometers on the adjustable base plates, ready to shift the sixty-five-ton units in any vertical direction required. There were jacking bolts on the sides of the equipment to adjust the horizontal attitude of the units by levering against the concrete. These were the final adjustments to be made before piping and electrifying the units.

Matthew went over to one of the millwrights staring through the level.

"Hi. Do you know Sloan?" Matthew asked. The man shrugged, grimaced, and went back to leveling. Matthew wandered over to the millwright on the other level.

"Hi. Do you know Sloan?" Matthew asked again.

"Sure do. You Matthew?"

"Yes. Can we talk when you get a chance?"

"You bet. Want me to bring Mickey? He's the other millwright from Sloan."

"That would be great." Matthew shook his hand. "What's your name?"

"I'm Phil. Do you also want to meet the others? We can all come over together if you want."

"Sure. Where would be the best place to meet?" Matthew knew it would be unlikely for them to get together during the workday or off-site.

"How about we meet outside the rec center at the camp and we can find a quiet spot away from the units." Phil was easy to talk to.

"Sounds great. How about tomorrow evening at seven?"

"We'll be there, Matthew. Take care. Oh, how do I find you if I need to?"

"Do you know James Peters? The site engineer."

"Sure do. Always comes round to see what we're up to."

"He's the contact for me. If you need me, just let him know." Matthew patted Phil on the shoulder and turned away.

He was pleased with how this was going, and the next evening he would find out what else was going on that could upset operations. Matthew headed back to his trailer to pick up his things and head back to the hotel to freshen up.

*   *   *

"Hey, Emma. What are you up to?" James had arrived at the project site gate at about the same time as Emma strolled over from the camp.

"Meeting someone, same as you," Emma said as she raised her eyebrows. She wasn't 100-percent sure of what James knew about her and Matthew, privately or otherwise, so she decided to wait until he arrived and he could do the introductions.

It was just a few minutes after six when Matthew drove up and Emma piled into the car while James followed in his. They drove through Sari to a discrete location on the east of the city. The Haj Hassan Restaurant was located off the main highway to Neka in a quiet retail area that accommodated locals and foreigners with a Middle Eastern and Mediterranean menu. They didn't need a reservation, the restaurant wasn't busy, and they managed to corral a table near the back corner of the restaurant where they could talk openly. They chose the buffet so they wouldn't be interrupted by waiters.

"If you haven't guessed already, all of us are on the ORB payroll, and we are all working toward the same thing on this project."

Matthew started as soon as they sat. "In case you don't know, there are another five guys on site that are also with us. I don't think you need to know their names, but you should know that we aren't in this by ourselves." Matthew unloaded the information before they could even lift a glass of water.

"Oh, and we three are on the same page when it comes to the Gorgan listening post and what we need to do with it. There are a few things I need to sort out before I move forward, but my thinking is to bring the commander's lady on board with us. I think we need her to pass on false information through the station." He waited for a response, but all he got were shrugs.

"What do you need us to do, Matthew?" James posed the question. He had the least amount of knowledge about ORB and who they were, but he wasn't going to ask any questions right now. He had thought he was just doing a special job for Dick Elliot, but clearly there was a lot more to this project than he had thought.

Emma was quiet. Her job was clear-cut, although she enjoyed mixing things up with Matthew, but she was already involved with the commander's lady friend, so there was little else she could see that could involve her... unless Matthew thought there was.

"James, do you remember that discussion you overheard between Plato and Ali over in Chalus? The one about the Russians?" Matthew eyed James.

"Sure do. Very interesting. A replacement for Tom Ardeghali and another guy coming in from Kabul. I don't know if they're here yet, but I know that Tom has already been moved out. I don't know where he is, or if he's coming back."

"He's not coming back, James. Ali has his hooks into him and wants to get him over to the US to help him with his business over there."

"Great." James smiled and looked from Matthew to Emma.

"Our problem here is figuring out who are the Russians, where are they on site, and what can we do about them before things start to go wrong with the plant." Matthew looked at both of them. He got up from the table and went over to the buffet. The others followed.

When they sat at the table again, it was Emma who spoke first.

"I don't know how much I can help there, Matthew. You know the place I'm working, and there's not much chance for me to move around the plant and interact with anyone else. Unless there's a Russian woman involved and I bump into her in the camp, I feel a bit useless."

"That's fine, Emma. I didn't think you would be able to help identify them, but I am hoping you may be able to help neutralize them when the time comes." Matthew stared at Emma. She knew what he meant.

"Just point them out and leave the rest to me." Emma broke out into a broad grin and put a mouthful of food into her mouth, followed by a generous helping of naan.

"Guess that leaves you, James." Matthew looked over at James, who was busily engaged in stuffing food into his mouth. He chewed, swallowed, coughed, and grinned.

"No problem, Matthew. Give me a few days. I'll start with the admin guys. I have some friends there who know how nosy I am. Maybe they've heard some Russian around the place. Then I'll move on the plant managers in the field and see what they know. The admin records will help identify who's new to the payroll."

Matthew was nodding as James went through his thinking process.

"It should show name and country of origin. That may be crap, but it's a start. At least the date should be right." James paused. "Two, you say? Yes, that's what I heard as well." James looked at Matthew, who had nodded. "I'm guessing that one of them might be working on the ponds where Ali was working with Mana. Maybe I'll check that out first. It wouldn't surprise me if that's exactly where one of them is because that's where he should be. Now, the other one, I'm not so sure. Let me think about it."

"That's good, James. Let me know as soon as you identify either or both."

They all scooped more food into their mouths and sipped the chai. This was good.

*   *   *

The Guys at Site

Matthew met Mickey and Phil at the project gate at seven the next day after supper, and they strolled over to the recreation hall where the other men met them outside. They introduced themselves.

"I'm Arnie, one of the electricians. Good to meet you, Matthew. Heard about you." They shook hands and smiled at each other.

"Hey, Matthew, I'm Walt, the other electrician."

"Pete, the instrumentation tech." Pete held his hand out to Matthew.

"Let's take a walk, guys. Mickey, why don't you lead the way to somewhere out of sight."

Mickey led them around the back of the camp to the east of the site and into a clump of trees away from the river. It was a blind spot from the camp and road.

"This should do, Matthew. Okay?"

"Looks good. Let's sit and talk." They settled themselves on the grass. A couple smoked. It was starting to get dark.

"Guys, I know you've all been told about what we're doing here, so I won't go into that unless someone wants more of an explanation. Maybe I can tell you, but maybe I can't. It depends on the question."

Matthew stopped and looked around at the five faces. No one showed any sign of wanting to ask questions, and Matthew knew that the less they knew, the better it would be. He was pretty sure they agreed.

"Mickey, Phil, tell me what you're doing and what your plans are going forward. And remember, we only have a few months to finish things off and I don't want anything to show up until they try to start up the steam system. The other utility systems are okay, so you don't need to mess with them. I also have the boilers set up for failure and someone is working on the control system, so that sets you free to cover almost anything else that will make a real difference. It has to be effective to the point of disaster, but we're not here to harm people other than those who may be especially selected for any reason any of us have to be suspicious of them. Like getting too close to see what any of you are up to or asking provocative questions about your presence here. So, go on guys, tell me about your work."

Phil started. "Mickey and me are both working on setting up the compressors and generators. The other millwrights are looking after the turbines, so we can't mess with them. We're setting them so each is off-centre in different directions by more than the allowable tolerance in the horizontal plane. No one other than a millwright with an instrument, maybe, will be able to spot it. We're doing the same in the vertical plane—offsetting turbines in different directions from each other. That's the first major thing, but if, or when, they catch onto it, it'll be an easy fix unless the equipment rattles itself to death.

"Now, there's a plug in each of the lube oil units located on the ground floor. The plugs are in the oil supply lines to the turbine. Not enough to raise the 'no oil' alarm, but enough to stop the system from lubricating the turbine like it's s'posed to. So far, that's it. It all pretty well gums up the works, and we'll be looking for more things to do once we get our next site assignments from the site super."

Mickey picked it up from there. "My guess is we'll be working on the final set for the condensate pumps, and then maybe a lot more. There's a spare in every circuit, so it's not so easy to deploy methods that would hit the plant as a whole. Now, the distillation unit has some pretty complex pumping systems for the various products as they come off the column, and that's maybe where we can look for something a little more 'fulfilling,' shall we say." Mickey raised his eyebrows at Matthew and looked over at Phil, who was nodding as he thought.

"The other thing we need to do is to take some of the essential spares and bury them someplace they'd never think to look. There are the infuser jets for the distillates, which we can gum up, and the solenoid valves for the small-bore injectors, and without spares, there'll be months to wait for replacements. Essential things, but small and easily lost."

"Make sure you remember everything you do, guys. We may have to put it all back together someday." Matthew turned to Arnie and Walt. "Anything so far?"

"We're working on the motor control cabinets, the MCCs," said Arnie, "so there's a lot of cross-wiring and wrong tagging going on there. Once we get that done, we'll move over to the local control cabinets in the field and mess with them. Nothing dangerous but highly effective in delays."

Walt just nodded.

"We didn't intend to poke around in the high-voltage area," Arnie said, "but we were thinking of tinkering with the main transformer protection. There are four 3,000-MW transformers sitting out there that need some attention."

"And you, Pete. Anything you can do?"

"Calibration's the key, Matthew. I'm on the bench, working my way through all the instruments—gauges, controllers, sniffers, etc. All are being set out of whack as I go through. Again, nothing dangerous—especially on the high-pressure circuits—but enough to throw the chemistry off. That's really about it for me."

"That's great, guys. As you move through the plant, keep your eyes open for folk looking over your shoulder. Someone could spot a calibration error, Pete. Or any obvious mix-up with tagging, Arnie, so keep things from prying eyes and watch out for someone, anyone, looking over your shoulder when you swap those wires, Mickey. We know they're out there, and you likely won't know who they are. For all I know, they could be doubling up on critical systems to check on what you're doing."

Matthew looked at the faces in front of him. They all nodded; some looked a little taken aback at the prospect of being discovered. "Thanks, guys. We better get back. I may need to get hold of one or two of you as things progress, but once you think you've done your job, don't hesitate to get out of here. You don't want to be around when the shit hits the fan and they start looking for who fucked them up." They all laughed, shook their heads, got up, and sauntered back to camp.

Matthew chatted with Mickey on the way. "Make sure you stay in touch with James. He's my go-to guy on site, and Emma—she's working on the boiler tubes—can also be trusted in case you need help with anything. She and I have worked together on a number of projects."

"How long are you here for, Matthew?" asked Arnie.

"My guess is we'll be out of here in less than sixty days. They start the utility commissioning next week, and that will keep them busy for a while. After that, we should see operations move to the steam systems and that's the most complex, so it will take them a month just to set them up for the testing. Then the fireworks will start, and I'd give security another two weeks before they realize they have a dud on their hands."

They reached the gate, shook hands, and Matthew got into his car and started up. As he was leaving the project gate, he noticed a beautifully clean Land Rover parked off to the side with two guys in the front seats. It followed him back to the turn off to the hotel but carried on as though going to Sari. He couldn't help but feel as though he was being followed. As the Land Rover passed, he spotted the driver looking over at him. A hard-looking man with a thick black mustache and matching eyebrows. It wasn't easy to see anything more and Matthew decided to make a U-turn and follow them into Sari at a discrete distance, far enough back that he might even lose them but it was a chance he was prepared to take.

The Land Rover headed into the center of Sari with Matthew in pursuit. At this point, he wasn't about to let them out of his sight and with the relatively heavy traffic it was easier to shorten the distance between them so he could be sure he wouldn't lose them. They took three turns and Matthew recognized the area. They were heading to the Revolutionary Guard barracks and, sure enough, the barrier was raised and they drove in as Matthew drifted past without turning his head in their direction. Whether they had really been following him or not was unclear, but he had that niggling sense that something just didn't feel right.

* * *

Those Ruskies

A few days later, James called Matthew. He had identified one of the Russians, who had taken Ali's place over at the lagoons. He was working on locating the second one and was fairly sure the guy was in admin working on expediting materials and equipment. He apparently spoke good English, had started on site only a month prior, and spent a lot of his time on the project site looking at everything as though he was searching for missing parts. Well, that was the story he gave but James just wanted to be sure.

A few more days passed before James called Matthew again but this time, he confirmed the identity of the second Russian. They had rendezvoused a couple of times to talk about the project. The way the other guy was smoking Russian cigarettes, talking about his home country, and gesticulating in an animated way confirmed James's suspicions.

Both the Russians had been spending time wandering through the plant, examining various components, and standing and watching workers as they went about their jobs. One had even climbed up onto the turbine mezzanine, talked to some of the millwrights, and then headed into the boiler areas, searching out the fitters and spending time just watching. James had followed both at various times and the second one, who was supposed to be over in the lagoon area, had drifted over to the control room to talk to some of the programmers as they set up the equipment. He had even gone up onto the crude oil cracking unit and sauntered around, touching the instruments, looking at the valves and their spring hangers, the pipe joints, and the electrical junction boxes. Whether either of them was technically smart enough to understand what they were doing was debatable, but the fact was that the casual eye could not see most of the plant's problems. They were inherent in the systems, completely hidden from view, or cunningly set in such a way that even the keenest of eyes would not be able to detect things like level misalignment—in either a horizontal or a vertical direction—of any of the equipment or towers.

James was confident in his findings and Matthew invited him and Emma back to the same restaurant on the east side of Sari, where they sat at the same table as previous and enjoyed a buffet supper.

"Good job, James. We don't need to know their names but the photos you took are invaluable. Now we need to deal with them as discretely as possible. Ideas?"

And so it was that a few days later one of the agents accidentally electro-cuted himself as he bent and touched a carbon steel check valve. The valve casing squashed up against the sliced protective casing of a high-voltage hot wire in the distillation area of the plant, where no other workers were at the time. The emergency siren had sounded and all personnel dropped their tools and collected over by the warehouse until an inspection was carried out to determine whether the problem had been resolved. It had, and everyone but the dead Russian went back to work.

Three days later, the other Russian "fell" through the temporary wooden rail installed on the turbine operating floor. The permanent handrail had not yet been installed but was sitting off to one side, waiting for an ironworker to finish the job. The Russian fell sixty feet onto a condensate pump, bounced off, and fell another ten feet over an open sump pit where the vertical rebar was waiting for the concrete cover to be poured. The half-inch-diameter rebar pierced his upper body in four places before he came to rest with his head hanging over the open sump. The emergency siren had sounded and once again all personnel dropped their tools and collected over by the warehouse until an inspection was carried out. It was found that the restraints holding the temporary fence in place had been released from the concrete columns on either side in anticipation of having the permanent handrail installed that afternoon. Once the inspection was completed, everyone but the dead Russian went back to work, and the first item on the agenda was the installa-tion of the permanent handrail.

Matthew called both James and Emma and congratulated them on their work. Emma had organized the handrail failure since it was close to where she worked. She had a bird's-eye view of the Russian as he came up the stairway to the mezzanine. Coincidentally, she happened to be in the area and had sidled over to the handrail when the opportunity arose. But it was just the gentle push from Emma that sealed his fate. The Russian had been far too mesmerized by her approach and hadn't realized how close he was to the temporary rail. Emma's hand on his chest was not something he wanted to ignore but he failed to react as she gently pushed him backward and his feet disappeared past the concrete floor.

James had arranged for the electrocution of the first Russian, since he had control of the power source in that area and brought the high-voltage wire down to contact the carbon steel as soon as the Russian put his hand on it as though examining whether it had been installed correctly. It had, but the Russian never found out.

"Wonder if they will be replaced," Matthew said to himself as he sipped his vodka.

* * *

Leila

It was almost two weeks before Matthew found an opportunity to intercept the commander's lady. He didn't want to wait for Emma to bump into her accidentally. It could take weeks with Emma only able to go into town on Fridays. That would be too long to wait and too much of a coincidental risk.

He had used Ali to flesh out some personal details about the lady: why she was in Sari and her name, family, home base, and whatever else. It was easy for Ali to find these things out, and he had even visited her parents on the pretext of needing to contact her.

Ali had called Matthew just a day after they had talked about getting information. Leila was her name. She was from the US and was in Sari to visit her parents. There was nothing much else to it.

Matthew was at Leila's apartment early on Friday morning and positioned himself at the junction corner so he could keep an eye on her movements from either the front or rear entrances. It was just before noon when she showed herself, complete with chador and a shopping bag slung over her shoulder. Clearly, she was not a mosque-goer.

Matthew followed her to the bazaar, made eye contact (what else was there?), closed in, and said, "You have the most beautiful eyes."

"Thank you. Do you think you should see?" came the reply in fluent, sarcastic English. He wasn't surprised, from the little he knew of her, and had expected some exchange like this. He knew she was Westernized and had a sense of humor.

"Of course. Where? When? Maybe a coffee?" He didn't want to appear overly promiscuous, at least not yet, so he made it all sound like fun.

"We have no Starbucks here, but there's a little place over by the fountain. Are you American or English?" An odd sort of question, but he went along with it.

"A bit of both, I suppose." He responded with that charismatic, white-toothed smile.

"Okay. How about 7:30 tonight at the clock tower." She smiled impishly, turned, and got lost in the crowd. Matthew was left to ponder where the clock tower was, but his ignorance was quickly dispelled after a discussion with the hotel manager who told him the Sari Clock Tower Square was an open area in the center of the city, which had a tower with a large clock and a bell that rang on the hour. It was where everyone, particularly the younger generation, gathered to gossip, laugh, and meet without too much interference from the Revolutionary Guard or the mullahs. According to the manager, one could not miss it if one aimed for the center of the city. Easier said than done but nevertheless a very good teaser.

Matthew was intrigued and excited. There were crowds of young people around the base of the clock when he arrived, sitting on the steps, drinking coffee, and laughing raucously. Some held hands but most flirted in a guarded way as people do when they are being watched. But youth had a way around these things and did what young people did when they didn't know if they should touch the other person or not. It was a very cute dance to the elders (over twenty-fives) who knew full well what that dance could lead to. But Matthew was focused and he spotted a chador-clad person who seemed distracted and searching for someone on the periphery of the group of young people.

It had to be her.

Matthew sidled up and spoke.

"Hey, the lady from the market. Is it you?" he asked with that white smile.

"Yes, yes, of course." She smiled back. There was no censorship or negativity in her response.

"You never know with so much body disguise." He laughed.

"It's me." She seemed coy. "Are we going for coffee?"

"You bet. Would you lead the way?" Matthew was playing cool. "Do you know the commander?" Matthew carried on smiling, not wanting to frighten the lady off too quickly. His stance was not threatening and he kept a space between them as they carried on walking.

There was a long pause. Clearly, she was taken aback, surprised, and then froze momentarily before answering.

"What are you talking about? I know of no commander." By this time, her whole demeanor had changed from that of a relatively compliant and happy-go-lucky female to one who sensed danger. Her hackles were up, and while Matthew couldn't see her face, he could tell from the look in her eyes that she was not amused. She waited and offered nothing.

"Are you aware you may be compromised?"

"What? What do you mean?"

"Do you realize your family could be in danger?"

"What?? What are you talking about? You're making no sense and I don't like where this is going. I want to leave now." She was nervous and started to look around as though being followed. Matthew had that same feeling but he wasn't about to stop now that he had come this far.

They had walked from the square into one of the adjacent lanes.

"We have access to your whole family, Leila."

"How do you know my name?"

"We know all about you."

"What's happening here?" Her voice had climbed a few decibels and was on the point of a shriek.

"Listen, we know that you're being used. We know that your family is being threatened if you don't comply with the Revolutionary Guard, and we know that you have no choice but to work with them." Matthew had based his assumptions on the little information he had. "You have the attention of the American commander from Gorgan," he continued, "and we know you're using him and passing the information on to the Revolutionary Guard. We need to know what information you're passing on and what your orders are."

"I don't know what you are talking about. I have no orders and I don't know a commander. I'm just here in Sari to see some family and I'm going back to the States at the end of the month, so I don't have time for this, whatever it is." She turned to leave.

"Leila, we know you're being used and we want to help. But before we can do that, we have to know what's going on. The commander is under constant surveillance, as are you, as well as the guy you go with back to the barracks."

"You're following me?" she asked naively. "Why would you do that? What's going on?" She was starting to show some interest but was still half turned away. "Who are you?"

"I'm not sure that matters right now, Leila, but I can tell you that you're in danger. Believe me, as soon as your usefulness is finished, they'll get rid of you. You aren't going back to the US. I bet you don't even have your passport, do you?"

"No. I was told they needed it to get my visa sorted out. Apparently, there was something wrong with it."

Matthew gave her a knowing look and pursed his lips. "Think you might want to talk to me now?"

"What if they're watching?" Her eyes gave away her fears.

"They probably are. Now they're wondering what is going on, so you need to act naturally and pretend we're just a friendly couple that struck up a conversation. I'll contact you in a few days to set up somewhere we can talk. In the meantime, you have to just carry on as though nothing has happened or will happen. Can you do that?"

She laughed and patted him on the arm. "Of course, I can," she said, quickly getting into the role he had described. She took him by the arm and walked him back into the square, where they strolled around, laughed a little, and eventually said their goodbyes, obvious enough for anyone who may be watching to be convinced this was just an innocent meeting. Perhaps someone she had known from back in the US. Leila wandered off away from the square and into the lane on her way home.

Matthew walked for a while around the square, trying to show some interest in the local goings-on but really keeping a lookout for anyone that could be tailing him. He picked up on two men in shabby casual clothes, starting and stopping whenever he did. From then on, he had to be on guard. He had no idea at that point whether they would continue to tail him, or if they were only doing so because he was meeting with Leila. He guessed at the second but needed to prepare for the first.

Matthew took a few turns, down a few lanes, a couple of rights and a couple of lefts, eventually arriving at his car. He fired it up, looked in the rear view mirror and didn't see anyone tailing him. He took off back to the hotel. Now he had to wonder whether they knew who he was, whether Leila would report the incident, or how much of a dilemma he had created. Maybe he was being overly cautious but better that than give anything away. He would have to talk to Stockman and they'd decide whether to pull him out or leave him in play.

*   *   *

Four days later, Matthew climbed over the wall to Leila's apartment and into the courtyard. He got himself up onto the third-floor balcony in the same way as James when he had got into the apartment during one of the commander's and Leila's meetings. He let himself in through the sliding doors, kept the lights off, and settled down to wait for her return sometime over the next hour or so.

The light in Leila's apartment came on at about 1:30 a.m. when she returned from the Revolutionary Guard's office after another rendezvous with the commander. Matthew was waiting. Leila jumped but didn't seem particularly surprised to hear him say, "Don't be afraid, it's only me—Matthew," as he sat in the chair on the other side of the room, facing the front door. Hopefully, that positioning would stop her from screaming out. It seemed to work.

Leila switched on a small lamp on a side table and switched off the overhead light. She did this in a few rooms as though to indicate to anyone who might be watching her movements that all was normal and she was getting ready for bed. She didn't engage Matthew in any talk until she had gone into the bathroom, came back out, switched off the excess lights, got into bed, and turned off the bedside lamp. Matthew had followed her into her bedroom, making sure to keep himself away from the windows, still not talking.

"Well, you may as well get in if we're going to talk. It'll be safer than standing in front of the window. You never know," Leila said as she threw half the bed covers to one side and waited for him to get in.

Matthew did as he was told. He slid into bed and moved toward Leila but didn't bother to cover himself up. She reached out and made sure there was at least a narrow separation between them.

"Okay, let's talk." She giggled wickedly.

Matthew gulped and had trouble getting focused. Leila kept her hand on his chest.

"Remember, we're just talking," she whispered. "Nothing more. Right?"

"No problem," Matthew replied in the nervous voice of someone who was anticipating something else. But he regained his composure and settled down. He had no idea if her apartment was bugged but doubted it. That was likely a level of sophistication too much for what Leila was doing with the commander. The Revolutionary Guard was likely more interested in her talks with the commander than what she did, although they might be watching her at times in case she met the commander clandestinely.

"Listen," Matthew started, "as I told you, we know about you and the commander. We know about your 'meetings,' shall we say, and that if he tells you anything about his work over in Gorgan, you pass it back to the Revolutionary Guard. We know about the guy in the closet with the recorder. We guess that they also tell you what they want you to tell the commander for him to pass back to his people. Understand?"

"Not really." She wasn't sure what to make of this situation. "Who are you? Okay, so you know I'm having an affair, but so what?" Leila sounded annoyed. "They just told me to get friendly with this guy and get to know him. They want whatever information I can get from him about his work and they threatened my family and me if I didn't cooperate. So that's what I did. We figured out a way to get together and every now and then he says something they seem to think could be important. Really, I think he's just a regular guy working over at the Chalus listening post. We all know it's there. Other than that, I don't think he knows much. He's nice enough but he doesn't understand Farsi or Russian or Chinese, so what can he really tell anyone?"

"So, what does he tell you that they think is so important?"

"Well, he sometimes jokes about the information going back and forth, and sometimes he has his people leak information into the network as though they are some Russian or Chinese official, passing on information that's really false. It all sounds like a bit of a game to me, but what do I know? All I do is have a little fun with him and report."

"Does he tell you what false information he passes on?"

"I think at one point he mentioned that they had passed on some false information saying that Iran was irritated by the lack of Russian and Chinese help to guard the site at Neka where the refinery terminal is supposed to be. It turned out that the Russians sent in two warships to Neka without the Iranians knowing and that set off a huge diplomatic spat that the boys over at

Chalus had a good laugh about. There've been a few things like that."

"Does he ever give you anything to do with his work, like documents?"

"Never. But why are you so interested?"

"You probably heard about the cinema in Chalus that blew up." Matthew drew an inch closer to her.

"Yes, it was dreadful, and everyone seems to think it was someone to do with the Tudeh Party."

"Could be, but that was a group of young revolutionaries that were killed. They wanted to change the way things are done in Iran. They've rebuilt but they can't move forward without some serious help. That is, in part, why I'm here," he lied.

"You know, I knew a couple of those guys from when we were kids together. I can't believe it."

"Well, you have to believe it. If you want to get out of the country safely, you have to play along with us."

"Okay, let me know what to say." She had cuddled in closer and Matthew put his arm around her shoulders for physical support, although there was, perhaps, just a touch of animal instinct.

"For now, just carry on doing what you've been doing with the commander. But we need you to tell him what we need him to know, and we want you to report back to the Revolutionary Guard some things we want you to tell them. As for your safety, we have our plans in place to get you and your family out of here fast if we even sense a problem. Got it?"

"I think so. But I have to tell you, the moment I get the feeling that someone is trying to make trouble for me or my family, I head to the other side."

"Understood. Now I have to leave."

"I have a lot to think about," Leila's voice softened.

"Understood," Matthew replied, somewhat relieved, and fell gently to the floor and went out through the kitchen window, dropped to a balcony below, then to the next balcony, and then to the courtyard before disappearing through the back gate. It was past 3:00 a.m. when he reached his car and drove out of the city with his lights off until he reached the outskirts. No one followed.

* * *

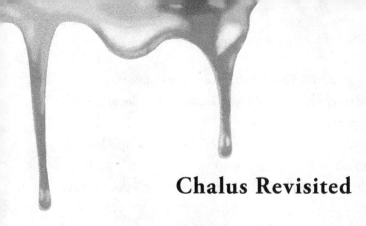

Chalus Revisited

It was a beautifully clear blue-sky day with the humidity chased away by a northeastern breeze that blew the moisture over the Alborz, where it quickly evaporated and mystically made its journey back up into the sky to once more advance onto the Caspian coastline. But, for now, the air was fresh, the road was clear, and Matthew and Emma made their way slowly west over to Chalus for a weekend to meet up with Plato and Margaret.

After his time in Sari, Matthew was more than ready to return to the casualness of Chalus, where he really felt as though he could relax with newfound friends. He sensed their affinity for friendship, together with a feeling of mutual interest. A little like how he felt with Emma. A comfortable closeness.

They turned into the driveway through the cypress trees to the house. Margaret was pruning and picking flowers, taking a few of the larger blossoms for the house. She was dressed in a loose, flowing, see-through white cotton wrap that started at the shoulders and fell to her ankles, with a light blue chiffon scarf wrapped around her waist. There was no intent for it to be a chador and the transparency only showed a white bikini-style outfit underneath. She looked up as their arrival crushed the gravel. Her smile was as wide as Matthew remembered it.

Margaret came over to the car, reached over, and put her arms around Matthew's shoulders while at the same time reaching a hand over to touch Emma on the shoulder. They shook hands as one as Matthew and Emma tumbled out of the car.

They stood together as Margaret wiped her hands on a cloth from her basket and threw her arms up to invite her visitors into the house. Plato appeared at the front door in reaction to the noise in the driveway. Ali was close behind. They were both all smiles with their hands and arms out in welcome. It seemed as though Matthew and Emma were long-lost friends, they'd all missed and were now reunited.

The Caspian was calm. The color of the water reflected a special serenity compared to the dismal gray it more often had to offer. Even the sand looked more golden than normal as the group sat in a circle around the fire pit on the patio and laughed at nothing in particular, exchanging nondescript greetings that were little more than skin-deep. But that was all it took. After all, they hardly knew each other, and Emma was at the bottom of the pole when it came to familiarity with the group. Nevertheless, the camaraderie seemed genuine and the interest in each other well-founded.

"Plato," Matthew eventually became more serious, "the two Russian replacements on the project are dead."

"Oh." Plato didn't seem to be overly concerned. He knew it was going to happen sooner or later, and it wasn't likely to affect him in any way. "I did know that Tom was going to be replaced—we talked about that a few weeks ago, so it doesn't come as a surprise to me that the issue has been dealt with, Matthew." Plato paused and looked around at the faces. "Any thoughts on the issue, Ali?"

"Not really." Ali hesitated. "I have already arranged for Tom to head over to the States."

"Do you think there will be others, Matthew?"

"My guess is yes, Plato. But I hope it won't be for a few weeks and by then we should have most of our plans in place."

*   *   *

It was late, and Matthew and Emma strolled out to the sand and sat a while watching over the Caspian. By now, it had become a dark, unfriendly sea with no welcoming harbor lights or boats out on the water. It was as though it was dead to enjoyment. Very different from where they had come from, where the sea invited recreation, ships anchored and waited their turn to unload in port, and activity was rampant and continuous. Here it was still, dark, and uninviting.

Matthew and Emma lay together on the hard, gray sand and listened to the crackling of the low waves as they broke, or rather set, upon the shoreline.

There was nothing interesting in their sounds but Matthew was quite happy to spend a few moments with Emma, talking about nothing in particular other than who they were, where they had come from, and their brief history. That was comfort enough for them in this frigid, insipid world of nothingness where no amount of imagination could conjure up any kind of love for one's environment. It was no wonder the shoreline was deserted. There were no memories to hold on to and no one to share them with. The Caspian was a deserted sea of nothing, at least on the Iranian shoreline.

It was after midnight before Matthew and Emma went back into the house. The fire pit was flickering, the logs were spitting sparks, and the others were laughing and sharing the hookah. They laughed and hugged and slouched until they slept on the rugs and pulled covers over themselves. Heads rested on shoulders, in laps, and legs intertwined with legs as the flames rose and fell with a friendly warmth that encompassed them all. It was difficult to tear away, but Matthew and Emma eventually headed upstairs to their room, collapsed on their bed, and slept, then slept some more.

* * *

"I met with Jafaar Sazesh a couple of days ago." Plato chose a few pieces of fruit from the oversized plate that Margaret had prepared for everyone and placed on the table out on the deck area for breakfast. The breeze coming off the sea was magnificently refreshing as everyone gathered outside just before noon. Plato and Margaret had already had their swim in the Caspian.

"Oh, and what did you find out?" Matthew asked as he complemented his plate with pineapple. Emma did the same and looked over at Plato.

"Not a lot more than we've been told already, although he doubts what they're saying," Plato offered.

"How so?" Emma asked.

"There's more to this than the Tudeh," said Ali. "For a start, we now know for sure that the guy they nailed was a well-known young intern for the Revolutionary Guard. He was devoted to them by all accounts. As committed to the Islamic cause as they come. That in itself tells a story but his ID has proven false, although it isn't going to be published, if you know what I mean. The inside story is that he was an Islamic Regime sympathizer used by the Revolutionary Guard to put a dent in the rally. He certainly did that, but the group recovered. I think the cinema incident backfired on the Revolutionary Guard, and the Friends of Iran have come back with a vengeance—especially now that they believe the Regime was behind it." Ali stopped and looked over at Matthew.

"I think the chatter from the Gorgan outpost confirms that," Matthew offered.

"If one can work one's way through the traffic noise, I think the Islamic Republic are claiming a success to the end of Friends of Iran. Apparently, the Ruskies were pretty disturbed by these guys. Too much to lose. But that's just the chatter. I don't think those young guys are giving up that easily. In fact, there's another session coming up in one of the school gyms. We need to keep our eyes on it." Plato was clearly concerned.

"Will you do that, Plato?" Matthew asked.

"Between Ali and I, we'll be monitoring the situation very closely."

"Great. Make sure you keep me in the loop but keep a very low profile." The others nodded their understanding.

"We need to make sure the Friends of Iran succeed in their mission, but they can't know we are pushing them along. I need you to make sure that anyone who presents a threat to them is dealt with."

"What do you mean, Matthew?" Ali sked.

"Ali, it's time to combine our efforts at the refinery with the political efforts that our young friends are pushing for—change! If that means by force, then so be it. Tell me what you need, and I'll arrange things." Matthew was almost animated now and Emma leaned in closer, wondering if the help he was referring to was her.

"Matthew," said Plato, "do you mean using force? If so, we are moving into substantially different territory from what we've been involved in so far."

"I mean force, Plato, my friend. Remember that the Friends of Iran and, I suspect, the newly formed unions, have been the subject of forceful and ruthless actions by the Revolutionary Guard. We have to help them push back if we want to move the Regime away from associating with Russia and China. We have to drive a wedge between them, and our young friends are the way forward. In the end, it doesn't matter if the Islamic Regime stays or leaves.

What matters is their affiliation with the West or with the East." Matthew paused and waited for a response.

"What kind of force?" Ali asked.

"Watch for shadows that appear at rallies. Have your people listen for messages and chatter among the crowds that could hinder the cause. Whatever it is, identify the perpetrators and shut them down—by force if necessary. If you need help, let me know, but let's get it done. We can't let anything stop the youth at this point."

The others went rigid, sat back, and pondered what Matthew was telling them, yet they knew he was right. There were no half measures. Get it done.

Matthew changed his focus. "What do we know about the Islamic Regime's financial world, Plato? Anything more we need to be concerned with?"

"I don't think so, Matthew. It's pretty transparent, although I'm sure that's not what they intend. What we know is the Regime is getting richer and the Iranians are getting poorer. Sure, they consistently advocate for the poor but in the end, they're the ones getting richer and no one else. Same old, same old. It is truly frustrating, but their followers are brainwashed into believing their supremacy. This is truly far worse than the Pahlavi dynasty." The frustration in Plato's voice was palpable and disarming.

Matthew interrupted.

"Plato, what do we have to do to interrupt the flow of money into the Cayman account?" Matthew looked over at Plato.

"Which one? The Regime or the Mansourian?" Plato asked.

"The Mansourian account. That is, any money destined for the Regime's own pockets."

"Well, without me being on the foreign desk, it will be difficult but provided I get some high-tech help, I think we could do it. We'd open another account and siphon the Mansourian money into that, then link the new account to another offshore one so we can camouflage the trail." Plato seemed satisfied but the look on his face belied his discomfort in executing the strategy. It wouldn't be that simple—would it?

"I'll talk to Stockman and see if we can get a crypto man in with us to mess with the system." Matthew turned to Ali. "Ali... what's happening with the Friends of Iran these days?"

"They're still all pumped up and moving forward," Ali responded and stared at Matthew as though he was also waiting for instructions. "I mean, they're still gathering supporters, still meeting, and still alarming the Regime."

"Any physical problems? Anything more like what we saw in Chalus at the cinema?"

"There have been a number of skirmishes, and I think there's going to be a substantial backlash soon, but nothing as serious as the cinema incident. I don't know when it will come, but I know it will." Ali looked despondent.

"Are you hearing anything from your contacts in the Revolutionary Guard?"

"They're nervous. They don't want to turn on their own young people, and there are many sympathizers in the ranks, but I don't know what will happen if they're ordered to take action."

"Okay. I'll try to find out more from the listening post in Gorgan. Meanwhile, move in deeper and keep as close as you can to the Revolutionary Guard in particular. I think we know where the Friends of Iran are heading," Matthew added.

"Yes, and they're also peaceful, as far as I can tell. I'm sure they know that won't work. They need to keep on track with their mandate to revolutionize society without war. They have to. I don't think they have any choice. The moment they turn to violence, it'll be the end for them and they know that."

"I hope you're right, Ali. We can't afford for them to create another civil war here." Matthew paused and looked around at his friends.

"As for the union, that's also gaining substantial traction, Matthew. My guess is that there's a secret plebiscite going on as we speak. Thousands are going to be involved and I think they'll be ready to declare themselves as a solid movement of workers, united for the first time, over the next two months." Ali looked at Plato and Matthew.

"Ali, you need to be sure and not just guess. Get closer to Jafaar. Become one of his supporters and work with him to make sure he's successful. The stronger his movement gets, the more they'll be able to support the Friends of Iran, and that would mean common ground across the age groups." Matthew seemed excited at the prospect, although he wondered whether it was wishful thinking or a real possibility that it could all come together.

"You know, I think I can get this to work," said Plato. "I mean hijacking the accounts without them knowing it's happening." He had been deep in thought while Ali and Matthew had been talking. Clearly, he had been thinking about what he had to do. "There's something like $25 billion in that account!" Suddenly he seemed excited.

"What about the Regime's account? If we could cripple that, everything would come to a stop, including any payments to the Revolutionary Guard." It was a new idea that Matthew was throwing out.

Plato had a broad grin on his face. "I don't see why we couldn't make that happen, Matthew, and I'd suggest we do it at the same time as the Mansourian account so they don't have time to distribute the Revolutionary Guard funds before we can get to them. It will mean alerting some of our banking friends in Europe as to what's happening, but I think Stockman is our man to do that, don't you think?" Plato looked over at Matthew.

"I think you're right. Now we need to establish when to pull the trigger." Matthew, Plato, and Ali smiled, and Emma let out a "Yow-eeee" and clapped her hands. Margaret had been quietly sitting by the fire, poking at the logs, and just listening to the men plot and plan.

"Should I tell Daddy?" Margaret asked when the hubbub died down.

"Why would you do that, my dear?" Plato asked as he looked over at his wife with a questioning frown.

"Well, for one, someone will need to alert the Russians and the Chinese that the bottom has fallen out of the agreement."

They all laughed as they realized the importance of what Margaret was suggesting. It would take someone like her father to be convincing enough to persuade both powers that everything they had been working on with the Islamic Regime was about to be laid to ruin. It would never be enough for them to hear it only from the listening post or their operatives on the ground.

"What a great idea, Margaret," said Matthew. "Do you think he would help out like that?"

"Absolutely, Matthew." He knows there has to be change and, to be honest, he doesn't think that much of the arrangements the Chinese and Russians have been involved in with the Iranians. I know the US is really concerned and this might be just what they need to throw a spanner in the works, so to speak." Margaret picked away at the pieces of food that were left on the plate. She picked some up, licked her fingers, and looked up at Matthew. "Okay?" she asked.

"You bet, Margaret. Just wait for my word, though. Don't want to unload too quickly." Matthew wiggled his eyebrows at Margaret and they all laughed at the innuendo.

Margaret smiled and carried on chewing the fruit.

It was time for Emma and Matthew to head back to Sari. They said their farewells, kissed a few cheeks, shook a few hands, and headed out through the cypress trees to the main road and headed east. There was a lot for Matthew to think about.

"Good people," said Emma understating the importance of the group they had just left.

"Better than good. Those guys are carrying quite a load."

They both sat back and focused on the road ahead while not seeing it, lost in their thoughts.

*   *   *

Matthew dropped Emma off at the gate to the camp, kissed her goodbye, and headed back to his hotel. She had loaded him up with a couple of bottles of vodka on her last visit, and now he sipped at the three ounces he had poured into the bathroom glass while he put a call in to Stockman. He had no idea where he was, nor what time it was wherever that was.

"Stockman." A distinctly succinct response was followed by, "Hello, my boy. What are you up to?" It didn't take long for Stockman to re-focus and realize it was Matthew calling.

"Hi, Stockman. Where are you these days?"

"In London. At least the time zones are close. What's up?"

"I took Emma over to Chalus to visit with Plato."

"Great. How is she doing? I haven't heard from her for a while now."

"She's doing really well and has her corner of the project well under control. I wanted her to meet with Plato and Margaret, and Ali was there, so we had a chance to go over things in more depth, but I wanted to run a few things by you."

"Shoot. I'm all ears." Stockman was obviously in a good mood.

"I told Plato I wanted to divert both of the Regime's offshore money, including the Mansourian accounts, into a European account of our choosing. We'll need some technical expertise as well as account numbers. Can you set something up as soon as you can? Plato's preparing to be ready whenever we pull the trigger, so perhaps you can send him whatever routing numbers you need, and he'll look after the diversion once we get him that IT person." Matthew paused.

"No problem. Colin will look after it. We have special accounts set up that we use for these kinds of things, and he's just the chap to organize the technical side of the transfers. Just let me know when to actually pull the trigger. In the meantime, I'll have Colin communicate with Plato over bank account numbers and wire details. Leave it to me. Of course, the shit will really hit the fan once this happens. If the Regime can't recover fast enough and change accounts in time, you can bet things for them will fall apart pretty fast, so we have to make sure it all comes together at the same time. What else?" Stockman fell silent as he waited for Matthew.

"Okay, Margaret will talk to her father about contacting the Russians and Chinese as soon as the cat's out of the bag. He has an incredible relationship with them, but I also want to make use of the Gorgan listening station to send out a few cryptic messages to our eastern friends."

"Like what, Matthew?"

"I think we need to lead up to the finale by laying a trail. Margaret's father will finish it off, but we have to send some of our own messages and I'm thinking we can use Leila to put the ideas into the commander's head and he can transmit the messages."

"Well, we could just go directly to the Americans in the Pentagon and have them do it, Matthew."

"Yes, we could. But I think we need to play this as close to our chests as possible and keep the level of reaction below nuclear. For instance, if I recruited the commander, there would be no telling if he would spill the beans to his superiors, regardless of our credentials."

"I understand what you mean. There's always a chance that the information would slip out or, if the big boys are involved, they'll blitz the place with propaganda and no one's going to know what to believe." Stockman sighed.

"You got it, Stockman. If they even have a whiff of us asking them to get involved, they'll be in there with all guns blazing and you can bet that's going to mean our Iranian friends will tighten up with Russia and China, and we'll have one hell of a mess on our hands. Let's just control all the moves our pieces need to make." Matthew was happy with Stockman's agreement.

"What about the Friends of Iran and the unions? What's going on with them?"

"Not as controllable as I would like, but Ali is doing a good job of staying ahead on that. There have been some skirmishes but nothing serious, and the Russians seem to have given up questioning the apparent Ukrainian interference. I think everyone knows it was a Revolutionary Guard setup, but no one's saying anything more. I can't discount the possibility that there won't be any more violence, but it appears as though there's sympathy for both the Friends of Iran and the unions, even among the Revolutionary Guard. We'll just have to wait and see; with Ali in play, we should stay pretty informed. He has a huge group of sympathizers working with him." Matthew paused.

"Sounds good," Stockman said. "Now, how about the plant and pipelines. Any progress?"

"As I mentioned, Emma's doing a great job on the boiler tubes, so I've no worries there. I don't know what's happening, if anything, on the overland pipeline. I haven't got into it yet, but my plan would be to be somewhat passive there. Maybe mess with the control systems. What do you think?"

"I think you should sabotage the pump houses. Forget the pipelines. They can be easily repaired and put back into action. The pump houses are the key. Take them out and it'll take forever to get the parts needed for replacements. I've talked things over with Brian and he has a really good handle on the overland pipe from Tehran as well as the reversing systems on all the other collector pipes. They're heavy-duty, high-head pumps and controllers. In fact, why not do both—the pump houses and the control system." Stockman seemed to be getting into detail he didn't normally get involved with these days, but his old habits were coming to the surface.

"I think you're right, Stockman. In fact, we'll get rid of the pumps first and they won't realize the control systems will have gone AWOL until they are mechanically ready again. If they ever get that far. As for the new pipeline heading north from Tehran, our guys have already started to mess with it, so I think we can leave that to sort itself out."

"Okay," Stockman conceded. "What about Neka? Anything on the power plant? Ken has been in touch with the design team and they're on board. They have already incorporated into the control design a failure-to-operate feature. But they haven't gone as far as doing anything with the equipment. That should come from the field level."

"Did you manage to get us a contact at the power plant that we can coordinate with?" Matthew asked.

"Yes. You need to be in touch with Hans Zimmermann. He's the guy who coordinates with the Sari plant, so he should already be in contact with James, although they may not know that they're both part of ORB."

"Okay, I'll meet with both of them and find out what Hans is up to over there. It should be pretty straightforward to stop that plant from working." Matthew waited a moment. "Any thoughts on timing, Stockman?"

"It seems as though the Regime has instructed its people and advised their partners that July 4 th will be the start-up date. That's three months from now. We should target no more than a month before that to bring the place down." Stockman paused.

"That's a fast track for a societal revolt by the Friends of Iran, Stockman. But on the other hand, I don't think we're looking for that so much as a strong signal that the Iranian population demand change and that the Revolutionary Guard aren't going to go along with any strong-arm tactics—hopefully." Matthew sounded concerned but seemed to be reconciling things as he thought more about it.

"You're right, Matthew, and the last thing we want is a revolution." Stockman paused. "What we need is a strong signal sent to the Islamic Regime that the Iranian people aren't going to put up with the continued religious and social intolerance. There has already been enough unrest in the streets, so most of that message has already gotten out from the masses. The Revolutionary Guard can't cart everyone off to jail so long as they stay strong. So, the Regime will, hopefully, reconcile."

Stockman was right. The demonstrations over the last ten years had been significant and a reminder to the Regime that an Arab Spring could be just around the corner for them if they pushed too hard without real force behind them. There would be no help coming from the Russians, and certainly not the Chinese, especially once they knew there was no money in the Iranian bank. And the Americans... they would only fan the flames. There would likely be no way the clerics would be able to control the masses of young people who wanted change this time around, and they weren't going to wait or accept any other way. Provided the unions were behind them, it would be too great a force to be reckoned with.

"Anything else, Matthew?" Stockman waited for him to respond.

"I think we've just about covered it. It seems as though I have a good friend in the ranks up at the Sari plant. A guy called Hossein Daneshkah. He got his master's in political science about five years ago from the University of California and married Liz, an American woman also with a poli-sci degree. They lived in Oakland until about a year ago, when they got their visa to come back. They live right here in Sari, and Liz is expecting their first baby. I think they're both about thirty-six years old. Both are working at the plant but heavily involved in local politics. I think he's close enough to the Russians in play there to keep an eye on them for me if we need. He doesn't have a clue what we're doing there, but he seems to appreciate us being around for whatever reason. Could be a ruse, could be a double agent, or he may just be playing things straight and really has no idea what's going on. Can you see if there is anything in his background that we have to be careful of?"

"Sure. It should be easy enough given the information you have. I'll have one of our people run a trace. Anything else?"

"I think that's it for now. But let me know when you have the offshore banking issue sorted out so we can get Plato planning."

"Okay. Oh, by the way, is Sloan supplying you with good manpower?" Stockman asked.

"He sure is on the ball, Stockman. One word to Dick Elliot and, before you know it, we've got another ex-pat on the ground. I can't believe how easy it is for him. I think they're all on-site now."

"You have to know the right people, Matthew. Talk soon." With that, Stockman was gone.

Matthew had another vodka, stretched out on the bed, and mulled over where he was with things and where he needed to be next. The timing had been established for plant start-up and that meant he needed to figure out a schedule for the other things to fall into place. He worked it through his mind and went over things again. He would go through the same routine in the morning just to see if there were any twists he hadn't thought about. He needed to get back to Leila with some instructions.

*   *   *

Matthew drove into Sari just before midnight and parked close to the Revolutionary Guard barracks. He could keep his eye on the security gate from there and spot when Leila came out from her usual grilling with the agents. Fortunately, it was one of the four days when the commander did his duty and visited his lady friend.

It was just before 1:00 a.m. when Leila appeared, wrapped her chador tightly around herself, and hustled off down the road toward her apartment. Matthew would give her thirty minutes to get home and get ready for bed before he went in.

Leila didn't seem to be the least bit surprised when Matthew carefully made his way into her bedroom, avoiding the windows despite the pulled curtains, and sat on the end of her bed.

"Nice to see you too," she said with a crooked smile. There was a look of anxiety on her face as she anticipated a request from Matthew that she was not looking forward to and at the same time realizing this might be her only way out of Iran with her family. Despite her requests, she still hadn't gotten her passport returned to her. She was really starting to worry.

Matthew smiled and reached over and put his hand on her shoulder.

"Turn your radio on."

"What? Why?" Leila searched his eyes for an answer. She didn't get one but still reached over and turned the radio on to her favorite music station.

"I need you to do something for me, Leila," Matthew whispered to her.

"I knew it was coming. I just didn't know when. What do you need me to do?" Leila focused on Matthew with a worried look on her face.

"Tell the commander that you heard things he might be interested in. Then wait to see if he bites. If he does, let him know that some high-ranking friends of your parents were overheard talking about the Russian and Chinese alliances and they were very derogatory. Tell him that once the refinery is operating, the intent is for the Iranians to raise the oil prices dramatically. In fact, the expectation is that they'll be 40 percent higher than previously agreed, with payment up front." Matthew paused and watched Leila for a reaction.

"Is that true?" Leila's eyes were open wide as she stared at Matthew.

"It's a fact," Matthew lied. "We have the information from one of our people in the Regime's inner circle in Tehran. There's no doubt about it. Their plan is to complete the plant, have the Russians and Chinese provide their tankers and complete their funding, load up the first few tankers, and then push the prices higher after the Ruskies cut off their contracts with the Saudis." If he could convince Leila, she'd do a better job of convincing the commander.

"My God. I don't believe it. It could start a war." Leila's eyes were still out on stalks. Clearly, she believed the story and, clearly, she didn't know what to think.

"Listen, if you convince the commander and he passes it on through channels, you may be able to prevent a war, Leila. Think of it like that."

"Yes. Yes, I could. I have to tell him as soon as I can. Tomorrow. I'll do it tomorrow night." Her lips trembled and there were tears in the corners of her eyes.

Leila didn't know that Matthew knew about the guard in the closet and he didn't want to tell her; she might take exception to such a private intrusion and think Matthew had heard and maybe seen everything that went on between her and the commander. It was essential the guard not hear what she was going to tell the commander.

"I'm thinking that you should tell him away from the apartment where you two meet, just in case it's bugged." Matthew didn't really believe there was a bug in the room but he needed to keep her worried, as well as get the commander away from the eavesdropper in the closet.

"You think it could be? Why would anyone do that?" She knew the apartment was bugged, but the bug was the guard in the closet.

"Well, you're seeing a commander in the US communications service. You can bet the Revolutionary Guard knows it's going on. They're not going to bother you as long as it's all innocent, but they'll certainly have wanted to make sure, so you can bet there's a bug in here somewhere."

"You could be right." Leila looked thoughtful for a minute. "I know. I'll convince him to take a walk around the block with me. I'll tell him I have a headache and need some fresh air. He won't like that but he won't want to miss an evening of pleasure either, so I think it'll work."

"Sounds like a plan. I'll be back in a couple of days to find out how you managed. Meanwhile, let's hope the commander gets on board and passes the information on."

Matthew wanted to contact Stockman to go over the plan so far, so he could contact his people in the Pentagon to be on the lookout for any message coming from the commander and any response. The seed had been sown and Matthew just needed to wait and see if it grew.

"I'd better go, Leila. It's getting late and you need your beauty sleep." He smiled at her.

"You think I need that to be beautiful?"

"I didn't mean it like that. It's just an expression. You're beautiful enough already, but some shuteye can't hurt."

"Get out of here, you. I'll see you in a couple of nights. But listen, it doesn't have to be this late. The day after tomorrow, I don't see the commander, so you can come earlier. Perhaps as soon as it gets dark."

"Sounds good." Matthew got up from the bed, edged around the perimeter of the room and out through the doors to the back balcony, where he climbed down to the yard and disappeared through the gate to the lane.

He smiled to himself as he drove back to the hotel. It was a good night's work. Hopefully, it would work. It should. If it did, there should be a lot of chatter going back and forth between Iran, Russia, and China. Ambassadors would get involved. There would be threats and counter-threats. There would be meetings and the distrust would grow into self-preservation. That's all Matthew needed. He didn't need a war, just discontent with no reasonable resolution. Then, when all was ready, Margaret's father would contact the parties with commentary designed to further widen the gap between them.

* * *

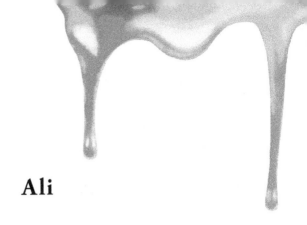

Ali

Jafaar Sazesh was pleased with himself. He had just received the informal results of another hurriedly organized national plebiscite that showed continuing support for the unionization of workers in Iran.

It was a dumbfounding victory after all these years of talk, persuasion, negotiation, argument, tears mixed with laughter, and now celebration at the success—so far—in such a religiously driven and now tyrannical country.

Jafaar celebrated with his wife, Saphir, who fully supported her husband for all the right reasons. The country deserved it, the workers had earned it, and it could soon be time that some kind of social welfare system would be introduced for the masses—provided the Regime allowed it. And that was the next and possibly impossible obstacle. But Jafaar not only had the support of his new membership, which counted in the hundreds of thousands, but also the Friends of Iran, the youth-inspired group that his son, Amir, had started. They also counted in the hundreds of thousands and had been even further inspired by the Chalus cinema massacre.

It had taken Jafaar's son, Amir, over a year to recover from the cinema blast. While he escaped debilitating physical harm, he suffered incredibly from the mental images and their effect on his emotional state, including his intense feeling of guilt upon having discovered that almost everyone in the cinema had died but him. And it was an event *he* had organized for the Friends of Iran. His nightmares seemed never-ending and had little desire to go back out into the world for six months. But gradually, with the help of his friends and family, Amir slowly came back to life. Losing four brothers in the blast had a monumentally miserable effect on his family. They all suffered for many months, but it was Jafaar who coaxed them out of that misery and set them back on the road to recovery.

Amir had worked hard to re-establish his control of the Friends of Iran, traveling throughout the country and talking to youth groups and universities about his vision. There was huge support, propelled further forward after what had happened at the cinema in Chalus and the suspicion of who was to blame. There were feelings of anger, disgust, and retribution, but Amir calmed the crowds and reminded them that violence was not the way. He also let it be known that it was not the Russians that had planned and executed the blast but more than likely their own Regime. The outcry was enormous and emotional. The youth, many of whom had come back after their education abroad, were ready, able, and willing to spread the word, gather supporters, and present a unified, organized, and intellectual front to confront the Regime. The days of violent street demonstrations were over. It was a time for peaceful marches and to act with intelligence and planning.

The Islamic Regime was cynical, affronted, and intent on retribution. They would not allow a group of young intellectuals dictate to them. Word was sent to the Revolutionary Guard to be armed and deal with any rebellious group that gathered in any public place and in the privacy of their own homes, if necessary. It was as though SAVAK had never left. What the Regime didn't realize was that even the youth of the Revolutionary Guard were dissatisfied with their situation, more educated than their SAVAK cousins, and sympathetic to the Friends of Iran—that is, everyone other than the older soldiers who remained close to the religious beliefs of their faith and the Regime established by their leader, Khomeini.

But still, the extent of the retribution they were prepared to extol was less than expected and, while there were skirmishes with the Friends of Iran and their supporters, there was no serious intent to stop or injure them.

The Revolutionary Guard might have been reluctant to punish the Friends of Iran, but it was the union membership that would stop them in their tracks.

Ali called on his good friend Jafaar. They had known each other since their school days in Chalus. That was many years ago now, and as they grew into young adults, Jafaar had gone his way to the fields and followed in the footsteps of his father and grandfather, while Ali went on to become educated and eventually head to America, where he eventually prospered in business, doing much the same as what Jafaar was doing in Iran but in a much larger and more mechanized way. As Jafaar got older and some of his friends were leaving to spread their wings and see how other people lived, he too got restless. But he couldn't leave Chalus. He had a family to support, a standing in the community, and a thirst for improvement in his society.

That's when he started to talk about a cooperative, a social- and work-sharing network that could improve everyone's life. At first, people listened with amusement and weren't interested in pursuing his suggestions. But then, they did start to listen to him and his followers as they worked their way through the issues and discovered and discussed solutions with them. Ali had always visited Jafaar whenever he came back to Iran, and he helped consolidate Jafaar's ideas about unions as he knew about them from living in the US. After all, Ali now had experience in collective bargaining and working relationships, and Jafaar lapped the information up.

"Jafaar, my good friend, are you making progress with your union philosophy with the employers?" Ali asked a few days after he had talked with Matthew in Chalus.

"Oh, very much so, my good friend. There are so many of us with the same thoughts now and we are strong. Incredibly strong. We have had meetings with some privately owned companies and most of them welcome our ability to communicate as a whole, rather than them having to negotiate with each person. That is complex and cumbersome and open to a lot of grievances, and those who don't do well in bargaining get jealous of those that do and then start to argue and fight." Jafaar smiled, dropped a sugar cube into his chai and sipped the piping hot drink from the small glass.

"And what about government agencies? Are they as keen as the private companies?"

"Well, they're resisting. They don't like to see us communicating and meeting. They look on it as some kind of subversiveness. But they don't want to understand." Jafaar looked down at the floor and averted his eyes from Ali.

"Do you think they'll come around?"

"They have to, my friend. They have no choice. We have come to that time when we will perform an act of solidarity if they continue to ignore us. Do you remember what you told me about the Polish workers in the 1980s and how they fought for an independent, self-governing union? Remember what they were fighting—martial law and political repression? That story has been told over and over again, but our membership knows they succeeded, so they are buoyed by that same prospect." Jafaar paused.

"I remember indeed, my friend. Are you strong enough to go through that yet?" Ali asked, getting close to where he wanted to go with the discussion.

"Yes, we are, my friend. We are ready at a moment's notice, but it will depend on the employers and what their reaction will be to our proposed union agreement."

"Oh, and when will that be, Jafaar? Soon?" Ali was getting excited at the prospect.

"Within two weeks. The first meeting will be with NPC when we'll test our strength." Jafaar looked serious and adamant.

"And what about your son, Amir, and the Friends of Iran? What are they doing?"

"What do you mean, my friend? They're now a powerful group, but they also have to test the political climate. I don't know what their plans are at this time, only that they are continuing to gain strength and frustrating the Regime."

"Perhaps they can somehow join your movement. There would be substantial strength in those combined numbers." Ali looked at Jafaar with a twinkle in his eyes.

"What are you up to, you old fox? I've seen that look in your eyes before." Jafaar smiled a broad smile. He knew his friend well. There was something more in Ali's mind than just a casual interest in Jafaar's business.

"My good friend, I must tell you that there's a move afoot that has a very good chance of changing the direction of this Regime. I cannot go into the details. You have to trust me on this. I can tell you it's not an invasion by foreign powers, nor is it anything that will harm the people of our country. Quite the opposite. But it is something aimed at the very heart of the Regime to drive a wedge between it and the Russians and Chinese. It will also create a time for you and your son to establish a strong base for the future of our country. While it doesn't necessarily mean an overthrow of this Regime, it is intended to, shall we say, tame it. And, if it cannot be tamed, it will have to be replaced." Ali paused and looked at his friend.

"Go on." Jafaar was stuck for words.

"We need to coordinate your efforts and those of the Friends of Iran," Ali paused again, "and all the better if Amir is working with you."

Jafaar's jaw had dropped. He seemed speechless but recovered quickly.

"If you say it is, then it is so, my good friend. What do we do?" Jafaar spread his hands out, palms up, on the table between him and his friend.

"The timing of your meeting with NPC, combined with action by the Friends of Iran on a national scale at the same time, is really important for the cause. The Regime will be caught totally off balance. And when that happens, we will do what we have to do, and then you will know." Ali stretched his hands across the table and placed them over Jafaar's.

"When? When are we supposed to meet with NPC?" Jafaar listened intently.

"We need you to move your meeting out a little. I am not sure for how long, but it could be only a couple of weeks. Can you wait that long?" Ali asked his friend.

"It will give me time to work with Amir and for him to make whatever arrangements he has to make to get ready for a national move. What kind of action do you think he should organize?"

Ali had thought this through and knew it would be a question his friend would put to him.

"Tell him we want them to occupy the mosques in all the major cities. Tell him to arrange for guest speakers to keep the crowds occupied. Tell him to contact their friends in the Revolutionary Guard and have them join in. All is to be peaceful but disruptive. No one would dare hunt them down in places of worship. Make sure their membership includes females. Tell them to bring their children. Tell them to make noise and invite the local and international press. Make sure photos and videos are made and distributed. Make sure that the day is held secret, so the Regime has no chance to take down the internet feeds too soon." Amir was finished. He stood, held Jafaar by the shoulders and hugged him. "The time has come, my friend."

Jafaar couldn't speak but stood watching as Ali left his home.

Ali looked back over his shoulder. "Wait for my call."

* * *

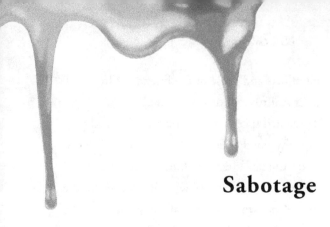

Sabotage

There were so many ways to sabotage the Sari plant during the construction phase that Matthew was sure he could manage the physical part of the job with the help of his associates on the site. It didn't take many, and the few that were there were more than capable of landing a powerful blow.

Clearly, Emma had the sabotage of the boiler tubes under control and the failure of those alone could mean months, if not years, of retrofit and delays. Squeezed under the steam drum and hovering above the supply drum, Emma had to fit the purposely designed and configured thin-walled supply tubes into each of the drum shells and then weld their connection points. The weld positions were the most difficult, and every high-pressure weld had to have a 100-percent x-ray taken to ensure compliance. It was the most grueling and demanding function in the entire plant. The welder's body had to contort into unimaginable shapes and positions to weld each tube with a circumference that was only one inch in diameter, and there were 3,000 tubes and only two welders.

Emma had managed to block over 60 percent of the tubes she was responsible for welding. Every weld came through with a 100-percent x-ray validation with no weld scours or over-burns on the drums that could cause concern. She raised no flags and the blockages were a lot more than needed to cause a collapse of the entire steam system without drawing the attention of the uneducated Revolutionary Guard until well after Emma had left Iran. The system would need a complete and exhaustive inspection and even if the operators caught everything on their first inspection pass, it could take a year to repair. New tubes would be needed, the old ones cut out and replaced. It was a far more exhaustive task than when the original tubes were installed.

But it was the control system where the sabotage would cause the greatest amount of subversive damage. It was an area of the plant that was easily penetrated by would-be saboteurs but difficult to monitor or control and easy for an expert to demolish. While Matthew didn't have that knowledge, James undoubtedly did. In fact, he had superior knowledge in the field of process control and reveled in the ideas he could concoct to bring the plant to its knees in an instant. From the first moment of commissioning the utilities, it would become clear there were serious problems with the plant. Cooling water would be far too hot, and the cooling tower would become overloaded; instrument air pressure would run too high for no obvious reason and the filters would be blocked and the specified size of the supply tanks far too small; and water systems would run at erratic pressures and temperatures and lubrication systems would be clogged with debris and flaking paint in the tanks. The problems would appear to be insurmountable. Each would have to be forensically diagnosed, repaired, and re-tested. With the hijacking of the control system, things would not go well, and even when all seemed to have been corrected, spikes of inconsistencies would plague the plant. The lack of dependable utilities meant it was impossible to commission the process systems that relied on air, water, and steam.

James and Matthew had spent several evenings considering the potential project failure by controlled missteps in graduated ways. James knew how, Matthew knew when and to what extent, and together they devised a plan that few could penetrate, least of all the Revolutionary Guard who monitored them. Matthew was far more interested in a tortured and drawn-out plan of failure than James, who advocated for a complete and massive control failure. Matthew won the argument, although there was really none to be had; James was quite happy to execute as instructed.

James spent the next two months re-writing the instructions sent to him by the Montreal-based process engineers to deliver a process instruction manual that was replete with counteractivities for plant start-up and control, sufficient for the users to get totally screwed up without realizing what they were doing. It could take years to sort out and the plant could still operate, but it'd be at less than 10- or 20-percent efficiency. It would be considered an utter failure and while it remained only in Iranian hands it might never recover. Meanwhile, the oil would still have to flow—but from the Straits of Hormuz and not from the Caspian.

But the control system was only one of the components of failure. Physicality was another and had an immediate impact.

Clearly, the boilers would never operate at capacity given the sabotage initiatives. There was no possibility of replacing them within any kind of a reasonable time frame—that is, if the problems could even be identified. There was little point in replacing boilers if the tubes were the problem. And who could tell if that was where the problems were without thoroughly searching for faults that seemed implausible.

The physical assets of the refinery were easy to deal with compared to the political issues. When the time came, the Tehran pipelines through the Alborz Mountains were a straightforward target for sabotage. Like the boiler tubes, they were subject to weld x-ray, although to a lesser extent; it was easy enough for the experienced welder to pass the x-ray but leave the remnants of sabotage materials in the pipeline that would end up blocking the pump stations and clogging the downstream pump filters. It could be as easy as rags left in the pipe or as sophisticated as weld scours on the pipe joint areas so that even the watchful eyes of the inspectors—who were charged with visual inspection before the pipes were finally wrapped—would not be able to detect the gap in pipe protection from the cathodic reaction.

While Matthew was originally thinking of leaving the pipelines out of the sabotage plan and focusing on the control system and pump stations, it was too easy to create havoc with them. Matthew had brought in one more person with his welding rig to tackle some of the pipeline welding and do whatever damage could be done.

The sabotage of the plant assets was a relatively easy accomplishment now that the saboteurs had everything in place and their instructions. They were professionals, and professionals knew how to succeed in whatever they were instructed. In this case, it was a matter of sabotage, and all the saboteurs took their assignments seriously. It was a matter of professional know-how, and healthy respect came with the success of their mission. It didn't matter if this was a mission of sabotage or not; it was a matter of success.

And so it was that the new plant was armed with total destruction as each system was commissioned. Even the utilities, the first of the circuits to be brought up to operating level, failed their initial tests. Valves had been installed in a reverse position and pumps had been plugged. But they were all small issues in the scheme of things, just to keep operations on their toes. The situation would get worse, far worse, as commissioning progressed to the more complex areas of process circuitry.

It was a three-month operation by Matthew and his associates to plan the purging of the plant of operational capability before it would all come to a grinding halt as the new owners realized they had a plant-wide problem that needed some serious attention. These were not going to be just commissioning "bugs." They were going to be substantial problems that questioned the very worthiness of the operational ability of the plant.

Each area of the plant would be shut down as it was re-examined, repaired, re-programmed, restarted, and declared inoperable to the extent expected for the full operation of the plant. Nothing would be successful as inherent problems planted by the original programming governed whatever retrofitting was undertaken. It would all be a disaster and the plant would never achieve optimum operating capacity sufficient to undertake the planned objective.

Even the supply pipeline would be plagued by problems with plugged pump filters plugged, failing weld areas incapable of handling the volume coming through, and damaged controls acting erratically. In itself, the 150-mile-long pipeline from Tehran would be rife with problems, with each section needing a forensic evaluation before any could be repaired. That alone was a lengthy and complex program of repair and retrofit.

Hopefully it would be all too much for the Regime. The new refinery would be incapable of delivering the requisite volume of processed products on time, and the Regime would have no way of knowing when they would be able to fulfill their contractual obligations and would be unable to retain any sense of reliability to their new and favored friends. While the Neka Power Plant would continue to put out the power it was contracted to supply to the northern coast, the seaport operations would be suspended with no known timeline for rejuvenation.

The Regime would have to look for alternatives to supply the Russians and Chinese the easy way. But were there any?

* * *

Matthew had worked the sabotage schedule through his mind a number of times since his last visit to Chalus and his subsequent discussion with Stockman. He now stared out of his hotel bedroom window over the Sari Valley as though looking for inspiration. But he didn't need it. He had rolled the plan over and over again in his head and seemed content.

Clearly, the most unknown factor was the effect the Friends of Iran and the unions would have on the Regime, and what reaction it might evoke. It was imperative that Ali work his way into those groups and alert them of what could be coming and what help he could offer them. It would be most effective if a national call to action by both groups occurred two weeks before the plant was taken out of operation. At the same time, Plato should be working with Colin to make the financial transfers from the Cayman accounts into the ORB account and doubling down to divert incoming funds. During the ensuing week, the Russians and Chinese would be continually alerted to the Iranian funding problems, and the lines of communications with the Iranians would be curtailed as they worked to consolidate their positions and examine the effects on their investments. No one would be focused on the Sari plant and it would be assumed that the start-up date would be maintained.

Meanwhile, system testing at the plant would be in full swing and while the general utility systems would eventually pass inspection and be accepted by operations, it would only provide them with a false sense of security. The first of the problems would be the commissioning of the high-pressure steam systems, also considered a utility, which would include the start-up of the boilers, turbines, and compressors. The plant would need the steam to provide heat for various processing requirements in the plant, and the generators would provide the supplemental power while the compressors would be on standby, ready to process the final by-products. At this point, there would be no need to rely on the power from the Neka plant. The grid would be sufficient for commissioning in the short term. But the Neka Power Plant was on the sabotage shortlist for Matthew to coordinate with once the steam systems at the refinery were dealt with.

Then there were the overland pipelines. The first of the storage tanks at the refinery would be scheduled to be filled from them while commissioning of the plant was ongoing. There was no problem in allowing that to happen if the pump stations were sabotaged close to the time that the steam systems were being tested. It was imperative that the sequence of failures was fast and caused as much chaos as possible throughout the plant in as short a time as possible. As soon as the first failure occurred, IDRO would be searching for other problems and, while they were quite ignorant of the technicalities involved, it would make Matthew's work that much more difficult to have them poke around to a much greater extent than normal.

The collector lines from the oilfields would be the last on the list of sabotaged items. They would be operating up to the point when the overland pipeline pump houses failed and as the first of the oil storage tanks at the Sari plant was being filled. The control system programming would stop the flow through the collector lines. It would not be possible to reverse the flows immediately—that would need manual adjustments to the pipeline bypasses that were used for oil flow in either direction. Immediately before filling the first storage tank at the Sari site, the bypasses would be adjusted to reverse the south-flowing oil to the north. Matthew had no intention of sabotaging the collector pipelines that would be needed once the direction of the oil flows was changed back to supply the south coast terminals again.

Once the steam systems were declared non-operational, the first processing unit in the refinery—the crude oil distillation unit, where decreasing heat was used to separate the crude oil fractions—would be inoperative. When there was no steam, there was no heat, and no ability to distill. Since the steam turbines contributed to the power generation for the compressors, and with them now out of action, there would be no ability to refine the various fractions once they were eventually distilled.

Matthew sat back and sipped on his vodka. Things were coming together, but a number of pieces still had to be put into play.

* * *

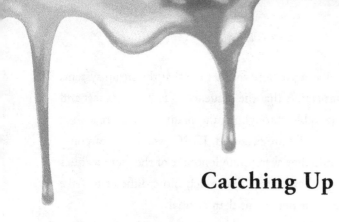

Catching Up

The phone rang several times before Stockman answered. "Oh, hi there, Matthew. I was just on the other line with Plato. I think we have everything organized between him and Colin for the electronic heist. He just needs the word. Where are we with that?"

"The plant has started to commission the utility systems, so we're still a month or so away from D-day, Stockman. There are a few things we still need to cover off. Did you run that check on Hossein Daneshkah?"

"Yes. He's all clear. Good credentials; solid background. Education checks out, and no affiliations we can find with radicals. Seems he has kept his nose clean, and his younger years were trouble-free. It's not a definitive shakedown given that these days there are all kinds of ways to doctor credentials, but on the surface, all's good. What are you going to use him for?"

"He's still an unknown to us, regardless of the background check, Stockman. I'm going to have Ali talk to him and figure out which side he plays on. If Ali thinks he's good, then we'll use him to coordinate the efforts between Jafaar's group and Amir's. I could do with a little help. If Ali is suspicious for whatever reason, we'll drop him, and move on."

"Sounds good, Matthew. I'll leave that up to you. Now, I don't think there's much more to say about the financial side. Everything's set. You just have to give me the word and I'll pass it on to Colin and Plato, and they can do their things. The Regime is going to find out pretty fast that there's something wrong, so be sure the other things fall into place as quickly as possible." Stockman let Matthew respond.

"That's fine. The first signal will be the testing of the steam circuit at site. When that fails the wet test, there's going to be some panic before they discover the full extent of the problem. During that time, the Friends of

Iran will be holding their national demonstrations and Jafaar's union will be meeting with NPC. That'll keep the Regime busy, and their attention won't be on the plant. Now, what have you heard from our friends in the Gorgan listening station?" Matthew was eager to find out whether the messages being passed from Leila to the commander had been relayed to Russia and China. He knew from the last talk he'd had with Leila a couple of weeks before that she had passed the information on to the commander and he had swallowed it hook, line, and sinker. In fact, he hadn't stayed with her that evening after their walk around the block but had called Richard to get him back to base immediately.

"Ah yes. Haha. That really put the cat among the pigeons. The lines were hot with calls going back and forth. Ambassadors were visiting each other, and presidents were talking and sometimes shouting at each other. It sounds as though no one trusts anyone. The Chinese think the Russians are at the bottom of it all, the Russians think the Chinese have made a secret pact with the Iranians, and the Iranians are just proclaiming to be the innocent bystanders in everything and denying, denying, denying. Now, we have the Turks involved, and they want to broker talks to get the sides back to the table again. I don't know if or when that might happen, but it's out there and we're waiting for more fallout. Just wait until the money has disappeared, and then we're really going to see fireworks."

"Wow. That's great, Stockman. I know Leila kept giving the commander more and more information that I fed her, but essentially the story stayed the same. I was just reinforcing the position. We told them that the Iranians had already revised their financial forecasting for the next five years and had built the oil revenue price increase into those calculations. Then we let on that the Regime had published instructions to NPC letting them know about the change. In fact, we even had a set of those instructions made up to give to the commander. I never expected anyone to check with the NPC and they obviously didn't, and I don't think the NPC would have told them anything anyway. Now, we need to get Leila out of the country with her family. That was the promise."

"We're working on that. Let her know to get her things together and get down to the airport in Tehran. They'll be flown to Frankfurt or Munich and on to the US. Anytime they're ready, Matthew. I'll leave the timing up to you. Just let me know when they're on their way. Leila's family will have US visas organized once they arrive in Tehran."

"Thanks, Stockman. Remember that she doesn't have her passport. The Revolutionary Guard still have it and they aren't going to give it back."

"No problem, Matthew. We got another one from the US State Department. They have all her information on file. Hopefully, her parents have theirs."

"Yes, I checked. They have theirs, and they're current. She's going to be very relieved. I think I'm going to have her get ready over the next week and hustle her and her family out before the shit hits the fan. When it does, you can be sure there are going to be some very serious investigations and people all over are going to have to face a lot of questions." Matthew let out a sigh and paused.

"Yes, I know. You need to make sure our people are out of there and off site as well, and that includes James and his family. The trades guys, as well as Emma, need to leave as soon as their jobs are done. Plato and Margaret will have to leave too. It won't be long before the Regime finger Plato for his interference through the Melli Bank and Margaret's meddling through her father. I don't know about Ali, but my guess is that he'll be able to look after himself. What do you think?"

"I think you've nailed it, Stockman. I'm not sure about Jafaar and Amir, but I don't think they are going to need our help. They're going to be up to their necks in establishing some control over the people and calming them down. If we are right and the majority of the Revolutionary Guard sympathize with them, there should be few if any reprisals. The old guard may be inclined to fight for the Regime but if our estimate is correct, 85 percent of the Revolutionary Guard are under the age of thirty. That means there's not much of an 'old guard' left." Matthew paused as he thought about what he was saying. "God, I hope that's true," he but I think Ali will have some reasonable handle on those things over the next week or so. He's doing one hell of a good job traveling around with his group and talking to the civil leaders of the local populations. So far, the news is positive and there's certainly more than just a desire for change—there's an insistence for change. Let's hope it sticks when the going gets tough." Matthew stopped.

"Good. Good, Matthew. Now let's not forget Hans Zimmermann over at the Neka Power Plant. He's going to have to get out as well. Have you talked to him?

"I talked to him a few weeks ago, Stockman. Not much to tell. He's totally on board and has his side of things well under control. The last thing we want to do is to shut the power down to the northern population, so we've focused only on the expansion. The new transformers have been, shall we say, tampered with, and the controls have been set to cause the substation protection to fail. Two of the four boilers are going to fail, and the generator chain is misaligned just the same as at the Sari plant. No way they're going to work for long, and they'll shake themselves apart before they operate fully. There's also been some pretty fundamental built-in problems with the cables. Some of the largest high-voltage cables have been changed to a much lower rating so they're going to fry pretty soon into operations. The cooling tower can't really be messed with other than it has been deliberately undersized for the expanded station. Without being the right size, the cooling water will be a lot warmer than it should be. Anyway, Hans will be out of there in about ten days. He's heading back home."

"Good. Listen," Stockman was clearly satisfied with what he was hearing, "Ken has been keeping his ear to the ground on the port and shipping, but there's really nothing to report other than they are almost ready, but we haven't interfered. There's no point if they don't get a chance to be used, is there?"

"Haha, you're right, Stockman. It'd be a waste of time and talent. Let's just concentrate on what we have in hand. Listen, I know we're getting together next week in Istanbul, but I wanted to tell you that I think I have a tail. I'm not sure whom but they share space with the Revolutionary Guard in Sari. I've spotted them a number of times now and they seem intent on following me everywhere."

"What are you going to do, Matthew?" Stockman sounded a little worried.

"Nothing, at least not here in Sari. I'm just going to go about my business. Go to the site to work. See my friends. Go to the restaurant. And maybe I'll even wave to them now and then. My guess is they do this with most senior *ferengies*, especially if they aren't staying in camp. Let's let it go and see what happens; as long as nothing questionable is happening at the plant, why should they be suspicious?"

"I'll leave it to you, Matthew. Listen, I have to go. Let's talk again this time next week and see where we are."

"Will do, Stockman. Take care. Give my love to Lucy." The cell lines went dead.

Matthew thought about Hossein and what he could use him on to help the cause, but he was still not convinced he should do anything. Something was nagging at him. It was likely intuition more than anything solid. He put a call in to Plato.

"Hey, Plato. Matthew here. How are you?"

"Great, Matthew. I'm in Tehran, as you probably know. What can I do for you?"

"I need to speak to Ali, but I don't have his contact number. Can you send it to me?"

"Of course. Here, I'll do it now, and you'll get the message in a split second." There was a pause. "It's gone to you, Matthew. Have you got it?"

"It just arrived. That's great. Thanks. I talked to Stockman a little earlier, and he told me you and Colin have things all set."

"Yes. Colin's a good man. Very, very good with computers. He had everything worked out and ready yesterday. So, we're ahead of schedule and will just wait for you to give the word."

"That's great, Plato. I have to go. Looking forward to coming over again, but I'm not sure when. If I don't get a chance, I'll see you on the other side." Matthew smiled, and he heard Plato laugh as they ended their call.

"Ali, it's Matthew here. How are you, my friend?" Matthew had called Ali right away and fortunately got through on the first ring.

"Matthew. Good to hear from you. How are things moving?"

"On track, Ali. And you? I hear you've been doing some traveling."

"Oh boy. I've covered a lot of miles and met a lot of people, Matthew. But the news is good, and I haven't met anyone who is not prepared to fully support Jafaar."

"That's great, Ali, but I need you to do something for me."

"If I can. Shoot."

"There's someone working up on the Sari construction site—Hossein Daneshkah and his wife Liz—who seems to be very close to the ideals that Jafaar and Amir are promoting. James is keen on them. They've shared supper a few times. But he's an unknown. He checks out fine with Stockman. I just don't know whether to bring him into our tent, so to speak, or..."

"Let me talk to him, Matthew. I'll be in Sari the day after tomorrow and get James to introduce Hossein to me, and we'll go from there."

"Great. Let me know what you think as soon as you can after you've talked, Ali."

"Of course." Their cell phones shut off.

*   *   *

"This is it, Leila. Time to move." Matthew sat on the end of her bed.

"What now? Why the rush all of a sudden?" Leila was shocked, although she really had no reason to stay in Sari any longer. Her family kept skipping through her thoughts and now it all appeared too much to take on this fast. But she knew that when she left Iran this time, they would have to come with her. That reality had initially thrown her parents into a panic when she first broached the problem with them a couple of weeks ago. Of course, they wanted to know why, how, where? And when. They didn't want to go. Everything they knew was there in Sari. But gradually they realized it had to be. The Revolutionary Guard was starting to act nervously in the streets, looking at each and every person with a degree of suspicion. There was word of coming unrest and it seemed as though there was an odd, unsettled feeling in the air.

But they were comforted by the thought that they would be returning and had started to distribute what they had accumulated over the years to their friends and family, who would take care of their possessions while they were gone. Their apartment would be rented out. They found their passports and got clearance from the tax officials, who stamped their documents to show they had paid their taxes. They transferred what money they had over to Leila's bank account in the US. It was all done over a couple of weeks. Low-key. Below the radar and nothing that should raise the eyebrows of the authorities who had the power to stop them.

"We've been over this, Leila. There's going to be trouble over the next few weeks, and you need to be well away from here when that happens. If the authorities run rampant, and they probably will, they'll round everyone that is the slightest bit suspicious, and your rendezvousing with the commander will surely raise some questions."

"What do I take? Where do I go? What about plane tickets? I have questions, you know." Leila became sullen and had tears in the corners of her eyes.

"Listen, Leila, just get yourself ready. Pack whatever you brought with you. Have your parents take a couple of suitcases each. Your replacement passport is already in hand, and I have someone who's going to take you all down to Tehran and take care of you until the plane leaves for Frankfurt or Munich. Someone will be waiting for you at the other end in New York, give you some money to take care of the folks, and provide you with contact information for us all to stay in touch. Once things settle down here, we'll get your parents back to Sari, but not before it's safe. Okay?"

"Okay." Leila wiped the tears from her eyes and started to perk up. "They're gonna love New York, Matthew. All those lights, all that food, all those people. They won't know what to do with themselves. But we'll only spend a few days there and then head over to California. Did you know there's a Little Persia near Westwood Boulevard? They call it Tehrangeles! I'll get them an apartment in that area and settle them down while they wait." Leila was taking in the excitement and her tears disappeared as she started to babble about what they would do and where they would go.

"Listen, Leila, I have to go. I probably won't see you again but I want to say it's been great knowing you and thank you for your help with the commander."

"Oh, what am I going to say to him? And what about the guards?" She was almost back to tears as her mind went round in circles, trying to figure out what to do.

"Make sure you leave for Tehran on the first free day you have from the commander three weeks from now at the latest. That way, he's not going to know you've gone for three days. The same with the guards. Let them find out you've gone at the same time as you're supposed to meet the commander. By the time they figure out that you and your family have left, you'll be on your way to Frankfurt. Make sure that when you head down to Tehran, it's immediately after you have seen the guards on the last of the four nights with the commander—even if it's in the middle of the night, which it will be. You will be in Tehran by dawn and on a plane that afternoon. Here's the number for the contact who'll pick you up and make all the arrangements." Matthew handed her a piece of paper with Plato's number on it. He would be on standby, waiting for the call. "Call him as soon as you can to introduce yourself, and he'll set things in motion."

Matthew kissed Leila on the cheeks, hugged her, and then let himself out in the usual way and made his way to his car a couple of blocks away. He drove back to the hotel with a smile on his face until he noticed the low beams of a car that had come out from a side road a couple of miles from the hotel and followed him at a constant distance. They had been waiting for him to return, which meant they didn't know where he had been. He gave a sigh of relief as he turned onto the short road to the hotel; the other car went slowly by on the main road. Matthew pulled over to the side of the road and turned his lights and engine off. He faced the main road but was around a slight corner, hidden in the dark. The same car that had followed him returned and slowly went past the junction on its way back to Sari. *Coincidence? Not likely*, thought Matthew, but he daren't precipitate anything here in the local community. He would have to wait things out and see if anything came of it.

* * *

Breakfast was light. Yogurt, toast, sweet pastries, and coffee. Matthew's phone rang. It was Ali.

"Hi, Matthew. Ali here." He didn't sound his usual jolly self.

"Good morning, Ali. What's up? Any news?" Matthew asked almost cheerfully.

"I met with Hossein Daneshkah last night, but not his wife. James invited me over to his place for supper and Hossein was there. We had a good chance to talk while James and Jenny were putting the children to bed. James knew I needed the time."

"And? What do you think?"

"Leave him out, Matthew. I don't trust him. He talks the talk, as you say, but I have a feeling he may be playing both sides." Ali was clearly concerned.

"Okay... what makes you say that? Something he said?" Matthew was really interested now, especially since Hossein had passed the ORB smell test. But his intuition had been right. Hossein had been flying under his radar.

"He was raised in Rasht. His parents are, or were, devout followers of Khomeini when he first came to power. They influenced him a lot and he can't shake it. It comes out in everything he talks about. Yes, he would like reform, but not at the cost of the Regime. No way. I don't know if he is on the Revolutionary Guard payroll, but he certainly identifies with them and has a number of close friends that are part of the Guard. He doesn't seem to know anything about what we are doing, nor is he that interested in Jafaar or Amir's groups, although he's against any demonstrations they hold. This man is a conundrum, Matthew. I think his vision for the future of Iran is good, but in no way will he work against the Regime."

"Well, that settles it. We'll just leave him alone."

There was a moment's silence. "You may need to do something about him, Matthew. If he gets even the slightest whiff of a problem at the plant, believe me, he'll be the first one to raise the alarm. Unfortunately, he's positioned in the plant such that he hears a lot, says little, but is intelligent enough to put things together. James did mention he had seen Hossein with the Russians when they were on site. Could be innocent, but you never know. If he hears anyone talking suspiciously while he's on site, I think he's very likely to let security know, and I think they may be using him, perhaps against his will."

"Wow. Do you think he's reporting to them, Ali?"

"Yes, I do." Ali went quiet again.

"Okay. What makes you think that?"

"Something he asked during our meal together. He wondered about you and what you were doing on site. He said that it seemed a little odd that you would be there in that position when Charlesworth was really doing the work."

"Well, I'd say we need to do something about our friend Hossein, Ali. And soon... I'll take care of it. Many thanks for your help. What about his wife, Liz?"

"Neutralize them both, Matthew." Ali went silent.

*   *   *

Two days later, there was a horrendous crash on the highway into the project site as a semi-trailer, loaded with building materials for finishing off the on-site warehouse, jack-knifed on a large patch of engine oil on the road surface and hit the oncoming Paykan as it left the site heading for Sari. Hossein and his wife, Liz, died instantly. There was no investigation, no Revolutionary Guard action. It was an accident. A terrible one that brought out so many grief-stricken friends to the funerals. A sad loss for the community; two bright stars that had faded so early in their lives.

*   *   *

"Hi, Plato?" Matthew put a call in to Plato on his cell while he was at work in Tehran.

"Hello, Matthew. How are things going? Are we ready to move forward?" Plato asked.

"Not quite yet, my friend. Another couple of weeks and we should be there. The utility testing is still going on at site, and they haven't got to the steam circuit yet."

"Oh, okay. What can I do for you?"

"You probably know that there are no British or American embassies in Iran these days. There hasn't been since '79. But there is a French embassy, which we work through when needed. I need you to organize a pickup of three people in Sari and get them down there. It'll happen on a Friday morning in a couple of weeks—three at the most. They need to get their visas and clearances and fly out that day. We have all their tickets and paperwork being sent over in the French diplomatic pouch from Washington."

"No problem, Matthew. Just send me the details; names, addresses, contact number, and flight information, and I'll have my friend in Sari pick them up."

"One thing, though, Plato. You have to have them picked up at about 1:30 a.m. from her apartment in Sari and make a hasty retreat."

"I'm good with that, Matthew. Can I ask what's going on?"

"It's Leila and her parents. Time for her to leave and go back home. I don't want her here in Sari when the Revolutionary Guard finds out there's trouble with the plant or anything else. I don't think they would link her to anything we're doing, but I can't be sure. And I don't know what they might conclude about the commander if they find anything wrong about him. Let's get her to safety. I'm working on the timing for getting the rest of the crew out of here as well. You and Margaret will have to do the same as soon as the money gets transferred."

"We have our plan in place, Matthew. We're in good shape; tickets in hand, and Greece is waiting. We have a lovely place rented on one of the islands. You should join us." Matthew was sure that Plato was serious about the invitation, and he was very tempted to accept.

"Maybe I will, Plato. Is there room for a little one like me?" He laughed.

"Of course. You are most welcome. I'll send you our coordinates once we get there and you can decide."

"How's Margaret?"

"She's in a great mood and quite excited about the future of Iran. Just waiting for your word before she calls her father."

"I should get the word out over the next couple of weeks, Plato. Tell her to be patient for a little longer."

"Great. Thanks, Matthew. I look forward to your call." The cell phones went dead.

Matthew tapped out a message to Leila. "Send the full names, passport numbers, and addresses for you and your parents to Plato as well as your best phone number for whoever will be taking you to Tehran to contact you when the time comes. I need to get the airline tickets organized, and the information will be sent to you over the next week. Plato's friend will pick the three of you up at 1:30 a.m. from your apartment—unless you tell him otherwise—in two or three weeks on a Thursday morning. I'll leave it to you and Plato to finalize, depending on what's happening in Sari. You'll be flying out that afternoon, so be prepared for a long day. Love, Matthew." He tapped SEND.

Next was a note to Stockman. "Will send names, addresses, and passport numbers tomorrow for Leila's parents to fly out from Tehran to Frankfurt or Munich in two weeks, three at the most, on a Friday afternoon, then to New

York, and stay in hotel rooms there for a week. Please make sure someone meets them in New York on arrival and provides them with $10,000 for expenses. They'll need flights to Los Angeles one week after arriving in New York and will find their own way from there." He tapped SEND, and the message left.

Matthew sat back, pleased with himself for covering so much ground over the last couple of weeks. He needed to decide when to head over to Istanbul for a final meeting with the group before he gave the signal for the plant shutdown. By the time he returned to Sari, the steam system should be going through its paces, the unions would have met with NPC, and the Friends of Iran would have started their peaceful disruptions across the nation. Only the diversion of the finances would be needed to complete the plan.

* * *

Istanbul Revisited

A week later, Matthew arrived at the Hilton Istanbul Bosphorous in preparation for the meeting with Stockman and the team. It was time to cover the project, go through any final details, and find out if there were any issues that still needed to be covered.

The Iranians had become interested enough in Matthew that the Revolutionary Guard had dispatched two of their agents to follow him to Turkey. They stood out from the crowd and couldn't help but stare at Matthew constantly as though he would disappear if they should blink. While he led them to the hotel, he had no intention of allowing them to get too close and decided to do something about it now rather than let them pursue him farther. In fact, it would likely become necessary to get rid of them altogether, and while that would be difficult on their own soil, it was entirely possible here in Istanbul. He had the rest of the afternoon and evening available to deal with them.

Once he had checked in at the front desk and picked up a copy of the *Financial Tribune*—the first daily English-language financial newspaper in Iran—he took up a position in the lobby where he would be clearly seen by the agents when they came away from reception and went toward the elevators. They spotted him without knowing that he had spotted them as well, but they had no time to think before Matthew led them out of the hotel and across the road to the tramway station. He purchased his ticket, lingered a little to let the agents catch up, and then stepped on the first tram heading west toward the city.

Matthew disembarked at the first station over on the other side of the Galata Bridge. He walked northwest for 100 yards or so before he came to the hustle and bustle of the Golden Horn canal, where enterprising boatmen had built grills and fryers right on the decks of their gaudily decorated boats, built fires in them, grilled fish fillets, stuffed them in one-foot-long bread rolls, and handed the fish sandwiches from the boat to the hungry mob of thrifty Istanbulites every day. Matthew could hear the shouts from the fishermen as he came within 100 feet, "*Balık! Balık ekmek!*" Patrons tossed coins for the fish sandwich to the catchers on the boats as they frantically rocked back and forth sideways across its beam. Matthew threw his coins to the boat catcher and a fish sandwich was pushed into his hand in return. He went to the seating area, grabbed some napkins, salted his sandwich, and walked off to catch the sights around him while chomping on his lunch.

He headed toward the last of the four boats tied up to the dock, two abreast—one to collect the tossed coins and distribute the fish sandwiches and the one farthest from the dock that handled the fish preparations and the grills. It was a scene of chaotic organization. No one seemed to be pushed out of line, miss the boat with the coin throw, or not catch the sandwich.

The agents had not bothered to stop at the boats but instead sauntered closer to Matthew, trying to avoid eye contact with him. The Bosphorous was alive with watercraft constantly on the move around them, particularly the ferries that went back and forth to the east side of the canal in a frenzy of activity and speed. Combined with the fetch from the wind and the narrowing of the channel as the water came around the Golden Horn, the water was choppy at best and frenetic most of the time. It was a challenge for the fishermen, cooking on their boats, but over the years they had found more than just sea legs. They found sea bodies instead that swayed with the rolling of their boats as they cooked and served. Great coils of hemp rope prevented the sides of the boats from damage against the concrete dock as the Bosphorous tossed them about.

Matthew got close to the dock where the last of the four boats was secured in a line. All were cooking fish and serving the crowds. Meanwhile, the throng of people vied for position to buy the fish sandwiches; everyone was completely engrossed in this task and focused only on the boats. There was a persistent loud hum that hung over the crowd as they talked, laughed, and shouted as comrades do when they're playing sports together.

Matthew looked over the side of the dock. As the boat he was closest to rolled with the water, it crashed against the rope coils that stopped the boat just inches away from the side of the dock, a vertical face of concrete. The agents closed on Matthew, wondering what he was looking at but not close enough to be noticed. As the three of them stood staring down into the water, hypnotized by the swaying of the boat and the crashing against the coils, a group of excited young Turks, pushing and pulling each other, closed in on them, each with their fish sandwich and excited by the prospects of enjoying themselves on such a beautiful day by the water and caught up in the hysteria of the situation. As they got closer, the agents tried to get out of their way but got caught up as they drifted toward Matthew. He took advantage of the distraction and pushed hard against one of the agents, who silently toppled off the dock and down between the boat and the concrete. The fallen agent cried out from the water but not loud enough to overcome the noise of everything around him as the boat thrashed him against the thick rope coils over and over again. The young Turks hadn't noticed. By now, they had turned *en masse* toward the sitting area, having decided they wanted to sit and eat, and maybe go back for another sandwich.

Meanwhile, the other agent stared down at his associate but had no idea how to help as his friend struggled to avoid the crush of the boat against the coils. He couldn't get clear and slowly got swallowed up by the water as the wash sucked him under. It was all so quick, but Matthew had the wherewithal to turn away without letting the other agent notice him staring. He walked hurriedly away toward the spice market across the square. By the time he reached the entrance to the market, the agent had seen him and came running across the road while Matthew slipped into the crowd.

Matthew smelled his way through the vividly colored spices displayed alongside Turkish delight, caviar, dried herbs, honey, nuts, and dried fruits. He almost stopped to take in some of the delights more intimately but couldn't right now. He was taller than the average Turk, and his light-colored hair was a giveaway to the agent who followed. The stalls were stuffed in so close together that it would be impossible to walk between them to the outer edge. All one could do was keep walking to the other end. Neither could one run. The throng of people was so tight. Matthew slowed, and the agent got closer while at the same time keeping his distance to avoid bumping into Matthew.

Suddenly, Matthew ducked down into the crowd. His head disappeared under the mass of Turkish heads, but he watched the legs as they came close and then passed him. Then it was the agent's turn. Matthew shifted off to one side and hid behind the legs of the people on the side of the throng. They ignored him and continued with the business of talking, testing the goods for sale, and buying. Once the agent went by, Matthew got up immediately behind him and jabbed an ivory shiv between the agent's ribs and through his back at heart level. Matthew quickly drew his shiv out as the agent started to collapse and pushed it in again, but this time through the agent's neck as it came level with his hands. The agent went down to the ground while the throng pushed over and around the body. The initial spurts of blood soaked into his layered clothing. At some point he would be discovered but for now, Matthew was safe and heading out of the market in no apparent rush.

He headed back the way he had come but turned farther west, looking for a local hookah café for a raki and Turkish coffee. He found one close by and slipped into the uncrowded room. Deep cushions surrounded the walls and Matthew plonked down on one. A hookah with a single pipe was placed in front of him and he selected an apple-flavored tobacco while the host heated the charcoal, placed it in the crucible, tamped it a little, and placed the guard over it. It would last an hour with the host occasionally coming by to tamp the charcoal a little more, offer more coffee, raki, and an assortment of sweets. Matthew felt himself relaxing, and as the hour drew to a close, he rose, a little weak-legged, paid for his service, and headed back to the hotel on the same tramway as he had arrived.

It had been a very long day, driving down from Sari in the early morning and catching his flight to Istanbul. There was no time for a Turkish bath this time. Sleep was the remedy Matthew needed.

*   *   *

Clearly, Stockman was not aware of the problems Matthew had experienced with the two Republican Guards. Not that Matthew expected him to be. It was likely not even in the local papers. He guessed that even the Iranian authorities were not aware yet.

Matthew headed down the hotel corridor to the same meeting room they used the last time. He caught up to Stockman as he was heading in the same direction.

"Hey, Stockman. How are you, my friend?"

"Great, Matthew. Looking forward to jumping the final hurdles. And you?"

"Had a little trouble with a couple of Revolutionary Guard people, who followed me here from Sari."

"Oh. I wouldn't have thought they had enough on you to warrant them coming all this way. Did you deal with them?" Stockman glanced over at his friend.

"Well, let me just say that they won't be bothering me again. Of course, I can't say what will happen when I get back to Sari, but I couldn't let them follow me in here. They got as far as the reception before I realized they were here, and I had to get them out of the hotel as fast as I could. One landed in the Bosphorous and the other went down in the spice market. As far as I know, there was no one around who took any notice and I headed toward the bazaar. I stayed in a little hookah café for an hour, just to make sure no one was on to me."

"Good man. But keep your eyes open in Sari and get ready for a fast exit. If necessary, I'll have a plane come in and get you from the local airport. Can't let the buggers catch us now, can we?" Stockman turned his head toward Matthew and gave him a wink.

They pushed their way through the door to the meeting room, where the other members of the ORB group were gathered. They all sounded their greetings but settled down quickly at the meeting table while Stockman took a thumb drive out of his pocket and pushed it into the laptop that one of the others had already set up for him.

"Let's take a look at what has happened so far, gentlemen. And, by the way, I can't praise you all enough for the work you have done on this project. It has been invaluable."

Stockman turned to the screen and pressed a couple of keys on the laptop.

"I have the project divided into a number of targets that we have pursued, so let me summarize things for you all." The screen showed a slide with a number of bullet items that Stockman referenced, starting with **Power plant**.

"We've been working with the German engineers on this. The existing plant will only function to provide power to the local communities. The expansion has been hijacked and won't operate to the full design capacity.

Does that about sum it up, Ken?"

"They were great to work with. Very innovative and full of ideas. I think they really relished a way to play rather than build! Anyway, everything's ready for when the button is pushed." Ken looked pleased.

Next was **Tehran pipeline**. This time it was Ken who summed the situation up. "Pump stations have been compromised through the control system, and there has been some welding that has been compromised on the pipelines. So all's good." He sat back.

"Great. Thanks, Ken." Stockman looked happy.

Refinery. It was Matthew's turn. "Steam system is seriously compromised, compressors and generators are misaligned and will rattle themselves into submission; all instruments have been mis calibrated; power cables are undersized and control panel connections compromised; plant control system is programmed to fail." It was a very short description of a huge issue but well understood to mean: "the plant is screwed."

"Thanks, Matthew. We really appreciate all your efforts, and I know you were involved with every one of these points." Stockman picked up his coffee.

Friends of Iran. "These guys are ready to take to the streets and the mosques as soon as Matthew gives the signal. Dave, have you got anything to add?" Stockman looked over at Dave.

"Nothing really. As far as I can tell, they're well put together, know what they're doing, and have been able to protect themselves from interference. If Matthew's good with giving them the green light, I don't see any issues with that." Dave sat back.

"Okay. Good. Thanks, Dave. I know that there have been a number of fingers in this pie, including yours. Our in-country rep, Ali, has also been closely following, and from what I can gather from him, through Matthew, he has also given the green light." Stockman stopped in case there were more comments. He moved on.

Unions. "They are ready to meet with the NPC to test their readiness to accept unions, and they fully support the Friends of Iran. We fully expect that to distract the Regime and keep them hopping now that they'll realize it's serious. Does that sound about right Matthew—and Dave?" Stockman waited and got the thumbs up from both of them.

Communications Center. It was Matthew again. "This is the Gorgan listening post manned by the Americans. We have been successfully broadcasting false information to Russia and China about the oil pricing structure with Iran, creating a lot of serious conflict between them. I am pretty sure it all worked for us, so we have some interesting days ahead." Matthew smiled and looked around at the other smiling faces.

Financials. "We're ready to move the Iranian funds to our international accounts, as well as all future payments we deem necessary to cause a serious financial crisis that will affect the Russian and Chinese relationships with the Regime. Plato has done a remarkable job, but I also wanted to thank Colin for his input. You two worked incredibly well together." Stockman sat back in his chair and looked over at Colin.

"Thanks for that," Colin said. "I can also report that James has done an incredible job on site with the control system. I didn't have to do anything but listen to some of this thinking. All good." He put a thumb up.

"Good. Have I left anything out, Matthew?" Stockman looked over at Matthew.

"The only things I can think of that we held back on were the port and shipping arrangements. There's no point in spending time there."

"True. Thanks for reminding me, Matthew." Stockman looked around at the others. "Okay, any questions or things we need to consider?"

It was Colin. "What's the timeline for all this to go down?"

"As soon as Matthew gets back to Sari, unless we have any serious objection coming out from this meeting. If not, he'll assess the situation at the plant site and if commissioning is going as he thinks, he'll put the Friends of Iran and the unions into action. Within a week or two of that, the plant will start to show its problems and the financial hack will happen. Within three weeks, all of this will be behind us, and we'll have to see where the chips fall. Hopefully, the Regime will revert back to shipping oil from the south and come crawling for money. By then, we expect the Russians and Chinese to have pulled up and moved out." Stockman looked around, searching for more contributions.

"I'm a little concerned about the power plant expansion, Stockman. I haven't heard from Hans in a few weeks now, so I can't tell if he's on track or has been discovered or . . ." said Ken, who had been looking after the power plant initiatives, as well as the port and shipping.

"Not to worry, Ken. James met with Hans a couple of days ago, and he's all ready with his stuff. It will take a while before the refinery needs more power than the existing power plant can provide but when it does, and if they are somehow able to operate, they're going to find that the power expansion isn't going to be very cooperative," Matthew reassured him.

"That's great. Thanks, Matthew. As for the shipping, I can report that the Russians have already dispatched two of their largest oil tankers to the Caspian port and anchored them offshore, waiting for the signal to load. I understand that the two captains have also gone ashore to inspect the control systems at the port and get comfortable with the piping system they're going to have to tackle when the time comes—or should I say, if it comes."

Ken leaned back in his chair, satisfied with what he had heard.

"Dave. Anything on the political side of things yet?" Stockman turned to face Dave, who had been keeping his eyes and ears on the Islamic leadership.

"Not a thing. It's all pretty quiet, so I don't think they know anything. I'd heard from our friends in Gorgan that there are some financial concerns the Regime is grappling with. Did you already know that, Stockman?"

"Yes, Dave. Both Matthew and I've been getting the reports from the Pentagon as the listening station sends and receives information. The Ruskies are getting antsy, and that means the Chinese would be as well. The Regime is trying to downplay things, claiming they know nothing about the potential for higher oil prices than they all negotiated, but that's the information we put on the streets for them all to worry about." Stockman sat back as the group smiled their appreciation of the situation. "The fact is, none of them trusts each other, and even within their own groups there are those not fighting on the same side. So, they're a little messed up at the moment, shall we say." Stockman smiled again.

"Boy, there's going to be a lot of shit hitting the fan when the funds are re-routed." Dave laughed. He was soon joined by the others.

"I should report that our legal boys are quite happy with things. They've been busy making sure our agreements with governments are all in order and sanctioned by the right people. I think everything has been worked out, so we have no reason, from a legal standpoint, not to move forward. What say all of you?" Stockman waved his hands around the group.

"Aye, aye, let's get this done."

"That's it, fellas. Next time we meet, it should be in a bar in London to celebrate. Matthew, I know you still have a lot of loose ends to coordinate and have to head back right away. Make sure you don't attract the wrong types, and if you do and can't shake them, let me know, and we'll yank you out of there. We have a plane stationed in Ankara, just waiting for instructions. And, by the way, it's capable of landing in Sari. No point in trying to get you guys down to Tehran when the time comes to evacuate. Now, I don't know if any of you are staying in Istanbul for the night but if you are, be sure to go your separate ways after this meeting and keep a low profile until you get out of Iran. Matthew was followed by a couple of Revolutionary Guard people, so it could happen to any of us."

Stockman went around the table and shook everyone's hand, patted them on the shoulders, and thanked them for their participation. When he reached Matthew, he bent in low over his shoulder.

"Good luck, my boy. Get out of there as soon as you can and call me every day between now and then." He patted Matthew on the shoulder but before he could leave the room, Matthew interrupted him.

"Stockman, is everything arranged for Leila and her family?"

"All set, my friend. I got a call early this morning from Plato. She has been in touch with him and confirmed the arrangements should be made for next Friday. Tickets are being arranged as we speak, and the French embassy has been alerted for the visas."

"That's great. Much appreciated. Have a good flight back. Where are you heading to?"

"London. See you later." With that, Stockman sauntered down the hallway to the hotel lobby.

* * *

Final Impact—Mid-2020

Matthew didn't bother staying at the Tooba Hotel, where he had a small suite. Instead, he drove straight through to Sari after he arrived in Tehran on his flight from Istanbul. He wanted to size things up as soon as he could, and now that he knew the Revolutionary Guard was suspicious of him, he felt a more urgent need to complete the project and get out of the country. He wondered if the Sari branch office of the Revolutionary Guard knew about the demise of their two agents. He doubted it, but as soon as they realized he was back in the city, they would be sending more agents to track him and then discover the agents they had sent to Istanbul weren't coming back. Obviously, they would conclude that Matthew had something to do with their disappearance. At most, it would take them a few more days to get their facts in order and then they would come looking for him.

Matthew contacted James.

"Hey, James. What's happening on the commissioning?"

"Ah, yes." James was just a little taken aback, having assumed that Matthew would be away for a few days. "They started the steam circuit last night. Filled one of the boilers with distilled water and fired it up this morning. They couldn't build pressure enough to get steam, so by lunchtime today they were going through the system, looking for problems. My guess is they'll realize they are at a loss by this time tomorrow; they'll be filling the second boiler and getting ready to crank up the pressure. By the day after tomorrow, once they figure out that the second boiler has problems, they're going to be really pissed that they can't fix things as easily as they thought. After that... who knows."

"Are you all set with the control system?"

"All set and turned on, my friend." James was suddenly back to his usual cheery self. "There's nothing that can stop it from doing its thing now, and

I can't imagine anyone from IDRO is going to mess around with it. I'm just getting Jenny and the kids ready to make our exit. I think my job is done here, Matthew, and I have to get us all out of the country. Plant operations have essentially taken over and seem comfortable with doing everything themselves, although my guess is they just want us out of there.

"We're going to make it to Tehran tonight and head out to Ankara first thing in the morning. You'll need to organize some airline tickets for us to get out of there."

"Good job, James. Listen, why don't you head to the Tooba Hotel in Tehran? I have a suite there. You can dump the car in the parking lot and get a cab to the airport. Let me know when you get to Ankara, and we'll get you what you need."

"Great. Take care, Matthew. Hope to catch up with you again one of these days."

"Good to have had you on the team, James. Look after yourselves and give my love to Jenny and the kids. Don't say anything to Richard. Just leave."

They ended their call.

Matthew called Ali.

"Ali, how are you, my friend?"

"Good, Matthew. How did the meeting go?"

"Good. We're all set. Everything's in place. You need to get hold of Jafaar and have him set his meeting up with NPC as soon as he can. The same for Amir. Have him get his people together at the mosques and wherever else they can make an impact and make sure the news outlets are there, particularly the internationals."

"Will do, my friend. Jafaar has already set a date for NPC tomorrow, in anticipation. He could have easily postponed it if the timing wasn't good. Amir is ready, and his people have started to collect in the areas they're most needed. The universities are also on board and ready for peaceful but disruptive demonstrations. The whole country will essentially be shut down. I just hope the Revolutionary Guard won't be able to fully mobilize, but I think many of them will be sympathizers with the Friends of Iran. I will give Jafaar and Amir the word to go, so expect things to get pretty disruptive over the next few days. If you're intending to leave from Tehran, you need to do it tomorrow or have an alternative."

"That's great, Ali. Many thanks for all your help. I don't know if we'll meet in Iran again, but let's keep in touch and get together somewhere, perhaps with Plato and Margaret in Greece."

"I look forward to it, Matthew. Good luck, and don't stay here much longer. The noose is going to tighten very fast, very soon."

"I hope to be out of here in two days, Ali. It's become a little more dangerous right now, so we need to wrap things up sooner than later. No time to waste. Are you going to be okay?"

"I'll go to ground for a few weeks and then head back to the US, provided I can get flights. If not, I'll head east and go the long way around. I'm quite sure my activities here have been well under the radar."

"That's good, Ali. Take care, my friend, and many thanks for your help." Their call ended.

Matthew called Plato next.

"Hi, Matthew. I was just thinking about you and expecting a call. Is it time?"

"It is, Plato. Put the computers on overdrive and get that money moving out of there. Let Margaret know she should tell her father we're ready for him to put the right words into the Russian and Chinese ears, but not before you have made the transfers and organized the re-routing of any future payments. Maybe give it a couple of days before he talks to them. By then, the Regime will be up to their eyes in problems all round and they're going to be slow off the mark to take any action."

"Got it, Matthew. Take care, my friend and don't forget, come visit."

"Are you going to have any trouble getting out?" Matthew was concerned with what Ali had mentioned about Tehran potentially coming to a grinding halt the day after next.

"Don't concern yourself, Matthew. Margaret and I will be heading to the French embassy compound in Tehran in the morning. That's where we will be until I am happy the transfers have been made, and then we'll leave under French embassy protection, with Margaret's father, and head over to Mehrabad airport for a charter flight to Greece. Mehrabad is really for internal country flights, so I doubt there'll be anyone there that could cause us a problem."

"That sounds like a plan, Plato. Good luck. Give Margaret a hug for me and thank her for her help on this."

"You're welcome, Matthew. Make sure you don't stay around too long. See you on the other side."

"Oh, Plato, wait a second."

"What is it?"

"Did you get Leila and her parents organized?"

"Yes, my very good friend will meet them early in the morning and take them down to Tehran. He has all the instructions, and I've given his name and cell number to Leila. They have been in contact. All is ready. Now, you go and look after yourself."

Matthew was happy with things, but he still needed to get to Emma and the guys on site. He knew they were preparing to leave before he had gone to Istanbul, but he needed to make sure they had done what they had to do before he gave them the word to leave.

He called Stockman.

"Hi, Stockman."

"Hello, my boy. How are things going?"

"Very well, but I'm making sure everyone gets out of here over the next forty-eight hours. James and his family are leaving tonight, and someone needs to be in touch with them when they arrive in Ankara to arrange for flights from there. Plato and Margaret are heading to the French embassy in Tehran until the day after tomorrow when they'll head out with her father under consular protection. Amir will find his own way out, and I'm about to get with the Sari team to make some arrangements."

"Sounds good. Anything I can do?"

"That's the reason for the call, Stockman. That plane you mentioned that was on standby in Ankara—how many can it take?"

"Well, we decided on a Gulfstream 650. It has a capacity of thirteen, plus two pilots and one cabin-crew person. It has plenty of range to get you out of Iran to Ankara. Do you need it?"

"Yes. I may have seven of us come out the day after next from the Sari airstrip. Can you arrange that?"

"Sure. We checked the airstrip length at Sari and it has plenty of capacity

290

for the Gulfstream. Do you think you can handle the customs and passport control over there?"

"I hope I don't have to, Stockman." Matthew paused to collect his thoughts. "But listen, would you have the plane sit at the north end of the runway just off the apron. I think there's a turning bay there that I spotted when I came in. I also saw a secondary road off the highway that goes up that way and then heads around the end of the airstrip and back down the other side. We'll stop at the airstrip boundary. There are some kinds of commercial buildings we have to pass through, and I may have to take a trip up there tonight to check it out. I think it's a maintenance facility, but you never know. We can walk over to the plane from our drop point. It'll only be a few hundred feet. I don't think there are any fences, and I don't expect any patrols. We may have to bust through a fence if there is one, but we'll make it. Hopefully, it'll be a peaceful event, but you never know. I don't really want to cause any trouble at this point, but I may have no choice. If you think of an alternative, let me know."

"Okay, Matthew. When do you think you'll be at the airstrip?"

"I think we need to do this early in the morning after next. Say, 2:00 a.m., when the airport is asleep. I doubt they even have controllers in the tower at that time, so you may have to come in on IFR."

"Good thinking. We'll be there. Anything else?"

"That's all she wrote for now, Stockman. I'll talk to you again tomorrow. Not sure what time: it all depends on how the day unfolds."

"Understood. Take care, my boy."

Neither of them said goodbye.

* * *

"Emma?" Matthew listened to Emma's cell phone ring a few times before she picked it up.

"Matthew. When did you get back?"

"Early this morning."

"How's Daddy?"

"Yours or mine?" Matthew joked.

"Mine, you nut case."

"He's in fine form as usual. We really didn't spend a lot of time together. Just the meeting. It was brief, so that was good. It means everything is on track, and we all agreed to move forward. I had a little trouble with some Revolutionary Guard but managed to get rid of them."

"Oh, anything you want to share?" Emma was all ears.

"Maybe later, hon. For now, I need to focus on arranging for all of us to head out. Where are the guys?"

"Two of them left for Tehran last night and should be flying out today. Arnie and Walt are still messing with some of the electrical, and I think Pete has finished up on the instrumentation. Do you want me to round them up for a get-together?"

"Yes, do that, Emma. Maybe best if we do the same thing as last time and meet over there. I don't want to risk anyone being followed. See you at seven at the gatehouse. Make sure it's just you who meets me there, and we'll pick up the other guys outside the rec center."

"Got it. Listen, I'd better get back. I've finished my stuff, and I want to pack my things. I may even come out with you this evening. Sound okay?"

"Good idea. We'll come back to the hotel for the night. I think tomorrow's going to be quiet for us all, but I want to head into the plant just to take the temperature of things, so to speak."

"See you soon." Emma ended the call.

*   *   *

Matthew headed over to the construction site and parked inside the gate. He waited a few minutes before Emma came by, and they headed toward the camp.

"Want to tell me about Istanbul?" Emma asked.

"Well, there were these two goons that had followed me from Sari. I wasn't 100-percent sure until I picked them up outside the terminal and then again at the hotel reception area. I got them out of there pretty fast, though. We went over to the docks, and that's where I managed to dump one in the Bosphorous. The other one followed me into the spice market and I managed to get rid of him there, with the crowds cutting off the action. And that's about it." Matthew shrugged and looked over at Emma. Hopefully, she didn't want to go into depth on the situation because there wasn't much more to say.

"Oh, okay. Glad you made it out all right." She shrugged, made a face, and let the subject go. "Think they'll catch up to you here once they find out what happened to their guys?"

"Yes, I do. That's why we're going to increase the tempo here and move out the morning after next," Matthew responded.

"Hey, that's good. Got a plan?" Emma was persistent.

"Let's go through it with the guys when we're all together."

"Oh, okay. I can live with that. And here they are." Emma looked over to where Arnie, Walt, and Pete were hanging around outside the rec center.

"Hey, guys. Good to see you. Let's take a walk." Matthew didn't bother with handshakes.

They sauntered over to the clump of trees they had adopted as an informal meeting room in the fields.

"So, let's see what we've got. But before we do that, I should tell you that we're heading out together at 12:30 a.m. the morning after next. Five of us can fit in one vehicle, so Emma and I will pick you up at the gate. I'm not going to give you any other details right now, so you'll have to be patient and trust the plan is a good one. We should all be out of the country and likely home by the weekend."

The small group smiled.

"Okay. What's been happening? Arnie, have you and Walt finished?"

"We wrapped it up yesterday, Matthew. We also had a session with Mickey and Phil just to catch up in case they needed us to pass on any information to you before they left. I think if they had known you were going to be here today, they would have stayed, and we could have all gone together."

"No problem, guys. I'm glad they managed to finish their work off and head out. They're probably in Frankfurt by now." Matthew looked at his watch. "Did everyone do what was needed?"

Walt took a piece of paper out of his pocket.

"This is what Mickey and Phil gave us:

Arcing against machined components

Rags in the lube oil system

Tape on the pipe threads to fractionators and the demister pads

Watering down the sulfuric acid storage

Tightening the pressure relief valves to over pressurize the piping systems

Not completing the stress-relieving cycle on high-pressure piping systems

Screwing up the calibration on spring hangers

"I think that's about it, Matthew." Walt leaned back against a tree with a cigarette hanging loosely from his lips.

"Wow. Busy boys. And that's not including the misalignment of the compressors and generators. Wow again. Hey, what's the sulfuric acid deal, Walt? I haven't heard of that one before."

"There's sulfuric acid in some of the pipes," Arnie said. "You probably know that, but if it's diluted to, say, 90 percent of its strength, it actually corrodes the pipe. So, after a very short time, the pipes give way and you're left with having to bring in a fresh supply of undiluted acid as well as replace the pipes."

"Okay. Sounds good. What about you three?" Matthew looked at each of them.

"I'm all finished," said Pete. "Not much more I can do. I helped with installation after the calibration and switched quite a few where they would fit. They're all sized for the piping they are attached to, so there's only so many you can move around. But it's done. I looked over the sampling systems and messed with them a fair bit, so site testing is going to be a headache." He had a way of understating and was nonchalant about what he had been doing.

"You ready to leave, Pete?" Matthew asked.

"You bet. I'll be there at 12:30 a.m. Thursday morning, waiting for my ride." Pete smiled, just thinking about heading home.

"Arnie, what about you guys. Anything new?"

"Not really. Just more of the same. Switching things out, messing with tagging, neutralizing the backup systems, and compromising the substation. Nothing dangerous, just inconvenient. They're going to blow a few secondary transformers and the like. Anything more you can think of, Walt?"

"Just the backup generators. We messed with the trips, so they aren't going to fire up if needed. Other than that, nothing to add."

"All good guys. Pack your bags, lay low tomorrow, and wait for us to pick you up. Make sure you have your passports!" They all laughed and headed back to camp.

"What do you think, Emma?" Matthew asked as they drove back to the hotel.

"It all sounds almost too good, Matthew. Can it be true? Apart from your run-in with the Revolutionary Guard in Istanbul, it's as clean as it could be."

Matthew watched the rear view mirror for signs of anyone following. There didn't seem to be, and he turned into the side road to the hotel.

They spent a couple of hours eating supper and deliberately avoiding talking about work or what had been going on with the others at ORB. Matthew furtively looked around now and again but didn't notice anything that looked out of place. Emma noticed his nervousness and put a hand on his leg as though to steady him.

"We'll be out of here in just over twenty-four hours, Matthew. Now is not the time to lose faith."

He smiled at her. "Just checking."

They signed the check and headed down to his room. There was a half-bottle of vodka left and he poured them both a few ounces.

"Listen, Emma. I need to go over to the airport. I want to check out the routing to the north end. Want to come?"

"Of course I do, silly." Emma downed her vodka and got up. Matthew hadn't intended to be in that much of a rush, but he suddenly got caught up in her eagerness and threw his vodka back. It gave him a few ounces of devil-may-care and they left the room, went down to the other end of the hall, and out through the fire door to the parking lot.

It took forty-five minutes to get to the airport and find the junction they were looking for on the east side of the airport entrance. There was no fence separating the airfield from the road. There was a ditch that would prevent traffic from getting onto the runway but other than that it seemed clear. They reached the buildings near the northern end, which looked like a fire station and warehousing. There was nothing more and at this time of night there was no one around. Matthew had checked the airline timetables and noted that the last flight was scheduled to arrive in Sari at 5:45 p.m. That time had come and gone a number of hours ago and everything was quiet, although he could make out the lights at the terminal end of the runway.

They drove past the buildings to the end of the short road that drifted off in two directions. One headed farther north and they could see it curve around to the west. The other was shorter and ended at the edge of the airport property. They parked the car where it couldn't be seen should any vehicle be passing and made their way across the ditches and onto the runway perimeter. Everything looked doable and Matthew was relieved. They stood there and turned in all directions as though something was about to happen. Nothing did and Matthew put his arm around Emma and led her back through the ditches to the car.

Matthew was tired and needed some rest. It had been an exhausting day and the vodka had just about finished him off. He only had one more thing to do before he would shut his eyes.

*   *   *

They showered together, slowly rubbing the soap over each other's bodies. The hot water soothed, the soap soothed, and the hands massaged while the lips caressed. They stayed in the warmth of the hot water for more than just a few minutes, washed each other twice, and then a third time, looking for excuses to touch and feel, rub and pinch, turn and thrust.

They almost fell out of the shower and laughed as they tumbled over to the bed, wrapped in towels. It took seconds to get rid of the towels and fall into bed, leaving the covers to one side as one mounted the other and then the positions were reversed. It went on for several rolls before they found their most comfortable position and Matthew leaned in to find her. It was a suddenly delicious and mind-numbing strength of coupling that only two lovers knew.

Matthew and Emma stayed in a tight embrace on top of the bed for a few minutes until Emma rolled off and headed back into the bathroom. Matthew had a slug of vodka, poured one more, and one for Emma. He went into the bathroom and cleaned himself before heading back to the bed with Emma close behind. She found the vodka, climbed into bed, knocked back the drink, and pulled the covers over both of them.

Their glasses emptied at the same time and Matthew leaned over to kiss Emma goodnight.

*   *   *

There is nothing so alarming yet delightful as a cock crowing in the early morning. It wakes the dogs, announces a new day, and makes people get ready for whatever they have to get ready for. In the case of the hotel location, it was also the Salat al-Fajr prayers at dawn echoing over the local mosque loudspeakers to remind the faithful of their first of five obligatory prayers to set the rhythm for that day. It was a sound that announced to everyone that this was a Muslim land in tune with Muslims throughout the world at this particular time of day. The ethereal quality of the melodies lingered over the villages, towns, and cities just like church bells used to do back in the old country on a Sunday morning.

Matthew opened one eye and looked over at Emma, who seemed oblivious to the sounds outside. He rested with his hands behind his head and considered the day before him. Emma would stay back at the hotel while he went over to the plant to take a look around, talk to Charlesworth and gauge the reactions of the operating team as they managed the first of the major problems.

He needed coffee. He dressed without bothering about a shower or a shave and headed down the hallway to the reception area, where he knew there would be a fresh brew waiting. They made an excellent coffee here in the hotel.

No coffee is grown in Turkey and, just like the Italians and French, it is the Turkish process of roasting and preparing the coffee beans and then brewing that gives a cup of coffee the distinct flavor of the country. Turkish coffee is made from high-quality arabica coffee beans from Central and South America that are blended and carefully roasted, then very finely ground. The coffee is mixed with water and the desired amount of sugar and cooked in a *cezve* or Turkish coffee pot. The coffee is served in small cups. The coffee must be left to stand for a short time after serving to allow the grounds to settle to the bottom of the cup. It has a unique taste, froth, aroma, brewing technique, and presentation... in other words, it has its own identity and tradition.

Matthew had two steaming hot cups of coffee, carefully avoiding the bitterness of the coffee grounds that collected in the bottom. The effect was powerful. Matthew came alive with the boost it gave him. He suddenly felt invigorated and eager. He took some naan and cheese and headed out to his car.

As Matthew went through the site gate, he could see a group of workers over at the turbine mezzanine structure, but he didn't comment on it when he met Charlesworth in the office. Charlesworth was bent over the stack of drawings and specifications and had a very perplexed look on his face.

"How's it going?" Matthew deliberately sounded happy-go-lucky. "Got it all in hand?"

"I don't know what's going on here, Matthew, but we can't get the first three boilers to produce enough steam. Can't figure it out, but I think it may be the size of the tubes. Sure hope it isn't because it would be a total plant shut down while we change them out. I'm having the design team check it out in Montreal."

"Are you firing up the fourth?" Matthew asked innocently.

"I think we'll hold off until we figure out what's wrong with the others. It would be a waste of distilled water." Charlesworth still hadn't looked up at Matthew, but he didn't seem to be showing any signs of suspicion at this point. Matthew wondered what the IDRO people were up to.

"Do IDRO have any thoughts?" Matthew asked.

"They're going into panic mode and realizing they don't have a clue what to do. It's all up to us at this point. I think they're getting nervous about not being able to get the plant up and running. There's a lot of pressure on them from the Regime, and the Revolutionary Guard is getting itchy."

"I'm just going to take a swing through the plant." Matthew took his hard hat off the peg and walked out the door. His cell phone rang.

"Matthew? It's Plato."

"Hey, Plato. How are things going?"

"Well, you can expect to see the shit hit the fan at any time, Matthew. The first two pairs of the major transfers have been made. Two for the Regime's account, and two for the Mansourian account. That's billions from both. We had no problems and have confirmation of receipt in the ORB accounts. So far, so good."

"Great. Have you told Stockman?

"I messaged him. It was the middle of the night for him when we did the first transfer."

"Okay. Make sure you get out as soon as you have finished."

"Matthew, we're about to leave for Tehran and will do the next transfers from the French embassy."

"Okay. Let me know when it's done. How many transfers are you expecting to do?"

"There are four accounts in each of the two groups and we will have done two pairs by the time we leave, so two pairs left."

"Thanks, Plato. Keep in touch."

"How's it going over there?"

"Well, the shit hasn't quite hit the fan yet, but they are getting pretty nervous. The first three boilers aren't putting out steam, and they're looking at the designs of the tubes to see if they're the problem. It's going to take a while. I'm just heading out now to take a look around."

"All sounds like a bit of a party, Matthew. Take care." Their call ended.

There was no way that Matthew could check on the Neka plant or the pipelines. Their problems wouldn't be discovered until the plant was running, and that could be months, or years, from now. But if they decided to operate at the lowest efficiency they would find problems everywhere, and that would shut the whole place down.

Matthew walked out onto the site and made his way over to the boiler area. There was a group of overall-clad operators working their way in pairs through the systems with their clipboards and drawings in hand. Everything was being checked and double-checked. There was no way they could see inside the plant equipment, piping or electrical systems, and they could only check whether it was built to the design specifications.

Matthew walked past a group of operations personnel who were huddled closely in animated conversation and gesticulating with frustration while a couple of guards eavesdropped on them in case there was anything they needed to get involved with.

There appeared to be nothing at this point, but Matthew figured there would be something really problematic by tonight when word came through about the money. There would be frantic attempts by the Regime to salvage what they could of their offshore accounts, but the system had already been corrupted and at the press of a button by Plato, the next and final tranche would be transferred overnight. By then, the airwaves would be frantic with calls between Iran, Russia, and China, all trying to figure out how one was screwing the other. By the next morning, the calls would be tripled as news rolled in about the demonstrations by the Friends of Iran and the unions, as well as the inoperability of the new refinery. The country would be plunged into chaos.

Matthew continued on his tour of the plant and wandered up to the control room. The operators seemed calm and unaware that their systems would not perform. At this point, they had no plant to operate, and the faults remained anonymous for now. But at the first sign of anything other than the simple utilities like air and water, they would quickly realize there were problems they would be unable to compensate for. That was likely a few days away if the plant operations crew decided to carry on with commissioning any more of the plant that did not rely on the boilers, compressors, or generators. There wasn't much since almost everything in the plant was intertwined, but there were some things they could test. Matthew would have left the scene of the crime by then.

There wasn't much left for Matthew to do at the plant. He wasn't intending to say goodbye to anyone. He would just drift off, but it was too bad he had to leave Charlesworth behind. *Oh well, they'll desperately need Charlesworth if they ever want to get even the minimal amount of the plant operating, as well as to help with a forensic inspection when the time comes. He'll be safe,"* Matthew told himself and headed to the IDRO offices.

There was pandemonium in the owner's offices as the finger-pointing and rhetoric flew in all directions. People had been fired for insubordination and others relegated to their desks, told to stay quiet, and do as they were instructed. The IDRO chief, Abbas, had broken out in a sweat but still managed to offer Matthew some chai. He gratefully accepted and wandered into the chief's office for a sit-down.

"Abbas, what do you think the problem is with the steam circuit?" Matthew asked innocently, while keeping a straight face and soaking his sugar lump before plopping it into the small glass chai cup.

"Matthew, I don't know. Charlesworth is certain all the components are in place, and while he has asked for a review of the tube design, he doesn't think that's where the problem lies. I think he senses, rather than knows, there are fundamental fabrication problems with the boilers. No one can spot where they may be, but perhaps there are weld torch scores and the like, or misfit flanges, or hatches, or whatever. But no one can see any steam escaping. On the other, we can't build up enough steam to test even that." Abbas sat back, pressed his lips together and seemed lost in thought.

"Have all the tube welds been tested?" Matthew asked.

"Of course, and every one of them tested with 100-percent success."

"Are the check valves in the right orientation, and are they the right size with their relief valves set correctly?" Matthew wasn't about to touch on what Emma had been up to, but he wanted to at least shine some positive light on himself for trying to help.

"I think so, Matthew." Abbas had sunk farther into his chair and was thoroughly dejected. "I'm sure our team is checking and re-checking everything out as we speak."

"Listen, Abbas, this point in a project is always stressful. Everything'll turn out fine. Don't worry." Matthew stood and held his hand out to Abbas, who just nodded but did not smile as he normally would. Abbas just reciprocated with a handshake and walked Matthew to the door.

"Thank you, my friend. I'm sure you're right and in a month all this will be over and we'll be shipping product." Abbas smiled.

Matthew went back out through the gate and drove over to the hotel. He noticed a black Mercedes behind him. It had pulled away from outside the perimeter fence when he came through and came up behind him. For a moment, he felt a surge of anxiety but he calmed down and kept his eye on the road. When he turned off to the hotel, the Mercedes followed him and parked on the far side of the lot where the occupants could keep their eyes on the main entrance to the hotel. Matthew parked by the fire exit at the back of the hotel but walked around and deliberately went in through the hotel reception area. No one had gotten out of the Mercedes yet. He wondered but kept his cool as he walked down the hallway to his room. He knocked on the door and Emma let him in.

"What's happening, Matthew? Everything going okay at the plant?" She was now concerned.

"I think we have some friends tailing us. Pack up, and let's move out. The car's parked over by the fire door and they're not going to see us leave. Let's go."

They grabbed their things and headed out through the fire exit, glad to see that no one was watching. Matthew headed to the highway and on to Sari.

"We're going over to Leila's place."

"But she's not there, is she, Matthew?"

"She's leaving first thing in the morning, so we can stay there for a few hours until it's time for us to move out."

They drove through Sari and over to Leila's area, where Matthew parked two blocks away. He called Leila. She sounded nervous but calmed when she heard Matthew's voice.

"Come on over. I'll go down and let you in through the alley." Leila slipped on her headscarf and went down the two flights of stairs. Matthew and Emma were coming down the alley when she looked out of the gate and waved them into the courtyard.

"I've been looking through the curtains all day whenever I heard the faintest noise. I think everyone in the downstairs apartments has already left for the weekend." She smiled a sort of restrained smile.

Matthew pecked her on the cheek and quickly introduced her to Emma.

"My parents will be here soon and we can have a small meal here while we wait for our ride. You must join us." Leila seemed happy to have the extra company and fortified by the thought there were friends around.

It was good for Matthew and Emma to relax on the sofa and just zone out while Leila was in the kitchen, getting the meal ready before she left for Tehran. Her luggage was waiting by the front door. Matthew and Emma had left theirs in the car. They had four hours to wait.

*　　*　　*

One Last Call and It's Off We Go

Matthew and Emma shut themselves in the second bedroom and put the call in to Stockman.

"Matthew here."

"Hello, my boy. How are things progressing? Are you all set to get the hell out of there?"

"I get the feeling we may be chased out, Stockman. I think I've picked up a couple more tails. We managed to lose them at the hotel, but they'll be searching for us and they know the car by now. We're over at Leila's place, and she's all ready to get out of here about the same time as us."

"What does your gut feeling tell you?"

"I think we're good, Stockman. Emma and I checked out the airport last night, and it should be straightforward. A couple of ditches to cross, and we'll be on the airstrip. The plan stays as is but tell your boys to fly in as close to pick up time as possible so it doesn't give anyone nosing around an opportunity to dig deep."

"Will do. They're all set. A couple of pilots and someone to look after you in the cabin. How's my girl?"

"She's right here. Do you want to talk to her?"

"If I could, yes."

"Hi, Daddy." Emma had taken the cell phone from Matthew when she heard his question.

"How are you doing, my darling? Got things under control?" Stockman laughed, and Lucy shouted, "Hello darling," from somewhere behind him.

"Hello, Mummy," Emma shouted although, since the call wasn't on speaker, there was no way Lucy could have heard.

"Job done?"

"All finished, Daddy. We're out of here. Can't wait. Dying to see you both."

"Good job. Matthew tells me you did pretty good."

Emma laughed and handed the phone back to Matthew.

"What's happening on the money front, Stockman? Any reaction yet?"

"There are a few conversations shaking up the airwaves. I don't think they believe it yet. They probably think it's a banking glitch. My guess is it'll be the next transfer that will set the cat among the pigeons."

"And the demonstrations? Any feedback yet?" Matthew asked.

"There are rumblings and threats, but nothing of great substance. It's all pretty peaceful and no guards out, so we'll just have to wait and see."

"Margaret's father should be on the phone to the Russians and Chinese by this time tomorrow, and that should send a lightning bolt through the Regime."

"I'm sure it will. Are you all finished up at the plant?" Stockman asked.

"Yes, the guys are laying low until tonight when I pick them up, but everything—and more—has been done. That plant will be a graveyard for a long time."

"Great. Let's hope we can get it up and running when the time comes. I need to consult with Domar. Make sure everyone has a detailed description of what they did so Domar can put it right when the time comes."

"As long as we use the same guys, things should be good. It'll take a long time, but it'll be worth it. Still, they could get on and order what they need from the descriptions the guys provide."

"Great, Matthew. I think we've covered what we need to, so lay low, take care, and our boys'll see you in the morning."

"See you soon, Stockman." Matthew signed off.

Matthew put his arm around Emma's shoulders and stretched back on the bed. They dozed for a couple of hours before Leila called them to eat. Her parents had arrived and introduced themselves as best they could. Everyone was smiling in that universal way of saying, 'I'm very pleased to meet you.' They all sat down. The next hour was spent gesticulating, laughing, and making facial expressions to encourage each other to understand what was being said. Leila was the translator.

It was time to get ready. At midnight, Matthew and Emma headed out to the construction site to pick up the guys. There was no traffic and, while

Matthew kept looking in his rear mirror, there was nothing to see. The goons had clearly not yet figured out where he was.

Arnie, Walt, and Pete threw their bags in the trunk and climbed into the rear seat, cramped but happy to be getting out.

"Okay, guys. I guess I can tell you what we're up to now. Sorry to say this, but I didn't want you to know before, just in any of you got caught and spilled the beans."

"Oh, thanks a lot, Matthew!" It was Walt. "Nice of you to think of us. Thank God you didn't tell us that before."

"Okay, we're heading to the Sari airstrip." Matthew paused for the guys to get their brains in sync with the thought. "There's going to be a plane waiting for us at the north end of the runway. We'll park the car close by and walk over to it. It's easy going with a couple of ditches in the way. Emma and I tested things out last night, and it's all good. The plane will take us to Ankara, where we'll pick up our flights back home. Good?"

"Sounds great, Matthew," said Arnie. "I thought we may have had to go down to Tehran and out that way, but this is much better."

"Any questions?" By then, they had reached the city limits and were working their way along to the road to Neka with plenty of time to spare.

Suddenly, Matthew caught sight of a reflection of something behind him about 100 feet away. He stared at it and nudged Emma.

"We may have company. My guess is they were waiting at the project gate in case we turned up there. Wild guess, but I could be right. Otherwise, they wouldn't have known where we were."

Emma strained her head around and moved Walt's shoulder out of the way so she could get a better look.

"I think you're right, Matthew. Judging by the shape, that's a Mercedes, and if it's the same guys, they're going to be looking for blood this time around."

"Any thoughts?" Matthew wondered.

"I'm thinking." Emma's brain was churning.

"What's happening?" asked Arnie.

"Looks like we've picked up some interested parties, and they're not the friendly types. We're just figuring out what to do." Matthew went quiet as he thought.

"Well, they don't know where we're going, so maybe we should head toward Tehran, lose them, and then turn back." It was Emma.

"I like the idea of leading them in the direction of Tehran," Matthew answered, "but these boys aren't about to lose us again. The moment we speed up, they're going to be on our asses and maybe they'll want to stop us with gunfire. They may even have some help waiting for us along the route."

"True, but it'd likely be on the route to Tehran, not to the Sari airstrip." Matthew went back to thinking. They were coming up to the junction where a turn to the left was the road to Tehran and to the right was the road to the airstrip.

Matthew made his decision.

"We can't waste time heading toward Tehran. We'll draw them toward the airport and as soon as we're off the highway and headed to the north of the taxiway, I'm going to take a dive and deal with them. In the meantime, Emma, I want us to change positions. You can drive. I'll be in the passenger seat and get myself ready. As soon as we round the corner, slow down just enough for me to bail, and then speed up. Only turn around when you get to the end of that short road and before you reach those buildings. Then come by and see if I made it. Let the guys out before you come back, just in case, and at least someone will make it out of here if it isn't all of us. Got it?" Matthew glanced in his rear view mirror at the three guys in the back. They each nodded.

No one argued or voiced their opinion. What choices were there?

"Okay, Emma, get over here." They twisted and turned over each other without any loss of vehicle speed. Matthew settled in the passenger seat. They were on the eastern limit of the city, heading toward Neka and looking for the turnoff after the one to the airport, which would take them on the road that paralleled the strip. The Mercedes' headlights were still off but the car was gaining on them slowly. Fortunately, it still stayed far enough behind for Matthew to have time to make his jump, roll, and rise.

Emma turned the car to the north onto the even narrower, little-used side road and headed toward the bend that would take them to the edge of the airstrip. It was a sharp left that let Matthew roll into the hedgerow and onto the side of the asphalt. He rolled to a standing position, pulled a gun from his jacket pocket, and leveled it at head height as the Mercedes rounded the bend. Two bullets into the windshield made the car swerve into the bank before it got to Matthew. The impact threw the car into the air, and then it rolled a half circle and bounced onto its roof in the middle of the road.

Matthew didn't stay around long enough to check the pulses of the occupants. He turned and ran up the road toward Emma as she drove to meet him. The front passenger door flew open as Arnie leaned over and pumped it open. Matthew had a fleeting thought where he remembered telling Arnie and the others to get out of the car before Emma turned back. But he didn't dwell on it and dove into safety instead. Emma put the vehicle into reverse and sped back to where the buildings were. She whipped the car around and gunned it to the first ditch, where she pressed hard on the brake, jerking them all violently but harmlessly forward and came to a sudden stop.

"Okay, let's go." Matthew spotted the Gulfstream coming to a stop in the turning bay off the north apron. The steps were coming down, and the five of them hurtled themselves forward with their baggage and climbed up into the cabin, ignoring whatever effects they had from the car coming to such a sudden stop. The stairway was raised as the last person entered the cabin. The plane had hardly stopped as they came on board, and it now moved forward to a taxi position and hurtled down the runway toward the terminal. It only needed 1,200 feet of runway for takeoff, which was almost a mile away from any eyes that might have been watching from the building's windows. There were only some dim lights on in the building and the control tower. It seemed deserted, and the lights had only been just sufficient for the pilots to get their landing position adjusted correctly.

The Gulfstream quickly climbed as Matthew watched the lights of Sari disappear. He could just make out the glimmer of lights at the refinery and wondered how things were going—or, rather, not going. He smiled.

* * *

What—No Refinery?

Matthew and Emma wandered arm in arm down the hill from the Ankara Hilton on a beautiful fall evening and went into a small restaurant just around the corner from the bustle of a thriving line of stores and crowds of evening shoppers. A trio of old musicians was playing in one corner of the restaurant, and the air was tinged with nostalgia, romance, and the smell of good food. This was one of Matthew's favorite restaurants when he was in Ankara and the only one he returned to each time he visited. It had the best, most succulent, thinly cut barbecued lamb chops and deep-fried whole mushrooms. His mouth watered just thinking about it as they were shown to a table in the courtyard, next to the open doors, and just far enough from the trio for the music not to be intrusive but close enough for them to appreciate it. The air was still warm, the lighting was low, and the place was filled with animated talkers enjoying the food, company, and surroundings.

They had been in the city for three days, luxuriating in the comfort of all that the hotel had to offer. The best breakfast buffet in the city, a heated swimming pool, comfort all round, and a hammam on the basement level with a full-service spa. They were thoroughly relaxed and catching up on the world news. There was a lot about Iran, and more came every day.

It had been interesting reading as they sat in the deep, comfortable armchairs in a secluded corner of the spacious lobby lounge, picking away at the finger foods, sipping Efes beer, thumbing through the local English newspapers, and snatching looks at the news on their cell phones.

"I think they got the message, don't you?" Matthew noted as he read a piece about the crumbling financial state of Iran and the mystery of the missing money. People were taking money out of Iranian banks at a rate that wasn't sustainable. Russia and China were only just getting to grips with the problems and wanted out of their deals with the Regime. They just couldn't be trusted. Meanwhile, the Regime went from one crisis to another as all the major cities dealt with demonstrations by the youth that were supported by the new union movement. It was chaotic and although the Revolutionary Guard had been called out, some journalists wondered about its strength since it was clearly outnumbered. In fact, it seemed, to some journalists, as though the guard had actually become more tolerant and willing to let the demonstrations go on. There were photos of guardsmen tangled up in the crowds with arms around each other, smiling and dancing in the street. It looked as though nothing could stop them all. These were not the same days as the shah had encountered when he could call in the Israelis to help, when his own people in the SAVAK refused to kill their own. This Regime had no such friends, especially now that word had gone out about their deteriorated financial position.

"Oh, Matthew, listen to this. It's a small piece I found in the *Tehran Times*, dated today."

> *"Sources say the new Sari refinery, located in the northern province of Mazandaran, currently being commissioned, and destined to become the principal export point for nearly 60 percent of the petrochemical products produced by Iran to places such as Russia and China, appears to be having some substantial teething problems getting up to speed. While these are early days, our understanding from people in the field is there are serious issues with the process design. We will continue to follow this story, but we also understand that support for the project by the Russians and Chinese is dwindling as Iran experiences financial uncertainty. Requests for comments from NPC remain unanswered."*

"Sounds like things are going according to plan—" Matthew was interrupted by a call on his cell.

"Hello."

"Hey, Matthew. Plato here. How are you, old boy?"

"Hi, Plato. Are you out yet?"

"Not quite, my friend. We're still in the French embassy in Tehran. I wanted to make sure all the money was out and the blocks worked on future transfers. As it happened, there was a fairly large sum coming in from Syria in payment for a couple of shipments of oil. That managed to bypass the Iranian accounts and end up with ORB. So, I'm happy everything's working, and we'll be heading out to Greece in the morning with some of the consular staff."

"It'll make for good reading, Plato. Great job. Many thanks. Give my love to Margaret—from both of us. Emma is here with me."

"Oh, HI EMMA!" Plato shouted into the phone for Emma to hear.

"She heard you, Plato. Take care." Their call ended.

"Hey, Leila says hi," Emma announced, looking up from her phone messages. "They all got to New York and are heading over to LA tomorrow. She says the local Sari newspaper is full of news about the refinery, as well as about a couple of Revolutionary Guard who got tangled up in a bad accident at the north end of the airstrip. Both the occupants died, but it doesn't say what they were up to. She wants to know if you know anything about that. She sends you a big thank you, with what I think is an emoji kiss." Emma looked over at Matthew with her eyebrows raised in a knowing way.

Matthew laughed. "That's great to hear. I guess the guys made it back home as well. I don't expect to hear from them, but I may give Dick Elliot a call sometime to confirm." His cell phone rang. It was Stockman.

"Hello, Matthew. How are things? And how's that daughter of mine?"

"All's good, Stockman. Emma's here with me, and we're catching up on the news. It all sounds like it could be going our way. Any thoughts?"

"Well, the Iranians have been banging on the doors in the US and the UK looking for buyers for their oil! It sounds like they are going to have to reduce their prices if they want to keep the old customers, though. I also happen to know that the Russians and Chinese have backed away from the Iranians and are making arrangements with others for their long-term supply."

"What about the financial issues?"

"Well, the Iranians haven't come out and said it yet, but there are hints they are in serious trouble and wondering who has been messing with their finances. The word on the streets is that the Russians have been playing games and likely hacked into their accounts. Of course, nothing can be proved, but that's what the chatter is, coming from the Gorgan station."

Matthew laughed.

"When are you guys back in Vancouver?"

"I think we'll be heading out at the weekend. Why, have you got another assignment lined up?"

"It so happens that I am just working on one right now. I'll tell you about it when you get back. We'll be down in the West Country for a while at the cottage. Maybe you can visit. It's a beautiful spot and I love the English countryside so much, especially when it's by the sea."

"Sounds very nice, Stockman. Can I bring Emma?" He laughed.

"Don't come without her, my lad."

*   *   *

Six months later, Dick Elliot was dining in Blanchette, his usual small French restaurant in the Soho district of London. As he dipped his first piece of crusty bread into the liquid of the *moules marinière*, he felt a pat on his shoulder.

"Hello, Simon," Dick said without looking up. "Would you like to join me?"

"Ah, yes, don't mind if I do." Simon pulled a chair from the table, plonked himself down, and extended a hand to his friend. "Boy, that looks good. I think I'll try some." He waved the waiter over and placed an order. "With bread, of course," he said as an afterthought.

"Of course, monsieur." The waiter scurried off to the kitchen.

"What brings you here, Simon?"

"Oh, I thought you might like to know how things ended up with our friends in Iran."

"Yes, I would. I heard some stories, but nothing firsthand. What's the news? Did it all turn out okay?" Dick stayed engrossed in his mussels.

"Well, they came back home, shall I say. The southern routes are open, and it's business as usual. Seems they ran out of money and had no choice, what with all the public pressure as well. I don't know what has happened to the refinery in Sari, but I'm pretty sure they mothballed it until they can figure out what to do. We'll let things lie low for a year or so, and then offer to go back in and put things right. That would be a very inexpensive plant for us after the Russians and Chinese essentially paid for it the first time around, and your fellows did an excellent job putting their notes together for us. We even have a list of the tubes that were blocked, as well as the alignment records for the equipment. So, provided the Iranians don't mess with things too much, it shouldn't take a lot to get everything up and running."

"So, that means you're happy?" Dick looked over at his friend.

Simon nodded. "Very, very happy, Dick. We want to thank you for all your help on this. ORB did a great job. Only a few casualties, but otherwise well-executed."

"Well, I'm happy to say I don't think I'll be here in another forty years when there'll likely be another Iranian catastrophe. I don't think I could take more than two in a lifetime." Dick laughed, and Simon joined in, knowing what Dick had gone through all those years ago and had come almost full circle for him.

The second *moules marinière* arrived, and Simon wasted no time in dipping his bread into the liquid and savoring the wonderful taste of the garlic-laced broth.

They both smiled in satisfaction, although it was difficult to know if that was a result of the food or the success of the project. It was likely both.

THE END

Printed in the USA
CPSIA information can be obtained
at www.ICGtesting.com
LVHW051512221124
797276LV00001B/101

* 9 7 8 1 0 3 8 3 0 1 1 5 4 *